MABEL GOES TO THE DOGS

Mysteries of Medicine Spring

Book One: Mabel Gets the Ax
Book Two: Mabel Goes to the Dogs

MABEL GOES TO THE DOGS

By

Susan Kimmel Wright

Mabel Goes to the Dogs
Published by Mountain Brook Ink
White Salmon, WA U.S.A.

Scripture taken from the Holy Bible, NEW INTERNATIONAL VERSION®, NIV® Copyright © 1973, 1978, 1984, 2011 by Biblica, Inc.® Used by permission. All rights reserved worldwide.

The Author is represented by and this book is published in association with the literary agency of Hartline Literary Agency, www.hartlineliterary.com.

© 2022 Susan Kimmel Wright
ISBN 9781-953957-21-4

The Team: Miralee Ferrell, Alyssa Roat, Nikki Wright, Kristen Johnson, Cindy Jackson
Cover Design: Indie Cover Design, Lynnette Bonner Designer

Mountain Brook Ink is an inspirational publisher offering fiction you can believe in.
Printed in the United States of America

DEDICATION

For my husband Dave—a practical-minded engineer who became a de facto patron of the arts when he married someone who spends her time making things up—with many thanks for his support.

ACKNOWLEDGMENTS

Many thanks to the following:

Editor and publisher, Miralee Ferrell, and the incredible team at Mountain Brook Ink.

Lynnette Bonner, who designed my stunning covers.

Agent extraordinaire, Jim Hart, and Hartline Literary.

Heather Houlahan, for letting her brilliant dogs find me. Whatever inaccuracies Mabel and I introduced are entirely our fault. Anything we got right is thanks to Heather and the gang. Thank you for the work you do and for my day in the woods—I'll go out again anytime.

All my wonderful readers. If you've bought my books, read my books, shared them with others, recommended them to your book club, written a review, or rated them, thank you from the bottom of my heart.

My family (both human and animal) and all my dear friends, for their unfailing loyalty and support.

The Lord God, from whom "every good and perfect gift" comes. (James 1:17, NIV)

Chapter One

MABEL'S BEST FRIEND LISA HAD WARNED that the TV cameras would add ten pounds to her appearance, and anything with a pattern would strobe. Mabel's black pants, white shell, and black-and-gray tweed blazer looked sharp, if she did say so herself. Hopefully the generous scattering of dog and cat hair she'd brought from home wouldn't show up, but still...

"Excuse me," she said. The only other guest in the green room, a fortyish woman with short brown hair and fresh, pink cheeks, looked up. "Do you have a lint roller?"

The big dog lying at the woman's feet thumped its tail. The woman smiled and shook her head. "Isn't that hair awful? It sticks to everything."

Mabel smiled back. "You're smart. Black clothes—black dog."

"I didn't actually plan that." She laughed and stuck out her hand. "Rachel Marciniak. This is Sammy—he's a coonhound. You might look in that basket over there."

"Mabel Browne." She shook with one hand and held out the other for Sammy to sniff.

Sure enough, Mabel found a lint roller, along with hem tape, safety pins, dental floss, Vaseline, and other emergency supplies for guests of WXAT's Country Morning show. Unfortunately, not much tape was left on the roller. She did the best she could. "Is your dog going to be on the show too?"

"Yep. We're with Bartle County Canine Search and Rescue."

Mabel studied the dog's friendly face, with its reddish jowls and eyebrows. "I thought bloodhounds did that."

"Nope. Pretty much any breed can do search and rescue, but some dogs have more natural talent for it, especially nose hounds."

"So, you find lost people?"

"We sure try, don't we, Sammy?" Rachel petted her dog. "Once we found a suicide victim, which was sad. But it's part of the job. Not all dogs do cadaver work as well as live tracking, but Sammy's multi-talented. Aren't you, guy? We've been lucky to locate a couple of lost hikers and that little boy who wandered off from the harvest festival last week."

"Wow." Mabel remembered the lost little boy. The search had gone on into the darkness, and it had been a damp night, with temperatures dipping into the thirties. "That must feel really good, to know you saved someone's life."

"It does. What are you being interviewed about?"

Mabel modestly lowered her eyes. "I solved the Sauer ax murder case," she said. "Maybe you read about it."

"I did!" Rachel's eyes widened. "Here I am, talking about Sammy and me, and you're the real hero. You nearly got killed, didn't you?"

"Twice," Mabel admitted with a little shrug. "My next book is all about it."

Mabel knew "next book" was a slight stretch. The only other "book" she'd ever written was a biographical booklet for the historical society.

"Wow, you're an author too." Rachel pulled a card from her pocket. "Put me on your mailing list when it comes out. I'll be looking forward to it."

Mabel accepted the card. "Sorry, I don't have any cards with me."

Again, this was a minor stretch. Mabel made a mental note—*order business cards*. What should they say? Maybe *Author, Speaker, Volunteer Expert*.

She thought about that last part. Maybe it sounded too much like she was offering to volunteer as an expert, instead of saying she was a writer who was an expert on the topic of volunteering…which, she also had to admit, was a slight exaggeration. Her short-lived gig as a historical society volunteer didn't exactly make her an expert.

This in turn reminded her she still needed to come up with her next volunteer job. After getting fired from her twenty-three-year career as a low-level attorney on the brink of her fiftieth birthday, Mabel hadn't been able to find another employer who could look past her age and forceful disposition.

Luckily, she had a nice severance package from her former law firm, as well as a rundown house and a sizeable bank account, both inherited from her late Grandma Mabel, along with a big, old dog named Barnacle. Relieved of the immediate need to take whatever subsistence employment she could scrounge up, Mabel had decided to reinvent herself by launching a glamorous new career as an author.

Her original plan had been to write about the benefits to seniors in volunteering. She'd gotten a bit detoured by the Sauer ax murders, but she still needed to keep that other book project moving forward.

"Nice talking to you, Mabel."

Mabel realized she'd zoned out and totally missed whatever Rachel had been saying. "Sorry. I'm not used to getting up this early. Guess I drifted a bit."

Rachel grinned. "That's okay. I know what you mean. We've got to go now, but listen. If you're ever interested in coming out with us, we can always use volunteer 'lost persons' for Sammy to practice on."

Mabel watched as Rachel and Sammy went to wait in the hallway for their interview. She'd be next.

Mabel took a deep, calming breath. Maybe she should rub some Vaseline on her teeth, so her dry lips didn't stick to them from all the smiling she'd be doing during her interview. That's what beauty contestants supposedly did.

On the monitor mounted high in the corner, the Country Morning hosts, Bee Novak and Doug Constantino bantered. Their teeth were unnaturally large and white. Mabel bared her teeth at the mirror. They looked almost yellow by comparison. She practiced smiling like the Mona Lisa.

"Well, this is looking more like Crime Morning than Country

Morning, Bee. Cadaver dogs and ax murders. Is that a Halloween thing?"

Bee Novak giggled. "It certainly seems that way, doesn't it, Doug? I don't know about you, but I'm so excited to learn how these dogs do their important work. And Mabel Browne—facing down a killer?" She shuddered delicately. "How brave would you have to be?"

"I hope I never have to find out, Bee."

"Coming up after our news and weather break on the half hour, we'll be chatting with Rachel Marciniak and her partner, Sammy." Bee beamed into the camera. "Part of the team that located four-year-old Noah Poellot, who strayed from his family at the county harvest festival."

Mabel turned as she looked in the mirror. The right seemed to be her good side. She'd have to try to keep it toward the cameras.

The Morning news anchor, a baby-cheeked young man who Mabel suspected had grown his wispy mustache to make himself look more credible, read the local headlines, changing expressions to suit the subject. He frowned as he reported another missing person, an elderly nursing home patient, believed to have wandered off the night before.

Following the news segment and commercials for the farm supply and Coffee Cup Diner, the weather forecast came on. More cold temperatures and bouts of rain—Mabel hoped the missing old man wasn't somewhere out there in the elements.

The camera shifted back to Bee Novak and Doug Constantino. "Now please join us in welcoming Rachel Marciniak and her amazing dog, Sammy, to Country Morning."

Mabel watched the interview with interest. Bee Novak seemed to take the lead in asking the questions. None were very tough, but Mabel couldn't help admiring how relaxed and natural Rachel appeared to be on camera. She didn't rush her answers, Mabel noticed. She'd have to remember to take her time too. She tended to babble when she got nervous.

Why had she drunk all that coffee? It certainly hadn't helped her nerves. Did she have time to run to the restroom?

"So," Bee Novak was saying, "this missing person case. Is that the sort of thing you and Sammy might be able to solve for the police?"

Rachel smiled and shrugged. "Certainly, that's the type of thing we do. Sammy is very good at finding missing persons. However, we'd need a place to start. When we did the search for little Noah, we knew he'd wandered from the picnic area at the park. We even knew which table his family had been using. There has to be a scent to follow."

"Could you start at the nursing home?" Doug asked.

"We could try, but if he stepped into a car or onto a bus, that would be the end of the trail. We aren't entirely sure when he disappeared, either. He could have traveled all around town for an hour or more, for all we know."

The entire interview only lasted about five minutes—maybe less. Surely, Mabel could be poised for five minutes. *Did* she have time to run to the restroom? No, probably not.

The green room door opened. "We're almost ready for you, Ms. Browne." The page held the door. "Would you please follow me, and we'll get a microphone on you."

Mabel passed Rachel and Sammy in the hallway. "Break a leg," Rachel said. "Don't forget to put me on your mailing list. And if I can ever answer any questions for your writing, give me a call, okay?"

"Thanks." Mabel blotted damp palms on her pantlegs. She tried to slow her breathing as someone attached a lapel microphone to her jacket.

The Country Morning set looked like a farmhouse parlor, right down to the view of autumn fields painted behind the fake window. Ivory duck slipcases covered the overstuffed chairs, and a coffee table of distressed pine held crockery mugs and a blue speckleware coffeepot. Only the blinding, hot lights spoiled the illusion of a visit to the farm.

"Welcome!" Bee Novak, looking shorter and tinier in real life than she did on the screen, pumped Mabel's hand with both of hers. "I'm so excited to meet you, you brave thing."

"Um, thank you." Mabel began to sit in the first chair, so her right side would be to the camera.

"Over here," a blue-jeaned young woman in headphones tugged Mabel to the opposite chair.

"My right is my good side." Nobody seemed to hear her.

"We're on commercial now." Doug Constantino shook her hand. "Have a seat and try to relax. Have you ever done this before?"

"Um, no. Only a couple radio interviews."

"You're going to be fine. Relax and try to enjoy yourself."

Mabel found a glass of water at her place and took a sip. Now that this was happening, she realized she wanted to be anywhere else. She was going to say something ridiculous. The camera was going to add another ten pounds to her already overweight frame, and she would look like a different species altogether from Bee Novak. What was she, anyway—a size 0? Was there something smaller than 0?

Suddenly, they were live. Bee beamed into the camera. "Welcome back. Today, we have the pleasure of talking to out-of-work lawyer Mabel Browne, who recently solved the decades' old mystery of the Sauer ax murders." She turned and focused her toothy smile on Mabel. "Welcome to you, Mabel. Doug and I are thrilled to have you join us in the farmhouse this morning."

"Um, thanks." Mabel was starting to sweat under the lights, and she had to quit saying "um." She frowned. "Actually, I'm an author. I did spend a number of years practicing law, but I recently made a career change. I completed a biography of Margarethe Sauer this fall, since leaving my law firm, and I'm working on a couple of other books right now."

"How fascinating." Doug Constantino looked anything but fascinated as he interrupted her. "Can you tell our viewers how you finally figured out Bartle County's case of the century?"

"One book," Mabel continued stubbornly, "is a nonfiction exploration of volunteering for seniors, and the other is a true crime book about the Sauer killings. And, of course, the more recent murders connected to them."

Bee leaned forward, touching Mabel's hand. "Let's talk about that. In fact, you nearly became one of the victims, didn't you?"

"That's right, Bee. The killer had me cornered. Twice."

"I'll bet that must have been terrifying. I cannot even imagine. This man had already killed two previous victims, but you escaped. Can you tell us about that? How did you survive?"

Mabel tried to look courageous but humble. She wondered if anybody she knew was watching.

"I didn't have time to be terrified." Mabel shifted in her seat, realizing that statement was not 100% true. She might not have had much time to think, but there had been plenty of time to be scared out of her mind. "All I knew was I didn't want to die. I knew if this killer was ever going to be stopped, it was up to me. The whole story is in my upcoming book, *Bloodstains*."

Bee and Doug seemed to exchange a look. Mabel was sorry, but she was simply not going to blurt out her whole story on Country Morning and spoil the best part of her book.

"Is it true you didn't press charges?" Doug asked.

"I'm sorry." Mabel sat back, arms crossed. "Since I'll be a prosecution witness for the murder trial, I can't comment on any specifics related to the cases."

Doug cleared his throat.

Bee smiled. "Of course. We understand and would never want to interfere with the upcoming trial. Can we get that archive photo up for our viewers, Ed?" Bee addressed somebody offstage. "The one of the crowds surrounding the Sauer mansion in 1939 after the discovery of the bodies?"

She turned back to Mabel. "Let's go back to the historic case then, shall we? I'm sure our viewers will be as fascinated as I am to hear how you came, after nearly a century, to solve the world-famous Sauer ax murders."

Mabel lowered her hand. She had been trying surreptitiously to wipe sweat from her upper lip. These lights were too much. Had Bee had her sweat glands surgically removed?

"Again, I'm so sorry, Bee. That's a fascinating, but very long story that's best told in my upcoming book."

This time there was no mistaking the irritated look passing between the two hosts. "Well, thank you, Ms. Browne," Doug said. "We'll certainly all be looking forward to the release of your latest book."

"And Volunteering for Seniors," Mabel added. "That's a working title at this point. It's a nonfiction handbook for seniors. About volunteering."

Bee reached across the corner of the coffee table to shake her hand. "Unfortunately, that is all the time we have right now. I'm sure we're looking forward to getting our hands on both your literary efforts in the very near future. Thank you for joining us this morning."

"And coming up in our next hour," Doug announced, "we will be treated to a live performance by the Grannies with Attitude hip-hop group. I hope I can rock out like they do when I'm that age. Or like Mabel here," he added a bit meanly.

Bee laughed. "Oh, Doug! You can't rock out like that right now."

Let Constantino be annoyed. Mabel tossed back her mane of still mostly chestnut hair. She hoped her former law school classmate—the one who'd fired her—had caught the Country Morning show.

As Mabel left the set, she had to squeeze past the Grannies with Attitude in the narrow hallway. *"Like Mabel," huh?* The youngest of the four women was at least seventy—old enough to be Mabel's mother. She had to admit, though, she was not and never would be half as toned as they were in their black leggings, ball caps, and Chuck Taylor high tops.

One of the Grannies offered Mabel a fist bump. Mabel fist bumped back.

"Proud of you," the woman told her. "We're showing younger people that growing older's a wonderful thing, aren't we? It's all in the attitude." She turned to display the Grannies with Attitude logo on the back of her black moto jacket.

"If you're interested," another Grannie interjected, "we offer classes down at the Second Presbyterian church on Tuesdays at 7 pm. If you take to it, we can always use a few back-up members."

"Thanks." Mabel edged toward the door. "We'll see." Being recruited as a possible second-string Grannie, at barely age fifty, stung. Plus, she was forced to recognize the probability of her breaking a hip if she was foolish enough to try launching a hip-hop career.

Mabel felt around inside her pocket for Rachel's business card. Maybe she'd follow up on that instead. It would be exciting to add saving lives—or at least helping train dogs who saved lives—to her bio, along with capturing killers.

As she headed for the studio exit, Mabel imagined herself tramping through the autumn woods, wearing boots and flannel. Dogs baying like they did on shows about tracking escaped convicts, while Mabel scanned the bushes, searching for a lost person or maybe even a fugitive.

Or a dead body? An image flashed across her mind, reminding her of the last time she'd stumbled upon a corpse.

Mabel shivered. As she did, she heard Grandma Mabel's voice in her head. "Somebody just walked across your grave."

Chapter Two

THE NOVEMBER AFTERNOON WAS BRISK AND overcast. Mabel looked around the parking lot for her car. She clutched her blazer to her chest, wishing she'd worn a coat. A breeze tossed the treetops, scattering a few remaining yellow leaves into puddles left by last night's rain.

How had her interview looked? It felt as if it had gone okay, but Mabel knew the AM hosts were frustrated she wouldn't talk about the murder case or the big reveals in her true crime book. At least, she'd gotten in a couple of good plugs for both her books. Not to mention an invitation to join Grannies with Attitude.

When she finally located her car and slid behind the wheel, she got the heat going and turned her phone back on. Her best friend Lisa, a kindergarten teacher, would still be at work for hours. But two texts popped up—the first one from her younger sister Jen.

You were great!

She fumbled with the buttons on her phone but finally wrote out a reply. Thanks! Glad you liked it.

The other was from John, her maybe-boyfriend of the past several weeks. John was a private investigator on what he said was a temporary hiatus, ever since his license had been suspended for reasons as yet unknown to Mabel. She'd been reluctant to pry...maybe because she wasn't ready to hear a potentially upsetting explanation. Since he currently worked as a substitute high school teacher and adjunct professor of criminology at the local community college, she reasoned he could pass a background check, at any rate.

John had texted an hour earlier, wishing her a good interview. Mabel dialed his number, and John picked up. "Hey." She heard the smile behind his warm, slow greeting. "There's my TV star!"

"Did you watch?"

He laughed. "Sorry to say, I just got out of class. Since you're already in Bartles Grove, you want to head over to campus and let me buy you lunch?"

Thoughts of food replaced Mabel's disappointment. "Sure. Where?"

"Maybe Pinto's? If you're in the mood for pizza. And don't mind all the kids."

Mabel couldn't recall ever having turned down pizza. "I can be there in ten."

It had started to rain again, so Mabel decided to drive the four blocks. She parked around the corner and ran for it.

Noisy students crowded the pizza place. Smells of garlic and oregano mixed with the sour, hoppy scent of the beer taps, a sign above which read, We card EVERYBODY. Be prepared to show ID.

Mabel worked her way across the room as John turned and smiled. Every time he did that, she felt her stomach go squishy. She gave him a little wave.

John stood for a quick hug. He was only a couple inches taller than she was, but at least forty pounds lighter, and more muscular. He had a close-cropped head befitting someone working with law enforcement, and his intense hazel eyes made her heart beat faster.

"I went ahead and ordered mushroom and artichoke. Our favorite, right? I figured with this crowd the orders would start backing up."

Mabel was pretty sure that was *his* favorite, but whatever John ordered would always be fine with her. As the waiter dropped it off, she had to admit it looked and smelled appealing.

"Your thing went good?"

She nodded and swallowed a bite. "I think so. They kept wanting me to tell how I was 'cornered by the killer.'" Mabel made air quotes. "I'm sorry, but I don't want to spill all the good stuff before my book comes out. So, I mostly talked about my writing."

"Sorry I couldn't watch. I recorded it, though, so maybe we can watch together."

"I think they'll send me a copy in a few days, anyway."

"I'm sure you were outstanding." John leaned across the table for a quick kiss.

Immediate noise erupted from a corner booth. John laughed and made a little head bow in that direction. "Kids from my class."

Mabel flushed.

"They're jealous."

Mabel doubted it. They probably wondered, like she did, why a handsome, fit, former PI was involved with an ever-so-slightly chubby fifty-year-old unemployed lawyer. Well, she reminded herself, they didn't know she was unemployed, anyway.

"Did you enjoy it?"

Mabel flushed again. "I kissed you back, didn't I?"

John laughed. "I meant the TV appearance, silly goose. Would you do another one, if you got the chance?"

Mabel considered. "I believe so. I'd probably develop the knack after a while, don't you think?"

He squeezed her hand as it rested on the table. "You're a lawyer. If anybody has the gift of gab, you should."

"Well…" After spending twenty-three years in a back room of the law firm, drafting documents, and doing research, Mabel had hardly had any opportunity to develop a court presence. "I'm sure it's only a matter of getting used to being on camera. You know what was really interesting this morning? I met a woman with a search and rescue dog. She talked about how they find missing persons. It was amazing."

"They really are. A good search dog can come along hours later and follow our trail by nose alone. No matter how many times I've seen that, it always blows me away."

"You used them in your work?"

"No—my ex-girlfriend, Victoria, volunteers with Shawnee County S & R. She's been doing it for years."

Shawnee was the county to the south of Bartle. Mabel's mood soured. There was no ex in her life. Until John had come along, nobody had seemed to appreciate an outspoken plus-size woman like herself. Of course, she'd realized John would have had other girlfriends, but hearing the specifics was unexpectedly unsettling.

"Victoria's dog—he's a Malinois named Cap—has found a lot of people over the past five years. It's their passion."

Mabel was glad Victoria wasn't in Bartle County. This county wasn't big enough for the two of them. "I'm thinking about calling her up. Rachel, I mean. I need another place to do some volunteering, and she said they need people to play victims."

John nodded. "I've done that for Victoria. It's fun."

Mabel tensed at the thought of his being out there, alone in the woods with this Victoria, who must be a horrible person. *ANT*, she thought, giving herself a firm mental shake. This was a therapy method she'd read about online, which advocated "talking back" to automatic negative thoughts or "ANTs." Ever since reading that article, Mabel had found she had many such thoughts, which needed a stern talking-to.

Victoria is probably a very nice person. She and John are no longer together. John and I are together, she told herself. *Maybe.*

"Mabel?" John waved a hand before her eyes.

"Sorry. Maybe I'll see if Barnacle has any talent for it, while I'm at it."

He grinned. "Barnacle may or may not have the nose for it, but he definitely has too much couch hound in the mix."

Mabel sniffed. "You don't know that. He may be older, but he's mostly cattle dog, and at least when I used to visit Grandma years ago, he was a ball of energy."

"Well, I do know *you* well enough to know you wouldn't be able to handle the grind."

ANT, she told herself, trying to drown out the other voice in her head screaming, *Oh, Victoria does search and rescue, but I can't handle it?*

He tapped her hand. "They train most every weekend. Think about that. In all kinds of weather. And go out on searches 24/7/365. That takes dedication."

Mabel opened her mouth, ready to argue she could be every bit as dedicated as any old ex-girlfriend of Mr. John Bigelow. Then he added, "You have a different calling. Every bit as important. Just different. You're a writer. You need to concentrate on that, right? Having people to practice on is essential. Why not go out and hide for the dogs first and see how that goes? Then, you can write about it too."

He was right. She had to keep her eyes on the prize. But writing had turned out to be so much harder than she'd expected. And all this volunteering was work.

Mabel's phone rang. "It's Acey Davis." Her heart sank.

John grinned. The handyman Mabel had hired to help bring her grandmother's place up to code was more colorful than competent.

"Hey, there, little lady," Acey drawled in her ear. "We got us a problem over here at the home ranch." Ever since starting the job, he had persisted in referring to Mabel as "little lady" and her place as "the home ranch." And he never called unless there was a problem. For a man she'd hired to solve a problem, he seemed to cause twice as many.

"What seems to be the matter?" Mabel resisted adding, *This time.*

"Y' know my pickup? Well, she's been havin' brake trouble, y' know?"

"Yep." Acey's truck was endlessly plagued with an assortment of grave issues. Mabel had given up trying to keep track of them.

"Well, I was aimin' to cut the brush back in there today, as y' know."

"Yep." The township insisted the overgrown field behind Mabel's house be cut back, but she could not see how it was contributing to any public health crisis whatsoever.

"So I was haulin' my little Cadet tractor, and I backed on into the driveway with it, to make it easier to unload, y' know?"

"Yep." *Blood pressure.* Mabel feared where this was going.

"You know it's on a bit of a downhill. So I backed her on in, and when I tapped on the brakes, there was nuthin' there."

"Oh, no."

"Yes, ma'am. I'm afraid I run your shed down."

"You ran into my shed?"

"I run it all the way down, ma'am, and I am truly sorry."

"All the way down?"

John snorted.

"Well, the back part's still standing, but you know it was not in the most sturdiest condition to begin with."

The shed, old like the rest of Grandma Mabel's property, could have used a coat of paint. Otherwise, it had looked okay to Mabel. "I don't think it was ever built to withstand a truck assault."

"No, ma'am, that's what I'm sayin'. It sure was not."

Mabel's jaw dropped. He said that as if the damage was the shed's fault.

"I can fix it for you," Acey told her. "We can add 'er onto the job, if you like."

Was he planning on being paid to fix the damage he himself had created? "We can talk about that later. Just tell me, is my lawnmower okay? Was anything else damaged?"

"Oh, not too awful bad."

"There are a couple tarps toward the back. If you can get to them, would you please cover my mower and tools and stuff? Then, why don't you call it a day? It's too wet to be out there cutting right now, and I'm sure you must be shaken up after the accident."

"Oh, it don't bother me none. I've worked in worse. And I feel okay. Sorry about my equipment, though. My Cadet and the truck both took a little damage from your shed."

Mabel couldn't imagine how he'd distinguish any new damage to his truck from the preexisting dents and scratches. "Please. Just cover my stuff and go home."

Acey required more cajoling, but Mabel finally convinced him to wrap up his efforts before any further damage was done. She hung up, feeling drained.

John slid a pizza slice onto her plate. "Sorry about your shed."

"Thanks. His intentions are good, but every time I deal with him, I feel as if Helen Thornwald is still poking at me from the grave."

Helen, Mabel's cantankerous late neighbor, had departed the mortal plain with one final stab at Mabel. She'd reported the rundown property Mabel had inherited from her late grandmother to the township. To get the work done, Mabel had ended up having to hire Acey Davis. She hadn't had many peaceful moments since.

Mabel had lost her appetite. "I should get home and let Barnacle out." The big dog would be watching out the window for her by now.

"And check on my shed," she added with a grimace. "How about you?"

"Oh, I need to grade some papers." John called for a box and picked up the bill.

Moments later, he walked her to her car. The temperature had continued to drop, and a few snowflakes now drifted in the air.

"Let me know if you're doing the search dog thing. Maybe I'll come out with you."

After he'd given her a hug and tucked her behind the wheel, Mabel sat watching the swirling snowflakes while her car warmed up. She imagined the missing old man, out in this weather, and shivered.

Chapter Three

DRIVING BACK THROUGH MEDICINE SPRING, MABEL glanced at Lisa's apartment windows above the Coffee Cup. Ulysses, the gray tabby Lisa had recently rescued, stared out at the snow and drizzle. Mabel felt him cast a disapproving eye her way. In fact, it was the only eye the big tomcat had, the other no doubt lost due to a mean life on the streets before his rescue. Mabel still marveled that her friend had bypassed the sweet kittens and ended up with this animal.

She passed the square, turned at the next corner, and again at Carteret, the one-block street where she lived to the left of the dead end, where the woods of the park began. As she did, her heart sank.

The damage to Mabel's shed was every bit as bad as she'd feared. Acey's truck had left deep ruts in the grass all the way from her side driveway to its target. On his path to destroy her shed, Acey had also taken out Grandma Mabel's treasured Dr. W. Van Fleet rosebush, which had stood at the edge of the driveway since at least the 1920s. She bent in the sleet which was now falling, studying the battered rosebush. Hopefully, it would survive.

Acey's runaway truck had shoved the front wall of the shed into a big U shape, rimmed by shattered boards. Above the point of impact, the roof sagged, slushy rain dripping off the edge. The side walls, having lost some support, leaned inward. Inside, she saw the tarps, one gray and the other bright blue, haphazardly spread over about half the shed's contents. Wind riffled their edges.

Mabel waded puddles for a better look. If she had more tarps, she might be able to do a better job, but she didn't. She considered ferrying stuff to the covered front porch, then threw up her hands. She was getting wet and cold, and it would take forever to move all that heavy stuff.

In reality, most of the shed contents were probably pure junk, which she'd soon have to sort through, anyway, and end up tossing most of it. Maybe Acey, in his unique way, had saved her some trouble.

Barnacle was barking and scratching at the back door, so she abandoned the mangled shed and went to let him out. On her way, she had to skirt a couple of dark-brown globs of Acey's chewing tobacco. He'd recently informed her he'd switched from hand-rolled cigarettes to an occasional "chaw" for health reasons.

Barnacle greeted her with mad excitement before launching a thorough exploration of her hands, feet, and pantlegs. He probably smelled Sammy. Would Barnacle's nose be up to search and rescue?

Mabel clipped his collar to the run-out cable, slipped inside the kitchen, shook out her wet blazer, and kicked off her shoes. Koi, her fluffy black-and-caramel tortoiseshell cat, leapt from the Hoosier cupboard shelf and plopped at Mabel's feet.

"Hey, pretty kitten. Are you looking for a snack?"

Koi sat and launched a grumpy string of complaints. Clearly, she hadn't been having a good day, and considered Mabel to blame.

The animals often played together, but when Barnacle was cooped up too long, he tended to continue the games past Koi's limited tolerance. Not to mention Acey's racket irritated the cat, and today must've been worse than usual, what with the truck crash, plus Barnacle's inevitable barking about it.

Mabel set the pet bowls on the counter, shoving accumulated mail and food cans aside to make room. She poured kibble into each and set Koi's down for her. When she looked outside, dirt was flying. Barnacle was busy digging in the back corner. *Perfect.*

She opened the door. "Barnacle! Leave it." She tugged on the cable, and with a show of reluctance, he finally turned and came bounding to her.

"Whoa." She caught and unclipped his collar, then grabbed a rag from the bottom drawer next to the door. Before she could touch his muddy paws, he gave a mighty shake, sending rainwater over both the floor and Mabel.

"Aagghh!" She didn't dare let go, since at this point his feet were big clumps of mud with toenails. She wiped at her face with the back of an arm.

While Mabel scrubbed at his massive feet, Barnacle stretched his neck as far as it would go, sniffing at his dish up on the counter. "Hold on, mister. You asked for this."

Koi, meanwhile, had finished eating and sat watching the show. She picked up one of her front paws and commenced a ladylike cleaning operation of her own.

It took a good ten minutes to get the worst of the dirt off Barnacle's feet. He still left faint mud prints on his romp across the room to gobble his food.

Mabel headed upstairs, Koi leaping ahead on the shadowy staircase. The Victorian still had high ceilings and limited lighting. Grandma had been Depression-era frugal, and her lightbulb preference ran to forty watts.

Since inheriting the house six months before, Mabel had been replacing bulbs in the rooms she spent most of her time in. So far, she hadn't figured out how to reach the entryway ceiling fixture without killing herself. When the low-watt bulb eventually gave up the ghost, she might have to ask John to help change it.

Or Acey. The thought made her shudder. Knowing Acey, he'd break a hip and end up spending the winter on her couch. She'd be running to bring him pillows and cups of tea every time he rang the bell, like *The Man Who Came to Dinner*—and probably get a bill for his trouble too.

After changing into dry clothes, Mabel headed back downstairs. She should work on her writing—either the "upcoming true crime book" she'd promised the Country Morning audience, or her series of volunteer-related articles she hoped would also lead to a book.

As always, Mabel felt disinclined to start. A writing career had sounded glamorous and even kind of easy when she'd lost her longtime—but dead-end—job as an associate lawyer several months ago. She had envisioned herself sitting at a desk in her cozy old farmhouse, looking out across the back yard as she meditatively sipped her coffee, then flew into a frenzy of inspired typing. She'd expected to love being her own boss, setting her own hours, and being invited to sign books for a long line of adoring fans.

Reality had been less kind. Mabel didn't even have a desk with a view, and her cluttered kitchen table wasn't conducive to flights of creativity. Plus, she was frustrated with trying to think how to phrase things that always sounded better in her head than they did when she finally got them down in black-and-white.

One thing she could do for her writing career—while avoiding actual writing—was call Rachel about volunteering with search and rescue. It was a good cause—and as John had suggested, after she'd been out with them once, she ought to know enough to write about it as a volunteer opportunity.

She dug through her big, slouchy purse, and came up with the crumpled business card. Mabel squinted and dialed.

"Rachel? This is Mabel Browne, from the TV station this morning?"

"Oh, hi—I hoped you'd call."

"Hey, I've been giving some thought to maybe coming out sometime, if you're training?"

"That would be wonderful. How about this weekend? We'll be out on a joint training exercise with the Shawnee County S&R at the state park Saturday morning. Clear Creek—you know where that is?"

Mabel hadn't expected anything quite that soon—and she definitely hadn't expected to be involved in any activities with Shawnee County, which might include John's ex-girlfriend. She found herself automatically running through excuses, before giving herself a mental shake. "Uh, sure. In fact, my family has a cabin up in that area. What time?"

"Eight o'clock, okay? We'll already be there. We like to get an early start, so we can run a bunch of searches with different dogs."

"In the morning?"

Rachel laughed. "Is that too early for you?"

Yes.

"Er, no. Eight is fine. Where should I meet you?"

Rachel promised to email directions, along with instructions so Mabel could arrive ready to do her job.

"Am I allowed to bring my dog?"

"Sorry. It would be better if you don't. Would he be excitable if he had to wait in the car and you disappeared into the woods without him?"

"Yeah, probably," Mabel admitted. "How long should I plan to be out there?"

"We'd love to have you for the full day, if possible. We'll have more than one dog we're working with, and some are more experienced than others. But as long as you're able to give us even half a day, that would be great."

"What happens if the weather's bad?"

Rachel laughed again. "We get wet. Or cold. Or cold and wet. When we go out on a search, we don't get to wait for better weather. The dogs have to be ready for anything."

Seeming to accurately interpret Mabel's silence, she added, "There's a front coming through. The end-of-the-week forecast is dry and milder."

Sleet rattled against the wavy old windowpanes.

After hanging up, Mabel groaned. What had she gotten herself into? *It's a good cause*, she reminded herself. *And this will make my second volunteer job.* Plus, she might get the chance to check out John's ex, Victoria, with no one the wiser.

The idea of writing about volunteering for seniors had lost a lot of its initial appeal, once she'd started the actual work. After the excitement of solving the Sauer murders and almost getting herself killed, writing a true crime book felt a lot more interesting. Mabel found herself wishing, not for the first time, that she could dump the whole volunteer thing. Could she make a career of true crime? Doubtful.

Her phone rang in her hand and made her jump.

"Mabel Browne?" a female voice asked. "This is Marie Passantino. The activities coordinator down at the senior center? I saw you on the Country Morning show and wondered if you might be interested in coming and speaking to us about volunteering."

A few minutes later, Mabel had a speaking engagement to write on her calendar. Of course, they hadn't offered to pay her, but Mabel had managed to squeeze a small honorarium out of them that would at least cover her gas. Maybe this was the start of something, she reasoned. She'd begun the morning on TV and already had invitations to give a talk and join a hip-hop group.

After straightening the kitchen, sorting the messy stack of mail, and wiping up Barnacle's pawprints, Mabel ran out of excuses for not writing. She settled herself at the kitchen table, her de facto desk. Barnacle, her faithful assistant, lay down on her left foot. He was still wet, and the damp soon penetrated her sock and pantleg. But he was snoring, and she couldn't bear to wake him.

Once she got started, her writing session went pretty well. She managed to finish most of a chapter outline for her now famous, but still unwritten, true crime book.

The sleety rain had stopped, so Mabel also managed to get Barnacle out for a short walk. It was already nearly dark. Since the recent time change, it seemed dusk fell practically in the middle of the afternoon. Koi, lounging in her basket, yawned and watched them go.

They walked up the long block from Mabel's house, which sat at the wooded dead end of Carteret Street, to the Sauer house at the corner. The two houses were the only structures on that side of the street, with Mabel's overgrown field between them—the field the township had ordered her to cut. Three other houses sat across from the Sauer property, but the rest of that side of the street was taken up by more woods, opposite Mabel's house.

The Sauer house, home of the local historical society, was also the site of the infamous 1939 ax murders of Walter Sauer, Sr., and his son,

Walter Sauer, Jr., as well as the more recent murder of Helen Thornwald, who'd been Mabel's neighbor on her back-property line.

Mabel couldn't pass the Sauer house without remembering everything that had happened there—and what had happened to her as a result. In the end, she'd prevailed. She might still be an unemployed lawyer, but she'd also solved the most notorious cold case in the history of the state, if not the entire country.

They turned left at the Sauer house and walked up another block before turning home. Barnacle pulled to go farther, but Mabel resisted. "I'll make it up tomorrow," she promised, wrapping her coat tighter around her.

The phone rang as they entered the kitchen. "Did you wow them?"

"Hey, Lisa." Mabel hesitated. "It went okay, I guess." The further she got from the interview, the more uncertain she felt about her performance.

"Come on, I'm sure you were the star of the show—solving murders, confronting killers."

Mabel couldn't help noticing the hint of envy in Lisa's voice. Having missed most of the action she was describing had been a bitter pill for her true-crime-fancying friend.

"Well...oddly enough, we didn't get into much of that."

"Really?"

"The whole spot was less than five minutes, and of course, I couldn't discuss a lot of it because of the criminal case. And my book."

"Of course." Lisa cleared her throat. "You want to come over this evening and watch a movie?"

"Sure. I can tell you about my new volunteer thing. I'm going out with the canine search and rescue this weekend and help them train."

"Not to sound rude, but how?"

Mabel reminded herself Lisa was her oldest friend. "I'm going to be lost in the woods, and the dogs are supposed to find me."

"Make sure you use your tick spray. But seriously, good for you. You know they found that missing old man this afternoon."

"No kidding? They said they had no place to pick up a trail."

"Yeah, a clothing article turned up, and the dogs took it from there. I guess he's going to be all right. Poor guy has dementia, and he walked as far as he could into a thicket of briars till he got stuck."

Mabel felt a combination of relief and pride. Of course, she hadn't done anything…yet. But maybe she was finally going to do something valuable as a volunteer. Her gig at the historical society had ended in homicide, so it should be fairly easy to top that, anyway.

When Mabel left that evening, Koi was nowhere to be found. Mabel searched, called, and shook the treat container, but only Barnacle came drooling. Clearly, the feline princess was snubbing her. "Look, I'm sorry. Tomorrow I'll be home all day—I promise."

Barnacle planted himself by the door, his face reflecting a desperate plea to come too. He hadn't been named Barnacle for nothing. "Oh, all right. You can ride along."

Mabel's petite friend was waiting when Mabel arrived. Ulysses still sat on the windowsill, his gaze following Mabel's every move as she hung her coat over a chair. "That cat's planning to knife me in the hallway."

Lisa tossed her dark hair. "He only needs to get used to you. Him's a big love muffin, aren't you?" She rubbed the cat's chin, and he stretched for her to pick him up.

Mabel glanced down at her car. Barnacle had moved into the driver seat, lying with his snout against the side window. A patient rider, he seemed to be napping, having learned she'd return for him.

Lisa wanted to watch *The Lodger*, an ancient Alfred Hitchcock thriller, on the classic movie channel. She explained the plot, revolving around Jack the Ripper and a naïve young woman, convinced her family's sketchy boarder was innocent despite all evidence to the contrary.

Sure, the guy has a picture of one of the victims in his room. Sure, he goes out for the evening, and another body turns up. *Girl, get a clue.*

Mabel had no appetite for suspense, but friendships required compromise. She only hoped she'd be able to sleep tonight in her lonely house. At least Lisa lived in the middle of town.

While they waited for the movie to start, Mabel told Lisa about her interview and what she'd learned about search and rescue. "I kind of want to see them do it," she concluded. "I mean I know they can do amazing things, but at the same time..." She searched for a way to explain.

"It almost seems impossible," Lisa suggested.

"Yeah. It's like a real-life superpower."

"I guess it is a superpower from our perspective. We humans sure can't do it," Lisa said.

Ulysses, draped across Lisa's lap, opened his eye at her and purred. He seemed to appreciate her humility.

"You want to make the popcorn? I don't want to disturb his lordship. It makes him so sad."

"Of course." Mabel curtsied deeply and rolled her eyes. For a cat who'd been getting his meals out of dumpsters until a few months ago, he certainly had an exacting list of requirements for his new roommate.

The movie was every bit as suspenseful as Mabel had feared, and she watched a fair chunk of it with her eyes closed. After bidding Lisa good night, she stepped back out onto the deserted street with her heart pounding. Every dark alcove seemed a potential hiding place for an attacker.

She fumbled the car door open then had to shove Barnacle back into the passenger seat. When she finally clicked the lock, relief flooded over her.

Home was only a few blocks away, but her street seemed darker than ever when she turned in, especially her tree-shrouded dead end. The phone rang in her cupholder. *Hot-Blooded.* John's ringtone. She'd have to change that—it had already embarrassed her more than once.

She tucked the phone under her chin and gathered her stuff so she could dart inside.

"Hey. You home?"

"Just got here. Hang on."

With leash and keys in hand, she tugged the reluctant dog, who'd decided it was time to explore the spooky, overgrown bushes, toward the door. "All right," she panted. "I'm going inside now."

They chatted as she settled her things and put Barnacle on his cable for his bedtime potty stop. Koi emerged from under the cupboard, stretching. She rubbed against Mabel's legs as if to say all was forgiven.

With the dog back inside, Mabel set the alarm and dispensed evening treats, including some cookies for herself. Funny how much safer she felt when she was on the phone with somebody, especially John. She yawned, already dreading the early drive up into the mountains Saturday morning.

"Maybe I'll go out with you," he offered.

"Seriously?"

"Sure. It might be a nice thing we could do together."

"Like you and Victoria did?"

"Well, yeah, sort of."

Mabel scowled. "Rachel said this is a joint training exercise. Won't that be awkward for you?"

"Why?"

She stammered. "Well, you were...she was..."

"Victoria and I are only friends. Truly. We went out together a long time ago and soon realized we were a lot better as friends than a couple. She's married now, for goodness' sake. You'll like her."

Doubtful.

"And she's going to like you too."

"Sure she will."

"So, you're jealous?" She heard the grin in his voice.

Mabel sniffed. "Don't flatter yourself."

He laughed out loud, then turned serious. "Listen, if you don't want me along..."

Mabel wanted to snub him, but somehow heard herself mumble, "I guess you can come if you really want."

Chapter Four

RACHEL'S WEATHER PREDICTION PROVED TRUE. BY Thursday, the temperature had crept into the sixties. Friday afternoon was cooler— yet sunshine still bathed the fading, early November landscape. Mabel even had to slap at a couple flies as she stood, watching Acey move a wheelbarrow full of ancient paint cans and rusted tools to the curb.

Mabel was relieved at least she wasn't paying him by the hour but wondered how much this shed incident was pushing back the brush-cutting project. For what had started as such a tiny project, it had certainly dragged on, as Acey repeatedly took days off to work elsewhere or go "huntin'." The yard and flowerbeds were better, but she was going to have to call the township again and beg for more time to get the field cut.

Acey had tried to squeeze her for the cost of body work to the dented back end of his truck. Her refusal had put him into a bit of a snit, and he didn't glance her way as he pushed the wheelbarrow past her, huffing as if he were pushing a boulder up a mountain like Sisyphus. If chutzpah were cheese, Acey would cover a whole lot of pizzas.

"Well," she said, "it looks like you've got this under control for now. If you don't think you're going to get to the brush this week, I guess I'd better go have a chat with the township."

"I'll be lucky if I get to 'er by next week." He cast a forlorn look across the overgrown back field. "Plus, it's so tall now, I'll prob'ly have to rent a brush hog, especially now my Cadet got damaged."

More money. While the weeds would die off in the next hard frost, the brambles and shrubby stuff were only going to lose their leaves. "Look, I'm going to run over there right now and file something to get us more time. Try not to burn the house down or anything while I'm gone, okay?"

"I ain't burning nuthin'. It's too dry. I'll have to haul stuff away when I get to cuttin'."

"Good." Mabel had learned Acey was extremely literal, and sarcasm tended to fly over his head like a flock of geese.

Next morning, a heavy fog cloaked the road as John drove into the mountains, and frost encrusted the grass and weeds. Mabel cradled a travel mug of coffee and nibbled one of the doughnuts John had brought along for the ride.

John, as always, appeared oblivious to the yummy pastries. He also seemed to be incubating a cold. "Maybe you shouldn't have come," Mabel ventured.

"I'm okay—just a bit snuffly. Most likely my allergies."

It was impossible to see where the road was about to bend next, so John crept along, pulling off at one point for the impatient driver of an oversize pickup with tires that would have come up past Mabel's waist. "Godspeed, buddy," John said wryly.

"Some people have a death wish." Mabel licked sugar off her fingers. "There's no way he can see what's in front of him."

A brown wooden sign with white lettering loomed up in the mist—*Clear Creek State Park 21 Miles.*

Mabel checked the time. "We're going to be late."

"This is as fast as I can go in this pea soup." John crouched over the wheel, as if that would help him see better.

Mabel sighed. "I know. I still hate being late the very first time out. I seem to get off on the wrong foot every time I volunteer."

John snorted. "You've only volunteered two places so far. We won't be all that late. That's why we left early, right?"

Mabel tried to relax. There was nothing she could do to get there any sooner. She checked her phone. As fast as she could, before they went out of her service area, she texted to let Rachel know they were swimming slowly through fog.

Mabel felt a frisson of apprehension. What had she gotten herself into?

The temperature had dipped again, but it did remain dry, as Rachel had promised. As recommended, Mabel had dressed for the woods in old jeans, rubber-soled boots, a flannel shirt and insulated jacket, both of which bore snags and rips of unknown origin.

The closer they got to the park, the more Mabel questioned her attire. While Rachel had told her to dress for bugs, briars, and broken branches, she now dreaded meeting John's ex, Victoria, who she knew would be skinny and dressed like a model in a wilderness outfitting catalog.

"Ha." John signaled for the park entry, at last. "Ten minutes to spare."

The entrance road wound between towering hemlocks, then split. A sign to the left said, *Look-Out Point, Carver Point, Mayfield Picnic Area, Primitive Camping.* A rustic ranger booth at the intersection was closed for the season, with boards over the windows. On the right branch, Mabel saw a larger log building with a parking lot around it, empty but for a green Parks pickup truck.

John made the left turn, and they bounced through ruts filled with standing rainwater. The overhanging trees—mostly maples and oaks—were bare, apart from a few tired hangers-on, brown and faded gold. Above them, a few old-growth hemlocks stood like sentinels. Rachel had said to meet at Carver Point parking lot.

Mabel cracked the window for a whiff of the clean air. The fog had lifted, apart from ribbons of mist still hanging in the low places, and the sun seeped between the trees like honey. Hemlock scent mixed with the musk of wet, fallen leaves.

John smiled across at her. "Nice, huh?"

Mabel smiled back.

About a mile into the woods, a small sign appeared on the right—*Carver Point 1.5 Mi.* A larger sign in stenciled block letters read, *Carver Point Look Out Closed to Public, Dangerous Landslides, Road Open to Trailhead Parking.*

The side road was narrower and nearly washed out in places. John's car lurched in and out of ruts and over rocks. They crossed a rustic bridge over a sparkling stream, and the road began a sharp climb.

Circling a bend, Mabel held her breath. Between them and the drop-off into the treetops below, stood only a flimsy-looking guide rail. She couldn't help noticing the soft dirt at the edge of the road had eroded away.

They survived what Mabel, mumbling under her breath, called "Dead Man's Curve" and climbed a more gradual arc in the other direction. Soon the trailhead parking sign appeared on the right.

A cluster of sport utility vehicles and trucks sat scattered around the crushed stone lot. Several large branches, probably brought down by the last storm, lay on the ground. A few men and women stood talking and sipping from take-out cups.

Inside the vehicles, a couple of dogs barked, voices high and excited, while most sat or lay at their people's feet or paced at the end of leashes, tongues lolling, faces happy and expectant. All wore little blaze-orange vests like miniature squirrel hunters—except theirs all said, "Search & Rescue."

"Victoria's here," John said, at almost the same moment Mabel pointed. "There's Rachel and Sammy."

Mabel swiveled for a look at John's ex. Victoria was tiny—a compact maybe five-footer, with a tousled cap of short, red curls. She was laughing out loud at something, her head tossed back. Victoria had a wide, generous mouth, and she struck Mabel as the sort of person who was happy and fun to be around.

She was wearing worn jeans, like Mabel—though perhaps four or five sizes smaller, along with a form-fitting stone-gray T-shirt and businesslike hiking boots. As Mabel had feared, she looked great.

Victoria's dog focused as they pulled in, following them with his eyes. "Cap sure knows this car." John grinned.

They pulled into a space near the other vehicles. Mabel caught Rachel's eye and Rachel smiled broadly, waving. "I'm going to check in," Mabel said. She didn't want to admit to herself that this was partly a way of postponing her introduction to the great Victoria.

"Okay. I'll go hang with Victoria for a couple minutes, while you get your marching orders…or should I say, 'hiding orders?'"

With a little pang, she watched him walk off to stand with Victoria's group. *ANT,* Mabel thought. *ANT, ANT, ANT, ANT.*

"Mabel!" Rachel greeted her. "You pumped up for your first outing?"

"Yes?"

Rachel laughed lightly. "You're going to have fun. Sometimes it's a bit uncomfortable, but it *is* always a lot of fun."

A nose nudged Mabel's calf, and she looked down to see Sammy greeting her. She bent to tousle his soft ears. "Hi, sweetie. Are you going to show me what you've got?"

"He's raring to go."

"Mabel."

She turned to see John approaching with Victoria and her Malinois. "I have somebody I want you to meet."

Rachel smiled. Of course, she and Victoria knew each other, if they did these joint training events very often. Their dogs wagged at each other too.

"Hey." Victoria stuck out her hand as John made the introduction. Mabel towered over her. She felt like a different species—like Bigfoot meeting a chipmunk.

John just introduced her as "Mabel." Had he referred to her as his girlfriend when he was talking to Victoria? Or as his "friend?" She wished she knew.

"Glad to meet you." Mabel wondered if that counted as telling a lie.

"You too," Victoria said. "This is Cap. Cap, shake with Mabel."

The beautiful sleek dog had a taupe coat and melting brown eyes in a black-dipped face. He lifted a paw. Mabel shook it. "How do you do, Cap?" The last time she'd taken Barnacle's paw, she remembered, was to scrub off mud clumps. Even Victoria's dog was winning.

"John tells me you're going to help us train. That's awesome. It can be hard to get people to come spend a whole day crouched in the underbrush."

"I'm glad to do it," Mabel said, and it was true. She hoped she still felt that way by the end of the afternoon.

She introduced John and Rachel. While they'd never met before, they seemed to have a certain automatic camaraderie as people who knew search and rescue.

"Ready?" Rachel asked. "I'm going to let Millie try to find you first. She's young, but she's already been out searching, and had some training as a cadaver dog. She's amazingly talented. Certain dogs are born to do this."

"Okay, sure." Mabel looked around, wondering if Millie was one of the dogs milling around the parking lot. "What do I do?"

"You're going to hide in the woods. We'll walk you out a half mile or so, and then you'll have to sit and be quiet for as long as it takes for Millie to locate you, okay?"

"How long does that usually take?" Mabel was happy it was mild for November, but the woods might still be damp. She wished she'd brought something to sit on.

"Depends," Victoria said. "Heat or cold make a difference. Humidity. Wind speed and direction. Depends on the dog too."

"Millie's good." Rachel grinned. "Bet you'll be home for Thanksgiving."

John and Victoria laughed. Mabel managed a polite smile, but at this point, wasn't really feeling the humor.

"Here you go." Rachel handed her a camo tarp. "This is going to help hide you, so the dogs have to rely on their noses. You want to 'lose her,' John?"

"Glad to." The two stepped away to the hood of Rachel's SUV, where they conferred over notes and cell phones.

"Ready, Mabel?" John gestured toward the woods as he returned to her, swiping at his nose with a tissue.

"Um…"

"You need the bathroom?" Victoria asked. "Might be a good idea. Anytime I know I can't go for a while, it's all I can think about."

"Uh, yeah. That's probably a good idea."

She hated outhouses, but choices here in the woods were limited. Holding her breath, Mabel ducked into the nearest one and prayed there were no spiders.

As soon as she slipped back outside into the clean air, Mabel sucked down a big breath of fresh hemlock and fallen-leaf scent, grateful for good lung capacity. She also gave thanks for hand sanitizer. She might be way out in the forest, but one had to maintain a few standards.

John grinned and led on. She swallowed hard and prepared to face her wilderness ordeal.

Chapter Five

MABEL TRAILED JOHN INTO THE WOODS, following a trace marked as the path to Carver Point Overlook. Another "closed" sign sat at the trailhead, and brush intruded on the little-used path.

John pushed aside branches for her. Though most of the encroaching growth was rhododendron or mountain laurel, rather than briars, broken twigs snagged at her clothing.

The path was still damp, and in places, muddy. "Is it okay to be walking back here, if it's closed to the public?"

"Yeah. They're using it because the dogs need some practice in heavy brush and rough terrain. The only reason the trail's closed is to keep people away from the landslide area, where rocks have been breaking away from the old overlook. We aren't going anywhere near that. The rangers know we're here. They signed off on it."

"Well, they got the right place, if they're looking for rough terrain." Mabel puffed. The trail climbed upward, and Mabel wished she'd worn actual hiking boots. Every time she stepped on loose rocks or a protruding tree root, her ankles wobbled, and she grabbed at the back of John's shirt to keep from wiping out.

She was panting. John seemed to climb easily. She suspected clean living might be a factor. *If I survive this,* she promised herself, *I'm getting in shape. No more Farmhand breakfasts at the Coffee Cup.*

"You okay back there?"

"Fine." Mabel mumbled. "Are we almost there?"

"Maybe halfway. We're going off the trail now."

"What?"

He turned and flashed a grin. "I think you heard me."

The way got rougher, as they scrambled over downed trees and lurched in and out of holes hidden by layers of fallen leaves. Mabel fell, making her wipeout all the more spectacular by rolling as she landed, legs waving in the air like a helpless bug.

"Here you go." John pulled her back onto her feet. "Did you do any damage?"

Mabel gasped. "Just knocked the air out of myself." Her jeans and the left side of her shirt bore smears of dirt.

John turned her hand over. "Your palm's bleeding."

"It's okay." She tried to pull it back. Falling was always so embarrassing. Getting hurt only made it worse.

"Do you have some tissues for that, at least?"

"Yeah, it's fine." She squirted hand sanitizer on it and yelped at the sting. "It's just a scrape."

"All right, if you say so." John resumed thrashing through the brush with Mabel stumbling behind him. He paused from time to time to consult his phone for their course.

Mabel felt weak with relief when he called a halt. "Okay. Here's your spot." He handed her a folded rain poncho to sit on. "Sit right here and throw that camo tarp over your head. Then all you have to do is wait. Try to stay as still and quiet as you can."

She looked around. A sizeable fallen oak had landed in the middle of a sprawling patch of green briar and multiflora rose. Leafless now but dense and tangled, the stand of brush created a semi-hidden nook. She supposed that tree trunk was her seat.

John handed her a walkie-talkie and explained how to use it if needed. "Now, sit tight. You're actually not far from the old overlook— we took the shortcut." John pointed uphill, where light showed through the trees. "You'll be fine."

With a sudden pang, she watched him leave. "John."

He turned.

"What if the dog can't find me? How will I know? How long should I wait? What should I do?"

He grinned. "She'll find you. Don't worry."

"What if she doesn't?"

"She will, but you can use the walkie if you get desperate. You know what? *I'll* find you."

Mabel watched him go. His dark brown jacket was already melting into the woods when she thought of something else. "John."

"What?"

"What if I have an emergency? Like a bear or something?"

"You won't."

"But I could."

"Walkie-talkie like I showed you. And you have your cell, don't you?"

Mabel checked. At least her phone still had a couple bars, and the battery was pretty good—but not great.

This spot felt so desolate. She knew there were bears up here and coyotes. Rattlesnakes too, but at least they had the decency to hibernate as soon as temperatures started dropping. Would the bears be hibernating by now too? Or had it been warm enough for the critters to come back out? Well…it had hit the thirties again the past couple nights, so…

She pulled out her phone to look up hibernation patterns but was distracted by the sensation of something crawling on her stomach. A bug must have gotten inside her shirt.

Mabel struggled to reach the bug, which might or might not have been real. This stupid spot in the woods stank too. Probably a dead raccoon or something, but since the breeze had shifted, it smelled pretty rank.

What if a pack of coyotes had brought down a deer? Maybe they had a den nearby. If they came back for it, would they see her as a threat?

It was rare, but Mabel knew of cases where a pack of coyotes had surrounded a large dog or even an isolated person. She jumped back up again.

No. It was more likely a carcass left by a hunter. It was always some kind of hunting season up here. Even if the park itself was off limits, a wounded animal could travel a long way before succumbing.

Mabel settled down to wait. It had taken so long to get this far into the woods. John had told her he was taking a different route back, so it might be a while before the dog headed out.

It would be maybe twenty minutes till John made it back to the group—at least. Would Millie make a beeline for Mabel? She hoped so.

The dog would follow a trail of Mabel's discarded skin cells. It was hard to believe she'd dropped them by the thousands while they were walking. All those lost skin cells, and she still had a body. Could Millie really sort out Mabel's scent from John's…and all this smelly wilderness? She pulled her collar up over her nose.

She no longer heard the distant crash of John's retreating footsteps. Something landed on her forehead, and she slapped at it. Barnacle's vet had told her to keep giving his preventatives through the winter months, because ticks and mosquitoes were still hanging around. She hoped she wasn't going to end up itchy. Or get West Nile or Lyme disease.

Mabel pulled out her phone and started searching West Nile virus.

You are offline. Please check your connection and try again.

She really needed a better service provider. Mabel sighed and eyed the time. John had only been gone five minutes. It was too cold for mosquitoes, anyhow.

Mabel stood and stretched. Why should she cramp up, trying to stay crouched, when the dog couldn't possibly get here for half an hour or more?

The walkie-talkie crackled, then went silent. She stared at it. Had someone been trying to reach her? She sat again.

There was nothing to do out here but think—and gag on that putrid deer smell. Too much for a raccoon, she thought—yet when a mouse had once died inside her kitchen wall, the stench had been nearly enough to drive her to a motel. She couldn't see the carcass, but she couldn't ignore it, either. Maybe she should move to another spot. The dog wouldn't care.

Mabel held her wintergreen lip balm under her nose. Better. She smeared a bit on her upper lip and covered her nose before checking the time again.

What would it be like if she were really lost? How scary to have to worry about weather, food, wildlife, and water. She hoped she could find her way back to the trail, but could she really? She'd read about people lost in the woods, who walked miles and miles, only to discover they'd been going in circles.

The temperature was supposed to drop even further tonight. Could she make a shelter with hemlock boughs? Or would she die of exposure?

Mabel was starting to hyperventilate. She stood and took a few deep breaths before choking on the smell. Thank goodness it wasn't warm today.

Her seat on the log was so hard and narrow. It also tilted to the right. Her bottom had been getting numb.

Crashing sounds erupted in the woods below her. Mabel's heartbeat skipped. Was it too soon for Millie to be coming? She looked at her phone again—another seven minutes had gone by.

Please don't let it be a bear. Once she'd made herself look as big as possible and made as much noise as she could, that was the extent of her anti-bear arsenal. Even if she called for help, John could never get here in time.

Mabel spun in a circle, looking for a tree to climb. Could bears climb? She thought maybe they could. There was nothing around her, anyway, but dense brush and big trees without low branches.

The crashing died away. Probably just a running deer.

Running from what? A bear? Coyotes? Bigfoot?

Ughhh. That smell.

Mabel made herself sit down and threw the tarp back over her head. She pulled the lip balm back out of her jeans pocket and inhaled. She could do this. It was for a good cause—search dogs saved lives.

After the longest, slowest forty minutes of her life, Mabel heard crashing again, but this time, she also heard voices. *Please let it be Millie and Rachel.*

Mabel crouched, trying not to leap to her feet, screaming for help. She buried her head with her arms, trying to hide.

Agonizing moments dragged by as the thrashing and voices came nearer. A cold, wet nose burrowed under the tarp and touched Mabel's cheek.

"Yes. Good girl, Millie." Rachel's voice came from overhead.

Relief surged through Mabel's body. She straightened to give Millie, a shaggy, young, black-and-white border collie, a hug of desperate gratitude. The dog sat alert and whining, focused on a spot in the bushes ahead. An instant later, she leapt to her feet and plunged on through the brush, not even waiting for her treat, the ball Rachel was holding out.

Abruptly, Rachel threw her arm out in front of John, who'd been following her and Millie. She nodded toward the dog, who was trying to sit, but having trouble settling her bottom in the heavy brush.

Mabel peered past Millie, through the makeshift path the dog had broken into the stand of brush and briars. A surge of bile rose in her throat, and Mabel staggered away, dropped to her knees, and vomited up her coffee and doughnuts.

She had been sharing her hiding place with a dead human body, and Millie had just found it.

Chapter Six

MABEL KNELT IN THE DAMP LEAVES, shaky, sweaty, and strangely cold. She wiped her mouth and blew her nose. She wished she'd brought more tissues—and something to rinse her mouth.

Dimly, she heard Rachel briefing someone on the phone and reading out coordinates. Mabel felt a hand on her back. John was holding out a bottle of water.

She wished she hadn't vomited in front of him. He'd certainly seen plenty of her at her worst.

His eyes were full of sympathy. He gently rubbed her shoulders. "Is your stomach settled now?"

Mabel nodded. Still, the combined smell of the dead body and her own upchuck made that questionable. A breeze lifted her sweaty bangs. It felt good, and it carried some of the smell away from her.

Millie came over, sniffing at Mabel. She carried her soft yellow ball in her mouth, and made it squeak. She shoved the toy at Mabel, looking hopeful.

John laughed. "You're a smart girl, Millie."

Sick and shaken as she was, Mabel had to smile. "Good girl." She stroked Millie's droopy ears. "Good job."

This amazing dog, little more than a puppy, had tracked her through the woods, right to her hiding place—then went ahead and located a dead body too. Still petting Millie's ears, Mabel stole a look at the body in question.

It appeared to be wrapped in a tarp, but a discolored hand had escaped the crude wrapping job. Despite decomposition—and maybe some animal damage—it looked like a man's, especially considering the overall bulk of the package. Flies swarmed around the grisly bundle.

John's gaze followed hers. "Hang on." He paused as Rachel

clicked off her phone. "Did you get the police?"

Though she bent to playfully tussle with Millie over the ball, Rachel's mouth was tight. "They're on their way. I can't believe this."

John gestured toward the tarp. "I'm going to take a look, all right?"

Rachel nodded. "Just be careful not to contaminate the scene."

John smiled thinly. "Don't worry. I'm a PI...or was." Using a stick, he lifted the edge of the tarp near the apparent head end.

Her embarrassing round of barfing had stifled Mabel's natural curiosity. She kept an eye on John but had no desire to move in for a closer look.

His back was turned. She thought she heard a sharp intake of breath but couldn't be sure. He looked down for a moment, then dropped the stick.

"Well?" Rachel asked as John turned back to them.

He only shook his head.

Rachel raised her eyebrows but didn't prod. Maybe she was hesitant because she didn't really know John.

Mabel didn't have those compunctions. As soon as she'd seen John's grim expression, she'd been wild to know what the deal was. She supposed seeing a decaying corpse at close range had brought down more than one tough guy. Still, she'd never seen John have an attack of the vapors.

"Are you okay?" she whispered, as soon as he got within range.

Again, just the head shake. She doubted John could smell much with that cold or allergies he had brewing, but he looked rather green.

Mabel grabbed his sleeve. "What?"

"We need to talk."

John's muttered "We need to talk" echoed in Mabel's head. She glanced at Rachel, who was back on her phone a few feet away. Mabel couldn't hear the quiet conversation and assumed Rachel couldn't hear them, either.

"Let's talk then."

He shook his head. "Not now. I need to think."

Mabel kept eyeing him, but he'd already stepped away, approaching the body again. A twig dropped from a nearby tree, and the plop sounded loud in the quiet.

For a few seconds, she considered following John, but he'd made it clear he wasn't going to talk for a while. She did wonder what he was looking for, though, as he stared at the tarp-wrapped bundle.

A graceful squirrel leapt through the leaf litter and scrambled up the tree next to her, carrying something in its mouth. Millie popped her head up and dropped her ball, watching it go. A muscle twitched in her shoulder.

Mabel smiled. Dogs were so basic. To Millie, this was obviously just another fun outing in the woods.

Rachel stuck her phone in her hip pocket. "Everybody back at base is dying of curiosity."

Mabel tipped her head at the tarp. "Have you ever found a dead body before?"

"Yeah, but not like this. A suicide or a guy who'd had a heart attack while he was out hunting. Not a murder victim."

Mabel swallowed. Of course, that was what this was. A person who'd died in an accident—or by his own hand—did not tend to wrap himself in a tarp. Somebody had to have rolled this body up that way. With a sinking sensation, she realized she was in the middle of her third murder in about a month. At any rate, the police couldn't try to pin this one on her.

At least, she didn't think so. Lieutenant Sizemore would hardly believe Mabel's showing up at another murder scene in a matter of weeks was a mere unfortunate coincidence. Then again, thank heaven, this was probably well out of Sizemore's jurisdiction.

She wondered who the dead guy was and wished she could take a peek without disturbing the crime scene. On the other hand, maybe she didn't want a peek. The sight of flies crawling over that mottled, swollen hand would be more than enough to give her nightmares.

"John—what you looking at?" Rachel called out.

"Trying to make sense of this, I guess. Why this guy's way up here, how he got here. I doubt anybody could've carried him up that trail."

"So, likely killed right here," Mabel said.

"Or nearby." John straightened, scanning the hillside.

"Even if he was killed on the trail, it would be hard to drag him back in this far, let alone rolled up that way."

"Now I'm looking for it, I can see some disturbance in the brush." John nodded toward the body.

At first, Mabel couldn't see whatever John did. He made his way back to stand next to her. He leaned close, pointing so she could sight along his arm. "Look right above the body. At the slope coming down."

"Oh, yeah. Look at that," Rachel said.

Mabel guessed she wasn't the outdoorsman John and Rachel were, because she still couldn't see much but leaves, rocks, downed branches—basic woods stuff. Nevertheless, after staring hard for a moment, she began noticing little things. A fallen branch really wasn't. It was a sapling bent down to the ground, with a split at the bent spot. And that good-sized rock had loose dirt on top, as if it had been rolled over.

"Looks like someone may have dragged the body down this way, huh?" Rachel squinted. "You thinking from the overlook? How close are we to that?"

"Oh, it's right there," John said. "Yeah, that's what I'm thinking. More likely rolled it, though, don't you think? Easier. Then tried to cover the marks that left."

Mabel's brain whirred, trying to catch up. Did having the tarp up here imply premeditation? Or might the killer have returned to gift wrap his victim...? "How did they get him wrapped like that?"

John shrugged. "I'd've probably laid out the tarp where I wanted him and rolled him right down onto it."

"Not sure if I should be proud or horrified at your murder cover-up skills."

John grimaced. "Me, neither..."

"Why use a tarp at all if you're not using it to transport the body? Doesn't it just scream 'murder'?"

John shrugged. "Maybe if you're afraid you'll need to move it later. Or to help camouflage it long enough for the body to deteriorate. Cause of death may be so obvious you wouldn't need the tarp to know it's murder anyway."

Mabel squinted upward, where horizon light showed through the trees. "Why not just send the body over the bluff?"

"Best guess? Either the killer was too smart to risk his neck getting that close to the edge and having it break away, or at this point the rangers have made it inaccessible."

"The authorities are on their way." Rachel's mouth twisted. "I'd say training's done for today."

"Do I have to stay here?" Mabel looked from John to Rachel to Millie.

She wanted out of here—out of the woods, and out of these clothes and barf-splashed shoes. Or sitting in John's comfy car, if not all the way back in her own sweet, messy home.

Rachel and John exchanged a look. Millie dropped her ball encouragingly at Mabel's feet.

"I don't see why you would," Rachel finally said. "John, why don't you take Mabel back to base and let her warm up? I think you guys better stick around till the cops arrive, but there shouldn't be any need for her to wait up here. If they need a physical escort back to the body, you ought to be able to lead them in."

John nodded. "That's what I think. Are you okay to stay here?"

"Sure. We're good. You can tell the others they might as well call it a day. I don't know if anybody else is still running a search. No one who's made it back to the vehicles is going to want to keep training with all the cops and coroner swarming around. They're not witnesses."

"Is Millie staying with you?"

"Of course. We're good here," Rachel repeated. "I'm sorry your first training exercise turned out this way."

44

Mabel waved a careless hand. "It's okay. It's not the first time. For a body, I mean."

Rachel's smile wavered. "I'd forgotten."

"I'm fine. Don't worry about it."

"Come on," John said. "Let's get out of here."

Mabel couldn't shake a strong sense of déjà vu. It hadn't been that long since people had been apologizing to her for the complication of a dead body on her first volunteer assignment with the historical society.

"Is it me?" she asked as soon as she and John were out of earshot.

He glanced over his shoulder. "Is what you?"

"Every time I volunteer somewhere, I trip over a dead body. I'm like Typhoid Annie."

John stopped and gripped her by the arms, looking deep into her eyes. "It's only happened two times—not 'every time.'"

"There's no 'only' about it. Who runs into *two* dead bodies? Wait—make that three, only a month apart? And, in this case, two times really are every time."

"It's a coincidence. You were out with a cadaver dog. You might as well blame her."

His attempted reassurances had little effect. Mabel couldn't shake the feeling she was somehow causing these corpses to pop up wherever she went.

John had started walking again.

"Do you think I might be like those teenagers who cause poltergeist activity? Because of their emotions and hormones?" she asked his back.

He laughed out loud at that and turned around again. "No. I don't think that. You are not causing dead bodies with the power of your mind, you goof."

He took a couple more steps and added, "And it's Typhoid Mary, not Typhoid Annie. Typhoid Mary was infected with a disease. Little Orphan Annie was a plucky inspiration."

Mabel stuck her tongue out at his back.

Neither spoke as they concentrated on navigating single file, back down the steep, rocky trail. When they finally reached a level stretch near the bottom, Mabel caught John's shirt. There had been something in his face when he'd turned from looking at the body. She'd simply been too shaken to process it.

"Did you recognize the…victim?" She could not bring herself to call that poor individual a "body."

He nodded, tight-lipped. "Yeah. I did."

Chapter Seven

"LATER," JOHN MUTTERED, AS HE AND Mabel emerged from the woods. A half-dozen search-and-rescue volunteers and five restless dogs still hung around the parking lot. The instant John and Mabel appeared, the people surrounding the open tailgate of an oversize black truck dropped their conversation and swarmed in. The group surrounded them, barraging them with questions.

John threw up his hands. "Hey, let this lady sit down and pull herself together for a bit. She's been out there a long time, and she's had a big shock. I'll be right back."

Mabel's relief at the sight of John's car almost brought her to tears. John started the engine. "I have almost a full tank, so you can let the heat run for a bit, till you start to feel better."

"I wish I'd brought a Thermos." She cast a longing look at her empty takeout cup.

John snapped his fingers. "I bet Victoria brought one. She's the most prepared person I know. Hang on."

She was about to tell him to forget it, but he'd already shut the door.

The heat felt good. Mabel lay back and savored the joy of a real, padded seat. She might still be stiff and smelly, but it was heaven not to be crouched on a log.

Mabel checked her reflection in the mirror on the back of the sun visor. *Good grief.* Had she started sprouting? Mabel leaned in for a better look. Dry leaves, seed puffs, and a large burr studded her hair. She began, hopelessly, weeding her crop of forest growth.

She was a horror—like she'd been volunteering with the annual Rotary Night of Fright, instead of search and rescue. Her pale face was puffy from lack of sleep. A miasma of barf rose in the warm car, and her hair had taken on a life of its own.

She watched John cross the lot to the cluster of other volunteers. Victoria grabbed his arm, said something, and he nodded. She held up her forefinger and opened the back door of her mud-splashed SUV. Her Malinois leapt inside.

A moment later, Victoria reemerged, toting a big Thermos. She gripped a yellow plastic grocery bag in her other hand. John excused himself from the group and the two approached the car.

"Hey," John said. "How you feeling?"

"I'm okay," Mabel said, although she knew she looked like Swamp Thing and smelled worse.

Victoria reached around him. "Pass me your cup." She filled it and passed it back.

"You poor thing." Her eyes were pitying.

Mabel wondered whether Victoria's sympathy was for the nightmare she'd lived through, or if it extended to her unsalvageable appearance.

"Here you go." Victoria held out the grocery bag.

Mabel looked inside. Apples, protein bars, baggies of trail mix, and similar healthy snacks abounded.

Nothing particularly appealed. Still, she was ravenous. And her nerves were rattled—a state she customarily treated with food. She helped herself to one of each snack and two of the granola bars. She ripped a package open and took a big bite.

"That must have been a terrible shock," Victoria said as Mabel passed the bag back.

Mabel nodded, mouth full of protein bar. It tasted like compressed cardboard and ground-up vitamin tablets, studded with desiccated raisins. She took a hard swallow, feeling the mouthful resist on the way down. "It was. I...never expected that."

"Neither did we," Victoria told her. "We've never had anything like that happen. It's plenty bad enough when it's what you set out looking for. Coming upon it the way you did—awful."

The sound of approaching vehicles made them all turn their heads.

Slowly jouncing over the bumps and ruts in the road, two police cars, a dark SUV, and an EMT unit came into view, pulled into the middle of the lot, and stopped. Most likely, the EMTs were only there to transport the body. She wondered if the dark car might be the coroner.

John gave Mabel an encouraging smile and stepped away, closing the car door. He and Victoria headed back to the cluster of waiting volunteers and milling dogs.

She reclined against the seat, watching as if it were all a play that had nothing to do with her. But it did. Soon, those police officers would be interviewing John, and then, they were going to turn and head her direction.

She had nothing to contribute. She'd been hiding, waiting for Millie to find her. Swatting at imagined bugs. Listening for predators. She had known zero about the corpse, with whom she'd been sharing her hiding spot, before Millie came bounding upon it.

Had come upon him, she corrected herself. That horrid sack of remains had—very recently—been a living, breathing human being. A person who surely hadn't deserved this terrible end.

Mabel was so sick of finding bodies.

Victoria headed her way with a cop following. It wasn't her nemesis from the Medicine Spring PD, Lieutenant Sizemore, at any rate. This team had come from the Shawnee County Sheriff's office, according to the logo on their car doors.

The tall, slim, dark-skinned officer was talking into his cell phone. Behind him, other police, along with the EMTs and a woman in jeans, split off to follow John toward the Carver Point Look Out Trail.

Great—she'd now been abandoned to her own devices. She guessed she'd be forced to rely on beautiful, young, capable Victoria for any support she was likely to get.

Mabel was calmer now. Somehow, she wanted to step into the fresh air and do her talking out there.

She clicked off the ignition, thrust the key into her coat pocket, and stepped outside.

"Hey, Mabel. This is Deputy Patel from the County Sheriff's Office. He wanted to take a statement, *if* you're up to it."

Mabel smiled wanly. "Sure." She appreciated Victoria's offering her a way out, but she didn't need it. Mabel's eyes followed Victoria, back to the small remaining cluster of volunteers.

Patel didn't smile. He flipped open a notepad and, after rummaging around under his jacket, pulled a pen from his uniform pocket. A hot pink feather pouf bobbed at the top, making Mabel wonder if he had a little girl at home, whose favorite pen was missing. She gave the officer respect for not commenting on it or even seeming to notice.

Mabel was able to give her account in a few minutes. She had little to offer beyond bare details of the discovery. Most of her account was taken up with explaining how she'd managed to spend so much time with a ripe body without even realizing it.

She also answered questions about her knowledge of the area— that she had grown up with a cabin only three miles away but had never been to this section of the park. Her knowledge of the victim—none. *But John knows something.* Remembering that, she felt her stomach do a slow rollover.

Only after the deputy had closed his notebook and headed off, making long, loping strides up the trail—most likely to join the rest of the team at the dead man's resting place—did Mabel realize Deputy Patel's questions hadn't all been so benign, after all.

She berated herself. What had she said? For a lawyer, she'd certainly let her guard down. Just because she'd discovered another dead body was no reason to get so flustered that she'd hand over information which could raise questions about John, if not herself.

It would all come out, anyway. Police would scour every possible relationship between the victim and his circle of family, friends, and acquaintances.

Mabel got back in the car and popped open a bag of trail mix. Absently, she watched the trailhead as she picked M&Ms and chocolate chips out of the mix before resorting to the raisins and nuts.

How had that body—that man—gotten all the way up that steep trail? Surely, nobody would have carried all that dead weight up that rugged climb, littered with big rocks and loose pebbles and booby-trapped with protruding tree roots.

Ergo, he must have walked up under his own power. Had he gone willingly, with somebody he knew and trusted? Or was he forced, making the climb ahead of someone with a gun to his back?

Mabel shuddered. Either scenario was too horrible to contemplate. Would she rather walk unsuspectingly, only to have the person she trusted turn on her, and realize she'd walked into a trap? Or would she rather struggle up that long trail, aware all the while of her jeopardy, maybe feeling that gun at her back, begging for her life?

None of the above. Mabel fervently hoped no one she loved ever had to experience such an end to their lives, herself included.

Chapter Eight

BY THE TIME JOHN, RACHEL, AND Millie finally plodded out of the woods, dusk was gathering. A crime scene tech unit, apparently borrowed from the neighboring—and larger—Bartle County had arrived and already made the trek up the hilly trail with their equipment, including what looked like lights.

The remaining volunteers, having resisted Rachel's initial advice to head home, were waiting to get all the details. They immediately mobbed John and Rachel.

Mabel had recovered enough to succumb to curiosity. She made her way to the cluster of people. Now that the sun had gone down, the temperature had dropped. A breeze stirred the hemlocks, releasing their scent on the cold air.

John beckoned her over to add her part of the story. Mabel attempted to be modest while telling the story with writerly flourishes, setting the scene in great detail.

Speculation was rampant as to what had happened to the victim. John and Rachel had heard the EMTs talking about an apparent gunshot wound, but of course, the coroner would be the final word on cause of death.

As they headed back to Medicine Spring, Mabel alternated between worrying whether Barnacle had peed on the floor by now and worrying about the murder. "John?"

He hit the brakes to avoid a deer that chose that moment to leap out in front of them. Mabel grabbed the dashboard.

After waiting a moment, in case more of the herd decided to try their luck, John resumed driving. Maybe the deer had distracted him because he didn't answer her. She studied his frowning profile and decided to wait.

Mabel's cell service had been spotty in the mountains, but as soon as they descended to where they could hop onto the interstate, missed calls and text messages began downloading.

Mabel listened to Jen's voicemail. "News travels fast," she told John. "The local news is already reporting discovery of a body in the state park."

She turned to the text messages. The first, from Lisa, simply read,

Again?!!

Another, from Jen.

Mom says body found in Clear Creek Park. Did you hear anything?

Jen's second message arrived seconds after the first.

Wasn't that up by where you were training dogs? Anywhere near the cabin?

John slowed to let a tractor trailer merge. "It's been a lot more of a day than you bargained for, hasn't it?"

"You can say that again."

Mabel texted Lisa and Jen.

A man's body in the brush near the abandoned overlook. No ID yet or cause of death.

Within a minute of hitting the "send" button, her phone rang.

Mabel toyed with not picking up but knew she couldn't avoid her sister forever.

"Mabel." Jen didn't bother with polite preliminaries. "Did you see that online somewhere?"

Mabel put the call on speaker.

"No. John's with me. We heard it from the police."

"The police? Why are they talking to you?"

Mabel shot John a helpless look, but he remained focused on the road.

"Well, actually, I was there."

"There, where?"

"I was there with…him. The body. I was up at Clear Creek Park, and—"

"Slow down. You were with the body?"

"I'm trying to explain. Today was my first training exercise with the canine search and rescue, right? Well, I was all by myself, way up in a remote part of the park, pretending to be lost…for the dogs, you know."

"Oh, good grief! You found him, didn't you? I can't believe it. You and your dead bodies all the time now."

Mabel ground her teeth but forcibly ignored the implication she was making some kind of sick hobby of searching for corpses. "No, I didn't find him. Not exactly. I mean I turned out not to be alone up there, because he was with me. The victim."

Silence echoed through the car. Then, another explosion. "What happened? How could you be with a body and not find it?"

"Well, you know how it is, out in the woods. You remember the raccoon that expired in the cabin crawlspace? Or when that hunter decided to gut his deer on the spot and leave the entrails? You just start out smelling something dead. An actual human murder victim isn't the first explanation that springs to mind. Millie, the dog, found him."

"Kudos to Millie, but are they sure this guy was murdered?"

"There's still going to be an autopsy. But yeah, it's pretty clear."

"Why? Maybe he was out walking and got lost up there. We've had a few pretty cold nights here lately. Maybe he died of exposure or something."

"I hear you, but the autopsy will sort it out. For now, I'd say wait for that. Or the later news reports."

"Hang on," Jen said. "Mom's calling."

Mabel chose that moment to "lose signal."

Her cell rang again. Lisa.

"You were there, weren't you? Start at the beginning and tell me everything."

"Have mercy, I'm exhausted," Mabel whined.

"Hey, give her a break," John said, loud enough for Lisa to hear. "We're still driving, and she's had a long, hard day, like you would not believe. I'm sure she'll be glad to give you all the details later."

Another silence settled over the car before a loud sigh from Lisa carried over the phone. "All right, sorry. I didn't mean to give you a hard time. Call as soon as you get home, okay?"

When Mabel hung up, she silenced the ringer, leaned back, and closed her eyes. After twenty-three years at the law firm and only a couple of months as a volunteer, she had to say volunteering was taking a lot more out of her than being a lawyer ever had.

Chapter Nine

JOHN PULLED INTO MABEL'S DARKENED DRIVEWAY to the sound of Barnacle's frantic barking. She was exhausted and dirty and hoped she wouldn't need to clean up any puddles before dragging herself off to bed.

John had driven down the mountain with barely a word. Though dying of curiosity, she'd been afraid to push him too hard—and maybe afraid to hear what he'd say.

"Thanks for coming. Sorry it turned out so..."

He shook his head once, hard, and tapped her hand. "Don't apologize. It had nothing to do with you." He hesitated. "I know you're wiped out, so we don't have to do it now. But I owe you a very long story, and that back there is part of it."

"Now's good," she heard herself saying. "I've got to let Barnacle out, though."

"Tell you what. I'll go grab us some food if you want to stay here. It's private, and you can get as comfy as you want."

"Sure. Whatever is fine."

Half an hour later, Mabel stretched out on the saggy couch in a clean oversize tee, leggings, and fuzzy slipper socks. Since she always used a fork, she'd figured out she could lean on one elbow and still manage to eat her Chinese shrimp-and-cashew without depositing too much rice on the upholstery. What landed on the floor quickly disappeared down Barnacle's gullet.

John, wielding chopsticks like a native of Kyoto, sat opposite, cleanly putting away a sushi sampler. "This is going to take some time. Just give me a minute to eat first."

"That's okay. Don't let your dinner get cold."

"You're funny."

Mabel finished before John, as usual, and shoved her covered takeout container across the coffee table beyond Barnacle's questing nose. "So…" She flopped back against her pile of cushions, landing on Koi, who sprang to the back of the couch. The cat glared down at her, flicking her tail, before pointedly turning her back and starting an aggressive grooming of her back leg.

Before continuing her thought, Mabel offered Koi a conciliatory nibble of shrimp, which was accepted without any promises. "You recognized that guy up there?"

John took his time, swirling his sushi roll in a mixture of soy sauce and green wasabi. He nodded, keeping his eyes on the food until he'd taken a bite. He dabbed his mouth. "Yeah."

"Who was he? If you're ready to talk."

"Sure. Give me a sec to put my leftovers in the fridge."

This was another thing about John. He always had leftovers. Mabel rarely did.

She watched as he cleared away trash, closed his container, and carried everything to the kitchen, Barnacle trailing after him, tail wagging. Of course, John was always neater and more orderly than Mabel. Still, she wondered if he was stalling a bit. Maybe he didn't really want to talk after all, or perhaps he was searching for the right words.

When he returned, he sank into the worn rust-colored armchair opposite her. Koi leapt neatly onto his lap. Holding his tea mug in one hand and petting the cat with the other, he took a deep breath. "I do want to tell you all this. It's hard to know which end to take hold of, though. I guess maybe the place where I came into the story."

Mabel studied John's face, half-cast in shadow by the old, fringed floor lamp. It struck her that was how he seemed to her—half the good guy and former private eye who seemed to like her, the other half a stranger she hadn't even begun to know. She knew nothing about his family, little about his romantic past, and certainly not the slightest clue as to why and how he'd lost his investigator's license. "All right. I guess if you lose me, I can always ask questions."

"Yep." He took another deep breath and blew it out. "Here goes. As you know, I was working as a detective up till a few months ago. I had an office in my house and mostly handled insurance work and domestics, skip traces, et cetera. Pretty boring stuff, but it paid the bills."

Mabel couldn't help feeling a bit disappointed. Practicing law had been like that, but TV, books, and movies had given her more hope for the world of private investigation.

"Are you listening?"

"Yeah, sorry. It's…you know…why does life always have to be so dull?"

John laughed, sloshing his tea. "Dull? After what you've been through in the past month?"

She sighed. "I guess I meant jobs. So far, volunteering has been pretty lively."

He snorted. "That's one way of putting it. But, no, if you were imagining me sitting in my office like Humphrey Bogart when in walks Lauren Bacall, then I'm sorry to break the illusion. My career wasn't as glamorous as the movies might lead you to believe."

On second thought, this struck Mabel as a good thing, because she knew she could never compete with Lauren Bacall.

"At least until…"

Mabel's head popped up.

"…About two months ago. I got a call from a woman who said she'd found my listing online. She told me her name was Amanda Johnson, and she needed someone to surveil her house."

"Why her own house?"

"I'm getting there. She said she'd been living in Kingman with her husband Mike, but their relationship was rocky. He beat her, especially when he was drunk, and a couple of times threatened to kill her. On top of that, she suspected he was mixed up in some bad—possibly criminal—stuff, and she didn't much like the people he hung out with.

"She'd put up with this for a while, but when she became pregnant, he accused her of being with other men. Denied the baby was his. One night, he came home roaring drunk, saw two cups in the sink, and decided she'd had a man in the house while he was out.

"He hit her pretty bad, and would likely have killed her, if she hadn't managed to lock herself in the bathroom till he finally passed out. She escaped with her toothbrush, a handful of clothes, and the money from his wallet."

Mabel sat all the way up. "Did she file for protection from abuse?"

John shook his head. "You know what they say about PFAs—all they do is tick off the offender and give the cops a place to start looking when the petitioner turns up dead."

That was all too true.

"Anyway, she decided to stay away till things died down, then file for divorce. She rented a place here in Medicine Spring...well, out near the Vo Tech...and got a cashier job at the mall. Then one day when she was returning from break, she was sure she saw him leaving the store. She finished her shift, watching the doors constantly. She didn't see him again but was afraid he'd be lurking in the parking lot."

Mabel was leaning forward at this point. "Was he?"

John shrugged. "She was too afraid to go to her car. She thought either he'd try to abduct her or watch and follow her home."

Mabel shuddered. This was exactly the type of scenario Lisa always warned her about. Thanks to Lisa's PhD-level expertise on true crime, Mabel avoided getting on elevators alone with strange men, parked in well-lit places and never next to big trucks or vans.

"Instead, she asked a coworker to pick her up at the back of the store and give her a lift. At this point, she was convinced he'd tracked her to Medicine Spring, and it would only be a matter of time till he found out where she lived."

"You were like her bodyguard or something?" Visions of Whitney

Houston and Kevin Costner flitted across her mind.

"No, she couldn't afford someone to follow her 24/7. Mainly, she was afraid at night and scared to sleep for fear he'd break in. I recommended she install at least a low-end alarm system, and she hired me to surveil the house overnight so she could get some rest."

"Like how?"

"Like I sat slouched down in my car in her townhouse lot and watched while you, she, and everybody else was sleeping."

"That must've been mind-numbing." Mabel frowned. "Uh... I have questions. How could you stay awake? What about the bathroom? Did he show up? Was she beautiful?"

Darn. She hadn't meant to say that last one out loud.

John laughed, despite the tight lines around his eyes. "None of that matters—I have a lot of story to tell you yet. But since you asked... One—it's hard. Two—you don't want to know. Three—I'm getting to that. Four—well, yeah, I guess she was."

I knew it. Lauren Bacall. "Did—?"

"Mabel. Please. Hold your questions, okay?"

She bit her lips.

"I did this for, oh, a week or so. Then, one Friday night, super late—like three in the morning—a car pulls in at the far end. Not that close to her place, and like I said, Friday night. I figure somebody who lives there was out partying, so I lay low.

"I see a good-sized, muscular dude get out. I keep watching, figuring he's going to let himself into one of the units down there. Instead, he goes around back. Maybe a rear door? Maybe a lost key, so he has to climb in through a window?

"Maybe. Maybe not. But it made my Spidey senses tingle, you know?"

Mabel nodded, keeping her mouth shut.

"So, I ease out of my car and tippy-toe toward the far end unit and around back. No sign of him. It's pretty dark back there. One pole light by the dumpsters in the middle of the block of townhouses.

"Then, my eye catches movement in the shadows down around where Amanda lives. He's trying to break in the back of her place. I can't tell if he's trying to jimmy the door or force a window, but he's sure working on something.

"I yell, 'Hey,' and he looks up. I figure he'll explain himself if he's innocent—or take off, if not. Instead, he rushes me. I was a lot closer to his car than he was. He had one way to get there, and that was through me."

Mabel felt her eyes bug out, but she clamped her lips.

"He was way bigger than me, and I guess he planned to knock me down and run for it. I was ready, and I tackled him. He fought like his life depended on it. When I tried to hold onto him, he swung around and hit me. Half my face was black and blue for a week." A smile twitched at the corner of John's mouth. "I think I broke his nose."

"Was it the ex? Did you get him?"

"Yeah. It was him." His smile faded. "He got away, streaming blood from his nose. I probably should've called the cops, but it all happened too fast.

"Amanda was okay. Freaked out when I told her what happened, naturally. Of course, he had no reason to be where I caught him. But she absolutely refused to call the police in."

Mabel's eyebrows rose.

"So, I went home next morning, and iced my hand and face. Next night, I was back watching the house—but from a different spot."

"He didn't come back." No way, Mabel thought, after being caught red-handed the night before.

He shook his head. "It was a quiet night. But, given what happened the night before, I thought I'd better call next morning and check in anyway. I waited a couple hours—I wasn't sure when she usually got out of bed.

"Then I called and called. No answer. I left messages—nothing."

Oh, no. Mabel clutched a throw pillow to her chest, gripping the brocade fabric with both hands.

"I wasn't sure what to do. I didn't have any contact info for relatives, and I didn't have a solid reason to call the police yet— especially since she'd been so against it. Still, something didn't smell right to me."

"What did you do?"

Barnacle barked and pawed at her leg. "Now? Are you serious?"

John yawned and stretched. "Sorry, Barnacle. You too, Mabel. You must be wiped out."

She got to her feet. Good grief, she was stiff. Was this arthritis setting in? As Mabel tried to straighten without groaning, she reassured herself that anyone would be bent like a paperclip after crouching on a cold tree limb forever, waiting for a dog to find them. "Don't you dare let things hang like that. I'll be right back."

When she returned, leaving Barnacle enjoying a night cap at the water bowl, John had moved to the couch. He slumped at the far end with Koi parked on his chest. His eyes were shut, and the shadows showed the stress lines on his face.

Mabel hesitated.

Was he already asleep? She slid back into her spot and stretched out a hand to touch John's arm. His eyes opened at the movement and met hers.

He took her hand and held it for a couple of heartbeats, turning it over, tracing the palm with a finger, seeming to study it. Then, he looked up, eyes serious.

"I'm in some trouble, Mabel."

Chapter Ten

WITHOUT THINKING, MABEL JERKED HER HAND back and sat up straight. "What kind of trouble? How much?"

John cleared his throat. "I don't know. It's kind of complicated."

Mabel frowned. Their relationship—if that was what it was—was "kind of complicated," in her opinion. If he *knew* he was in trouble, shouldn't he have a pretty good idea why and how much? She turned sideways to face him, drawing one foot up under her. "I'm listening."

"This is where things started to go seriously funky. I had a key to Amanda's place and also her security code."

Mabel's eyes narrowed.

"She wanted me to be able to check on her in case something went wrong. I went over there that evening, around nine. I hadn't been able to raise her all day, and when I got to the townhouse, there were no lights on, even though it was already dark out. I shone my flash into the attached garage but couldn't see her car. Okay, maybe she went somewhere. Then why wasn't she answering my calls?"

Mabel rubbed her hands on her knees. She was remembering once before, when she and John had gone to meet someone who wasn't responding. They'd checked her townhouse garage, and the discovery had been chilling.

"It felt wrong. So, after I'd knocked and rung the bell awhile, I finally decided to let myself in. The security system was already disabled, and the place was cleaned out—like nobody was living there at all.

"Except it looked as if somebody had forced the laundry room window. I saw a few suspicious specks on the kitchen floor, so I brought in some luminol—"

"You have luminol? Can you just buy that? Without being the police, I mean."

"Sure, and you can too, but I don't recommend it." John launched into a detailed explanation of chemical dangers and risks of crime scene contamination. "You have to be trained, and extremely careful how you use it. Anyway, I tried it on a single tiny area. A couple of specks lit up, and I could see a few more of what appeared to be bloodstains beyond the two-inch area I checked."

"What did you do?"

"Called the police. I still wasn't sure what happened, and maybe there was an innocent explanation, but even a little bit of blood—on top of that run-in with her ex only two nights before—made waiting too big a risk. Especially with signs of a forced entry."

"Did they take it seriously?"

He shrugged. "They took my report, including what she'd told me about her ex and about his trying to break in. But I wasn't her family. They took me seriously enough, but they pointed out what I already knew. The place was cleaned out and her car was gone. It was as likely—and maybe more so—that she'd decided to split once she realized her ex had tracked her down. And skip on my bill."

"You mean you didn't even get paid after all that?"

John grimaced and stretched. "Not a dime."

"Well, that stinks."

"That it does."

"What about the blood, though? And the laundry window?"

"They said, quite logically, that the techs would go over the place, but it was a small amount, and we all bleed from time to time for various non-nefarious reasons. She could've forced that window herself at some point. Then they lectured me on breaking into places—despite my having permission—and about using my PI license to justify 'playing police officer.'"

Mabel scowled. She'd had enough people patronize her to know how it felt. "You were only protecting your client. Obviously."

He grinned. "Thanks, Mama Bear, but things got worse.

"To make a long story—well, not short, but a little less long—I started trying to locate her myself but had no luck. It's a fairly common name, but in the end, it was like she never existed, which of course, also meant I couldn't follow up with family or friends. All the while, my mind kept going back to the guy she was so scared of, creeping around her back door and windows—and that blood in her kitchen.

"Since I wasn't having any luck finding Amanda, I figured my best bet was to look for him. But—funny thing—he turned out to be as hard to locate as she was. I kind of understood her changing her identity if she was trying to escape an abusive husband. But I was surprised she'd apparently changed his too—or he had. I wondered if she'd put one over on me."

"Why would she do that?"

"I don't know, but if she expected me to follow up and find her, it certainly made my job a lot harder. Anyhow, I was getting nowhere, till a few days later out of the blue, I happened to spot Mike's car. It was unmistakable, because of a big dent in the rear with a crack down the middle, like he'd backed into a pole at some point. It was sitting outside a dry cleaner over in Kingman, when I happened to drive by.

"I pulled around the block and walked back. It was still there, so I kept an eye out and did two things as fast as I could—took a quick shot of the license plate and stuck a GPS tracker underneath the frame."

"Hold up." Mabel tried to process what she'd heard. "You just happened to have a tracker in your pocket? Is that even *legal*?"

John had the grace to appear a bit shamefaced. "I had one in my car from another case. And no, it wasn't strictly legal, but you have to realize how worried I was about Amanda by that point. From everything she'd told me, she was in mortal danger from this guy. Domestics can go very bad in a hurry."

Mabel bit her lip. She might've been a marginal sort of lawyer, but she still considered herself an officer of the court, and as such, had the utmost respect for the law. Nonetheless, she understood John's anxiety, especially with the police barely showing any concern for what might've happened to his client.

"You don't need to look at me like that," John continued, "because the law bit me back. I was fast, but as I rolled out from under the car, I had the bad luck to get spotted.

"At that moment, Pete Underkofler, a Kingman cop who doesn't like PIs in general—and me in particular—came out of a barbershop two doors down. While he was interrogating me, Mike came walking up, still with a big bandage on his smashed nose." A small grin flickered across John's face.

"Interesting—he kind of froze before he got to us. Wouldn't you think an innocent man who sees a cop questioning a guy right next to your car would come running up and ask what was going on?"

"Definitely."

"Well, I pointed him out, and explained why I was concerned enough to try something the slightest bit questionable. Of course, then he had to come over because Pete waved him in.

"We both stood around, sort of shuffling our feet while Pete called in to the Med Spring PD. When he was done, all he said was he heard I 'like to play cop,' and said sticking a GPS on somebody's car requires a warrant. He asked Mike if he wanted to press charges.

"Well, Mike threw up his hands and said, no, so long as I leave him alone and stop harassing him. Suspicious, right? He couldn't get out of there quick enough."

"Not normal behavior. I'm a lawyer, and I know scumbags." *And some of them are lawyers.*

Koi, still occupying John's lap, yawned and stretched. Mabel extended a hand to the cat, hoping to make peace. Koi moved to John's far shoulder, turned in a circle and lay down with her back to Mabel. *Message received.*

John stroked Koi's fur. "I figured I wasn't going to get charged anyway, and I apologized to Underkofler. No way I was apologizing to Amanda's ex. I hoped Pete would take off and I'd still get a chance to trail Mike. Then he drove off before Pete was even back inside his cruiser. By the time I was able to retrieve my car, I'd lost him."

"A few days later, I found out Underkofler had reported me to the PI licensing board, and they were suspending my license for six months. Even my friends at the department wouldn't run Mike's plate for me."

"What's more, for all you know, your client is dead, and Mike's getting away with it."

He slowly nodded. "Yeah, except 'was' is the operative word. He's not getting away with it anymore." John's glance met hers and flicked away. "That body up there in the woods was him."

Chapter Eleven

MABEL'S MIND WANDERED DURING THE MORNING church service. Even with the benefit of the microphone, the visiting missionary's soft voice didn't carry.

She tried to listen, but her thoughts drifted to yesterday and the dreadful discovery in the woods. As horrid as that was, realizing John might be a suspect made it worse.

Last night, she'd tried to reassure him. "The police can't possibly think you'd bump someone off and go to all the trouble of hiding the body in the remotest possible location, then lead me and a pack of search dogs right to it."

"Weirder things have happened," he'd said. "What they're probably considering is how unlikely it is that a body shows up there at all. Moreover, that the guy who happens to find it way up there, the guy who had a major beef with the dead guy, would be completely innocent."

Valid point. However, it still made no sense to her.

Plus, at the time that body was most likely stashed, John didn't even know I was going to get involved with search and rescue, let alone go to Clear Creek Park this weekend. It could never have been planned.

Mabel gave herself a mental shake. She couldn't help John by refusing to consider every angle. She was acting like that girl in *The Lodger*. How would the police look at it?

Probably, they'd say when John found out the search and rescue team was going up there, he'd decided to try to get ahead of the inevitable. By accompanying Mabel, he could arrive along with everyone else and pretend to innocently stumble on the body.

But, she argued with herself, wouldn't the simplest thing be to move the body before they all got there? She shook her head. He'd only found out where they were going the night before. It looked next to impossible for him to not only get to that body in the dark but also move it very far from where it had landed. Not without help, anyway.

When the service ended, Mabel made her way outside, averting her eyes guiltily when she shook the missionary's hand. She also felt prompted to put a little bit more into the free-will basket, to support his work...and salve her conscience.

As she was speed-walking across the parking lot, a voice behind her boomed. "Mabel Browne."

It might've been the wrath of God, after her inattention to the guest speaker, but Mabel knew this voice all too well. Reluctantly, she turned around.

"Good morning, Cora." She smiled. "Nanette."

"Isn't it a lovely morning?" Nanette, Mabel's slim, seventy-something friend took a deep breath. "I'm glad it's cooler this weekend. Warm weather's fine for summer—at least in reasonable doses. All the same, I want fall to feel like fall."

"I agree," Mabel said, but as she'd feared, Cora wasn't there for chit-chat.

"You haven't signed up to work in November," the historical society president said bluntly.

Mabel's eyes darted longingly toward her small car, parked under the trees at the far end of the lot. "Er, no...I actually thought I might take a bit of a break. You see, I started volunteering with—"

"A break?" Cora brayed. She towered over Mabel, who was no Tinkerbelle herself. Cora's swirly, Creamsicle-colored Lilly Pulitzer wrap-dress was topped by an orange cardigan in apparent deference to fall. She reminded Mabel of the Great Pumpkin, which in turn reminded her that it might be nice to stop for a pumpkin-spice latte on her way home.

"How can you need a break when you barely started?" Cora asked. "You only joined—"

"Now, Cora," Nanette reproved. "You have to realize Mabel has been through…an unusually difficult time of it. It's no wonder she'd need a break."

Yes, Mabel thought. Stumbling upon the previous president's dead body in the society headquarters, the Sauer ax murder house, certainly ought to qualify as "an unusually difficult time." Not to mention—

"Exactly my point," Cora bellowed, illogically. "First, we lost Helen. Then, if you think about it, it's sort of Mabel's fault that Darwin's no longer with us, either."

"Now, really, Cora," Nanette protested.

Cora sniffed. "At least, we should have Linnea coming aboard before long. She has more than a bit of her mother in her, but we can work with that." The glint of battle sparkled in her eye.

Cora's rancorous history with the late, previous society president and Sauer granddaughter, Helen Thornwald, had been exceeded only by Mabel's. News of Helen's daughter Linnea's return to Medicine Spring, the historical society—and worst of all, Mabel's back property line—curdled her stomach.

"I'm sorry," Mabel said. "I do have to run. I'll be in touch," she promised, making sure not to specify when.

Mabel was glad she always wore flats. She was able to hot-foot it to her car and was already driving out of the lot by the time Cora and Nanette were unlocking their doors.

Truthfully, she wanted to make her "little break" from the historical society permanent. But—in a town this small, and with a president as forceful as Cora—she feared that ambition was doomed to fail.

Not that it seemed search and rescue would consume much of her time. From the beginning, Rachel had assured her it would only amount to an occasional Saturday. To be honest, that had been a major attraction for Mabel. Search and rescue was important, to be sure, but as John had pointed out, Mabel had her own calling in life to attend to.

Gloomily, she reflected that she hadn't been attending to that calling all that much lately either. Writing was so hard, and she was still on her learning curve. Not to mention she needed to keep chipping away at bringing Grandma Mabel's house and grounds—now her house and grounds—into compliance with township codes too. Maybe Jen was right that she should rent a dumpster and throw a fling-the-trash party.

The thought made her stomach twist. She knew she couldn't bring herself to treat Grandma's things that way.

On impulse, Mabel turned at Blue Hollow Road. She wasn't ready to face the mess at home. Her animals would be okay for a while, and it might be nice to stop at the farm market for a pumpkin and some cider—and maybe a thick turkey club sandwich on toasted farmhouse bread.

The lot was swarming when she arrived, with an actual police officer directing traffic at the entrance. A huge sign proclaimed, "Fall Festival Days, Weekends 10-5."

The crowd nearly deterred her, but at an impatient whistle blast and wave from the cop, she obediently turned in. She crept along, starting and stopping to allow cars ahead of her to pull into spaces, and families laden with pumpkins, balloons, and kettle corn to pass.

Absentmindedly, she slammed the brakes one more time for a couple crossing in front of her. The woman tapped on her hood.

Startled, Mabel focused, recognizing Lisa, casual in slim-cut jeans, boots, and red-plaid flannel. Mabel rolled down her window.

"Mabel—I was going to call you later. You never got back to me last night."

The driver behind Mabel honked. "Oh, for pity sake. Hang on—I see a space."

Moments later, she'd parked. Lisa and her fiancé, Tim Fielding, a big, shy woodworker with a dark, scruffy beard, stopped by the car.

"Tell me everything. First, the body, okay? Then the crime scene. Do you know the cause of death? Did the cops say anything?"

Tim, panting a bit, set their enormous pumpkin on Mabel's hood. He shuffled his feet and looked away.

"Honey, why don't you and the pumpkin go sit on that bench for a couple minutes? I won't be long."

Mabel considered her words. She couldn't say anything about John. Nevertheless, given her friend's nose for true crime—not to mention over forty years of knowing Mabel better than her own mother—would she be able to tell Mabel was holding back?

She sighed. "All right. Get in." Quickly, she ran through her time in the woods, Millie's discovery of the body, and the arrival of the police, skirting the awful look on John's face when he studied the victim's face.

Mabel was able to rebuff most of the questions by saying they'd have to wait for the autopsy, but already Lisa was sniffing like a search and rescue dog on the scent. "Honest," Mabel concluded. "That's all I know for now." *Or at least that I can tell you.* "Tim looks restless."

A quick glance showed Lisa's fiancé apparently dozing peacefully next to the pumpkin, but Mabel's suggestion was enough to make Lisa look guilty.

"Oh, all right. But you better keep me posted—no holding back." With a last stern look, Lisa gathered up her purse. "I also wondered if you might be free next Saturday to go check out the art museum with me. We're thinking of having our reception there. Tim says whatever I decide is fine, as long as he doesn't have to make the rounds with me."

Mabel cast through her possible commitments and, unsurprisingly, found none. "Sure, I guess so." She'd once felt the teensiest bit envious of Lisa's happy wedding plans. Now that Mabel had…whatever it was she had with John, she found herself more inclined to take mental notes. She wondered how John would feel about a reception at the art museum—or a wedding. With her. Anywhere. Someday…

"Mabel?" Lisa waved a hand in front of Mabel's face.

"Sorry. I was thinking what I have on my calendar. Nope, nothing. Sounds like fun."

"Great!" Lisa hugged her. "They have a café—I'll treat you to lunch, or tea, if you'd rather."

When Lisa and the long-suffering Tim had moved on, Mabel made her way through the festive mass of people. Wistful, she considered signs for cider-making demonstrations, hayrides, and apple-picking. If she'd realized this was going on, maybe she could've mentioned it to John.

Of course, with a potential homicide charge hanging over his head, who knew when he'd be thinking about something so mundane as a date with Mabel again? This was another reason they needed to figure out who'd killed this guy and do it soon. Having recently turned fifty, Mabel had no time to waste.

Chapter Twelve

WHEN SHE GOT HOME SUNDAY AFTERNOON, Mabel tossed her keys and a slip of paper onto the cluttered kitchen table. On the bulletin board at the farm market, she'd found a notice for a writers' group meeting in the Bartles Grove Library on Monday mornings, and she'd scribbled down the info. Now that she was a serious writer, this might be a good next step.

Barnacle bounced in front of the door and whined. She opened the door, then carried her newly purchased pumpkin out to the front porch railing and put away her other purchases. Koi supervised, sniffing each item and leaping up to pose next to the pumpkin, as if demonstrating her modeling capabilities.

Mabel brought her back inside before changing out of her church clothes with a sigh of relief. Then she clipped Barnacle to his leash and took him on a quick walk.

Finally, Mabel worked her way home, with Barnacle taking his time snuffling through the grass and fallen leaves. She shuffled through the drifts of yellow and brown. Her oaks were finally dropping their leaves too—another job that needed to be taken care of, and she'd have to do it herself. If she trusted it to Acey, she'd no doubt end up paying him for injuring himself with the rake.

As Mabel let herself in the back door, fumbling with Barnacle's leash and the code for the security system John had insisted she install, her pocket vibrated. Before she could get her phone pulled free, John's ringtone filled the air.

Mabel grabbed her cell. "Hey."

"You busy right now?"

She mumbled something about her utter lack of activity as she unclipped Barnacle and shrugged out of her hoodie.

"Not definitive, of course, but I ran some facial recognition, and I'm pretty sure I have a solid ID for Amanda."

"Really? You can do that?"

He laughed. "You always make me feel like a magician. Yeah, I messed around with it a while ago, but didn't really get anywhere since the only picture I have of her isn't that clear. This time, I got a hit that sure looks like her...especially considering the ear, which is one of the most distinctive points I look at."

"That's great." Mabel held the phone between chin and shoulder as she filled the animals' dishes. "What did you find out?"

"Not a whole lot. There's no real social media footprint, apart from a couple mentions of her in other people's posts, which seems odd. I did pick up a few things. Would you be interested in dinner tonight and maybe a little investigation?"

Mabel brightened. Not only was John asking her out, but she wouldn't have to eat leftovers–or work on her writing or the house this evening. "Sure. What should I wear?"

"Come as you are. I'll pick you up in a couple of hours if that's okay?"

Time flew by, because of course, Mabel wasn't going to "come as she was," in baggy sweatpants and a Tractor Supply tee. As soon as the animals were fed, she grabbed a quick shower and started trying on and discarding outfits, with Koi lending her fashion advice by scrunching her eyes when a combination seemed to please her.

By the time the bell rang, Mabel was dressed in slim dark-wash jeans, her trusty short black boots, and a loose, squash-colored sweater. The sweater was cheery and seasonal, as well as covering a multitude of sins.

"Where are we headed?"

"You know The Timbers?"

She searched her memory. "It sounds familiar, but..."

"It's a restaurant along the highway, out toward Kingman. Apparently, Amanda Johnson—or I should say Amanda Pedersen, which is her real name—has been a waitress up there pretty recently."

The Timbers managed to look both rustic and imposing. Set well back behind a busy parking lot, it blended into a backdrop of hemlocks and fading rusty oaks, all dark-brown logs sprawling under a forest-green roof. Camp-style lanterns, wired for electricity, flooded the entry with warm light.

Mabel spied expensive business casual wear among the crowd—tailored corduroys and twill with designer jackets and cashmere sweaters. "I feel underdressed."

John squeezed her hand. "You're perfect."

He seemed to mean it. John's attitude of fond approval continued to be a constant source of amazement.

He held back the heavy door, and Mabel stepped into a delicious-smelling cloud of garlicky roasting meat, and the soft buzz of voices. Vast rooms spread left and right of the hostess station. Straight ahead, behind a section of rough stone wall and lush potted plants, tables dotted a flagstone floor, with rustic booths along the walls and tables in the middle. A fieldstone fireplace, which could have accommodated an entire ox, dominated the far wall, a fire blazing beneath its massive hewn timber mantel. Mabel presumed it was burning gas, rather than the "logs" on the hearth.

More lanterns hung from the ceilings, shedding soft light on old Navajo rugs, photos, and prints lining the walls, and on the diners below. Mabel squinted. It was an inviting room, for all its size, but she wondered if she'd be able to see the menu. On the plus side, she guessed nobody could see what she was wearing, either.

The pencil-thin hostess, whose nametag read Buffy, was perhaps in her mid-thirties, strikingly tall, with the high cheekbones of a model. Her boyish, spiky cap of white-blonde hair, tailored black pants, white dress shirt, and black tie only seemed by way of contrast to accentuate her femininity. As they followed her to their table, Mabel sucked in her stomach and attempted to think sleek.

Seated at a booth halfway back in the room, Mabel scanned the menu. Everything looked delicious, and it was hard to decide. She moved her nose closer to the page, trying to make out the prices in the dim mood lighting, and gasped. She must be reading that wrong.

"Are you all right?"

"I'm okay, but these prices aren't. Should I order a cup of the soup? We can stop somewhere else for dinner on the way home if you want."

John snorted. "I may have lost my license, but I'm not selling my plasma to survive. Not yet, anyhow. It's okay. Let me treat you. Order whatever you want—we can always wash dishes if I come up short."

Mabel grimaced. "If you say so." Still, she couldn't help wondering if he'd read those prices. Maybe he couldn't see them, either. He'd said to order though, so she went with the trout amandine, hoping it wouldn't be full of bones.

Their waitress, Leah, looked to be late twenties, with a long, shiny brown braid down her back and a patrician face. It struck Mabel funny that someone who looked like her was waiting tables. She felt as if she and the waitress ought to switch places.

"Excuse me," John said as the waitress dropped off a breadbasket and small tub of butter, "we wondered if Amanda might be working this evening."

The waitress's head jerked upward. "Pedersen?"

At John's "yes," she shook her head. "She hasn't worked here in months. Is she a friend?"

"No. I did a little work for her a while back and wondered what became of her."

The waitress narrowed her eyes. "Did she stiff you on your bill or something? Sorry, I shouldn't have said that. But she was never that reliable, till one day she was on the schedule, but never showed up again."

"When was that?" Mabel asked, forgetting she'd intended to let John do all the talking.

"Three months maybe? I shouldn't say anything. I hope she's okay. Considering that boyfriend of hers."

As John opened his mouth to put another question to her, she glanced past him. "Oh, hey. Excuse me. I need to get to my other booths."

He touched her arm. "Could we maybe talk later? It's important," he added, as she drew back.

"Please," Mabel said. That kindergarten word was always a good idea, in her experience.

"Um, sure, I guess so. But I won't be done here for almost two hours." She'd already begun inching away.

"Perhaps after you get off, we could buy you a drink." John nodded toward the bar area.

"Sure."

Mabel turned to John as he watched her go. "Do you think she'll show up?"

He shrugged. "We can always catch up to her at some point. After all, we do know where she works. Plus, other people here might be able to tell us as much as she can."

Mabel paused in slathering butter inside a hot herb-and-garlic roll. "Would you like one?"

"No, thanks. You go ahead and enjoy."

She hated when he did that. It made her feel like he might be judging her eating habits. Of course, he'd never said anything like that—in fact, he always encouraged her to enjoy her food. Except he was such a fit freak. She set the roll down. Seconds later, she stole a pinch from it. It smelled so good.

"Sounds like Amanda bugged out right around the time she hired you as a bodyguard."

"Not exactly her bodyguard, but yeah. It does sound like the timeline matches up fairly close."

Mabel stole a bigger pinch. The roll melted in her mouth. "What do you think about the boyfriend? Wasn't she married?"

"Said she was. But she also said her name was Amanda Johnson. She wasn't the most reliable narrator. Seems like the boyfriend and the so-called husband had similar personalities, though, huh?"

"Some people seem to attract that type." Mabel pondered. "Or it might be the same person, and she was calling him her husband for some reason of her own."

"Or," John said, "she had an abusive husband who came after her precisely because she had this boyfriend."

"In either case, one of them might have had reason to make her disappear." Mabel gave up and bit off half the roll. They weren't very big, and she figured she might as well appreciate it while it was still hot.

When she'd swallowed her generous mouthful, Mabel dabbed her lips. "And, I suppose, either of them could have been the father of her baby—the way Mike claimed."

John nodded. "Another complication."

"How pregnant was she?"

He raised his eyebrows. "You *have* heard there's no such thing as 'a little bit pregnant?'"

"You know what I mean."

He shrugged. "She didn't say, and I can't hazard a guess. She wore these...things." He waved his hands around his body in a less than descriptive way.

"You mean like...?"

"Baggy. These long hippie tops."

"Tunics."

"Yeah, I guess so. Is that what you call them? I don't know a lot about women's clothing. And sometimes these really long dresses like sack things."

Mabel began to develop an image. "You said hippie. What they call boho. Bohemian. Artsy, sort of?"

He grinned and nodded. "I mean she wore sandals all the time. All the time. I guess what I'm also saying is the 'baby' could've been a fabrication too—maybe just to get my sympathy."

"You said you looked her up with facial recognition software. Do you have her picture on you? I ought to know what she looks like, in case I should run into her."

John scrolled through images on his phone. "Here." He slid it to her.

Mabel enlarged the image and squinted. It showed a statuesque ash blonde with one of those messy haircuts that somehow look charming on beautiful young women. She was emerging from a doorway, and her head was turned toward the camera, though she didn't seem to be looking directly at it.

"She didn't know the picture was being taken."

John grinned again, looking a bit sheepish. "I had a feeling I might need this and took it on impulse."

"Eye color?"

"Gray. Very clear gray."

Mabel looked up sharply from the image to John. Had he been staring into her "very clear gray" eyes?

He smiled.

She cleared her throat. "I see what you mean about the clothing. Hard to tell what's going on under there."

John's smile became a snort. "You make it sound as if she were toting an unruly band of performing squirrels inside her dress."

Mabel couldn't help smiling back. She passed the photo back to him, thinking she'd probably be able to recognize Amanda Pedersen if she ever met her. There was something distinctive in her features. It wasn't a conventional face, but none the less striking.

"Have you heard anything from the police up there since yesterday?" Mabel avoided John's eyes.

"Yeah, they picked up my gun to check ballistics."

Mabel sucked in air.

John's smile was crooked. "It's not a match. I didn't shoot the guy."

"I know that. It's...they're interested in you."

"Yeah. I don't blame them for doing their jobs, though."

"When it comes back negative or whatever, you should be in the clear then."

He shook his head. "That's the only gun registered to my name. They have to consider I might have used something else."

"It'll be okay." The lame reassurance was all she could offer.

For a while, they dropped the topic of Amanda Pedersen, as well as whether John was going to get out from under the cloud of suspicion, avoid jail, and get his PI license back. Instead, they talked about Mabel's frustrations with Acey and the complete lack of interest on the part of any other reputable handyman in the vicinity in taking over the job.

John offered to do as much of the work himself as he could, but Mabel couldn't let him take that on. Besides which, he was teaching during the day, the evenings were now dark, and the weekends too often rainy.

"I'll soldier on." Mabel sighed. "I have another extension from the township now. They seem to be fine, as long as they can see I'm working on it."

"I'm sure Acey's reputation precedes him. They probably pity you."

"I'm not above taking pity, if it'll buy me more time."

After the food had arrived, and Mabel had sampled everything on her plate, she took a deep breath. They suddenly had a lot of time to kill. She had to ask John the questions that had been burning a hole in her chest almost as long as she'd known him. Granted, she'd only known him a few weeks, but he seemed interested in starting a relationship. Yet she knew next to zero about his personal life.

"Uh…can I ask you a question? Or two."

His eyebrows went up, fork poised midway to his mouth. "Shoot."

Mabel pretended to inspect her trout for wayward fish bones— which was pretty much impossible in The Timbers' fashionable darkness. "I was sort of wondering. Were you and Victoria serious?"

"Not where I thought this was going. I'll probably never get my license back, and I may be going to the electric chair, but you want to interrogate me about my ex?"

Mabel looked up in shock, only to see him grinning again. She threw her napkin at him. "Come on. I'm serious. And may I please have my napkin back?"

He passed it over, gently grazing her hand with his. It sent a little shiver up her arm, and she forced her attention back to her trout, no longer sure she wanted his answer.

"Victoria was a girlfriend I had. I wouldn't say serious. We were together about eight months, a couple years ago. We liked a lot of the same active, outdoor stuff, and she's incredibly kind. I liked her—still do, in fact."

Blast. He would talk about all that "active stuff" Mabel didn't share.

"But listen." He took her hand across the table. "She and I never did click on that deeper level. She was all about her dogs, and I was focused on my cases. The only thing we really shared was doing all the outdoor stuff together."

Together. Aagghh... Mabel guessed she could try camping. She resolved to start using the fitness tracker John had given her for her birthday. If she could find the darn thing. Nonetheless, if he thought he didn't have much in common with Victoria, what on earth did he have in common with Mabel?

"Mabel."

"Huh?"

"You asked me a question, and I'm trying to give you an honest answer, but you zoned out on me again."

"Sorry. I have a problem with that."

"I've noticed."

"She was just one of my girlfriends, all right?"

One of how many? "Was there somebody else you were serious with?"

This time he hesitated, and her heart began to thump. She took a big, therapeutic bite of trout and choked. She had located a fish bone.

John jumped up. "Are you all right? Here, drink this." He handed her water.

Mabel sipped and coughed. Her eyes were tearing, so her mascara was probably running too.

"This is what you need. You'll never be able to cough up a fish bone." He passed her a chunk of dinner roll. "Swallow bread and chase it with water—it'll push it right down."

To her surprise, it worked. Mabel excused herself and fled to the restroom. The face in the mirror looked as if she'd been experimenting with clown makeup. She made a mental note—*Buy waterproof mascara.*

By the time she returned to the table, she'd decided not to pursue John's romantic history anymore this evening. He had clearly hesitated on her last question, and she realized she wasn't ready for whatever he'd been about to say.

Chapter Thirteen

THE RESTAURANT BAR WAS EVEN DARKER and more crowded than the dining area. The ceiling was lower too, as if the bar might've been the original building with the big room a tacked-on addition. Mabel nursed her heavy crockery mug of decaf, wondering if Leah the waitress would show. "This place feels like *Little House on the Prairie*," she muttered, glancing around at the log walls.

"Probably more like *Little House in the Big Woods*," John corrected, and grinned at her raised eyebrows. "What? We read those in elementary school too. Anyway, you'll notice these logs are coated in polyurethane, which was unavailable to Pa Ingalls, as I'm sure you know."

Mabel ignored him and looked at her phone. "She's late. You think she skipped out?"

He shrugged. "Only a couple minutes. She may have blown us off, but she has to know we'll be back—she works here, for goodness' sake."

Sure enough, Leah appeared in the doorway a moment later, scanning the crowd. She'd pulled a black motorcycle jacket over her white work shirt, and her long, slim purse strap across her body.

John rose and waved. She came over with seeming reluctance and didn't sit right away when he gestured for her to slide in next to Mabel. "Can I get you a drink?"

"Um, Coke, I guess. Thanks." Slowly, she sank onto the seat.

John stepped away to the bar, leaving Mabel alone with her. "Thanks for talking to us."

Leah met her eyes. She sat on the edge of the seat, as if poised to run. "Who are you guys? Why do you want to know about Amanda?"

Mabel darted a look toward where John was still waiting for the bartender to draw the drink. She wasn't sure how much he wanted to share with Leah. "Well, here's the thing. I'm Mabel, and my…boyfriend John…"— how she loved saying that, even if she was still not 100 percent sure it was true — "is a private investigator."

Leah's perfect full lips formed a silent O. "Is Amanda in some kind of trouble with the law?"

"Nooo…" To be entirely truthful, Mabel wasn't sure about that, either. But she had no personal evidence Amanda was in that kind of trouble. "I'd better let John explain." She breathed a sigh of relief as she saw him returning with a full glass.

Leah accepted the beverage and set it on the cocktail napkin he handed her but didn't drink. "So, what's you people's deal? Your girlfriend here says you're a PI."

"Not at the moment." John slid into the seat across from them. "I was when Amanda came to me as a client, and now she's missing."

Leah frowned. "She does tend to do that from time to time. I guess I'd say she's probably okay, if you're worried about her."

He raised a shoulder. "Could you tell me who she was close to here?"

"If by 'close' you mean intimate, I'd say Mike Hardy. He tended bar with Jesse over there. I know Amanda had a boyfriend when she came here—a guy she was in grad school with. Danny…sorry, I can't come up with the last name right now. But it didn't take her long to get tangled up with Mike."

John produced another photo on his phone. "Does this guy look familiar?"

Leah barely glanced at it. "Yeah, that's Mr. Big Stuff."

So Amanda met her abusive ex when she waitressed here, and he was tending bar. Mabel caught John's eye.

"You don't like him," Mabel said.

Leah sneered. "No, I don't like him. He has a bad temper, and he takes advantage of women. Single, married—it's all the same to him. Too young, or a bit older and easy to flatter—he goes after them all."

"When's he working?"

"He isn't. He left here not long after Amanda. Jesse might be able to tell you more. I think I heard he was moonlighting over at Peach's—that place a couple blocks from the art museum. Maybe he's still there."

"You know anything about Amanda's family or friends?" Mabel ran a finger over the rim of her mug.

Leah shook her head. "We weren't that close."

After a while, it became clear they wouldn't get anything more out of her. John thanked her, and she gave them a nod and left, leaving her drink untouched. They watched her go, and then John gestured toward the bar.

"Jesse?" Mabel asked.

"Might as well try to get what we can from him, as long as we're here."

The bar was still busy. It was going to be hard to have a private word—or any word, for that matter—with the bartender that evening. Finally, John caught him for a moment and slid a business card across the bar along with a folded bill. He briefly explained what they were interested in and said he'd be up late. Jesse promised to call after his shift, which Mabel calculated wouldn't be till about 2:30 am.

"So Mike Johnson and Mike Hardy are one and the same." She yawned as they walked out through the thinning crowd in the dining room. "It's going to be a late night for you."

John's mouth quirked. "I probably wouldn't be sleeping, anyway. Ever since this happened, I haven't been the most relaxed person in the world."

"You want me to sit up with you?"

John smiled and held the door open. "I don't think you want to sit up that late."

She didn't. She was dying to hear what the bartender had to say, though. "Tell you what. If you want to come over for tea, we can wait at my place. That way, I can let Barnacle out. We can watch a movie or something till he calls."

"If he calls," John said. "But sure. If you really want to."

When they returned to Mabel's house and she'd tended to her animals, she brought tea and joined John in the living room. He patted the spot next to him on the couch. He had found the original black-and-white *Mummy* movie with Boris Karloff on one of the film channels. "We should have popcorn." Mabel hopped back up.

"Aren't you full from dinner?"

Mabel hated to tell him no, but she really did want popcorn. "It's a movie. Of course, we need popcorn. I'll be back in a jiffy."

Moments later, the tantalizing, buttery aroma had Barnacle crowding her at the microwave, big paws up on the countertop. She filled a bowl and brought it back to the couch, Barnacle jumping at her as she walked.

"Come here, you." John patted the seat next to him.

"Ah, so now you do want popcorn!"

"Not exactly what I meant, but sure." He helped himself to a big handful, which disappeared quickly. He wiped his fingers on a paper towel Mabel had brought over with the snack, then reached his arm around her shoulders.

It was almost enough to make Mabel forget her popcorn.

She sighed as she settled against John's warm side, popcorn bowl on her lap. On the screen, Karloff's creepy eyes burned with evil. "This is such a great movie," John said. "Love the old horror flicks—*Phantom of the Opera, Nosferatu…*"

Okay. She had now learned one more thing about him this evening. "Hey, John."

His eyes shifted from Karloff to her.

"This Danny guy who used to be Amanda's boyfriend might be a good suspect. He had a darn good reason to be mad at the guy who stole her."

"I think so too."

"I wonder if anyone at The Timbers knows his last name."

"We'll ask around. We'll find out who he is." John's eyes were glued on the screen once again.

Suddenly, Mabel got it. He truly did love the old horror flicks. She suddenly knew he could handle the investigation just fine. He didn't want to be disturbed while he was watching because what he needed right now was an escape from thinking about it for a couple of hours. This movie was taking him away.

She snuggled into his side and slipped another fat kernel of popcorn into her mouth. So peaceful. Koi, who loved popcorn almost as much as Barnacle, sat on her other side, patting her hand for a share. Soon, Mabel was dozing in and out while the movie played on.

John's phone launched into the theme from *Peter Gunn*. Mabel thrashed, trying to remember where she was, spilling popcorn in the process. Barnacle scooted over to clean up, but Koi, full tummy to the air, couldn't be bothered. She blinked one slitted eye at the dog and yawned.

Mabel had been nestled against John on the couch, and a TV commercial blared. John seemed to be waking up too. The evening came flooding back, like a big file download.

She glanced at the time and muted the TV. This would be the bartender from The Timbers.

"Hey, Jesse, thanks for calling," John said. "I appreciate it, man. I'm sure you're tired and want to get home."

She couldn't hear the reply, but then John said, "Do you mind if I put you on speaker? The other investigator I'm working with is here."

He winked at Mabel and grinned. She liked that. She was his fellow investigator.

John was sitting up now, physically focusing on the call. "We'll try not to keep you. I only have a few questions about a couple people from The Timbers you might know. Here's the thing. I'm looking for a missing person named Amanda Pedersen, and I understand she worked there."

"You say she's what? Missing?"

"Sorry to tell you. Since about end of August. I'm trying to get a lead on her through people in her life, but haven't found any family members yet…maybe you know somebody?"

"Wow. 'Fraid not. Wish I could help you, man. She's not a bad kid. But, hey—how do I know why you're trying to find her?"

"You don't," John admitted. "You're right to be cautious. All I can say is I think she may be in danger, and we are who we say we are. Maybe you can at least tell me a bit about some of the other people in her life."

"Like who?"

"I understand from one of the other waitresses there—Leah?—that Amanda had a boyfriend named Danny? Then that ended somehow, and she took up with another guy from work named Mike. Do you know anything about that?"

Jesse laughed. "Oh, yeah. I worked with Mike in the bar. He's not, shall we say, a very stand-up guy. At all."

Mabel moved closer to the phone. And John. She found an envelope under the stuff on the coffee table and flipped it over to make a few notes.

"All the same, she liked him?"

"Yeah, she and a lot of other women. I don't get it—why women go for these creepos."

John grunted. "Me neither, man."

Mabel had to admit neither did she. Why would anyone choose to get involved with somebody who was not a good person...unless, of course, they didn't see that until it was too late.

"Good looks, maybe?" John suggested.

"Maybe. The girls seemed to think so. Anyways, yeah, he was a smooth operator. A lot—and I mean a lot of women—fell for him. They'd wait at the bar for him to get off work. Mostly really hot—and maybe some others not so hot, but they looked like they had money, you know?"

Mabel knew. She had never been what anybody might describe as "really hot." Of course, she didn't have money, either. She was glad for the millionth time that John seemed to see her with different eyes.

"He was also involved with a hostess here, Buffy Westermann. A bit older, but nice looking. Money too. Husband Chad's a lawyer—Chad wanted to kill him."

Mabel's eyes shot wide open, and she looked over at John, who winked again. She wrote the names down. They'd seen the very striking Buffy—there couldn't be two hostesses with the same unusual first name.

"Listen, Mike was a good bartender. He did a good job over here and worked at Peach's on the side. Never a complaint about him—always on time for his shifts, quick on the drinks, good with the customers. Especially the ladies. But he's a cheater, and he's sketchy, if you get me. Never saw him do anything here, but everybody knew about his little side jobs. You heard of Vin Perdue?"

"Yeah," John said. "Slumlord, right?"

"And small-time criminal. Mostly fraud. But there were rumors."

"Like what?" Mabel interjected.

"Oh, hi, ma'am."

Ma'am.

"Like Perdue wanted a piece of property over in Wilkie a while back, and the owner wouldn't sell. He didn't think it ought to be leveled. Or, maybe he thought Vinnie should pay a lot more for the privilege.

"Well, the house burned down one night, and the owner filed an insurance claim, but he ended up in prison."

"What for?" Mabel said.

"Aggravated arson. There was a guy sleeping there, which I guess whoever set the fire didn't realize. The DA figured the owner torched his own property for the insurance. There was nothing to connect Perdue to the fire, but most people thought he hired someone else to do the job—and some of us were pretty suspicious it was Mike."

"Did the victim survive?" John asked.

"He must have," Mabel said. "Or the charge would have been murder."

"As far as I know, but he was really messed up."

"You have a name on the homeowner? Or the homeless person?"

"No, sorry."

"That's okay. Good information. Can you tell us any more about Mike's relationship with Amanda?" John asked.

"I don't know. Like you say, she had a boyfriend when she started working here. She was taking classes, I think, at Charles Harding U, or maybe she used to, and he was a grad student. Art history guy. You know."

Mabel did not know. She looked at John, who shrugged.

"Danny something. Used to come in sometimes and pick her up after her shift. He'd sit in the bar once in a while and wait for her. Anyway, Mike put the moves on her. Guy was a master—gotta give him that. It didn't take long before the boyfriend wasn't coming around anymore."

"Did you ever see the two guys interact with each other?"

"Interact?"

"Talk to each other, argue, or anything?"

"Well, Mike used to wait on him sometimes. After she started up with Mike, I heard the boyfriend yelling at Amanda in the parking lot once. I don't remember him having it out with Mike, but it could've happened. I don't know. We didn't always work at the same times."

"Thanks, man. I better let you get home to bed."

"Almost there now. Got you on the Bluetooth."

After they hung up, Mabel grabbed John's arm. "Chad Westermann, Buffy's husband—I *know* him. Well, not personally, but definitely by reputation in the legal community. The guy's a hot shot trial lawyer. Got a reputation for arguments that can turn personal, and badgering witnesses as much as he can get away with."

"Is that unusual—or more like a job requirement?"

"You can be a trial lawyer with a calm demeanor and still win cases. This guy's known as a real hothead, and he doesn't always leave it in the courtroom. A couple years ago, he was all over the news— broke a guy's windshield with a lug wrench in a road rage incident."

John's eyebrows went up.

"Even before that, he had misdemeanor assault charges over bar fights, which all somehow got dropped. He ended up having to take court-ordered anger management classes after the road rage, though."

"We need to talk to him for sure."

Mabel clapped her hands with glee. "Three more suspects." She checked her notes. "The boyfriend, Danny, plus the Westermanns."

"Maybe more besides." John yawned and stretched out his legs. "Sounds as if Mike went around breaking up relationships just for the exercise."

"Mixed up in criminal activity too. Who knows how many people wanted to bump him off?"

"I'm interested in the arson. Wonder if that homeowner's out of prison by now."

"If so, he probably spent his whole time thinking how he was going to get back at Mike for getting him sent up," Mabel said.

"If he knew Mike did it."

Mabel nodded. "If."

"Sounds like it was the rumor among The Timbers staff. Whether the homeowner ever heard it, who can say?"

"Or if it was true to begin with."

John tweaked her nose. "There's no investigator like an investigating lawyer. You're right. Mike's coworkers might have concocted that story because they knew he was mixed up with Perdue— and Perdue's name came up in connection with the property."

Mabel yawned, and so did John. "I guess they really are contagious," she said.

"Being it's 2:30 in the morning might also be a factor," John said. "I guess I better hit the road."

"Careful driving." She followed him to the door, carrying the popcorn bowl and their glasses. Some women might have suggested he stay, since it was so late, but not Mabel.

John didn't suggest staying, either, which she found sweet and respectful. Or possibly disinterested. Everything seemed to have two sides when one was insecure.

Chapter Fourteen

ACEY ARRIVED MONDAY MORNING TO START shoring up the demolished shed. Mabel, exhausted from her late night, woke to the sounds of his hammering and drilling. This also set off Barnacle, who seemed to think they were under attack. As soon as she'd taken care of her animals and downed a couple of ibuprofen for her crashing headache, she headed for the Coffee Cup. Breakfast far away from Acey seemed the sanest start to her week.

Mabel was inhaling a second coffee refill after a sustaining breakfast—her last Farmhand Breakfast, she promised herself—when Grandma Mabel's lifelong friend, Miss Birdie came in. "You're late this morning, Miss Birdie." Usually, the spry ninety-year-old ate her breakfast around seven am when the diner opened, and then joined her friend, Ms. Katherine Ann, for their daily power walk.

"Yes, Katherine and I tried a new route this morning, and we decided to do that first, since it was a bit more challenging. What brings you out so early, baby?"

"Acey's trying to fix the shed he ran his truck into, and I couldn't handle the noise."

Miss Birdie shook her head. "That man. His work ends up pretty good, all right, but you best not be in any rush."

"I'd invite you to sit down, but I'm about done now."

"That's all right. Katherine's in the restroom. They're clearing our favorite table right now."

Mabel picked up the check and counted out a tip.

"You haven't forgotten your talk to the seniors' group, have you?"

"Uh, no." Mabel cast about, trying to remember the date she'd promised to speak.

"Saturday night," Miss Birdie told her, obviously realizing Mabel had forgotten. "Seven-thirty at the senior center. You can talk about whatever you like, baby—your experiences with those murders, or being a lawyer—or that writing you do. Whatever you like." She rested her tiny nut-brown hand over Mabel's. "You have a lot to offer."

"I'm looking forward to it, ma'am."

Mabel thought about it as she paid her check. Maybe the easiest thing to speak about would be the late Margarethe Sauer, since she'd recently written that whole biography of the town's leading benefactor. Or she could talk about volunteering for seniors and promote her book, since she was supposed to be an expert on that topic. Unfortunately, she wasn't really an expert yet—it was still more of a plan than a reality.

Maybe she'd wait and decide tomorrow.

Ms. Katherine Ann, a substantial figure in bold purple sweats and sturdy walking shoes, emerged from the back hallway as Mabel was heading for the door. "Well, hey, there!" she called. "How's that murder of yours coming along?"

Heads turned.

Miss Birdie shushed her.

Mabel gave a weak laugh and walked back to avoid sharing a shouted conversation with the entire diner. "Now, Ms. Katherine Ann, I'm not involved in any murder. As you know."

Both older women frowned, and Miss Birdie caught Mabel's hand. "We know, baby. But we did hear another murder found *you*. Being as this one was up there on the mountain, I hope you can steer clear this time."

"Nothing to do with me," Mabel assured them, as well as herself. "Don't you worry about me now."

After she'd managed to allay the ladies' concerns, Mabel considered going home. Then again, she couldn't bear the thought of trying to work with Acey crashing around outside. She had brought her laptop and folders. Maybe she'd head to the library and write for a bit.

While she was driving, a better idea occurred. Her niece Betsy might be working at The Grind. Mabel hadn't seen her in months, not since Betsy had started attending Bartles Grove Community College and working part-time at the coffee shop.

The coffeehouse sat on the corner of Main Street and Elm in Bartles Grove, next to Caravan Used Books, and across the square from the courthouse. Not for the first time, Mabel gave thanks for angled spots along the curb, as she would drive blocks out of her way to avoid parallel parking.

She fished for change in her big leather bag, but of course, found no quarters. After digging under her seat, she finally came up with some sticky change and a couple fuzzy breath mints. She locked up, fed the meter, and headed inside.

The Grind occupied a former dry goods store with wide, battered hardwood floorboards. Green plants—mostly small citrus trees in cans, sprouted from foraged orange or lemon seeds—lined the windowsills. Original pressed-tin tiles, painted dove gray, covered the high ceiling. Voices interspersed with the clatter of dishes and hiss of steam from the espresso bar. Behind the high counter, a colorful, hand-scrawled chalkboard listed available drinks and food.

It was barely ten am, and she'd already eaten a big breakfast, but Mabel's mouth watered at the smells of coffee and cinnamon. She really should get a little something since she would be taking up a table.

The place was crowded for mid-morning. Through the open door to the side room, she saw the ladies' book club group—which, these days, also included two men, despite the name—laughing about something.

All the tables in the main room were filled—some with people in business dress, others obviously students, and a few like herself merely fortunate enough to be able to frequent coffee shops in the middle of a workday. As Mabel squeezed her way up to the counter, a blonde in leggings and oversize BGCC hoodie gathered her books and left a corner table. Mabel changed course and hung her coat over the back of the newly vacated seat.

"Hey," she called, when she realized she'd been left with the job of busing the table, but her voice melted into the general chatter. She made a face at the girl's departing back.

After dumping a sticky latte cup and crumb-covered plate in the plastic tub atop the nearest trash can, Mabel aimed for the counter. Only two people appeared to be working—a young male barista, now tamping espresso, and a twenty-something woman with a nose ring, taking orders. Both wore dark brown T-shirts scrawled with The Grind in cream. Betsy was nowhere in sight.

Two people stood ahead of her in line. While she waited, she decided on her treat—a pumpkin cream latte.

By the time Mabel finally made it to the counter, she'd added a cranberry-nut muffin to her order, and Betsy had appeared from the back, carrying a double armload of napkins. Her face brightened. "Hey, Aunt Mabel."

"Hi, honey." Betsy was tiny, like her mother, with dark brown hair in a smooth, ear-length bob. "I'm glad I caught you."

"Almost didn't. I'm covering someone's half shift, and I should have been out of here at ten."

Mabel glanced at the time. Fifteen after. "Are you leaving soon?"

Betsy set the napkins down. "Pretty soon. After I do a bit of restocking. We got slammed this morning, and all the dispensers are empty."

"Why don't you come sit with me when you're done?"

While Betsy made her circuit of the tables, wiping spills, tossing trash, refilling supplies, Mabel collected her drink and settled herself at the table. Her laptop battery was low, so she found an outlet and plugged it in, then strung the cord under tables, where it would be less likely to trip someone.

"Here you go, Aunt Mabel." Betsy slid her warmed muffin across the table and sat. She had thrown a raspberry fleece on over the uniform shirt and was carrying a takeout cup of her own.

"Thanks, sweetie. I guess you didn't get to watch my TV debut last week?"

She shook her head and her shiny hair swung around her face.

"Sorry. We do have a little TV in back, but that was our busiest time of day."

"I understand."

"I'm sure you rocked." A frown crinkled Betsy's smooth brow. "Mom said you got mixed up in another murder."

"Well... 'mixed up' is a bit strong. I accidentally ended up with a body." Mabel waved an airy hand. Yep, just an accidental body. That's all it was.

"You better be careful, Aunt Mabel. Murders aren't a hobby for older people."

Mabel stared at her niece.

"I'm sorry. You know what I mean. I love you, and I don't want anything to happen to you because you're out playing detective. The police are trained to handle homicides, and they have to be able to run and climb over walls and stuff."

There it was again—the idea that Mabel was over the hill and out of shape. Out of the mouth of babes. She fingered the fitness tracker on her wrist guiltily. She was planning to start a walking program. Soon.

"I'm not 'playing detective.' I was a victim last time...or almost was. This time, I only happened to be there when a dog found the body. It's not like I'm searching for corpses. They come looking for me."

Betsy shook her head and rolled her eyes, as if she were the mature one.

A thought occurred to Mabel. "Hey, since you go to school over here, maybe you can help me out with something. Do you know Peach's Bar?"

Again, the eyeroll, this time with a grin. "Uh, Aunt Mabel, you do know I'm underage, right?"

"I didn't suggest you were drinking there. I simply wondered if you knew anything about it."

Betsy frowned. "Is this part of your new murder investigation?"

"You're worse than your mother," Mabel said. "And my mother."

"That's a yes, then?"

Mabel narrowed her eyes. Kids these days. She wrestled with her conscience. "Maybe. It's not really a murder investigation. The thing is there's a guy who supposedly moonlighted as a bartender over there, who was stalking one of John's clients. He and John had a run-in when the guy tried to break into the woman's apartment."

Betsy's eyes widened. "That's horrible. Nope—I do not frequent bars. I know a few people who've been there, though. The place is a little 'dive-y,' if you know what I mean."

After Betsy left, Mabel tried to concentrate on her search and rescue story. When she wrote about hiding in the woods for the dog to find, however, the memory of the stench of death nearly choked her.

Using the shop's wi-fi, she started scanning background material about search dogs. That, being less personal, went better. By the time she was done, she had a rough draft of an article—and possibly a new section for her volunteer book.

The Grind was situated in the original downtown area of Bartles Grove with the florists, a hardware store, diner, and the old Regency Hotel. Before heading home, Mabel decided to drive the other direction and check out the campus area where the art museum was also located. It was a scenic loop if nothing else.

The community college buildings were all newer construction, the original cream brick building dating from the 1960s and the rest from the eighties and later. In fact, a construction crew with heavy equipment was working behind an orange mesh fence, apparently building another one. All around it, green lawns sprawled beneath substantial oaks, maples, and sycamores, with curving drives beneath them, connecting all the college facilities. As she passed the faculty parking lot, Mabel craned her neck for John's car. Nope. Not there.

Bartles Grove Community College abutted the Charles Harding University campus, which was even more beautiful, since the buildings themselves reflected Mabel's romantic concept of what a college should look like. Built mostly at the turn of the previous century, they were all red brick and stone, lavishly draped with blankets of ivy.

Mabel took time to wind through the campus and emerged at the bottom of the hill, directly opposite the Art Museum of the Alleghenies, an amalgam of adobe-looking arches, vaulting glass, and stainless steel. It looked to her architecturally untrained eye as if a spaceship had crashed into a Native American pueblo in somebody's nightmare. Nevertheless, she could imagine Lisa having a lovely wedding there, as it looked as if light would stream through those floor-to-ceiling windows.

Beyond the museum things soon became less impressive. Here sat the sandwich shops, bars, and college-logo clothing shops that students and their families frequented. And there was Peach's, cater-corner from the museum.

Mabel pulled into a spot opposite. A neon sign flickered ominously above the unimpressive square building. The front looked like peach-painted concrete, with old-fashioned glass block framing the single window.

Not the trendy kind of place likely to appeal to students or office workers. More of a neighborhood bar where one might expect to find shift workers and older neighborhood guys. But it was close enough to the campus—and the museum—to pull some business from both.

She wondered if Mike had continued his habit of picking up women here—women who were already otherwise attached.

Chapter Fifteen

SATURDAY MORNING DAWNED SUNNY AND COLD. About as beautiful a day as one could expect of early November. Nevertheless, Mabel groaned as she contemplated getting up. She had overslept, because even Barnacle, who usually served as her canine alarm clock, didn't seem in any hurry to go outside.

As Lisa drove them to the art museum later, leaves swirled across the road. A lot of colored leaves had clung to the trees late this year, but the last frost had dropped most of them. Lisa was in high spirits. "Have you ever been to the museum?"

"Not since our class went there in like fourth or fifth grade."

"That was the museum in Greensburg. It's next to a different college campus."

"Oh...then, no."

"It's magnificent inside. The collection's amazing, of course, but the space itself is wonderful. I think it'll be magical."

"Mm-hmm." Mabel yawned.

"The Silver Mushroom does all their catering. We're going to get to try all the samples this morning."

Mabel brightened. "That's great."

Lisa laughed. "You're such a romantic."

"I meant the whole thing, you know. The venue and all."

This time, Lisa said, "Mm-hmm." She glanced over at Mabel as they sat at a stop sign, waiting for an ancient pickup truck, trailing blue smoke, to clear the intersection. "Tell me—I'm dying to hear what's new on your big murder case."

Mabel sighed. She wasn't sure how much she should share about John's situation. Of course, a best friend was always entitled to the inside track on anything important in one's life. Plus, Lisa, with her true-crime fascination, often knew a lot more about murder than Mabel did. If Lisa hadn't been so wrapped up in work and wedding plans, she'd have wormed every detail out of Mabel long before now.

Mabel decided she could at least tell her about the whole Amanda thing and how it all ended with John's fight with Mike and Amanda's disappearance. By sticking to the high points, she managed to convey that much of the story by the time the museum loomed up ahead.

"Wow. That has made-for-TV movie written all over it. You think she's still alive?"

Mabel shrugged. "It gets worse. At least, for John."

Lisa shot her a sharp look. "How?"

Mabel still couldn't bring herself to spill what was going on with his PI license. All the same, she had to tell her about John's connection with that body…his *entirely coincidental* connection with the body.

They'd been driving again, but Lisa pulled over, only scant yards from the museum parking lot. "He didn't just know the victim, but it was the same guy he had the run-in with?"

Mabel nodded.

"And now his client is missing, and this guy's dead?"

Mabel nodded again.

"Hoo boy. What's he going to do? Do the cops consider him a suspect?"

"I guess we don't know yet. At least, so far the police haven't called him in for further questioning." *Yes, but they ran ballistics on his gun.*

Lisa patted her hand. "Try not to worry. The vic sounds like a major creep. He must have enemies worse than John."

"Thanks. That's what we figure. It's…I can't help worrying."

"I know. We can solve this." Lisa had that Nancy-Drew-on-the-case gleam in her eye.

"I'm not sure you and I ought to get involved. We'd probably only get in the way and screw things up for John."

"Pfftt." Lisa dismissed Mabel's hesitation with a toss of her head before pulling back onto the street and driving to a closer spot in the museum lot. "Remember grade school—we were going to be the Dana Girls forever."

She parked and grabbed her purse from the back. "Well, anyway, we're here. Maybe all those nice samples will help take your mind off whatever the police are up to. We'll figure this out. I'm sure John will be okay in the end."

"I hope you're right," Mabel said darkly, though she did try to focus on those luscious nibbles yet to come.

The interior was cool and expansive, and the artwork stood out in sharp relief against white walls...all except the square of white canvas captioned "No. 2," with the "artist's" name. Mabel put the term in mental quotation marks.

A massive, curving glass-and-steel table sat in the center of the entry, with sprawling galleries to either side, and a few narrow hallways leading back. A wide, curving stair in the left corner led to second-floor promenade space.

Lisa identified herself to the handsome but sullen-looking young man lounging behind the front desk. He wore dark blond hair in a man bun and sported a trendy scruff of beard. Since she could see right through that glass table, Mabel couldn't help noticing his button-down oxford dress shirt was paired with worn blue jeans and scuffed boots. His nametag read, "D. Brannigan."

He pulled himself to a sitting position, apparently in no great hurry, and picked up the phone. A moment later, he told Lisa to hang on.

"*Hang on?*" Mabel rolled her eyes. She'd lost her attorney job because she'd allegedly been overly blunt with clients...well, they had used the word "rude." Others didn't seem subject to the same expectations.

"Good morning, Ms. Benedetti." A thin, balding man in a tweed jacket and navy turtleneck emerged from the back hall, beaming at Lisa and Mabel.

"Come along and let's see what we can do for you in the various price ranges." He led them back a narrow corridor, away from the galleries, past restrooms and offices to a door marked Fund Raising & Special Events.

Mabel accepted coffee in a heavy, cream-colored mug with the museum logo. After that, she mostly tuned out as the man, whose name was Mr. Comstock—"call me Phil"—spread out flyers and circled various options and prices.

"No, that's on the second floor—you take those broad stairs in the far corner of the north gallery. Or the elevator, naturally."

Mabel swallowed another yawn.

"Yes, that's the south gallery. I agree it's a wonderful space, but we have no feasible means of protecting the artwork against theft or damage."

"Excuse me." Mabel made a vague gesture toward the hallway. "I'll be right back."

Lisa and Phil would figure she'd gone to the restroom. Meanwhile, Mabel had had a brainstorm.

Was "D. Brannigan" possibly the Danny who'd been Amanda's boyfriend before she became involved with Mike? She and Danny had been fine-art students, presumably right here in Bartles Grove. Wouldn't this be the perfect place for an art student to work?

D. Brannigan still lounged at the front desk. An elderly couple browsed landscape paintings in the gallery to the left, but so far, she didn't see any other visitors.

Mabel sauntered up to the desk and smiled. "Quiet morning, huh?"

"They pretty much all are, except for school groups." He seemed to shudder.

"What a shame. People should appreciate access to art like this," Mabel said.

"Philistines. It's all wasted on this town."

Mabel felt herself bristle at his obvious contempt for the hard-working members of this very pleasant community. Then she remembered she had never before set foot in this museum herself.

She glanced down at the desk. A sketchbook sat open in the corner, with a pencil drawing of an angel.

He seemed to notice her interest and slid a folder over it. "Is there something I can help you with?"

"Sorry, no. I'm just looking around." She gestured toward the hidden sketchbook. "I couldn't help noticing the lovely drawing. Are you an artist?"

He snorted. "I'd be ashamed to call myself that when I'm surrounded by real art. I'm only a dilettante, copying pieces."

Mabel thought of the plain white square titled "No. 2" and stifled a snort of her own.

"Are you an art student? I understand most artists start out copying."

"For what it's worth. Grad student. No future in it, of course. No money. We all become computer programmers in the end." He spoke as if being a productive IT professional were a fate similar to the gutter.

"May I see your picture? It looked very good."

"It isn't. The perspective is off. Anyway, no, I'm actually not supposed to be drawing while I'm at work."

"May I ask you a question?"

"That is my job."

"Is your name Danny?"

His handsome dark eyes narrowed. She wondered if he thought she was hitting on him.

She pointed at the nametag. "I wondered if that was what the D stands for. I…" She stole a glance down the hall toward Phil's office. "I'm looking for a missing person. It occurred to me you might know her."

He scowled. "My name's Dan, but I have no earthly idea what you're talking about. Who's missing and why should I know her?"

Mabel leaned in. "Do you know an Amanda Pedersen?"

He jerked in his seat.

At that moment, a young couple came through the entrance, pushing a toddler boy in a stroller.

"Excuse me. Sorry." Danny didn't look sorry. He looked relieved.

Mabel wandered away while he took the couple's money and gave them a guidebook and an explanation of the different exhibits. She liked some of the landscapes, especially the mid-twentieth century ones that used sharply contrasting light and shadow and simple shapes. For some reason, they reminded her of the painting by Edward Hopper she'd once seen, called *Nighthawks*, showing people in a diner at night.

When she came back, Danny was doing something with his cell. She cleared her throat. "Excuse me?"

He jumped.

"Sorry. I didn't mean to do that. I was wondering if you knew whether the painters who did the landscapes along this wall were influenced by Edward Hopper."

Danny stared as if she'd sprouted a second nose.

"Right there." She pointed.

"Oh, yeah. Good eye." He seemed shocked Mabel had produced the name of an actual painter and knew something vaguely accurate about him. She wasn't sure whether she should be offended, however, given she'd already exhausted her entire fund of artistic knowledge.

"We have an Edward Hopper, you know."

"You do?" Mabel was surprised a small, local museum would own anything by such a well-known artist.

"Here." Danny got up and walked to the other end of the gallery. He gestured at a painting of a sun-splashed building at the corner of a city block. "Hopper was known as more of an urban painter, but he did landscapes too."

"Well, would you look at that." Mabel squinted at the signature. "I never realized this place owned anything this valuable."

Danny's face darkened. "They did own quite a few important works at one time." He glanced back toward the desk, but no one else had come in. He lowered his voice. "Amanda's really missing?"

"You do know her, then."

He laughed shortly. "Yeah, I know her. Or thought I did. Not that

I care, but what do you mean, missing?"

"Well, she hired my…friend, who's an investigator, to do some work for her, but then she disappeared a couple months ago. He's concerned about her welfare."

"Well, she's pretty flaky, so she probably just cut out. If you're worried you could check on her boyfriend, Mike Hardy. He's a real piece of work. You'll probably find him down at Peach's." He jerked his head in the bar's general direction.

"Why do you say he's a piece of work?"

"He's a hothead, for one. An actual criminal, number two. Shall we say he always lived better than his employment would indicate— supposedly, thanks to his 'odd jobs.'" Danny made air quotes. "Third, he's a liar and a cheat. Fourth…well, never mind."

"I heard you used to be involved with Amanda yourself."

"Look. I'm trying to work here."

Mabel rolled her eyes. *"Work" in a near horizontal position. Sure.* "I won't keep you. I only hoped you might have some insight into where she might be."

"I don't know, and to be frank, I don't much care. Yes, we were together for a while, but it wasn't all that serious. As she demonstrated when she took off with that tomcat. I'm glad I found out how shallow she was before things went any further."

"No suggestions?"

He inched toward his desk. "Nope. Other than the boyfriend. We, uh, haven't kept in touch."

"Peach's?"

"Or he might still be working at The Timbers. That's where Amanda met him when she worked there. You should know he was also involved with a part-time hostess named Buffy, last name Westermann. Husband's a lawyer with an even worse temper than his, and someone told me Mike got canned once Chad Westermann came after him. Heard management didn't want to put up with his romantic drama anymore, but it's basically all rumors."

When Danny walked away, Mabel scribbled a few quick notes. Then she sighed. Chad was a prime suspect, all right. Given Mike's roving eye and lack of respect for preexisting relationships, they could be chasing down enraged husbands and jealous boyfriends for months.

Chapter Sixteen

LISA GROANED. "AFTER ALL THAT DELECTABLE food, you want to stop where?"

Mabel's hand still rested on the car door handle. "Just for a drink—to celebrate signing the contract for your venue. I'll buy."

"Neither of us drinks. Plus, couldn't you come up with a better place?"

"It's right there, and so convenient. I'm sure they have soft drinks." She coughed unconvincingly. "I'm parched."

Lisa's eyes narrowed. "Are we investigating? Is that it?"

Before Mabel could reply, Lisa's eyes snapped wide open again. "Omigosh. We are investigating. I wondered where you disappeared to back there." Lisa popped the door locks. "I saw the body was released this week but no word on time or cause of death. Get in and tell me quick. It's freezing out here, and if I have to go in that sleazy place with you, I want to know exactly what this is all about."

"Deal," Mabel said, happy to slide in out of the cold. "The report could take weeks, but it's a pretty definite homicide. And he couldn't have been dead more than a couple days—unless it hit freezing up on the mountain for some period of time. Speaking of which, let's get that heater going."

In as few words as possible, she sketched out what she'd learned about Mike, including what Danny had told her. "I want to know what people down there can tell me about him and any enemies he had."

"One's super obvious," Lisa said.

"Danny, naturally—he sure acted mad for someone claiming he didn't give a hoot about Amanda or anybody she was with. Chad Westermann for a second."

Lisa waved an impatient hand. "Of course. But one more should be obvious right off the bat."

Mabel frowned. They hadn't discussed anyone else.

Suddenly, the old lightbulb went off in her head. "Oh, shoot. Amanda."

Lisa grinned and nodded. "She may have been taken in by this gigolo to start out with, but 'hell hath no fury,' and all that. Once she found out what a cheater and womanizer he was, don't you think she'd be every bit as mad as any jealous man?"

"Of course. You're right. Nobody wants to feel like a fool." Mabel blew her nose, which had started running from the cold. "If she gave up her old boyfriend—and who knows what else—to be with him, all the worse."

"I wonder where they were living," Lisa said. "It's common for these guys to move in with women they take advantage of. They live with them rent-free, drain their bank accounts, then bump them off once they've taken out a big life insurance policy on them."

Mabel pondered the classic true-crime documentary Lisa had outlined. "Except in this case, maybe Amanda figured him out before he got to kill her, right? And he's the one who ended up dead."

"Or maybe it was more than one of the women acting together. Sometimes that happens in real life."

"Sort of like Agatha Christie's *Murder on the Orient Express*." Mabel thought some more. "Though it seemed to John like Amanda was completely on her own and on the run. She was afraid of him."

"Then that fits with the theory that she might've found out—or suspected—that he planned to kill her for money."

Mabel snapped her fingers—or attempted to. It was a skill she'd never fully mastered. "Here's another thought. Amanda claimed to be pregnant, and she told John that Mike denied the baby was his. That would have given him another motive, if he didn't want to be on the hook for child support. It would also give her—"

"—Another motive for wanting him dead." Lisa finished her sentence. "Can you imagine trying to deal with being pregnant, and then, finding out your boyfriend is a no-good gigolo with a girl in every port?"

"Or, at least, every dive bar," Mabel said. "Speaking of which…"

"Yeah, okay," Lisa turned off the car's ignition. "I'm warm enough now to walk down there."

Together, they crossed College Avenue and trudged down the hill. The glass blocks of the sun-washed bar front glowed red and green, clashing with pinkish concrete walls. The sign above the door featured the bar name next to a huge fruit that appeared to be a dented orange but was surely intended to be a peach. Loud voices seeped around the warped door and into the street.

As they crossed the threshold, Mabel's courage wavered a trifle. They were the only women there at midday, apart from a muscular young barmaid and a woman perhaps in her seventies, seated on the end stool and drinking shots. Every male eye in the place focused on Lisa and Mabel as they hesitated in the doorway.

The smell of beer and stale fryer oil made Mabel hold her breath for a moment, before realizing what she was doing. Obviously, she had to breathe.

Lisa took a half step back, and the thought flitted through Mabel's brain that maybe she should return with John later on. Or send him without her.

There was no time to waste, however, and she and Lisa were already there.

"Shut the door!" a deep voice bellowed, adding a colorful expletive before the word door. Mabel stepped all the way in, pulling Lisa with her, and closed the door behind them.

"Sorry." She gave the roomful of men a cheery wave, but most had already turned back to their drinks, conversations, and game consoles.

"There should be a pool table," she hissed at Lisa. "In all the movies, when the heroes go into the dive bar, there are tough guys around a pool table."

"Shh." Lisa elbowed her. "They'll hear you."

They made their way to the bar and with a bit of a struggle, Mabel hoisted her bottom onto a stool. Lisa hopped up next to her.

"Hi." Mabel addressed the barmaid. "It's sure a cold one for so early in the season, huh? Especially after almost hitting the seventies there."

The woman, whose dull violet-black hair color did not occur in nature, looked up but didn't reply. Mabel was immediately hypnotized by a silver ball, seemingly inserted in a piercing in the woman's cheek.

Mabel forced her eyes back to neutral territory. "A hot coffee would be nice."

When the barmaid didn't respond, Mabel cleared her voice. "Do you serve coffee?"

"Sure. You want a cappuccino?"

"Oh, that sounds good." Lisa rubbed her hands together. "Could you make that two?"

The woman rolled her eyes and tossed the bar mop under the counter. "No, we don't have blinkin' coffee. What do we look like? Starbucks?"

Lisa giggled nervously and Mabel narrowed her eyes. She didn't appreciate being mocked. She was a customer—and wasn't the customer always right?

"No," Mabel said. "You certainly don't. But don't you think customer service should still matter? It wouldn't kill you to be polite."

Lisa jiggled Mabel's arm as the barmaid's dark brows came together in a thunderous scowl. Mabel sighed. "Never mind. I suppose you have soft drinks? I'd like whatever kind of cola you serve, no ice."

"Same here," Lisa said. "Unless you have ginger ale. I'll take that."

A moment later, the drinks slammed down in front of them, sloshing sticky bubbles over the sides. "Pay now." The woman named a price that seemed like a lot for flavored soda water.

Mabel held up her hand. "My treat." She pulled out some bills and laid them on the bar. "Keep the change," she said. "For the good service."

She couldn't afford to get thrown out of here for arguing with the barmaid. She took a sip. Mabel hoped the glass was clean. She tried to remember if there had been a County Health Department sticker on the door. At least the drink tasted all right.

"Sooo," Mabel said casually, "is Mike working this evening?"

The barmaid cracked her first smile since she and Lisa had come in. In fact, it was a snort of laughter. "Not you too? Aren't yinz gals a bit, uh, *old* for Mike? Think about it, honey, and save yourself some grief." She patted Mabel's hand.

Mabel pulled her hand back. "No, of course I'm not chasing after the guy. I can do a lot better than him, thank you."

Again, Lisa jiggled Mabel's arm.

Mabel cleared her throat. "I mean, it's...a...friend of ours is missing, and she and Mike were...friends, and—"

The barmaid waved her hand. "Yeah, okay, I get it. I know what kind of friends he has. What happened to your friend?"

She seemed to have loosened up a bit. Mabel wondered if the barmaid had seen bad things happen to women in her own life. Maybe they'd happened to her.

"She disappeared a couple months back. She and Mike had been...together, and things didn't go well, and she left him. Then, she up and disappeared."

"Geez, I'm sorry. Mike is a worthless piece of trash, and he might knock her around a bit, but I don't think he would ever, you know, kill anyone. At least, not on purpose."

Mabel's mouth dropped open. She hadn't mentioned killing.

"Do you think he might...hurt someone?" Lisa asked.

"Oh, yeah. But no more than a few ribs or whatever, you know."

The barmaid sounded as if she was trying to convince herself, more than Mabel and Lisa. "I hope your friend's okay. She mighta taken off, you know. If she got her fill of Mike's shenanigans. Anyways, he stopped showing up here weeks ago."

"Thanks, uh..." Mabel waited a moment for the woman to introduce herself, but a name wasn't forthcoming. "We really appreciate your help." Mabel patted her chest. "I'm Mabel, and this is my friend, Lisa."

The barmaid nodded. "They call me Kitten." She pointed to a tattoo of a snoozing kitty cat on her left bicep.

"Oh, that's cute." Mabel leaned in closer. "Now, here's the other thing, Kitten. Does Mike have any enemies you know of?"

"Huh? Like what kind of enemies?"

"That might want to hurt him?"

Kitten frowned.

"Hey!" The older woman at the end of the bar piped up. "Can I get another shot and a beer down here?"

"Now, I really think you've had enough," Kitten said.

"I'll let you know when I've had enough," the woman snapped back.

"Come on, Mom," Kitten said, with a despairing glance at Mabel and Lisa. "Parents—am I right?"

The older woman turned their way. "I heard that."

"How about some food, Mom?"

The woman shrugged. "Oh, okay. Burger and fries. Slice of onion on there."

She got up and moved down closer to Mabel's barstool. "Name's Bea." She stuck out a hand. Her grip was firm, and amazingly, she didn't seem intoxicated.

Mabel introduced them. "You're Kitten's mom?"

The woman, muscular like her daughter, nodded. Her dark hair was cropped short, and her blue eyes were clear. "Had her right out of the Navy."

Since Kitten had stepped away to put in her mother's food order, Mabel asked, "Are you in here often?"

"Course. I like to give Kitten moral support."

"I see. I was wondering if you knew Mike? The bartender?"

Bea snorted. "Don't bother looking for him, honey. Just keep stepping. He'll break your heart, take your money, and leave you flat."

"I'm not looking for him," Mabel said, with as much dignity as she could muster, "and neither is my friend. What we wondered is whether he had any enemies."

Bea stretched. "How much time you got?"

"All day," Lisa said to Mabel's surprise.

"Wait a minute." Kitten had returned and was drawing draft beers for one of the tables. She handed them over, and put her hand on her mother's arm, which Mabel noticed was tattooed like her daughter's. Except the mother had a tattoo of a smiling bee.

"Why you asking about Mike's enemies?"

Mabel cleared her throat. "Because, uh, he's—"

"Dead," Lisa chirped, and the women's eyebrows shot up. "Murdered." She drew a finger across her throat.

Seriously? Lisa had been poking at Mabel the whole time they'd been in here, trying to get *her* to watch what she said, and how she phrased things.

"No kidding?" Bea shook her head. "I guess it ain't true only the good die young."

Kitten frowned as if trying to wrap her head around the news. "Seriously? Mike dead?" She crossed herself. "Now I feel kind of bad I spoke ill of him."

Bea blew raspberries. "Now, that never did make any sense to me. He's not any nicer dead than alive, baby. Yeah, you better believe the guy had enemies. Besides any woman who was ever with him, you can count whoever they dumped to be with him."

"Plus, anybody he cheated," Kitten said. "Anyone he ripped off."

"Excuse me." A brown-haired man, perhaps in his forties, wearing a museum ID clipped to his belt, spoke up from Bea's other side. "Sorry for eavesdropping, but if you're talking about people with a grudge against Mike Hardy, you should probably add any of the criminal types he did business with, and that guy who went to prison."

"What guy's that?" Mabel asked. "The guy who went to prison?"

Another museum guy came up, hoisting his drooping pants. "Charlie Maier. The guy who owned that arson property, you're talking about—right?"

Although she'd already heard a bit about the arson, Mabel decided to play dumb and let them talk, figuring she'd probably learn more that way. Lisa, who hadn't heard anything about the fire, raised an eyebrow at Mabel.

"Something happened to Mike?" the first man asked.

"Dead," Lisa said. "As the proverbial doornail. Murdered."

"Whoa." Both men reacted visibly. "What happened?" Other heads went up.

Mabel sighed. She really should've stood on a table and called the place to attention to begin with. It would have saved all this repetition. Quickly, she gave the two men a barebones explanation, then waved away questions. "Sorry, but could you please go on with your story? It may be really important."

"Who *are* you?" Brown Hair asked.

"Yeah, at least tell us that much," Kitten said, with a hint of suspicion in her voice.

"Look," Mabel said. "I, uh, found the body up in Clear Creek Park. It really upset me."

"And the police want to pin it on her boyfriend," Lisa chimed in. "So, it's personal."

"Oh, honey. I'm sorry." Kitten frowned.

"I shouldn'ta said what I did about Mike's women. I had no idea." Bea patted Mabel's hand.

After a moment's confusion, Mabel realized the women thought she'd been having an affair with Mike, and John had killed him in a jealous rage. "No." Mabel waved both hands. "It wasn't anything like that. John was working for Mike's girlfriend Amanda and had a run-in with Mike when he tried to break into her house."

Kitten gaped. "Mike really came after her like that? I'm surprised the boy made that kind of effort. He has a temper, but I never knew him to do anything where he went to someone's house and tried to break in. He's more a 'blow up in your face' kind of guy."

"He must've actually fell for this one. Ha!" Bea cackled as Kitten set down her plate. "The fly caught the spider."

"Anyway," Mabel prompted. "You said arson? Maier?"

"Yeah," Droopy Pants said. "Mike would do different jobs for our local wannabe 'Godfather,' Vin Perdue. The story was, a year or so back, Perdue wanted a piece of property Maier owned. Maier didn't want to sell—said it was historic."

"I think it was a family property." Brown Hair took off his glasses and seemed to inspect them for smudges. "Then again, it was rundown and supposedly vacant. Perdue thought he'd get it cheap, but Maier refused. Said he wanted to hold onto it and fix it up."

"Yeah, that sounds right," the other man said. "I think part of Maier's problem was he wanted to do everything historically accurate—and that costs money he didn't have. So that's why it was sitting empty. Supposedly."

"Perdue didn't want to up his offer, and Maier wasn't interested." Brown Hair nodded before resettling his glasses.

"And then, it burned," Mabel said.

Both men looked at her.

"Well, you said arson."

Seemingly satisfied, they continued, talking over each other. "Next thing you know—"

"It was old frame construction—"

"—the house goes up in flames—"

"—so except for the frame, it pretty much burned to the ground."

Mabel's head swiveled between the two men, before she finally gave up keeping track of who was talking.

"Maier suspected Perdue, but Perdue had an airtight alibi. Maier, unfortunately, didn't. The DA made a case for insurance fraud. It was circumstantial, but it did look bad for him. Found some of the accelerant in his garage, and traces on some clothing…could've been planted, I guess."

"Was he convicted? I assume he went to prison," Lisa said.

Mabel nearly answered Lisa's question herself since Jesse The Timbers bartender had already told John and her that much. She caught herself and managed to turn her reply into a cough.

116

"Definitely." Brown Hair nodded. "Still there, in fact, far as I know."

Droopy Pants cleared his throat. "A homeless person had been using the place, but no one knew it. It was a miracle he made it out. He woke up in time to escape before the roof fell in, but he was burned real bad. Guy spent a long time in the hospital, but I guess he survived. I never heard."

"That would be plenty to make it first degree arson, whether he lived or not." Mabel looked at the two men with their museum badges. "I take it you know—or knew—Mike?"

"Sure, he worked here pretty regular."

"And we're here pretty regular," Droopy Pants said. Both laughed.

"You work at the museum?" Mabel asked.

Droopy Pants pulled out a badge. "I work IT, he's an administrative assistant. Bunch of us come down here. This place isn't pretty, but it sure is handy."

At a playful scowl from Kitten, the man who'd spoken pretended to duck.

"Anyway," Brown Hair said, "a lot of us figured since Mike did Perdue's dirty work, he might've poured the gasoline and lit the match."

"I'm guessing he didn't come right out and tell you he was involved with Perdue—and definitely didn't tell you he burned that house down, either." Mabel picked up her glass, but it was empty. Kitten reached across the bar and filled it.

Brown Hair laughed. "Not in so many words—not about the fire, anyway. But his relationship with Perdue was common knowledge, and he all but admitted that to us more than once."

"Admitted?" Droopy Pants snorted. "Heck, he almost bragged about it. He thought he was smarter than everybody else who worked for a living."

"Right after the fire, he seemed to come into a lot of money. Talked about going to the casino and dropping more than I make in a month. All the same, he seemed stressed—more than I ever saw him, at any rate. I think finding out someone was in that house when he'd torched it shook him up."

Mabel scribbled notes. Maier was an obvious suspect for Mike's murder—and who could blame him? Also, if the fire victim was still alive—and knew about Mike…big if—he would've had motive to go after Mike himself. Then there was Vin Perdue. Could he have wanted to shut Mike up about the fire—or other crimes Perdue had been involved in? It sounded like Mike had had a bit of a problem keeping his mouth closed.

When Lisa dropped her off later, Barnacle was barking. It was still half an hour early for his dinner, but he tended to freak out whenever she was gone long. He'd been Grandma Mabel's dog, and Mabel suspected he was afraid of losing Mabel too.

She said goodbye and hurried inside to assure Barnacle he wasn't an orphan. She felt a tad guilty, though, as she realized she'd only have a few minutes before she had to go speak at the seniors' group. Fortunately, she'd made herself take time last night to prepare remarks on volunteering. Ever since she'd become a successful writer-to-be, it seemed like she was busy all the time. It was flattering to be in demand, but so far, she hadn't noticed it making her any richer.

Oh, well, she thought, as she changed into her uniform of black pants and top—this one the green yellow of key lime pie—it wasn't like she could say no to the senior citizens. Miss Birdie and Ms. Katherine Ann had been girlhood friends of Grandma Mabel's, and she couldn't let them down.

"I promise I'll bring you a special treat," she told Barnacle. Koi pointedly turned her back and began a vigorous grooming.

Mabel gave herself a spritz of cologne. She was a writer. She was going to bring the glamor.

Chapter Seventeen

THE NEXT DAY AFTER CHURCH, MABEL managed to dodge Nanette and Cora. She nearly cackled to herself as she exited the parking lot. She should probably show up at this week's monthly historical society meeting but feared that would be the first step on the slippery slope back into volunteering.

Mabel truly did need a break from the society. In fact, she hoped never to step back inside the historic Sauer ax-murder house, which had nearly become the scene of her own demise. Besides which, she'd seen Nanette and Cora huddling by the steps with Linnea, who apparently aspired to become a leading force in the historical society. The last thing Mabel needed was to end up back at the society with a younger, more vigorous version of their late president—Linnea's mother and Mabel's nemesis, Helen Thornwald.

John had invited her to discuss progress on the case at the Coffee Cup. She looked forward to time with John and a delicious brunch. But, as she'd been thinking about the Sauer House, she realized meeting John at the Coffee Cup to talk about theories was also an uncomfortable reminder of the nightmare she had recently gone through.

The sky overhead was gloomy, but oddly, this was much warmer than the sunny day before. Cars packed the lot—Sunday post church was one of the diner's busiest times—so Mabel parked on the street.

She hoped John had arrived early as promised.

As she reached the glass-paneled door, she saw people jammed up, waiting in line. *Doggone it.*

"Excuse me." Mabel gently elbowed her way through the reluctant crowd. On her way, she collected a couple of dirty looks—one from a woman whose toes she'd accidentally smashed, the other from a man who glared as if he suspected her of line jumping.

"I'm so sorry," she told the woman.

"I'm meeting someone," she told the man, but doubted he believed her.

John was still waiting. He smiled and waved when he saw her. As she squeezed her way up next to him, he shrugged. "I tried. I saw them cleaning off one of the small booths, though, so we should be next."

He was right, and soon they were seated knee-to-knee at a two-person booth by the window. Mabel, looking at the menu, briefly considered the Farmer's Daughter combo, but couldn't bring herself to order yogurt and fruit, when her mouth was already watering at the aroma of bacon and onions.

Healthy changes were best made gradually because they tended to stick better. She had read that in a recent article.

A Farmer's Daughter would only lead her into a setback when she became ravenous an hour after eating. She'd order the Farmhand, but without the toast. Of course, if she substituted home fries for the bread, she'd be incorporating a vegetable into her meal—three, if she counted the diced onion and peppers that were mixed in. Four, with ketchup.

After they'd placed their orders—John, with his usual, aggressively healthy spinach and egg-white nightmare—they sat back for what promised to be a long wait. Mabel sipped the plain coffee the harried waitress had poured without asking. A nice pumpkin spice latte would have hit the spot but sacrifices sometimes needed to be made.

She tried to sketch out in as orderly a way as possible what she'd learned the day before, glad she'd taken notes.

"That confirms what we learned at The Timbers," John said. "I think I need a chat with the Westermanns."

Mabel made a face as the waitress set her plate down.

"Is something wrong with your order?" John asked.

"No. It's…ugh. I dread talking to Chad Westermann."

"You don't have to. This is my problem, not yours."

Mabel sighed. "No. I'll go. But he's such an arrogant gorilla of a man."

John laughed and speared a forkful of spinach and egg white. "From what I've been hearing, that's an insult to upstanding gorillas everywhere."

"At least I don't have to face him in a courtroom," Mabel said.

"Or a road rage incident," John added. "We'll try to keep it low key and not mention murder at all. I'll ask about Amanda and say we understand his wife worked with her at The Timbers."

That sounded non-confrontational enough. "When do you want to go?"

"ASAP. I need to get this resolved, so I can file to get my suspension lifted without the whiff of a potential murder charge hanging over me."

"Are you going to try to set up an appointment?"

He shook his head. "I'd prefer to catch him off guard. If we call ahead, I suspect he'll refuse to see us."

"Which he might, anyway."

"If he does, we'll have to move on to the wife. We can probably catch her at The Timbers—or one of her other haunts. That's basic PI footwork."

"So…like now? You want to go this afternoon?"

"No time like the present. I have a few things to finish up, but I can pick you up, say, four-thirty."

Half an hour later, Mabel was ditching her church clothes for detective wear—dark wash jeans and a loose black jersey top. Then, she settled on the couch for an afternoon nap. Koi nestled against her tummy and purred. Mabel ran a hand over the cat's soft back. "I know I've been neglecting you. This will be my last murder, all right?"

Koi opened one eye. Mabel was pretty sure she rolled it.

A few minutes after three-thirty, Mabel got up and stretched, feeling somewhat refreshed. She let Barnacle out to kill more of the remaining grass and topped up the animals' dishes.

Koi sat narrow-eyed, swishing her tail, as she ignored the food.

"Hey, I said I'm sorry," Mabel told her. "I have to do this."

The cat's glare only wavered when Barnacle, seeing an opportunity, shoved his snout into Koi's dish. Amid the hissing and flash of claws, Mabel took her leave.

John waited in his classic blue muscle car, splashed with patches of red primer, feeding the Westermanns' address into his GPS. "They live in Shady Glen," he said as Mabel slid into the passenger seat.

She whistled—or would have, if she'd been capable of whistling, which she was not. "Fancy neighborhood."

Mabel briefly reconsidered her detective clothes but decided it probably didn't matter. She and John were simply not Shady Glen material, however you sliced it. "Silk purse, sow's ear."

"What?"

"Oh, nothing. Let's get this over with."

Shady Glen was, surprisingly, exactly what the name said. Mabel had driven past the exclusive community many times but never had any excuse to turn in. A high stone wall guarded the wooded grounds from the public road. Iron filigree created an arch, forming an interwoven SG between massive pillars at either side of the entrance. Here, the drive plunged into a natural valley and over a stone bridge that crossed a tumbling creek fringed with hemlocks.

The road zigzagged through the trees. Individual drives, many secured behind gates, presumably led to houses not visible from the entry road. "It doesn't feel particularly welcoming," Mabel said. "If the Westermanns' house is gated like this, we might as well forget it."

"We'll see. They aren't all gated."

"Oh, hey." The road had climbed up out of the glen, and they'd reached an open hilltop, where sprawling houses looked out over the lush valley below.

John squinted at a sign and turned. "This is our street, and 105 should be coming up on our left."

The lots all must have been at least an acre—but with houses this big, they somehow managed to look sort of cramped. She was surprised when John hit the brakes at the foot of a long drive leading up to what appeared to be a luxury boutique hotel. Imposing iron gates stood open, framing the building on the hill.

"Why are we stopping at the clubhouse?"

John pointed. "See the number?"

"That's a house?"

"So it seems."

Once again, too late, Mabel had cause to rethink the blue jeans. She reminded herself it was just Chad Westermann. He might have money, but it wasn't like he was a movie star or Nobel laureate.

"He won a big verdict a few years back, and his contingent fee had to be massive." Mabel gawked. "Guess that's about when he started building his Taj Mahal."

"Maybe he'll invite us inside." John's eyes twinkled. "You want to get the tour?"

Three and a half stories of cream-colored stone blocks. Mabel counted three balconies and a promenade, ascended by sweeping palazzo stairs. A portico entrance on the ground level was surmounted by a great, curving, two-and-a-half story battery of windows.

"Holy cow." Mabel tried not to be awed. "Talk about cathedral ceilings. That's one room up there. Do you think Chad has a ballroom?"

John laughed. "Let's ask."

Mabel was glad John could be casual about this. It helped take the edge off her own nerves. What a contrast with Peach's Bar. She tried to imagine Chad's wife coming from this and getting mixed up with somebody like Mike Hardy. Of course, she'd heard of women who were attracted to bad boys. Still, it was hard to wrap her brain around that.

John pulled around the arc of stone-paved driveway and parked between an Escalade and an expensive-looking white sports car Mabel couldn't identify. "Maybe we shouldn't park so close to his cars," she whispered, then realized it was ridiculous to lower her voice with nobody around. She cleared her throat. "Seeing as how he has this road rage issue. Who knows whether that anger management class did him any good?"

"I didn't touch his cars. They remain unscathed."

"I hope he appreciates that critical detail."

Security-system signs bristled around the entry. Mabel wondered if they'd already triggered some kind of alert, merely by driving up here. Nobody had appeared so far, though.

John strolled up and pressed the bell, and chimes sounded inside the house. Moments later, the door opened. Struck again by Buffy's two-inch, choppy platinum coif, Mabel tried to imagine her own hair cut that way and involuntarily shuddered.

Buffy narrowed her eyes. "Are you ill?"

"Sorry. Must have been the cold breeze."

On Buffy, the haircut looked glamorous, like she should grace a magazine cover in her slim black pants and open-necked, orchid-colored silk shirt. "May I help you?" Her frown appeared dubious.

"Good afternoon." John flashed his charming, friendly smile. "Are you Mrs. Westermann?"

"Ms."

"Ms. Westermann, how do you do? I'm John Bigelow, and this is my associate, Mabel Browne. We're sorry to bother you at home, but we're trying to locate a missing person, and wondered if you might be able to help."

The woman's brows seemed to draw together slightly, but not much progress was made. Mabel wondered if she'd had already had Botox at her young age.

"I'm not sure what we could do. Do you mean like a search party...?"

"Nothing like that. Let me explain." John gestured toward the interior. "Might we come in?"

Buffy hesitated, blocking the door. "Sorry. Who are you again? Are you with some organization?"

"I'm active with Bartle County Canine Search and Rescue," Mabel said. It was almost truthful, given her recent disastrous training day.

"Do you have some identification?"

"Just my driver's license," Mabel said, but John produced his private investigator's license. She tried not to draw Buffy's attention by staring at it but couldn't help wondering if John had relinquished the actual physical license when he was suspended. Had he created this from a photocopy?

"I suppose it's all right. You can't be too careful these days. My husband would kill me for letting strangers into the house."

"You have a beautiful place." Mabel looked around. "It's, uh, really big."

Ms. Westermann almost smiled. Mabel could see it in her eyes and the slight twitch at the corners of her mouth. It would be wonderful to get rid of the lines that kept cropping up at the corners of Mabel's eyes and around her mouth. Just the same, she couldn't imagine giving up the ability to smile.

"Thank you. Yes, it's a lot of house for two people. We entertain a lot—clients and bar association bigwigs. Chad wanted space for that."

She led them into a side room near the front, where sunny yellow tiles covered the floor and bright prints punctuated white walls. What appeared to be a substantial, vintage farmhouse table, now painted white, sat in the center with chairs around it. A jungle of lush green plants crowded near the glass sliding door to an outdoor patio. "This is our breakfast room," Ms. Westermann said. "Not that we use it much— at least, Chad doesn't. His job is very demanding."

"I'm sure it is," John agreed.

Mabel nearly told her she was a lawyer too, and that even lawyers eat breakfast, but decided her input wouldn't be helpful.

"Please sit. Would you care for a drink?"

"Thank you, no," John said. "We won't impose any longer than necessary."

"I think I'll have a Bloody Mary. I could as easily do three."

"No, thank you," John repeated.

While Buffy Westermann mixed her drink at a bar along the wall, John explained why he was looking for Amanda. Mabel closely watched her reaction.

Buffy's back, unlike her face, was apparently not Botoxed, because Mabel saw the immediate movement. She turned, holding her glass of tomato juice in one hand and a vodka bottle in the other. "Amanda's missing?"

"You *do* know her?" John asked.

Buffy set the drink ingredients on the bar with hands that seemed a bit unsteady. "We worked together. I was a part-time hostess at The Timbers restaurant for a while—something to keep boredom at bay. Amanda was a waitress. I left recently—my husband doesn't like me working. I have no idea where Amanda went."

Mabel and John had just seen Buffy at The Timbers a week ago. Buffy hadn't left back when the jealous and apparently domineering Chad Westermann first discovered her blossoming affair with Mike Hardy. Odd, given Danny's suggestion Chad had created a scene over the relationship and gotten Mike fired.

What was the real reason she'd left now? Maybe chatter around The Timbers staff about two nosy investigators looking into Amanda's disappearance?

"You lost touch? No idea where we might look?" John asked.

Buffy shrugged. "No earthly clue. What happened?"

John sketched out the disappearance in more detail, but left Mike's name out.

"Do you know if she had family?"

Buffy sat, her drink seemingly forgotten. "She came from someplace out in the mid-west—or west maybe. Idaho? They were estranged. Civil servants, I believe. Perhaps a much younger brother. She was a fine arts major, which they didn't understand, and then she dropped out, and they refused to support her."

"Maybe Idaho" didn't narrow things down very much, even if they had full names. Which they also did not.

"Did you know she was pregnant?" John asked.

Buffy's face remained impassive, though that might've been the Botox. "No."

"She was living with a guy—"

"I know."

"What was his name again?" Mabel asked.

Buffy waved her hands in a show of confusion. "I can't remember." She got back up and returned to the bar. Suddenly, she froze, and her head came up, reminding Mabel of a deer alerting to a sound.

"Oh, man, he's home." Buffy's cultivated accent slipped. "Hey, listen, guys. I'm sorry, but Chad doesn't like unexpected company." She hustled toward the entryway, obviously expecting them to follow.

Mabel exchanged a look with John. He winked. "Now, it should get interesting," he whispered.

They trailed after Buffy. Mabel, taking her cue from John, took her time, looking all around as she went. "We never got the ballroom tour," she hissed.

John grinned. "We'll ask Chad."

"Buffy!" An irritated male voice boomed from the doorway.

Buffy's response was too low to make out, but when Mabel and John emerged into the entryway, she was clutching her husband's sleeve and talking rapidly. He looked over her shoulder and glowered.

"What in blazes is this about?"

Chad Westermann had the look of a campus football hero gone to seed. Broad-shouldered and around six-foot-three, but with a definite paunch, he was carrying too much weight to make the team these days. Expertly styled dark-blond hair looked to be thinning a bit on top. His golf clothes and Rolex had probably cost way more than Mabel's car. He must have come directly from the community's private club because a golf cart had appeared in the driveway, parked behind the sports car.

"Mr. Westermann, hi." John offered his hand. "John Bigelow. I'm a private investigator, and this is my associate, Mabel Browne. We're looking into the disappearance of a former co-worker of your wife's."

Westermann ignored John's outstretched hand, beyond glancing at it briefly with an expression that suggested he'd have liked to spit on it. "What exactly are you insinuating?"

Mabel struggled to control her irritation but failed. How dare this arrogant sack of hot air be so rude to John? She fixed him with steely eyes. "Look, *sir*. We aren't insinuating anything. We're following up on a missing person and hoping somebody can give us a lead. The logical starting place is family and co-workers. Since we aren't aware of any family, we hoped your wife could help."

Chad glared dismissively at Mabel and shoved into John's space. "*You* look, sir. I know why you're here, and we have no idea what happened to that man. Zero."

Mabel jumped reflexively and glanced at John. Surely, he'd been startled as well by Chad's misreading of what they'd said.

Calmly, John shook his head. "What man? We're looking for leads on a woman named Amanda Pedersen, who was a waitress at The Timbers restaurant, where your wife works—or worked—as a hostess. Has someone else vanished that we should know about?"

Red crawled up Chad's thick neck. He shoved John's shoulder. "Get out. You have no business on our property." Behind him, Buffy stood white-faced, hands clenched.

When John made no immediate move to leave, Chad flexed his fists as if itching to use them. "I presumed the missing person was male. We know nothing about this woman—or anyone else. Your business here is concluded."

Chad pulled out his phone as if to dial—presumably, the police or security.

John smiled and took Mabel's elbow. "Thank you for your help, Ms. Westermann, Mr. Westermann."

Their footsteps scratched on the paving stones as Mabel and John headed to the car. Mabel felt Chad's eyes on their backs as they walked away in the weighted silence.

She shot a sideways glance at John, who seemed curiously cheerful for a man who'd been thrown off the property. He opened her door and saw her inside, then came around and started the car, reversed slightly, and pulled out from between the Westermann vehicles, narrowly missing the golf cart.

Chad yelled something she couldn't make out, as they exited the other end of the semi-circular drive. As they headed down the long drive to the entrance road, John reached his left arm out the window for a cheery wave.

"Our boy Chad does have a bit of a temper," he said. "Isn't it curious he 'knew why we were there,' but didn't know anything about 'that man,'—then less than two minutes later, knew nothing at all, and merely presumed the missing person was male?"

"We know he had a beef with Mike." Mabel pondered. "I wonder if he's aware Mike's identity was finally released to the media. Even if he isn't, if you've killed and dumped somebody in a remote area, I bet you'd start sweating as soon as it's reported someone's stumbled over a body in the very place you stuck your victim."

"Does it strike you too," John said, "that Buffy's at least borderline afraid of her hot-headed hubby?"

"Maybe she knows he's capable of more than yelling and beating people up," Mabel said.

"Perhaps like what happened to her former lover."

"She reacted when she heard Amanda was missing. I wonder if she suspects him of that, as well."

John slowly shook his head. "Could be. Except we have a motive for Chad to attack Mike. We don't have that with Amanda. Why would he want her out of the way?"

"I got nothing."

Dusk fell early these late-fall evenings. As they followed the winding drive back to the road, the sun was already riding low behind the trees. It blazed orange red like the coals of a campfire.

On the way home, they approached a hilltop pull-off, where you could look out over the rolling fields and valleys. During the Depression, the WPA had built a stone wall along the edge. This vantage point offered a sweeping view of the fiery sky, now inscribed with swirling ribbons of aqua and gold, peach and inky blue.

John slowed the car. "You wanna park?"

"Park?" Mabel squeaked.

He took her hand. "Stop the car? Snuggle? Watch the sun go down?"

"I, uh, my animals…"

He gently squeezed her hand, and they drove on by. "Maybe next time."

The rest of the way home, Mabel mentally kicked herself.

Chapter Eighteen

THEY HAD TO PASS JOHN'S PLACE on the way to Mabel's. Mabel blinked as they crested the hill, and she spotted his house at the bottom. At first, she thought the setting sun was glinting off a window, but…well, maybe not.

"Huh. Looks like you left a light on."

John leaned forward and cocked his head. "No, I don't think so."

"Don't you see it?"

"Oh, I see it, all right." Grim-faced, he accelerated. "I just don't think I'm the one who left one on."

Mabel grabbed her door handle as the powerful V-8 engine growled, and the car shot forward. John's headlights bathed an arc ahead of them in their bluish beams, but long shadows swaddled the roadside, making hulking monsters of the trees and bushes.

He was about to swing into his property, when a white Jeep shot backward from the driveway into their path. John hit the brakes, and Mabel jerked forward as their car fishtailed.

As the Jeep changed gears to rocket away down the street, John's headlights struck the driver's startled face. Mabel had a confused impression of a young woman with shaggy blonde hair.

Mabel's heart thumped as John stomped the gas and his car leapt ahead, on the tail of the Jeep. She clutched the chicken handle above her door. "Who was that?"

"That appeared to be my client, Amanda Johnson. Or, as you know her, Amanda Pedersen."

Mabel's jaw dropped. She stared at his thunderous profile, hunched over the wheel. "Wait…what?

"Yeah. My dead client is apparently alive. The guy who was stalking her is definitely dead, and she was here at my house—but took off when she saw me."

"That's crazy. What's going on?"

"That's what I'm going to find out." John cornered, tires squealing, down a residential side street.

Mabel clutched his sleeve. John's car—for all that it was probably over sixty years old—had a powerful engine and had been built to run. Surely, Amanda's boxy four-wheel-drive Jeep couldn't outpace them. A residential street was no place for a high-speed chase, however.

John clearly knew that too. As Amanda shot through the next intersection, John's headlights lit up the back of the Jeep as he eased off the gas.

"Did you get that plate number, Mabel? Write it down, if you would."

Mabel rummaged in her purse and found her notebook. She scribbled the number and read it back to him.

"That's what I got too." The car eased to a stop as the Jeep's taillights disappeared around the next corner.

"You think she wanted to talk to you?"

"If she came to see me, don't you think she'd stick around? She wanted something—but nothing she cared to ask me about."

Sedately, John pulled into the nearest driveway, causing a dog inside the house to start barking. He turned around and headed back out to the main road at a respectable pace.

"Will you be able to trace her through the license plate?"

"Maybe, but I don't know if I can get anybody at the department to run it for me." He shrugged. "It may not even be her car."

When they returned to the bungalow, John pulled a flashlight out of the glove box. "Let's take a look."

John hadn't left any outdoor lights on, but as soon as they approached the house, they were flooded by the beam from a security light mounted on the roof at the front corner of the house.

He jogged up the steps with the ease of a teenager and tried the door. "Still locked." He turned on the flashlight and an intense beam shot out.

"Wow."

"Law enforcement grade." John ran the light over the front of his house. "No broken windows. Nothing looks forced. You want to wait here while I check around the side and back?"

"Are you kidding?" Mabel asked. "I'm coming with you." She didn't want to miss whatever he found, but mostly, she didn't want to wait by herself in the dark.

Immediately, a solid, warm hand gripped hers. "Come on then, Nancy Drew."

A second security light came on, leaving the back porch in deep shadow under its roof. They circled the house, feet rustling the fallen leaves. John's flash roved the back door and all the windows. Nothing showed signs of tampering.

"Hmm…"

"Maybe we surprised her before she could get in," Mabel ventured.

John shook his head. "She was already driving, and it looks like she hadn't even tried before we rolled up. My alarm would have gone off."

"We both saw a light, though."

He shook his head. "Not inside. What we saw was the back security light shining through the window. I was hoping an animal triggered it but figured that was unlikely."

"What do you think she was doing here?"

"I'd love to know. A reasonable explanation would be she came back to talk to me, but we seem to have eliminated that possibility."

"And no sign of a break-in," Mabel said. "Maybe we did interrupt her."

"Why break in? For what?" He unlocked his door and disabled the alarm. His cat Billie Jean slunk around the corner from the kitchen, froze at the sight of Mabel, and hissed.

"Nice to see you too," Mabel said, as the cat spun around and dissolved into the darkness.

"I better feed her. She's already mad enough. I don't want to get murdered in my sleep."

Mabel felt a shiver run over her arms. Murder had become all too real.

"I'll wait here." Mabel sank into the single armchair. "I don't want to contribute to your demise." Billie Jean had hated Mabel from the first instant, and thus far they hadn't progressed.

"You hungry?" he called from the kitchen. "I can warm up some leftovers or make us a sandwich."

"Thanks," Mabel said. "Sounds good, but I can't stay long. I left food for my animals, but they'll be wondering where I am." She hoped, as always when she left them longer than usual, that Barnacle would remember his housetraining.

"Which do you want?" he called. "Neither will take that long."

"Whatever." Mabel looked around the comfy living room. John's desk and a nice, old oak filing cabinet sat in the opposite corner.

"Hey, John."

"What?"

"You think there might be something in your files Amanda would want?"

He stuck his face around the doorframe. "I'd have to think about it. I don't have a huge file on her or anything like that. Just my initial notes—and time and expense records for the work she never paid me for."

"Maybe she told you something she was afraid would incriminate her or lead you to something she didn't want dug up."

"Incriminate her for what?" He'd gone back inside the kitchen, and his disembodied voice drifted back.

Mabel hadn't thought that far. A moment later, she and John both spoke at once. "Like maybe Mike's murder."

"Like murder?"

"Hang on," John called.

A moment later, he returned with a plate of turkey sandwiches. He set it on the coffee table, which Mabel noticed he did not have to clear off first. What would it be like to live that way? With no clutter?

When he'd fetched two glasses of water, he settled on the couch, across from Mabel. "It is possible that Amanda killed Mike in self-defense. But if it was self-defense, given their history, I'd think her best bet would have been to confess exactly what happened."

"Mmm," Mabel mumbled around a mouthful of sandwich. "Maybe. But just because somebody claims self-defense doesn't necessarily mean they'll be believed—even if the facts tend to support it." She paused. "Then again, maybe it wasn't self-defense."

"True. That tarp suggests planning. Anyway, I don't see what I could possibly have that she wants."

Mabel and John talked their way through the tray of sandwiches and half a jar of dill pickles. John took Mabel's plate. "Would you like some dessert before you go? I have fruit and cheese."

Mabel didn't consider fruit and cheese a dessert but sitting around with John a bit longer sounded nice. "Sure."

She had mopped up pee puddles on her kitchen floor before. Besides, Barnacle normally didn't go out till later in the evening. He'd probably hold on till then...unless he decided to punish Mabel, which was always a distinct possibility.

Mabel heard John singing in the kitchen. It sounded like *Some Enchanted Evening*, and his baritone was beautiful. For a moment, she let herself believe he was singing about her.

Once you have found him, never let him go. Mabel wanted to let herself trust him.

Suddenly, John's phone rang at her elbow. She jumped.

"Do you see a caller ID?"

"Just a number." Mabel read it to him.

"I don't know off the top, but maybe we'd better answer it. Could you get that, please?"

Mabel picked up. Before she could get a word in, a rushed and breathless female voice said, "John? Amanda. I'm sorry I ran. I, uh, freaked out and all I could think was I needed to get away. I, uh—"

"Wait," Mabel said. "Don't hang up. John's here—hang on."

She muted the phone and yelled. "John. It's her."

As he ran from the kitchen, Billie Jean dashed in front of him. He executed a leap that would have done the Bolshoi Ballet proud and grabbed the phone.

"Hello."

"It's on mute."

"Hello."

Apparently, she hadn't hung up because John continued to listen. After a moment, he spoke. "Whoa. Hold on. You know I thought you'd been abducted and likely killed? I lost my license over your little escapade. What was that about?"

Seconds later, he made an impatient noise. "That's not an explanation. Look. At the very least, you never paid my bill. In fact, I never even got a chance to present a bill, given you took off on me."

More listening. "That's it? That's why I found you in my driveway? So why didn't you stick around and talk to me?"

John's brow furrowed. "Listen. Do you know Mike's dead?"

A strangled sound on the other end of the line came through to Mabel, but after that, she couldn't pick up anything more. John ran a hand over his head in apparent frustration. "In that case, can you give me any idea where I should start looking? You know another part of the fallout of your flying the coop on me is now I'm a suspect in Mike's murder.

"…Yeah, that's right. And I'm not inclined to sit around and wait for the cops to figure it all out.

"…Okay. How do I get in touch if I want to reach you?"

After a brief silence, John said, "Hey. Hello?" He looked down at the phone screen.

"Blast. Lost her."

Mabel held up her hands to block John from returning to the kitchen. "Forget the cheese. What did she say?"

John redialed, but without apparent luck. He threw the phone down on the couch then ran both hands over his head. "She was literally babbling. Almost as if she were trying to spill a lot of stuff out while she could. I didn't understand what a lot of it meant. I'm wondering what the rush was about."

"Did she explain her first disappearance?"

"No. Said an emergency came up, and she couldn't explain right now."

"Well, how about that car chase—what was that about?"

John shook his head and released an explosive breath. "Didn't explain that, either. Said something about being embarrassed about skipping my bill, and not wanting to face me."

Mabel raised her eyebrows. "Soooo...now she ran off on you again."

He gave a brief nod. "Yup. She apologized for not paying me and promised she'd meet me for lunch tomorrow at Romano's Restaurant and take care of that."

"That's it?"

"She said she's still in danger but wouldn't say why. That she had some stuff she was worried would end up in the wrong hands, so she left it with me for safekeeping. Told me she'll be back for it, but I should use it to satisfy what she owes me, 'if something happens.'"

"What 'stuff?' That sounds ominous."

"She didn't say." John threw up his hands. "I don't know what to believe anymore when it comes to her. My gut tells me she really may be in some jeopardy, but at the same time, my baloney meter says she's holding back a *lot*—the part that answers all the questions and tells me *why* she's in jeopardy."

"And from whom, I'm guessing, now Mike's dead. You think she killed him?"

"Definite possibility. She did toss out some suspects to look at—or should I say toss under the bus—but nobody not already on our radar. Chad, naturally, and Danny—the jealousy boys. Vin Perdue."

Mabel nodded. "Maybe Perdue realized Mike was the weak link—and that he could put the finger on Perdue for the arson."

John leaned back. "From what we know about Mike so far, don't you think it's possible he decided he could improve his bottom line by hinting he could point the police in Perdue's direction?"

"Yeah...but if he did that, Perdue could as easily have pointed his finger at Mike."

"Which would still tend to implicate Perdue. I think Amanda was right. We have to consider Perdue a suspect. But he's one suspect you, my dear, need to steer way clear of."

Mabel was only too happy to stay away from hardened criminals. Nevertheless, she groaned. It was good they had a lot of strong suspects, but maybe there was such a thing as too many. Especially suspects with a criminal history and likely to be dangerous. It would take forever to work their way through investigating all these people, particularly if she wasn't allowed to help.

Then again, it would be worse if they crossed paths with a killer and wound up like Mike.

Chapter Nineteen

MABEL KNEW SHE SHOULD BE GETTING home but was so keyed up from the day's events that her mind wouldn't stop spinning, trying to fit the pieces together. John, in his compulsive way, was tidying up from their sandwich dinner. Billie Jean had reemerged from wherever she'd been hiding and glared at Mabel from atop the mantel.

"Are we going to go look for whatever Amanda supposedly left here?"

"I planned to," John called from the kitchen. "But I figured you needed to get home, and I was going to take you first."

Mabel popped up and headed to the kitchen. "Are you kidding?"

John turned from stowing lettuce in the crisper drawer and grinned over his shoulder. "Yeah, let's go take a look, Nancy Drew."

"Where do you think she put it? Should we divide up the house?" Secretly, she thought it would be interesting to get a peek at the less "public" areas of John's home.

He shook his head. "I can pretty much guarantee she did not get inside this house. Whatever she left is going to be outside—probably in the shed, since she mentioned valuables. She wouldn't be hiding them under a bush."

"Do you think she didn't want you to find it?"

"If she left something in the shed, she'd know there was a good chance I'd blunder into it at some point. But since she came over without calling first—and ran when we surprised her—I suspect she hoped I'd at least not discover it right away. Maybe she needed a quick place to stash something for that moment and took a chance she'd be able to get it back out, and I'd never be the wiser."

John held Mabel's coat, then slipped on his own jacket and grabbed a flashlight. "This way." He opened the back door from the kitchen, triggering his security light, which flooded the back.

Mabel followed him across the small, covered back porch. A couple of steps led down into a back yard big enough for a thumbnail patch of grass, an apple tree, and a cottage-like wooden shed. "How cute. Is that one of those Amish storage barns?"

"Yeah. I was going to run electricity out here and use it as an office. Now I may never need it."

"It'll work out," Mabel said stoutly. "This murder will get solved, you'll file for your reinstatement, and everything will be good."

"Thanks. You may be a little bit biased…or in any event, kinder than the police and the licensing board. But I hope you're right."

Mabel shivered. The wind had picked up, and indigo clouds blew across a near-full moon. John shone his flashlight on the shed door.

"No lock?"

"I never needed one. My yard's small enough, I can use a trimmer between the garden beds. I don't even have a lawnmower."

He opened the door, and his flashlight illuminated the one-room interior. Mabel peered around him. An electric weed cutter leaned against one wall, along with a rake, shovel, and a few garden tools stuck inside a galvanized bucket.

In the opposite back corner, several brown paper-wrapped, flat objects leaned against the wall. "Well, there they are." John pointed. "Shall we look?"

He hung his flashlight loop from a hook on the wall and began toting parcels forward. Mabel picked up a couple of smaller pieces. She didn't want to miss the first glimpse of whatever was in there.

"Here goes." John untied the string wound around the first parcel.

"Wow." Mabel tilted her head to study the painting that appeared. "It's a bunch of dots."

"I think it's called pointillism," John said. "If we step way back, we should be able to make out a picture."

Mabel scooted back and squinted. Then she scooted farther. The shadowy room didn't exactly have ideal gallery lighting. "Huh. I think it's a tree."

"Maybe. Could be a toadstool. See the polka dots?"

"I think those are blossoms."

Though Mabel's taste in art ran more to covered bridges and adorable cats and dogs, something told her Amanda's claim her stash was valuable might have been true. "You think this stuff's real?"

"I'm no expert, and even they can be fooled by a good forgery, but it looks that way to me."

"You think they're hot?" Mabel asked.

"Nobody we talked to suggested Amanda was rolling in money. She didn't dress like it or live like it, but sometimes rich people don't. She could simply be artsy and bohemian, and still be a trust fund baby."

"Not with what Buffy said about her background."

"No. Unless these are repros, I'd guess they're stolen."

Mabel rubbed her nose. She was starting to feel the chill of the unheated cottage. "The rest of these must be paintings too."

"Undoubtedly. You want to head out? I'll padlock this, and we can look at the rest in the daylight."

"Yeah. I've already pushed my luck with Barnacle's bladder."

"Maybe we'll get more of an explanation from Amanda tomorrow. She has a lot of talking to do."

Monday morning dawned with a thud. Now Mabel no longer had a job to drag herself to, she felt she should be able to accomplish all sorts of things, but reality had not matched her vision. After dawdling all morning over the newspaper and both crosswords, the "easy"—which was not—and the humiliating New York Times, and making herself a second pot of coffee, she finally turned to her notes for a true-crime book about the Sauer murders.

Mabel struggled with whether—and how—to include the modern-day murders as well as the historical murders. But she was sort of the heroine of the latter-day murder investigation—as well as the 1939 murders, which had remained unsolved until she came along. She needed to find a way to weave it all together. That was proving tough, since Mabel hadn't been around in 1939, and had to rely on old accounts with limited detail to bring them to life.

When she found herself repeatedly checking her messages, she gave herself a stern talking to and turned off her phone. John wouldn't even be meeting Amanda for another hour or so.

One good thing about having two different projects was she could switch back and forth. She opened her volunteer file and began editing her historical society article. She knew it was way too long, but it was hard to cut what she modestly considered some of her best writing. Maybe she should forget trying to turn it into an article. It would be perfect, she thought, as a chapter in her volunteer book.

She should find herself an agent.

Mabel got up to pour a cup of coffee from the fresh pot. As she did, her eye caught a slip of paper stuck to the fridge with a magnet—the information she had copied down about the writers' group that met at the library. Maybe they could help her get an agent. Or a publisher.

She looked up at Grandma Mabel's sunburst wall clock. *Darn.* There had been a meeting this morning at eleven, and even if she put her pants on right now, she couldn't get there in time.

At least, it was now late enough to check her phone again. She turned it back on.

John had texted. Two simple words.

No show.

Mabel dialed into her voicemail. John's was the only message.

"Letting you know Amanda blew me off again. I waited half an hour and finally went ahead and ordered lunch. Her phone's not answering. Probably a burner, anyway. Give me a call when you get this."

Mabel frowned. It was way too late now to join him at Romano's. That's what she got for being industrious and turning her phone off.

He picked up on the second ring. "Hey, babe."

Babe? She decided she maybe liked that.

"I heard your voicemail. What's up?"

"I'm back home, loading Amanda's stuff into my car. Since she told me I could use it to cover what she owes me, I'm protecting my security and taking it to my storage locker. It's completely secure and climate controlled, which the shed definitely isn't.

"...Plus, who am I kidding? If this stuff isn't hot, I'm a flying monkey."

"You need some help?"

"No, I'm good here. I almost have the car loaded right now, and I can drop them off on my way to my afternoon office hours."

Mabel felt a little dip in her heart that she wouldn't be seeing him.

"I don't have anything tomorrow. I thought I might go try to see Charlie Maier—you know—the guy who owned the arson house."

"In prison?"

"Yeah. No guarantees he'll even see me, but I figure if I put something into his commissary account, it might warm him up to the idea."

"How are you going to do that before tomorrow?"

"I know somebody. He's going to check in with him for me. I should know later tonight. If he agrees to add me to his visitor list, I plan to drive up early."

"Which one's he in?"

"Cold River. On the edge of the national forest."

"That's a long drive."

"Three hours, more or less."

Mabel thought of her neglected writing career and the looming disaster that was Grandma's house. Since inheriting the accumulated mess along with the house seven months ago, she'd been half-heartedly trying to get it cleaned out. She had to get that done—especially since she lived in fear of Linnea's reporting it to the health department. Still...

"Would you like company? Maybe Barnacle and I could ride

along. I feel guilty leaving him so much lately, and he'd love a walk in the woods. We can take my car if you want."

"I'd love to take you and Barnacle too—and he's always welcome in my car. But I've been monopolizing your time. You have plenty to do right here—going to Cold Water would shoot your whole day, and you wouldn't even be allowed in to see Maier."

Mabel hesitated. She knew John was right, but maybe he also thought she was being pushy. "If you're sure…" Her voice came out sounding a trifle stiff.

"Of course, you can come if you want."

Mabel chewed her lower lip. She couldn't help thinking about the first man she'd nailed for murder. Would he be at Cold Water? It was a maximum-security prison, where most capital cases were housed. What if she ran into him? She wouldn't want to end up on the wrong end of a shiv.

She shook her head—she was being silly. He hadn't even had his trial yet. And although he had killed two people—and nearly made her his third victim—she couldn't help feeling a bit sorry for him. After all, his first homicide hadn't been premeditated. And he'd always been kind to her…leaving aside the two times he'd tried to kill her, of course. Still, a prison would, by definition, be uncongenial. She didn't want to be reminded of the remote risk of John's being sent up.

Mabel was still reflecting when John cleared his throat. "Sorry," Mabel said. "You're right. I need to focus on getting some work done."

"Good plan. I promise to call as soon as I'm headed back."

Did he sound relieved? John made it sound like staying home was Mabel's idea, but they both knew the truth was he'd turned her down.

After they hung up, Mabel felt out of sorts. A day of writing or worse—decluttering—did not appeal.

When her phone rang, she jumped. Had John reconsidered?

"Mabel—you'll never believe it." Lisa. Mabel checked the time—Lisa should still be at work.

"Try me."

"A main water pipe broke. School's closed at least through tomorrow. Maybe longer."

"Lucky you—you can sleep in."

"What are you doing tomorrow?"

Whining to Lisa about getting the dust-off from John would be both pointless and pathetic. "Writing. Or working on getting the front junk room cleared out." Mabel sighed.

Lisa giggled. "You say that like you have more than one junk room."

"I kind of do. I mean the room across the hall from my living room. It used to be a parlor. Then, when Grandma's dementia got bad, her stockpiles kind of took over. Anyway, trash night's Wednesday, and I figure I can get some bags filled for pickup by then."

"You want some help?"

"A bonus day off just landed in your lap. I'm sure you can do better."

Lisa hesitated. "I'll be honest. I kind of have an ulterior motive here."

"I knew it. You want to get your hands on Grandma's *Reader's Digest* collection."

"Actually, I was eyeing that box of old margarine tubs."

"You're a friend in a million. Are you sure? You don't have to."

"I still have that ulterior motive, remember? And it won't even cost you a mouse-eaten *Reader's Digest*. I was thinking maybe you and I could do a little undercover investigation of Vin Perdue."

"Huh?"

"Vin Perdue. You remember he was the—"

"I know who he is." John's warning to stay far away from the local crime boss still burned in her ears. "Which makes him a very dangerous man—even if he isn't involved in Mike's murder."

"I'm not saying we confront him or anything."

"What on earth *do* you have in mind?"

"He's a landlord, right?"

"Slumlord."

"Right. So we're a couple career gals looking to rent an apartment. One that accepts pets."

Mabel rolled her eyes so hard they nearly completed the trip around her head. "Suppose we find him in the office. Does he have an office? What do you expect to find out, anyway?"

"Just watch me work. C'mon, Mabel, you owe me after keeping your last two murders to yourself."

Mabel grunted. "That wasn't by choice. Anyway, the Sauer murders were up for grabs seventy-five years at that point. You were more than welcome to solve those."

"You know the only reason you solved those was because somebody else went and got murdered on your watch. Please, Mabel."

"Are you driving?"

"I'll not only drive, I'll also come over at seven in the morning to work on your junk room first."

"Not till ten, at least. I can't face that room before I'm adequately caffeinated."

Lisa laughed. "I'll be there at eight."

True to her word, Lisa arrived on the dot of eight. Mabel sat and nursed the big, therapeutic go cup of orange mocha Lisa had brought her, watching, bleary-eyed, as Lisa sorted through old clothes and Grandma's stockpiles. By the time Mabel had the strength to join in, Lisa had already created a path down the center of the room and was ready to hand out bags marked "trash" and "Mabel."

"You can check the trash bags if you want, but the 'Mabel' bags are more important. You'll have to decide whether you want to keep any of that stuff or donate it."

Two hours later, a heap of trash bags waited by the driveway for Acey to haul to the dump. Another smaller pile sat on the covered front porch, destined for Goodwill. Lisa bit her lips when she looked at the remaining bags Mabel wasn't ready to part with. "Oh, well, at least we made a good start."

"We did, thanks to you." Mabel stood in the doorway and savored their progress. Koi and Barnacle seemed similarly impressed by the new landscape. Koi leapt upward on stacks of boxes to a new perch under the ceiling, where she blended into the shadows. Only green-gold eyes betrayed her location.

Meanwhile, Barnacle sniffed along the freshly exposed floorboards till he got to a spot that made him whine and paw at the remaining boxes. Mabel pointed. "He's alerting like a search and rescue dog."

"Probably a mouse nest back there." Lisa stretched and sneezed. "You ready to wash up and get going?"

"How are we dressing?"

"I think business casual. I brought a change."

A half hour later, they were on the road. Mabel, charged with navigating, squinted at the screen. "Unbeatable Real Estate. Is that supposed to be Vin Perdue?"

Lisa nodded. "He seems to be involved with several other businesses, but this one's based in Bartles Grove, and his picture's front and center, so I figured we'd start there."

"I know Unbeatable. More like 'unbelievable.' They're criminals. You name something you wouldn't want to ever live with, and they can rent it to you—broken locks, bedbugs, black mold..."

"Yep—that's why everybody calls him a slumlord."

Mabel's eyes narrowed. "When I was doing pro bono landlord-tenant cases for the bar association, I wrote a bunch of rent withholding letters to this company. I don't even want to 'pretend rent' from that guy."

"You promised."

"I know, I know. But you better do the talking. I'd probably get us kicked out in two minutes."

Lisa smiled. "No problem. I've got a plan."

A moment later, a thought struck Mabel. "Oh, wait. You better give me a fake name. In case he remembers those nasty letters I wrote to them…and the health department."

"Good idea. Just elbow me if I start to slip up."

Mabel liked this outing less and less. John had told her to stay away from this guy because he was potentially dangerous. Now she had to worry he might recognize her. She scanned her memory. Had she ever been at a magistrate's hearing when Unbeatable had tried to evict one of her clients? She couldn't remember ever running into him—his name hadn't even rung a bell the first time Jesse the bartender mentioned him. Most likely, he'd sent an underling to handle the cases.

She hoped.

The Unbeatable office sat in the middle of a block in downtown Bartles Grove. Little curls of baby blue paint peeled from the dingy, yellow-brick exterior. A film of grime covered the front window so that "Unbeatable," painted on the glass in a scrawling script, was nearly illegible. Weeds, now frostbitten, had sprouted in the crack between the building and pavement.

Lisa had already parked at the curb, but Mabel sat staring at the unwelcoming exterior. The office squatted between a sandwich shop and a purveyor of vape juice, neither of which looked to be flourishing. She was sorry she'd put on decent gray dress pants.

"Ready?" Lisa chirped, gesturing for Mabel to follow her.

She'd promised. And it was for John. Mabel got out.

When Lisa opened the office door, an old-fashioned bell rang overhead, and a musty breath of tired air laced with disinfectant wafted toward them. Mabel wrinkled her nose.

Two padded, steel-framed guest chairs, their dull, dark-red plastic covers veined with tiny cracks, stood in front of a utilitarian, cluttered steel desk. A plump woman with a messy salt-and-pepper bun looked up. "Help you, ladies?" She didn't invite them to sit, which was probably as well.

As Lisa explained their imaginary housing needs, Mabel let her eyes rove the office. The room was heated by an ornate, ancient radiator, and a dented, gray metal filing cabinet occupied the corner. She stared at the cabinet and wished she had X-ray vision.

Perdue hadn't wasted a dime on creating a prosperous façade for his clientele.

Unbeatable. Mabel snorted to herself. She had beaten him a time or two herself and stuck him with massive repair bills instead of overdue rent or an eviction. And admittedly, she was hardly Kathryn Hepburn in *Adam's Rib*.

Mabel couldn't help noticing the placard on the desk. *Edith Perdue.* "Excuse me, are you related to Vincent Perdue?"

Lisa's mouth was open. Belatedly, Mabel realized she'd interrupted and smiled an apology. "I'm sorry. I noticed your nameplate."

She'd tried to inject a bright note of admiration into her voice when addressing the receptionist. It seemed to work because Edith responded with apparent pride. "Yes, he's my son."

"How...great. He's involved in...so many different businesses. Uh, very diversified." It was hard to come up with anything specific about Vin Perdue that fell under the heading of "positive."

Edith didn't seem to notice Mabel's struggle. She glowed. "Oh, Vin has quite the head for business. Everything he touches is a success."

You sure wouldn't know it from looking at this place.

"Are these the grandchildren?" Lisa pointed to the bookcase behind the desk.

Edith spun around so fast, Mabel half-expected her to keep going. But she grabbed the picture frame and displayed it with a flourish. "This is Vinnie, Jr. The girl is Isabel."

"Oh, aren't they darling?" Lisa cooed.

"Is he in the office today?" Mabel glanced at the closed door in the back corner of the room.

Both Lisa and Edith looked at her. Belatedly, Mabel realized she'd once again interrupted Lisa's efforts to soften Edith up. "I'm sorry. I— wow, aren't these kids something, huh?"

Edith, her head clearly still in Grandma-land, proceeded to rattle on about difficult forceps deliveries, soccer championships, and Girl Scouts. *Being a teacher, Lisa must listen to this sort of thing from parents every day. I can do this.* Mabel kept a vague smile on her face and nodded from time to time, until Edith succumbed to the universal need to breathe.

"Is Mr. Perdue in today?" Mabel interjected.

With an air of reluctance, Edith smoothed over the photos with her hand before returning them to their place behind the desk. She frowned. "Did you need to see Vinnie for some reason?"

Mabel hadn't thought that far ahead—and thinking on her feet wasn't her greatest gift. After a frantic moment, she found her lips moving. "I'm a historical society volunteer, and it occurs to me Mr. Perdue might make a wonderful speaker for one of our meetings."

She groaned inside. Who'd ever believe she thought Vin Perdue had anything of interest to share with a historical society?

Someone with unquestioning maternal love for the man, of course.

"What a lovely idea. Would you like to ask him while you're here?"

"That would be great." Mabel beamed on Edith.

"Maybe he knows of some other apartments that might work for us too," Lisa added.

"Of course." Edith's smile rested on them both. "Wait here a moment."

While her back was turned to knock and ease the door open, Mabel and Lisa looked at each other. "Speak at the historical society? That's the best you could come up with?" Lisa hissed.

"I had to think fast," Mabel hissed back. "We couldn't talk grandkids and two-bedroom apartments all day."

Edith turned back with a smile. "He's very busy, but he can give you a minute right now."

"That's terrific—thank you." Mabel returned the smile and headed toward the door, Lisa crowding behind her.

The moment Mabel stepped inside, Perdue burst from his chair with so much force she blundered backward into Lisa, who squawked when Mabel crunched her toes. "Sorry," she mumbled.

Perdue grinned and shoved out his hand like a politician at a Rotary pancake breakfast. "Vin Perdue." He peered around Mabel while pumping her hand. "Are you okay back there?"

Lisa winced. "Fine, thanks." She introduced them, stumbling over Mabel's name as she seemed momentarily to forget her promise to fabricate a false identity for her. "M-Margie Barker."

"Sit, sit." Perdue gestured at two oak guest chairs upholstered in a muted green tweed. The contrast between the low-budget outer office and his own tasteful sanctuary could not have been more marked. Mabel noticed the separate rear entry. Presumably, the outer office, opening on the street, was only for the "little people" seeking affordable housing. She also noticed the back door was steel. With a deadbolt.

Perdue's substantial oak desk and credenza, which matched the chairs, would have looked at home in the Oval Office. He himself appeared to be a reputable, balding businessman in a subtle, mid-gray suit. Subconsciously, Mabel realized, she'd envisioned slicked-back hair, a loud shirt, and diamond pinky rings.

"So, my receptionist mentioned you were looking for a guest speaker?" Perdue split a smile between them.

"Uh…" Mabel had been so busy cataloging observations she'd nearly forgotten her cover story.

"Yes." Lisa returned the smile. "For the historical society."

Mabel's sluggish brain came back online, but only at low power. "Perhaps about the history of your business…empire."

Perdue's forehead creased, but his smile never wavered. He folded his hands on the desk. "Oh? Was there a particular aspect your group was interested in?"

She waved a careless hand. "Origins. Like what gave you your start? Is this a family business?"

The smile narrowed. "Interesting. I'm afraid I don't have much of historical interest to offer. This isn't like Roberts' car dealership that began in the 1800s as a carriage maker. I started this business right here out of college." He smacked the desk. "My 'empire' only goes back to the lemonade stand I had as a kid."

"Oh, how fun." Lisa gave an encouraging nod. "Everyone would relate to that—it's classic Americana."

Perdue grinned. "I was pretty shrewd for an eight-year-old. Watered down my lemonade, so I ended up with twice as many quarters."

Mabel laughed heartily with him. *Crooked all the way back to childhood. And Edith seems so nice.*

The office walls were basic white. Not a calendar or speck of artwork in sight. Not even pictures of the family, like Edith had. A notepad sat at his left hand, along with a blue Sharpie. Scrawled notes, likely from said pad, covered the desk—some herded into neat stacks, others scattered about like wandering sheep. They appeared to be the only evidence some kind of work was being done here.

"Unbeatable Real Estate was your first venture?" Lisa asked. "What led you to branch out?"

Perdue leaned back, hands behind his head. "Diversification. Not good to put all your eggs in the same basket."

Mabel arranged a bland expression on her face. *So, you branched into fraud, theft, and arson...maybe homicide. Got it.*

A hollow sensation filled her chest and her palms sweated as she steeled herself to introduce a tougher question. "While we're here, I was wondering about Mike Hardy." The name slipped out before she'd formulated a question to go with it.

Vin's reaction was visible, yet the change was so slight Mabel nearly missed it. "My—our friend. I think he used to work for you sometimes? Like an independent contractor?"

Perdue's cool blue eyes grew calculating, and his glance darted to the Rolex on his wrist. "Oh, yeah. He drove occasionally for my resale business. Heard he passed recently—sorry for your loss."

To Mabel's surprise, Lisa clutched her chest. "Mike's…?"

His lips thinned.

"What happened?"

"Tragic—surprised you hadn't heard. Look online, you'll find it."

He frowned and tapped his watch. "Look, ladies, I'm sorry too, to cut this short, but I just got a reminder for a conference. I'm not sure I have much to contribute to your meeting, but if you'd like to send me something, I'll mull it over."

"Thanks so much for your time. It's been fascinating." Lisa had already been tugging at Mabel's sleeve, so she got up, still trying to capture whatever impressions of Perdue's office she could on her way to the door.

"Margie." Perdue's voice caught her, two paces later.

He held out a manicured hand. "Do you have a card?"

"O-of course." Mabel fumbled through her bag before giving what she hoped was a convincing little shrug. "I'm sorry. I changed purses. All my info will be on what I send you." She felt a betraying flush climb her neck.

"And you?" he asked Lisa, hopefully having forgotten her name.

Lisa managed a wavering smile, befitting someone who'd just received a shattering piece of news. "I don't have cards. It was lovely meeting you."

They blew through the outer office with a brief apology for Edith. "We'll have to come back. We're late for an appointment," Lisa said. "Thanks for everything."

Once out on the sidewalk, Mabel pulled Lisa past her car. "I don't want them to see what we're driving."

Lisa was hyperventilating. "I need my car."

"And we'll get it. But let's pretend for the moment it isn't ours."

Lisa followed Mabel around the next block and collapsed against a brick wall. "You're right. That was awkward back there."

"You think? Now, he's suspicious of us."

"You could've been more subtle about bringing up Mike." Lisa scowled.

"Well, I never went to detective school."

"Me, neither. All the same, we did find some things out."

"Vinnie, Jr. was a week past his due date, and Isabel takes tap."

Lisa swatted her. "Perdue admitted Mike worked for him. What's more, it's obvious from his reaction he wasn't doing anything legitimate."

"Agreed. And he said Mike drove for his resale business. If anything funky was going on with the goods he was selling, Mike would have been in the middle of it. His handling of Mike's death was…unique. But let's keep walking." Mabel steamed up the street. "We confirmed that much. On the other hand, we've now put ourselves on his radar. John would've been way smoother."

She stopped abruptly and caught Lisa's elbow. "Does Edith have our addresses?"

Lisa shook her arm free. "No, they don't. I never got to the point of filling anything out."

Mabel realized she'd been holding her breath. *Thank the Lord.*

Why did I mention the historical society? Did I say which *historical society? Surely, he'll assume it's Bartles Grove or the county. Not Medicine Spring.*

A step later, she halted again. "Your name, Lisa—you told them your name."

"Give me some credit, Mabes—and pay attention when I'm talking. I told them I was Crystal Goldstein—how does that even sound like Lisa Benedetti to you? "

"Sorry." Mabel breathed again. "I freaked out a bit there—I should've realized you know your stuff. While you were talking, I was looking around for clues."

Lisa raised her hand for a high-five. "Dana Girl teamwork, right? Can I buy you a coffee?"

"Thanks. But let's get out of this neighborhood."

"Market Street's this way." Lisa pointed. "John will be proud."

Mabel's stomach soured. Somehow, she knew "proud" wouldn't begin to describe John's likely reaction to their escapade.

Chapter Twenty

IT WAS LATE AFTERNOON BEFORE JOHN called, and he still had a long return trip ahead of him. "Can you talk?" Mabel asked. "Or do you need to drive?"

"I'm at a place called Old Hippies. Figured I'd grab a quick bean burrito and an immune-booster smoothie before hitting the road. We can talk. I'm the only customer in here."

Imagine that.

"Great. Start at the beginning and tell me everything."

"First of all, I feel sorry for the guy, and I believe him. I don't know whether Mike started that fire, but I sure believe Charlie Maier did not."

That could be John, sitting in Cold River State Correctional Institution, day after day in a prison jumpsuit, knowing he was innocent.

"Does he know about Mike? That he's suspected of setting the fire?"

"Hang on, my smoothie's here. Thanks." She heard a slurp. "Yeah. Mike's name didn't come up till Maier was convicted and awaiting sentencing. Word on the street was Mike had done it, and Perdue was behind it, but there wasn't any evidence to tie either of them to it. Perdue never even bought the property after all. Guess after a victim turned up inside the building, Perdue couldn't distance himself fast enough."

"I'm guessing Maier's bitter?"

"Oh, yeah—but to be honest, he struck me as more depressed than vengeful. His marriage broke up over this, his name's ruined, and there he sits."

"Well," Mabel said, "it's obvious he couldn't have killed Mike himself. Still, he might have someone working for him on the outside."

"I know." John sighed. "I just didn't meet that man—the guy

who'd arrange a hit on someone. I realize you can't always tell, but I didn't see that kind of simmering rage. He has an appeal going."

Mabel thought. "Maybe there's a family member with their own ax to grind." It was hard to offer an opinion when she hadn't even met Maier, but John seemed convinced of his innocence. John, moreover, had every reason to try to find someone to blame for Mike's murder. He wouldn't be naïve and easily fooled by a good actor.

"Food's here."

Mabel waited till John said, "Okay."

"Were you about to say something before your dinner came?"

"Oh, yeah, well, I agree that while Charlie might not be out for a pound of flesh, he might have a family member mad enough to go after Mike on their own. Good suggestion. We could look into that."

Mabel sighed. "Guess the interview was a bust, though."

"*Au contraire.* Maier told me the man who got caught in the fire was still alive, last he heard, and rightly pointed out if anyone had reason to avenge himself on Mike it would be him. Whether Mike committed the arson or not, a mind bent on revenge might find the evidence compelling enough."

"Why now?"

John shrugged. "The same question pretty much applies to all our suspects. Something may have triggered him—or opportunity may have just presented itself."

Mabel pulled out her little notebook. She wrote, *Look up news coverage of arson, especially name of injured homeless man.*

"I'll try to do a little research tomorrow," she promised, "and see if I can get any info on him." Lisa's and her interview with Vin Perdue she kept to herself.

Next morning, Mabel slept late. That was one perk to having been fired from the law firm. No more 7:30 am commutes.

She'd have loved to sleep even longer, but by 8:30, a loud bang made her shoot upright and Barnacle leap to the window, barking wildly. Koi slipped under the bed, her tail blown out to never-before-seen proportions.

Disoriented, Mabel stumbled to join Barnacle at the window. Of course. Acey Davis had belatedly arrived to clear her field with his rented brush hog. He'd apparently let it drop as it came off the back of his truck and was now hollering colorfully as he checked for damage.

Mabel considered talking to him, but concluded Acey was best taken in small doses, and preferably not before coffee. By the time that was brewing, and she was letting Barnacle out, Acey had gotten the brush hog running. It seemed abnormally loud, possibly due to damage from being dropped—or then again, maybe because it was as ancient as it looked.

Instead of doing his business, Barnacle stood in the yard, barking at the noisy invader. The roar must have hurt the dog's ears. It certainly hurt hers and further intensified the low-grade headache she'd woken with.

She came inside for ibuprofen and coffee, shutting the door behind her. Koi sat on the windowsill with her ears pinned back, watching with an expression of feline disapproval. Acey was bouncing away from the house toward the Sauer mansion, and the noise was blessedly fading, but Mabel knew he'd be headed back their way soon enough.

As she drank coffee and filled the animals' dishes, she considered her agenda. Any day Acey decided to make an appearance was both a miracle and a good day to work elsewhere. Maybe she'd head out to the Medicine Spring Library. Or over to The Grind.

Mabel pulled out her notebook. On a clean page, she wrote a to-do list for the day. *1. Work on volunteer book. 2. Write Chapter One of Sauer Ax Murder book. 3. Online research arson fire.*

Barnacle had begun barking again. Mabel hurried to let him back inside. While he gobbled his breakfast, she rummaged in the cupboard for something for herself. She didn't have much, which meant she needed to add grocery shopping to her list. She reopened her notebook and started a grocery list under Item 4. Then, she grabbed the last doughnut on the kitchen table and tossed the plastic bag.

The doughnut was rather stale, so she dunked it, the way her long-dead grandpa had done. The reminder he had shared her bad eating habits was depressing, especially given his early death. Surely it hadn't been the doughnuts?

The idea his premature demise might have been due to something genetic was even less welcome. She certainly couldn't change her DNA. One could always change one's diet. Theoretically.

Koi now perched atop the high cabinets, flicked her tail and stared down as if to pronounce, "Nevermore."

Thinking dark thoughts about her own mortality, Mabel pulled out of the driveway twenty minutes later, aiming a cheery wave at Acey and applying her pedal to the metal. She'd already eaten a doughnut, she sternly reminded herself. She would resist the temptations of the Coffee Cup or The Grind, with their hot caramel apple ciders, greasy breakfast sandwiches, and Farmhand platters.

Feeling downright Puritan in her self-denial, she took the turn toward the library and parked in the side lot under the bare sycamores. The main reading room was mostly empty, apart from an old man reading the *Washington Post*, and a young mom with a stroller, leading her toddler toward the children's room. Mabel had forgotten how soul-satisfying a library could be. Like too many others, she had fallen away from the habit of using her library card regularly.

Medicine Spring Public Library was unusual in today's world, because it occupied a big, old house from the first half of the previous century. The only improvements were the addition of handicapped access and first-floor restrooms, as well as opening up the main floor to create the big reading room. Real oak paneling on the walls wasn't bright and cheerful like the newer libraries but gave the place a feeling of substance—of a place where knowledge and wisdom could be found.

The lack of patronage, at least this early in the day, meant she could pretty much pick her spot. Mabel selected a deep, leather-upholstered armchair in the big window bay facing the north lawn, where someone was throwing sticks for a small, scruffy, tan dog.

Mabel set her laptop bag on the table. Priorities suggested she start with her actual writing projects. But she'd already exercised so much discipline in skipping a diner breakfast, she figured she was entitled to reward herself by tackling the online research first. She could ease into the writing after she had—hopefully—gleaned some solid information to share with John.

Having a general idea when the fire had occurred helped Mabel narrow her search. It didn't take long to turn up a few articles online, concerning the trial and conviction of Charles Maier. When she had those, she was able to pinpoint the date of the fire, at which juncture she went to ask the librarian to help her get access to the articles about the fire and its aftermath from the *Wilkie Clarion*.

"Everything is digital now," people said, and that appeared true at the Medicine Spring Library. Nevertheless, when Mabel found the articles she wanted, she still printed them out and took her trusty highlighter to them.

By the time her grumbling tummy reminded her she'd missed lunch, she'd created a timeline from the articles, which she could share with John. The most important things she'd learned related to the arson victim, including his name, Frank Sedlak.

On impulse, she fed the name into the search bar on her phone, under both Frank and Francis. Then, she tried Franklin. No current address or phone number came up. Mabel sighed but was unsurprised. After all, the man had been homeless at the time of the fire, and given the severity of his injuries, he might even have passed away by now.

She pulled out her trusty notebook. Where could they go from here? John would know, but she could at least write up her own checklist.

1. Check homeless shelters and soup kitchens.

What if he had died by now? There had to be databases for that.

2. Check death records.

Mabel sat and stared at a geranium on a windowsill across the room, trying to decide if it was real or fake. As her mind wandered, a third bullet point occurred to her.

3. *Check databases for birth, marriage, military, etc.*

Okay, that one might require a subscription to a specialized database. Maybe John, as a private investigator—even a suspended PI—had a subscription they could search. Or maybe the library did.

Mabel stretched. She seemed to have reached the end of what she could do here, short of a deeper dive. Theoretically, her next task ought to be her writing, but according to the big wall clock, it was long past time for a lunch break.

Moments later, Mabel found herself driving up the highway ramp toward Wilkie. She hadn't planned to go that far for a bite to eat but reading about the cottage fire and its aftermath had made her itchy to visit the scene of the crime.

She exited the highway hungrier than ever and developing a headache. At a commercial strip on the way into town, she pulled into the first fast food drive-through on the right and ordered a combo. Her original plan had been to eat while she drove, but the first glob of barbeque sauce on her chest convinced her to pull back into a parking space until she was done eating.

Feeling revitalized, Mabel decided to visit the arson site first and get the feel of the place. The newspaper articles had included a street address, a photo of the cottage in better days, and another shot of it engulfed in flames, which the fire marshal later reported had been fed by an accelerant.

Mabel wasn't too familiar with Wilkie, but whoever had laid out the streets had been kind enough to follow themes. She was looking for Chestnut, so it should be a simple matter of working her way from Oak, where she now was, through the rest of the forest of tree names. Seeing Poplar Street down on the left, she turned that way.

Sure enough, only a couple more blocks to go. After passing Poplar, she crossed Linden, and then, Pine. The next corner was Chestnut.

From a block away, she could already see the blackened hull of the historic cottage Charlie Maier had refused to sell, but ended up losing anyway, along with his freedom. She shook her head. What a waste, if Vin Perdue had had it torched, only to let it stand this way in the end. She wondered how he slept at night.

Mabel pulled in across the street, rolled down her window, and stared. The house truly had been a cottage, likely one-and-a-half stories, with no more than four small rooms on the first floor, and maybe two on the second floor, under the eaves. The roof was gone and the windows broken out. The exterior paint was blackened and bubbled. Incongruously, a single dingy curtain dangled from a second-floor window. Sooty streaks ran up the outside walls.

"You lost?" asked a high-pitched female voice.

Mabel turned to see a plump, middle-aged woman in a red parka, clinging to the leash of a black Chihuahua in what appeared to be a matching jacket. The dog stood on its hind legs and growled menacingly at Mabel. "Down, Pepe." The command had no discernible effect.

"No, just looking at the house."

"It burned," the woman told her helpfully. "That house stood there a hundred years, and poof." She shook her head. "Arson. Now, you tell me. Why do people have to destroy nice things?"

"They said it was for the insurance money," Mabel offered.

The woman's lips tightened. "Yes, they did. Well, I for one, don't believe it. Charlie—he owned the place—was a good, hard-working man. He wasn't the type to do such a thing. His family owned that house for generations—his grandmother was born in that house, right on the kitchen table."

"We don't always know," Mabel said. "Sometimes people do unexpected things."

The woman shook her head. "I'd have thought the poor man who got caught in the fire started it with a cigarette or something. But it was no accident. The fire marshal was clear about that."

"Do you have any idea who might have set the fire?"

The woman seemed to have no thoughts on that topic. Either she'd never heard the rumors about Perdue and Mike or didn't believe them.

"Do you know what became of the man who got caught inside? Did he survive?"

As Mabel rearranged her arm on the bottom of the open window, Pepe lunged, flashing tiny fangs. "Pepe, down," the woman repeated without conviction or noticeable result.

Over Pepe's continued growling and yapping, the woman said, "I know they said he was expected to survive, but my goodness, those burns were horrible. He was going to need skin grafting and who knows what else? You could check Community Hospital. They have a burn unit. I imagine that's where they took him, but I doubt he'd still be there."

"Is there a homeless shelter here in town?"

The woman, who'd been so eager to chat, narrowed her eyes as if suddenly asking herself why Mabel was pursuing all these questions. After that brief flicker of caution, however, she resumed talking. "Not what you'd call a shelter. There's a soup kitchen-type place, but nowhere that takes them in overnight, except maybe down at the Presbyterian Church. Sometimes they might take someone in overnight if they're elderly or have a special need. Or if there are children. Then again, we don't have a big homeless problem here."

"Where are those located?" Mabel asked. Seeing the woman frown again, she added, "I think I'd like to make a donation. Winter's coming, you know?"

Darn. Now she felt an acute pang of conscience and the need to donate. Oh, well, it was a good cause.

"I don't know addresses. The Lutherans run the soup kitchen out of the church on High Street. The Presbyterians are at the bottom of the hill right where High and Market intersect. Oh—and I can't remember the name, but the synagogue between here and Carleton also offers some services…but I think that's mainly referrals, clothing, and so on."

"Thank you. You actually have a lot of resources for homeless people."

The woman shifted her grip to pull a tissue from her pocket. As she did, she dropped the leash. Pepe leapt and his teeth flashed, barely missing Mabel's arm. Mabel jerked her arm back, bared her teeth, and growled.

Pepe, clearly startled, yelped and jumped back. He darted behind his owner's legs, and cowered, trembling and snarling, his one visible eye on Mabel.

The shock on the woman's face told Mabel it was time to go. "Well, I'd better be on my way." She flashed a smile. "I appreciate the information. You have a great day, now."

In the rearview mirror, she saw the woman bending over, comforting her traumatized dog. "Hmph," Mabel muttered. "Pepe started it."

She came to Market Street Presbyterian Church first—a traditional red brick building with tall stained-glass windows. The Lutheran church, a gray stone variation on the same theme, stood at the top of the hill, its cemetery markers seemingly spilling down the slope toward the bottom. Mabel pulled into the Presbyterian lot. Only one other car was there. Mabel tried the nearest doors, which looked like they might lead to offices on the ground floor, but they were locked. She looked for a buzzer but saw nothing.

Committed to the mission at this point, she trudged around the building, trying doors, but ultimately had to give up. Maybe they'd open later, for a youth group meeting or choir practice. Or to let a few homeless people in to bed down for the night. But Mabel wouldn't be there. She might try calling in the morning.

She was luckier at the Lutheran church. St. Stephen's had an afternoon kindergarten program, and there were several cars in the lot, as well as a group of children running around a fenced play area under the watchful eye of a couple adults. Mabel parked and shuffled through fallen leaves from the overhanging sycamores.

"Hi," she called from the fence. A rosy-cheeked young woman with a perky brown ponytail, who looked barely eighteen, turned and smiled.

"May I help you?"

"I wondered if anyone's in the church office right now. I was hoping to make a donation to your soup kitchen?"

"Aren't you wonderful?" the teacher said. "That's so appreciated. There should be someone there right now. You know what else—they start serving in about an hour, if you'd like to stick around and help? I know they always need an extra pair of hands."

Mabel started to explain why she couldn't stay to work at the soup kitchen—that she had animals waiting at home and had only stopped to make a donation. But the teacher had left to tend to a squabble over a ball, and Mabel's words trailed off.

As she headed for the indicated doors, it occurred to Mabel that it might not kill her to lend a hand for a couple of hours. She was already there, wearing jeans and comfy shoes, and it would give her a totally unexpected volunteer experience she could write about for her book.

She thought hard. Lisa should be done for the day. She had a key to the house and might be able to let Barnacle out and do the evening feeding.

It only took a call and a few quick text messages to make her arrangements.

Mind now at ease, Mabel headed inside.

A sign pointed left for the church office. Another to the right—hand-lettered in bold red—said, "FREE DINNER THIS WAY," with an arrow. Since she heard voices, Mabel turned right.

In the sprawling social hall, volunteers were setting up tables and chairs. A young woman with smooth, dark cheeks, a full head of explosive black curls, and a St. Stephen's T-shirt gave Mabel a wide smile. "Hi, I'm Pam. I haven't seen you here before—welcome. Unfortunately, we don't begin serving for another hour, but you're more than welcome to wait. Can I get you a drink?"

Mabel looked down. Did she look like she'd been living on the street? Of course, homeless people could be tidy—they simply had a greater challenge in maintaining that on a daily basis. Mabel probably looked like a tidy homeless person.

"Sure," she said. "I'd love a Coke if you have that. Or whatever. But I'm not here for dinner. I, uh, came to volunteer."

Pam laughed. "I apologize. Let's get you that drink, and then we'll talk. Sorry we don't have Coke. The coffee for the volunteers is already made—we'll be making up the big pot for our guests in a little bit. We do have donated orange drink. And water, of course."

"Coffee would be nice."

"Follow me." Pam led the way into the kitchen, where a group of women and one man, all of whom looked to be in their sixties and above, were preparing what smelled like spaghetti. The man had the oven door open and was turning sheets of ground meat for even browning, while someone else stirred a vat of garlicky tomato sauce. Several people gave her a smile.

The coffeemaker sat on a metal utility table inside the door, along with cups holding powdered creamer and assorted sweeteners. "Please help yourself—I'm sorry. I didn't get your name."

Mabel filled a Styrofoam cup. "Mabel Browne."

"Do you go to church here?"

"No... I stopped to make a small donation, and one of the teachers outside suggested I could help in the kitchen while I was here."

Pam beamed. "Well, aren't you nice? Yeah, we can always use a hand, and the donation, especially. It costs a lot to feed these many people five days a week. We were lucky we got a bunch of ground beef donated that was about to expire. We brown it in the oven—less mess, but we'll dump that in the sauce, and it'll go a long way."

"How many do you feed on a normal night?"

"Around thirty. That number changes. They aren't all homeless. We don't ask a lot of questions, unless it seems like someone may be abusing it. A lot of families in this community are working poor, so they appreciate being able to eat here, especially when they get a small raise at work, and then, their food stamps get cut."

Mabel frowned. That sounded as if people were getting punished for trying to work hard and support themselves and their families.

"Do you only serve dinner?"

Pam made a face. "Yeah. We're only a small-town church. We don't have the resources to do more than that—or even do seven days a week. Thank the Lord for older people like yourself who have the time and are willing to do all this work."

Mabel didn't quite manage to stifle a glare. "Older people," her foot. She was at least fifteen to twenty years younger than anyone else in the kitchen.

Pam obviously noticed her expression. "Oh, hey, I'm sorry. I stuck my foot in it again. I'm so much younger than the rest of the crew, I'm just used to my group of retirees. Now that I take a look at you, I realize you can't be a day over…" She wisely hesitated for Mabel to fill in the blank.

"My forties," Mabel said, and automatically touched her nose to see if it had grown, as her mother had always warned her it would if she told a lie. "I mean I'm barely out of my forties."

"Wow. I'd never have guessed you were even that old." Pam continued back-pedaling. "Anyway, we appreciate your help. How would you feel about helping with the salad?"

"I can do that. Let me pull my hair back and wash up."

After Mabel was wrapped in a St. Stephen's bib apron, and had been introduced to her fellow salad maker, Mim, Pam excused herself. "Oh." Mabel waved. "Could I ask one more question before you leave?"

"Of course," Pam said.

"I wondered if Frank Sedlak ate up here. Do you know him?"

"Sorry. I don't know everybody we serve by name," Pam said.

"I saw the burned-out cottage in town, and I hear he was the man who got injured in that fire."

Mim, a plump woman with graying curls, paused in opening bags of salad greens and leaned over. "Oh, of course he ate here, poor thing. I didn't know his last name till it was in the newspaper. Isn't that sad? I saw him five days a week without fail, and he was such a nice, polite man. Always said thank you. But I never really knew him."

"Of course," Pam said. "We talked about how he'd been up here for dinner that same evening. It was a chilly night, and I guess he wanted a roof over his head. I wish we had an actual homeless shelter in this town."

"Do you know where he is right now? Is he still recovering?"

"Please excuse me." Pam headed for the service doors, where someone was struggling to bring in what looked like a sheet cake.

Mim handed Mabel several cucumbers. "If you wouldn't mind, could you rinse and slice these into the bowl?"

"Sure. Do you know what became of Frank?"

Mim shook her head. "Not exactly. He was treated in the burn unit for a long time, and then I suppose he got transferred someplace else for rehab. Burns like those can take years to heal, and a lot of surgeries and treatments."

"How would a homeless person afford that?" Mabel dried her cucumbers with a paper towel.

"I imagine a social worker at the hospital would have helped him qualify for medical assistance, wouldn't you suppose?"

"I've been thinking," Mabel said. "Someone with injuries like that could hardly be living on the street anymore, could he?"

"I'd think it would be unlikely. I haven't seen Frank here since the day of the fire."

Frustrated, Mabel sliced cucumbers on the cutting board Mim handed her. She wasn't getting anywhere fast. And she'd only learned here what she could have deduced for herself. She wondered if what she knew at this point might already have effectively eliminated Frank Sedlak as a suspect, anyway. A person with extensive burn injuries only a year or so ago would hardly be capable of running around on that rugged trail at Clear Creek Park and killing a healthy—and younger—man.

"You can toss them in here," Mim said. Mabel had moved on to cutting up tomatoes on the other side of the enormous salad bowl. "Then, you might get a bottle of Italian dressing out of the fridge."

Mabel found a half-full bottle and brought it back.

"We'll dress this ourselves at the last minute," Mim said. "It makes for easier serving and less waste, if we do it that way."

When the salad was made, Mim put it on a metal service cart, and Mabel wheeled it to the serving area. Trays, plates, napkins, and tableware were already in place. Mabel hoisted the salad onto the table at the opposite end, next to a platter of bread covered with plastic wrap. At another table beyond, someone was cutting the sheet cake.

"You know who you might ask…" Mim retied her apron. "Frank had a friend he often ate with. His name is Gary. If he's here tonight, I'll point him out."

Bless her heart. Mim was a helpful and unsuspicious soul, who seemed to accept Mabel's interest in Frank at face value.

The doors opened promptly at 5:45 pm. Mabel had been assigned plate-scraping duty, which seemed easy enough, though disgustingly messy—especially where spaghetti was concerned.

The crowd appeared orderly and familiar with the drill. Women and children came through first, then a few older men. The younger, able-bodied men brought up the rear.

When everybody had carried their trays to the tables, Pam—whom Mabel had learned was the parish assistant—led them in saying grace. After that, cheerful-sounding conversation and clinking of forks filled the hall.

Mabel had nothing to do for the moment, since nobody had had time to finish eating yet. She sidled over to Mim, who was waiting to dish up seconds of spaghetti.

"Is he here?"

"Hmm?"

"Gary. Is he here tonight?"

"Oh, I forgot. Let me look."

She scanned the crowd then nodded to the table in the far corner. "Right there. The man with the shaggy salt-and-pepper hair. Wearing a dark-blue jacket."

"Thanks."

Mabel grabbed a water pitcher and headed for the table. Gary looked to be in his sixties, skinny, with a mop of graying hair and a grizzled beard. He seemed to be eating by himself, a bit apart from a family with three young children at the other end of the table.

"Would anybody like more water?" she asked.

"Yes, please," the mother said, and Mabel poured.

"I want orange drink." The little girl looked about three. Her nose could have used a tissue, and there was already an orange ring around her mouth.

"That's enough orange drink, Sara. And you should say 'please' when you ask."

Mabel left the mom to do her parental thing and turned to Gary. "Water?"

"No, thanks. I got my coffee and I'm good with that."

Mabel set her pitcher down. After a moment's reflection, she also sat herself down and leaned closer. "Excuse me, but is your name Gary?"

He looked up, mouth full of spaghetti. Then, he looked to either side, as if she were possibly talking to another Gary. Seemingly deciding he was the Gary in question, he quickly chewed and swallowed.

He dabbed his mouth with the napkin. "Yeah?" His voice was wary.

Mabel stuck out her hand. "My name's Mabel Browne. I was asking some of the people who work here if they knew how Frank Sedlak was doing. They said you were his friend."

Gary hesitated, then shook her hand. "Yeah." He dropped his eyes. "Yeah, Frank and I...we go way back."

"How's he doing since the fire? Is he getting better now?"

Gary carefully set his fork down. "No. I doubt he'll get much better than he is right now. They put him in the VA for rehab, but he has some mental issues that got worse since the fire. Paranoia, like. He's better off in there than on the street."

"Which hospital is that?"

"Millerville. I went up to see him one time. He remembered me. He's a good guy. A vet. He didn't deserve what happened to him."

"I'm so sorry," Mabel said. And meant it. She'd been hoping this search for Frank Sedlak might lead her to Mike Hardy's killer—and clear John of suspicion. Now, she could feel nothing but sadness for the down-on-his-luck man who'd lost so much in that fire. She wouldn't have wanted anything more to befall him.

"I guess he doesn't get out much."

"Ma'am, he doesn't get out at all."

Impulsively, Mabel patted his hand. "Sometimes miracles happen, Gary."

"Wish you was right," he said. "Me and Frank haven't seen too many of those."

"Thanks for talking to me, Gary. I'd like to give you a little something."

"Nah, that's all right. I was glad to have somebody want to talk about Frank."

By the time Mabel had helped clean up, written a check for the soup kitchen, and returned to slip Gary a little money over his protestations, she was more than ready to head home. Her purse was a little emptier, but she'd learned a few things to report to John and felt good about helping out. For the first time, she realized she felt a glimmer of the satisfaction people claimed to get from volunteering. Who knew?

Chapter Twenty-One

THE NEXT DAY, MABEL MADE A determined effort to write. Acey hadn't shown up to work, but at least the field had been cut, which she hoped would help get the township off her back for a while, despite the alleged "standing water" area she still hadn't addressed. Her fond—thus far dim—hope was getting the state to declare the swampy patch a protected wetland.

So far, she'd been able to avoid the county's inspecting the inside of the house, but she feared when they did, she'd have far bigger problems than the grounds had proved to be. In any event, it was a quiet morning, and she was feeling inspired to write about her volunteer experience at the soup kitchen.

John was working at the college till noon and planned to stop at the rehab afterward to check on Frank Sedlak. While Mabel believed Gary's account, John had quite reasonably told her they needed to verify it. He'd promised to bring over a pizza afterward and report back.

Mabel made coffee and cleared the table. She opened her laptop, placed her notebook next to it and laid out her favorite pens on top of that. Next, she arranged her chair, so it lined up with a small chip at the edge of the table.

She booted up the computer, opened a new file titled "Soup Kitchen," and formatted it. Mabel glanced at the wall clock. She had at least seven hours till John was due.

She wasn't sure how to begin. Maybe if she started typing, inspiration would kick in?

As I walked into the soup kitchen, I was met with the smell of spicy tomato sauce.

She already had a powerful start for her ax murder book. Maybe she should come up with something stronger than tomato sauce for the soup kitchen story. Of course, it was harder to generate excitement over a soup kitchen than a double ax murder.

Every face told a story...stories of hardship, stories of...

Stories of what?

Perhaps she should start with an outline. That was the problem with writing. There were possibly a million ways to write the same tale, and how would she know which was the right one? She opened her notebook to a fresh page and wrote a header—Things to Ask Writers' Group. Below that, she wrote, "How do you know the right place to start your story?"

She pondered other questions she might want to ask, assuming she ever made it to a writers' group meeting. At her feet, Barnacle yipped softly in his sleep, and his legs jerked as he ran in his dreams. Her eyes wandered from him to the boxes of cookware and cutlery her sister Jen had helpfully pulled from Grandma's cabinets, to be donated to the thrift shop.

She should carry those out to her car while she was thinking about it. It was embarrassing Jen and Lisa felt they had to take time to help her—but the process did go a lot faster with them on the job. They were way more decisive than Mabel and far less inclined to sentimentality over things like kitchenware.

Mabel got up and stretched. She stepped over Barnacle's snoring bulk and walked to the window overlooking the field behind her house. Koi sat on the windowsill, so fixated on something she didn't even turn her head.

Through the woods beyond the field, Mabel saw movement. Koi's tail twitched. Even at this distance, Mabel could make out the bulk of a rental truck in the driveway of her late neighbor Helen's house.

Mabel's heart sank. Helen's daughter Linnea had been staying at the old house off and on since Helen's funeral, and Mabel had heard reports she planned to make it permanent. She just hadn't expected it so soon.

Mabel's relationship with Linnea was no better than it had been with Helen. It would be like Linnea to file an immediate complaint about Mabel's house with the health department, as both she and Helen had threatened to do.

Mabel drew the blinds. The sight of that moving van wasn't conducive to inspired writing. However, it did make her think maybe she should take a wee break and clean out the spice cabinet. Jen had poked her nose in there and nearly erupted at the sight of three cans and one bottle of curry powder. Mabel explained only the bottle was hers, but Jen was still emoting, waving curry powder and exclaiming they no longer marketed spices in cans.

All Mabel could think to say was, "Oh."

Jen had turned one of the cans over and squinted at the bottom. "This expired in 1974!"

"Wow," Mabel said.

She had promised Jen she'd toss all the old spices this week. But Jen sighed and said, "I'll probably regret saying this, because it's only going to feed your hoarding tendencies. Toss the cans in a separate bag. Antique stores sell those now. Maybe you can make a few bucks off Grandma Mabel's stockpile."

No. Mabel closed the cabinet door. She'd never get her writing career off the ground like this.

She checked the time again. Six hours and fifteen minutes till John was supposed to arrive. It felt like she'd been working a lot longer than the clock suggested.

Mabel was still trying to focus when her cellphone rang. She frowned at the unfamiliar number, thumb hovering over the off button.

Boredom got the better of her. "Hello?"

The piercing shriek made her jerk and drop the phone. Even as she scrambled to retrieve it, she heard a female scream.

"Hello?" Mabel gripped the phone with both shaking hands.

"Mabel Browne, come immediately. Bring your dog."

"Wh—?"

"Better wear boots. No, never mind. Just hurry."

"Hurry where? Who are you?"

It seemed her caller had dropped her own phone because all Mabel heard was muffled yelling. Her heart thudded. Should she call 911? What could she possibly tell them?

Koi leapt onto the table and sniffed the phone. She meowed loudly into the receiver.

Wait—that voice. Could it possibly be Linnea? What on earth...?

Barnacle had sprung to his feet, as if somehow sensing his services were required.

Mabel tried to steady her breathing. What did Linnea expect her to do?

If Linnea hadn't called 911 herself, perhaps she'd better wait and see what they were dealing with. As she ran through her options, Mabel realized she was already tugging on her muddy rain boots. Something in those commanding Sauer genes tended to spur one to action.

"Come on, Barnacle." She clipped the excited dog to his leash, stuffed her squawking phone in her pocket, and on second thought, reached back for Grandma's rolling pin.

She'd take the car. No time to jog across the field.

Pulling into Linnea's driveway, Mabel heard crashing inside the house. "Linnea," she yelled into the phone, but nobody answered. She hung up, prepared to dial 911, if need be.

The moment she opened the car door, Barnacle bounded outside, charging toward the tidy Victorian with Mabel in tow. To her relief, there was no sign of a strange vehicle in the driveway. Linnea's late-model hybrid sat near the house next to the rental truck, and her husband Duane's car was absent—presumably he was at work.

"We're coming," Mabel puffed as she and Barnacle scrambled up the porch steps. "And I'm armed." She clutched the heavy rolling pin against her body. "Police are on their way."

The last was an exaggeration, given she hadn't called for backup yet. But the cops could be there in minutes, whenever she did.

"Police?" Linnea shrieked. "No police. Just get in here."

Mabel eased the door open, and Barnacle burst inside. The spindly fern stand in the entry teetered as the dog plowed past it. Mabel caught it, dropping the rolling pin with a thud as she did.

She also lost her grip on the leash in the process, and Barnacle loped down the hallway, disappearing into the kitchen at the far end. "Down, get down," Linnea snapped. "Come get your dog."

Mabel scowled. For someone who'd been begging them for help, Linnea should treat them a whole lot nicer, in her opinion.

Mabel's jaw dropped as she surveyed the kitchen. Linnea stood on a chair like a cartoon character, wild-eyed and gasping for breath. A glass mixing bowl lay shattered on the floor. A generous dusting of flour had settled over the landscape, studded with a scattering of tableware, a timer, several potholders, and a couple of mixing cups. In the space between the refrigerator and counter, Barnacle was sounding his high-pitched prey bark as his paws tore at the narrow opening.

"Poltergeist?" Mabel guessed.

"No, you idiot—snake," Linnea panted. "I was about to bake some scones for the historical society meeting when I happened to look down. It was coiled right there." She pointed at the spot Barnacle was energetically attacking.

"I don't see anything now, so it probably slithered back downstairs. I wouldn't worry," Mabel told her. "A lot of old houses around here get snakes in the basement this time of year. They mostly mind their own business and keep down the mice."

Linnea's eyes bugged out and all but glowed red. "Are you insane? Maybe you can live with snakes, but I can't. Especially if they come right up into my kitchen whenever they feel like it."

"I didn't say I have snakes over at my place—just that it isn't uncommon. What do you expect me to do?"

"Kill it. Open the basement door and release your dog."

Mabel grabbed Barnacle's leash.

"Where are you going?"

"I'm sorry, Linnea, but we aren't the snake patrol."

Barnacle dug his claws into the flooring and whined. Mabel pulled harder.

"I'm sure these snakes are coming from your unkempt property. If you claim you don't have snakes, it's because you're sending them all over here. I expect you to deal with it."

Mabel heaved a sigh and swiped at her sweaty brow. "Not my snake." Seeing a notepad and pencil on the counter, she scrawled a number. "Call this guy. I'm sure he can help you out."

This would undoubtedly further delay her clean-up project, but Mabel couldn't help grinning when she envisioned Linnea trying to work with Acey Davis.

By the time John arrived, a few minutes earlier than expected, Mabel had recovered from Linnea's snake invasion. She'd even managed to concentrate long enough to finish a rough draft of her article, as well as walk Barnacle before the rain started again, and clean out the spice cupboard. The cupboard now contained her jar of curry powder, salt, pepper, garlic powder, and cinnamon, which rattled around in the middle of a lot of unfamiliar empty space. Since she rarely cooked, she couldn't imagine why she'd ever bought the curry powder.

"Do you want a jar of curry powder?" she asked as John came through the kitchen door, carrying a fragrant pizza box.

He laughed. "I'd rather have a kiss."

Mabel felt herself flush. "I was cleaning out Grandma's spice cabinet."

John set the box on the stove, since Mabel still had her writing material spread all over the kitchen table. Immediately, Barnacle stretched up for a sniff, and Koi vaulted onto a stack of papers on the adjacent countertop so she could investigate too. The papers shifted, and Mabel had to leap to catch them.

As she came back up, John ducked his head and gave her a quick kiss.

Every time John kissed her, which hadn't been many times so far, Mabel's heart did a swoopy thing, and her knees went wobbly. What if his attentions turned out to be a mere flirtation, and she woke up one day to find out she'd made too much of this?

To hide her rush of confused emotions, she lifted the corner of the pizza box lid to peek. "Mushroom, light cheese."

"There's sausage on the other side, the way you like it. At the risk of repeating myself, you might want to embrace your inner vegetarian occasionally. I want you to live forever, and the formula for that doesn't include sausage."

"I liked the barbecue chicken with red onions."

He tweaked her nose. "It's a start. I'll remember next time."

When they'd each transferred a couple of slices to plates and carried them into the living room, Mabel asked, "Did you find Frank Sedlak?"

John nodded, mouth full of pizza. When he could speak, he said, "I did see him, but let's say, he hasn't gone anywhere in a long time, and he isn't going anywhere in the near future, either."

Mabel sighed. "And probably no money for a hitman. Well, barring angry family members, that's that. We're down to how many suspects then?"

"Chad Westermann. Danny. Buffy. Vin Perdue."

"Are we scratching Charlie Maier off the list too?"

John shrugged a shoulder. "I still don't see him as a murderer—or hiring a hitman. I may be wrong, but I don't see it. Like you suggested, though, I can't rule out a bitter family member either doing it or taking out a hit."

"So where from here?" Mabel picked up a slice of pizza. "Are we going to look into Perdue? Or Charlie Maier's family? Maybe check out Danny some more?"

John got up. "Can I bring you a drink?"

"Sorry. I forgot to get us one."

"You were in a hurry to hear what I found out." John winked. "And eat pizza."

"Guilty on both counts."

John returned with two drinks, plus the entire pizza box, and plopped back down next to Mabel. "We have to follow up on all of them. But let me look into Perdue—I don't want you anywhere near that guy."

Mabel kept her head down and eyes on her pizza. She'd never been any good at concealing her emotions. If John knew where she and Lisa had been, mere days before, he'd erupt like Vesuvius.

In mystery books and movies, the heroine predictably bristled at any suggestion she couldn't handle every aspect of an investigation. However, despite Mabel's proud sense of woman power, she also liked to think of herself as possessing good common sense. Which was telling her it was a terrific idea to avoid Vin Perdue from here on out. Not to mention the warm fuzzies that came over her every time John behaved protectively.

She and Lisa should never have called on Unbeatable Real Estate. They'd put a target on themselves and, even now, their escapade could come back and bite them.

"I'm quite capable of handling myself, you know." Mabel dabbed her lips. "Well, fine, if that's how you feel. I guess there's no reason for us not to split up the work."

John grinned, and she knew he saw through her bravado. He set down his pizza and took her hand. "You're something else, Mabel Browne. This isn't your problem, though. You've been wonderful, but I should never have dragged you into it to begin with."

Mabel tried not to squirm with embarrassment. "If you hadn't been out with me on that dog-training exercise, you wouldn't have been there when the body was discovered. And you wouldn't have this spotlight on you right now."

"It's not your fault. Or your responsibility." He tilted her chin and looked into her eyes in that way that made her heart chug like an old prop plane trying to gain altitude.

"I want to help you," she said. Her lips were inches from his and suddenly her brain could no longer focus on anything else.

She closed her eyes and suddenly, she was being kissed. Mabel had never been kissed like that. To be honest, she had not been kissed very much at all, up to this point. But she very much liked it. Somehow, her arms ended up twined around John's neck.

She felt Barnacle's paw on her knee. He whined softly, apparently checking to see if she was all right in there.

John laughed and pulled away, with his arms still lightly wrapped around Mabel. "Your bodyguard doesn't want any more fraternization."

Mabel was shaky, and well aware her cheeks were flushed. "Yeah, well..." Darn. She couldn't even produce a comprehensible sentence.

"We make a good team," John said. "However it happened, I'm glad we ran into each other that day in the woods."

"Me too."

"Look. I'd better head home and feed Billie Jean. She's probably plotting my demise by now. I'll give you a call tomorrow. And I'll take care of Perdue. Why don't you hang on till then, and we'll see where we are?"

Mabel didn't reply. She had no intention of merely hanging on while John was facing the electric chair...potentially.

Chapter Twenty-Two

JOHN HAD HEADED HOME HALF AN hour earlier, after kissing Mabel once more at the door, and repeating his promise to call tomorrow. Rain rattled against the bathroom window while she brushed her teeth before bed.

When her phone vibrated to John's ringtone, Mabel smiled. Was he already calling to wish her good night and tell her he missed her? She rinsed her mouth and grabbed her cell.

"Hey." John's voice was excitingly breathless.

"Hi," she chirped.

"I've had an incident over here."

Mabel's fingers tightened on the phone. Apparently, his breathlessness wasn't due to her charms. "What kind of incident?"

"I surprised a burglar."

"Again? Are you all right? Did you catch him?"

"He was running away when I pulled up. All in black. Before I could get out of the car, he'd disappeared between the houses. I tried a while to pick up some trace of him, but he was gone."

"Did he take anything?"

"Nothing seems missing. The house was still locked tight, and the alarm was set. The shed was open, but there wasn't anything in there anymore."

Mabel sat on the edge of her bed. "Maybe Amanda was coming back for her stuff."

After a pause, John sighed. "From my quick impression, it was a man. I suppose it might've been her—I only got a quick glimpse. That would make sense. Unless it was completely random, I don't know who'd want to break into my place."

"Did it look like any of our suspects?"

"Not Chad, I don't think. He's way too big. Possibly Danny or Buffy. We still don't know what Vin Perdue looks like, either. If he's on the slender side, it might've been him. We still have to ask what any of them would want there. Maybe it was a random break-in."

Mabel bit her lip. It had been on the tip of her tongue to offer a description. "I guess it could've been. It's so weird. First, we surprise Amanda, and now you turn around and come home to another break-in. How would anyone else even know who you are?"

"What are the odds?" John said. "If it's *not* a coincidence, it must relate to what Amanda stashed in my shed. That stuff looked genuine. Anybody who knew about it might see a chance to make a big haul in one quick stop. But how would they know it was there in the first place?"

"Then most likely Amanda or somebody who knows her. Did you call the police?"

"There's no point in hauling out the police when nothing seems to have been taken, and there was no actual break-in. I'll wait till I can take another look in the daylight."

"Maybe I'll join you."

"It's not a very big yard. I think I can manage."

Was she being too pushy? Was he giving her the brush off again? Surely not, when he'd called her right away—instead of the police— after catching an almost burglar. Still…

"Whatever then," Mabel said stiffly.

"Don't be that way. I don't want this to consume your whole life. You're launching a new career, and I've been selfish. You're wasting entire days, trying to help me. I *am* a trained investigator, you know. Have some confidence in my ability to take care of my own problems, huh?"

While Mabel processed how she should feel about that, John cut into her thoughts. "How about this? Come by and I'll give you breakfast before I head over to school. How's that sound?"

"If you're sure it won't be a problem."

"Don't be mad. I'd love to see you. We'll have French toast with fruit and real maple syrup. My mother's recipe."

He sounded sincere. "Okay, then."

"Terrific. I don't work till eleven, so come when it suits. Just let me know when you're on your way over, all right?"

"Okay."

"Good night. Sweet dreams."

The next day was warmer, and the sun shone like melted butter, streaming down over everything. The prospect of seeing John soon and eating French toast put a smile on Mabel's face. She even caught herself humming.

She pulled along the curb in front of his bungalow, and a cardinal flew up from the hedge. That seemed a good omen. Last night, she had tossed and turned quite a while, feeling like an idiot for getting snippy with John. By morning light, she'd managed to convince herself—again—that everything was perfect between them, and all she needed was to not mess things up.

John's cat sat in the front window. Billie Jean's golden eyes glittered with warning, and for a heartbeat, Mabel hesitated. That cat hated her beyond all reason and showed no sign of cutting her any slack anytime soon.

As she reached the front porch, Billie Jean vanished. Possibly, she was lurking inside the door, ready to pounce. Or hiding under the furniture, waiting for Mabel's ankles to pass within striking distance.

As Mabel raised her hand to knock, John opened the door. "I heard the car. Come on in. The bread is already soaking in the batter. Let me stick it in the fridge while we take another look out back."

So, he'd decided to let her help again. She hoped she hadn't nagged him into it.

As she stepped into his unnaturally neat kitchen, the aroma of warming maple syrup greeted her. John stowed things in the fridge as she waited. She admired the rear view for a moment and then the beautiful breakfast set up. Bananas and strawberries waited on the table for slicing, next to a tub of softening butter.

He was indulging her with this break from his usual Spartan diet.

He straightened and gave her a smile. "Ready?"

"Sure."

Mabel followed John to the back door, but before she reached it, a tempest of lashing claws and mad hissing flew from under the old Hoosier cupboard.

"Aagghh..." Mabel thrashed to escape the vengeful claws of fury.

"Billie Jean." John scolded. "Stop it. Mabel has a perfect right to be here."

Billie Jean had already shot into the front hallway, probably to lie in wait elsewhere. Wrath had doubled her tail's normal size.

"She seems to be warming up to you a little bit. She gave up pretty quick this time."

Mabel rubbed at her ankle, thankful she'd been wearing jeans. It was too bad they were her nicest pair. The spandex was still nice and stretchy, so they weren't bagging at the knees. Now they had a big, fresh snag.

The back yard was a pleasant place in the sunshine, despite the chill. A few stubborn remnants of summer still hung on in the pocket-sized garden—one brussels sprouts stalk, a clump of parsley, and another of chives. Two white-painted Adirondack chairs occupied the porch. She guessed in warmer weather the chairs sat outside on that circle of bricks around the little fire pit. Between the fire pit and garden was a molded concrete birdbath, and a feeder hung from the bare tree beside the shed.

John had closed the shed door, but there was still no padlock on the latch. As he'd said, there was little worth stealing, now that he'd removed Amanda's treasure trove.

"Watch for footprints," John warned, "before you take a step. We probably won't find any in the grass but check the edges of the garden and the flowerbed along the foundation. There's a chance he might have left a print in the loose dirt there."

As John headed to the shed, Mabel decided to walk the perimeter. She'd hoped the intruder might have tried the back windows, but the mulch near the house appeared undisturbed.

Mabel focused on the hedge separating John's yard from the neighbor to his right—boxwood, squared up with a pruner. There were no shoe impressions, or telltale scraps of fiber caught in the bushes, like Nancy Drew or even Jessica Fletcher seemed to find.

She worked her way around to the back fence. No marks in the mulch here either. Seeing a gate, she wondered if the burglar had come in that way. When she tried it, it held firm.

John called over. "Yeah, it doesn't open anymore. I nailed it shut when people built on the vacant lot behind me."

Mabel continued to the next corner and glanced toward the street. The overgrown hedge on this side of the yard looked like holly. The contrast in maintenance between this and the boxwood was striking.

"My neighbor's supposedly in charge of his side, up to the middle, but I have yet to see him do much of anything. I clipped mine, as you can see."

"Mm-hmm," Mabel agreed. Given the lack of maintenance on her own property, she wasn't going to be critical of anyone's pruning.

As he'd said, his side of the hedge was well trimmed. But she could see debris caught in the lower branches, closer to the street. She supposed the wind might've caught it as the trash workers dumped a can into their truck.

In fact, a gusty wind was tossing the tree branches right now. Several twigs bounced into the grass.

"Where are your garbage cans?" Mabel asked. "You've got stuff blowing around your yard." She pointed to what looked like a purple plastic bag caught in the hedge.

John frowned. "The back porch."

He strode toward the stray bit of plastic at the same time Mabel did. It only took a couple steps before Mabel's heart lurched. She wasn't looking at a plastic bag, as she'd imagined, but the hem of a purple rain slicker.

John threw out his arm and she ran into it with an oof. "Is that...?"

"You better call the police." His face was grim.

Mabel pulled out her phone but ducked under John's outstretched arm and crept nearer the slicker.

As she'd feared, a body was occupying the purple raincoat. The body of a young woman with a shaggy head of streaked blonde hair, matted with what looked like dark, dried blood.

Mabel concentrated on deep, slow breaths of the chilly air. She should be getting used to finding bodies by now, but she'd begun to shake all over.

"Stay back," John snapped.

She stared at him in shock. He had never spoken to her that way.

He caught her shoulders gently. "Just get the police. Please."

It only took a moment for Mabel to connect with emergency services. As she tried to focus, she kept getting distracted by the sight of John, kneeling in the grass beside that horrid wreckage of what had recently been a living, breathing human being.

"I'm not sure," she told the operator, in the interest of total accuracy. "John. Is she breathing?"

John didn't turn around. He shook his head.

When she'd confirmed the police would be arriving soon, she crept back. John had sat back on his heels, but still hadn't moved away from the body or taken his eyes off it.

Mabel laid a tentative hand on his shoulder. "Do you...?"

"Yeah. It's Amanda. She came back. Just not when I expected her."

He pushed onto his feet, still looking down, as if answers might appear if he stared long enough.

"Are there any clues on the body?"

"I don't know. I can hardly tamper with a crime scene, no matter how desperate for answers I might be." He walked back to the porch and dropped onto the third step.

Mabel followed and plopped next to him.

"You think she was here for the paintings?"

He shrugged, elbows resting on his knees in an attitude of discouragement. "I'd say so—and watched for a time she wouldn't run into me."

"That's pretty crummy," Mabel said.

"I've got to agree with you. She wasn't the poor little runaway, abused wife I thought I was protecting. Not that it matters anymore."

"Well, it looks like she did need protection from somebody. But not Mike, I guess."

"No. Not Mike…at least not anymore."

"The intruder you saw must've done this." Mabel peered into his face. "He could have followed her here."

"Possibly."

She was puzzled at his lack of enthusiasm for the obvious solution. She jiggled his arm. "John, it has to be. Try to remember everything you can about the person you saw last night. We already pretty much narrowed it down to either Danny or Vin Perdue, right? Or Buffy, I guess. Well, and Amanda…but now we know it wasn't her."

"We *don't* know that. It could've been her, running away when she saw me come home. She could have snuck back later, long after I went to bed for the night."

"Well, she didn't kill herself…at least, I don't think so. I doubt she flung herself under that hedge. And I didn't see a weapon anywhere."

"Me, neither. Plus, what appeared to be the entry wound in her back didn't look self-inflicted."

"So we're most likely back to Perdue or Danny?"

"Or a family member or someone else we don't even know about."

Mabel slumped, feeling as dejected as he looked.

"She's in my yard. It doesn't look good." He sighed and got to his feet. "I think I hear the cops. I better go meet them."

Mabel got up too. When John went through the house to greet the police, she walked back to the body. She didn't see any weapon nearby but hadn't expected to. Slowly, she scanned the surrounding area, with no real hope.

The back door opened, and John emerged, along with Lieutenant Sizemore and another female officer Mabel had never seen. Sizemore grinned briefly. "You again."

"Um, hi." The red-headed female detective had treated Mabel as a suspect the last time they met. She hoped for an improved relationship this time around.

EMTs came around the corner and, at a nod from Sizemore, the other officer led them over to the body. The small yard suddenly seemed very crowded.

Sizemore halted Mabel and John. "Hold on right there." She walked across the yard and took a moment to look over the crime scene, taking care not to touch anything. When she returned, she came up the steps and headed for the back door.

"Both of you please come inside. I'll take you first, Ms. Browne."

Mabel swallowed. A wave of déjà vu swept over her. She couldn't believe this was all happening again. What John had said right before he left to meet the police gnawed at her. The last thing he needed was a dead body in his yard.

Sizemore glanced around as they walked inside. She gestured toward the living room. "You wait in there, sir, please. Browne and I shouldn't be long."

John nodded. His eyes met Mabel's, but his expression was unreadable.

Sizemore led Mabel into the kitchen. Involuntarily, Mabel's eyes drifted to the refrigerator, where their uncooked French toast sadly rested.

Sizemore gestured at a chair. "Have a seat, Ms. Browne."

Mabel had scarcely taken two steps into the room when a hissing dervish, claws flashing, burst from beneath the Hoosier cabinet and attacked her ankles. Mabel shrieked and jumped aside.

"Are you okay?" John called from the living room.

"Yes," Mabel called back. "Your attack cat got me again."

Lt. Sizemore, planted in the adjacent chair, covered her mouth.

Nursing her injuries, Mabel sank into her seat. "That cat needs a scratching post."

"Help yourself to coffee," John called.

Mabel raised her eyebrows at Lt. Sizemore, who nodded. "Thanks. Black, please."

Mabel was glad to have something to do. She hopped up and set two mugs on the countertop. She poured one cup and delivered it to the detective before carrying her own mug to the fridge for milk and started adding sugar.

"What are you concocting over there, Ms. Browne? I'd like to conclude this before darkness falls."

"Sorry." Mabel ferried her mug back to the table, suddenly aware of a tremor that was causing her to slosh hot coffee on her hand. She sat with a bit of a thud and grabbed a handful of napkins to mop up the mess.

"Did you scald yourself?"

"No. I'm fine."

"Do I make you nervous, Ms. Browne?"

"No. Yes. A little bit." Mabel started to take a casual drink, then realized she was better off not trying to control a cup of anything hot right now.

"Don't be nervous. I'm sure you were only a witness. Again." Sizemore set a tiny voice recorder on the table. "This is going to be less painful than your encounter with that cat."

Mabel didn't reply. Her glance drifted toward the door, as she imagined John, sitting in the living room, waiting for his turn to be grilled.

As it turned out, Lt. Sizemore had been telling the truth about her interrogation—at least, the part where she'd said it would go quickly.

She first methodically walked Mabel through the discovery of the body, which should in theory have been simple, but because of her worries over John, wasn't.

"What brought you and Mr. Bigelow out into his back yard this morning?" Sizemore asked.

Mabel hesitated, tempted to say, "Fresh air."

Sizemore looked up from the notes she was taking along with the recording.

Darn. That pause stood out like a cherry in a bowl of vanilla ice cream. "Sorry, my mind wandered. We, uh, came out to…what I mean is Mr. Bigelow surprised an intruder after dark here last evening. So we went outside this morning to get a better look—to see if anything was taken, or any evidence left behind."

"What's your relationship to Mr. Bigelow, Ms. Browne?"

Again, Mabel hesitated. Should she say he was her boyfriend? "A friend. He's a friend. I mean we're…friends."

"I get the picture." Sizemore's voice was dry. "Did you and your friend find anything relating to the intrusion last evening?"

"The body was all. We called 911 and sat down to wait for you."

Sizemore's eyes drilled into Mabel's. "You say 'body.' Do you know, as you sit here, the identity of the deceased individual?"

Okay. Can of worms fully deployed.

"Personally? Like firsthand, no."

"Has anyone else apprised you of the identity of the decedent?"

Since only she and John had been there, Sizemore was really asking whether John had told her who the victim was. Mabel looked around, as if seeking another source of knowledge, but then realized Sizemore would undoubtedly find that insubordinate.

"J-Mr. Bigelow identified the body," Mabel said.

Sizemore nodded and scribbled. She acted as if this information was no surprise, yet it surely must have been. "What's her name?"

Mabel muddled through the Amanda Johnson/Amanda Pedersen confusion, till Sizemore waved her off.

"Did Mr. Bigelow tell you how he happened to know the woman?"

"She was a former client."

"I see. And do you know any more about the circumstances of their acquaintance?"

Well, Mabel did know more, but that question was so overbroad, she imagined it would be open to objection in a deposition or hearing. She didn't think the evidentiary rules applied to police interrogations, however.

"Ms. Browne, did you hear my question?"

"Yes, but I'm not sure I understood it."

"Fair enough. Do you know what services Mr. Bigelow provided to the victim? Or the circumstances surrounding their no longer working together?"

"You should probably ask Mr. Bigelow that."

"Oh, I will, but I'd also like to hear what you know about it."

Mabel drew a deep breath. She'd rather take her chances with Billie Jean again than continue this dance with Lt. Sizemore. She threw a despairing glance toward the living room.

Sizemore took a big sip of coffee and closed her eyes in apparent appreciation for John's hand-ground French roast. She turned back to Mabel. "Is that question making you uncomfortable?"

"No, it's... I don't know enough to give you a good answer, and anything I know is only what J-Mr. Bigelow has told me. It's hearsay—"

"You're not in court, counselor."

Mabel tried to remember whether she'd ever told Lt. Sizemore she was a lawyer. Well, ex-lawyer...specifically, someone with a law license who hadn't practiced in nearly a year at this point. Maybe Sizemore didn't really know but was tweaking her for talking about hearsay.

"Well, yes, I know that. I'm only saying the evidentiary value of secondhand information is generally less than firsthand information," Mabel said. And immediately regretted it.

"Objection denied." Sizemore grinned. She seemed almost to be enjoying this. Billie Jean had nothing on this woman, who did cat-and-mouse with the finesse of a plush tabby. "You seem to be talking all around this, and I still haven't heard an answer to a simple question."

"Well, I know there's a question of client confidentiality—or was, when the client was alive. Mr. Bigelow is…was a private investigator, and that woman out there hired him for some surveillance work. He stopped working for her when she disappeared. I'm sure he only shared that much with me because she was missing, and he was trying to locate her."

"You've been very helpful, Ms. Browne. See, that wasn't so hard. Now, let's talk a bit more about your discovery of the body."

By the time Mabel stumbled out of the kitchen, she'd lost track of the time. She looked at the clock and was shocked to realize how brief the interview had been. She felt as if she'd been turning on the rotisserie of justice for hours.

John passed her in the living room entry. His face was grim as he walked into the kitchen for his sit-down with Lt. Sizemore.

Mabel gave him an encouraging smile, but it didn't seem to register with him. She plopped on the couch and closed her eyes. She could hear emergency personnel and crime scene techs going past the side window, and the staticky chatter of radio comms. At some point, she knew they'd be carrying Amanda's body out to the coroner's van. Were neighbors standing on their porches and in the street, rubbernecking and taking cellphone videos?

John's interview would, no doubt, run longer than hers. Mabel thought about her writing—which was not getting done. She thought about Barnacle, patiently waiting for his walk, and whether Acey was working on her demolished shed…or doing more damage, as only he could. Maybe she should use this quiet time to think about the murders and all the suspects she and John had investigated and see whether any patterns suggested themselves.

Mabel tried to concentrate, but soon, she jerked awake from a doze to something sharp, needling her stomach. Her eyes flew open to see her nemesis, Billie Jean, sitting on her, paws kneading Mabel's stomach as if they were the very best of friends.

"Ouch!" Mabel sat upright, dislodging the cat, who spat at her and leapt to the top of John's oak bookcases.

Mabel yawned and rubbed her tummy. The radios were still squawking outside, and she heard the back door from the kitchen open and close.

John stood in the hallway. "See any grill marks on me?"

Mabel grimaced. "Bad, huh?"

He sank down and threw an arm over her shoulders. "Not great. But we knew it wouldn't be pretty."

"I don't know why she has to be so darn smug," Mabel said. "It's as if she's made up her mind before she even starts talking to you."

John shook his head. "No. She's a good cop. Her mind's still open. But she'd be a fool not to hear alarm bells when a guy who has a history with the vic ends up with the dead body."

Mabel snorted, not so quick to give Lt. Sizemore any undue credit. "And a guy would have to be a fool to kill someone he has a history with and leave the body right in his back yard, then phone it in to the police."

"Weirder things have happened. The important thing is I'm not under arrest. Furthermore, I'm sure Sizemore and her team will conduct a thorough investigation before they charge anybody. Plus, I don't even have a weapon at present. Shawnee County hasn't returned my gun yet…though they did let me know the ballistics didn't match what they pulled out of Mike's body."

"I know that's not enough to clear you, but sounds like so far, so good." Mabel pointed to the kitchen. "Would it be gauche to ask about French toast?"

John slapped his forehead. "Oh, good grief. I totally forgot. Of course not. Let's get some food in us. You must be ready to faint—in fact, now I think about it, I'm about to keel over from hunger, myself."

If Mabel hadn't been so hungry, she might have regretted

mentioning their delayed brunch. Back in the kitchen, her eyes were inevitably drawn to the activity in the back yard. The body was gone, and none of the bustle out there told her anything useful. All it did was remind her of how much trouble John was in. Determinedly, she turned her chair around to face away from the crime scene.

"Here." John passed a colander of rinsed strawberries and a ripe banana. "Would you mind slicing these for me?"

Mabel was glad to have something to keep her hands busy, but it still failed to keep her mind off Amanda's murder. "Did you tell Sizemore about the stuff she stashed in your shed?"

John's back was turned as he tended the griddle. Slowly, he shook his head. "I told her she called and promised to meet me a few days ago, but never showed up. I said I didn't know what she was doing in my back yard, which is true. And that I was away last evening, which I can easily prove."

Mabel frowned, her mind going automatically to the holes and the problems, as if this were all a law school hypothetical. "I wonder when she was killed. Time of death could make a big difference as to whether your alibi holds up."

"I wonder too. Partly, for the reason you said. Also—think about it. I may have been upstairs sleeping while she was being murdered in the yard right below me. That's what's making me crazy."

"Well, we don't know. Of course, at some point, we probably will—once the coroner has completed the autopsy. Till then, it's all pure speculation, which only tortures us with possibilities. More than likely, she was already dead by the time you got home last night, or you'd have heard the shot."

"Right as usual." John presented her with a plate of golden French toast, dusted with powdered sugar. "All you need to add is maple syrup and berries."

"Where's yours? I can't eat while you're still cooking."

John raised his eyebrows dubiously.

"Okay. I could probably eat but it wouldn't be polite, would it?"

"Mine's almost ready. Go ahead while it's still warm. I'll be sitting down in less than two minutes, and probably still finish eating before you do."

Mabel doubted that but took him at his word. Food might not be the answer to all life's ills, but it did tend to take the edge off.

"So…" Mabel said, as John slid into his seat opposite her. "You're not going to tell the police at all about the paintings Amanda left in your shed?"

John loaded his French toast with fruit, then barely grazed it with a drizzle of maple syrup. She couldn't help shaking her head.

"I have to tell them. It could be material evidence."

"I'd think so."

"I only want one last chance to go through it before I turn it over. I can't help thinking there must be a clue in there."

"When are you planning on doing that? Do you have to stick around here till they all leave?" Mabel waved a hand toward the back yard. To her surprise, one of the crime techs waved back.

"No, I don't think so. But I'll have to be careful, because I'm betting Sizemore will be putting a tail on me."

"Really?"

"I would, if I were her."

"I'm going with you," Mabel announced, scraping her plate.

"Of course, you are. Let's finish breakfast first, and I'll check and make sure the guys out back don't need me for anything else."

"I hope you're right," Mabel said, "and there's some kind of answer in that storage locker."

Chapter Twenty-Three

MABEL HAD FORGOTTEN JOHN WAS SUPPOSED to work that afternoon, but he hadn't. "I had office hours scheduled from eleven to three, but I called and canceled. I hope the department secretary put a notice on the door."

"Where's the storage locker? Do you need to swing by school first?"

"It's the only place I know of around here with climate-controlled storage, out past the college, on the far end of town. I suppose we could stop by school for a minute, make sure there's no problem, and pick up my messages."

After John spoke with the police, he and Mabel headed outside. "Might as well go together." He gestured at his car. "It's probably as well we hit the school first, anyway," he said. "In case we do pick up a tail."

Mabel leaned back, watching the scenery slip by. "They'll likely pick you up again when we leave there," she said. "Won't they be watching your car?"

"Undoubtedly. They know I work at the college, so they'll probably accept my stopping there, but they may continue to keep an eye on me."

"What if I could get another car?"

John shot her a look, eyebrows raised. "Are you suggesting I try to give the police the slip?"

Mabel's eyes veered away. "Well, if you put it that way..."

"You're a devious woman, Mabel Browne."

Mabel opened her mouth to say to forget it, but John spoke first. "Where would you get a car?"

She stared back. "You're okay with evading the police?"

He quirked his mouth. "Look. I may suspect, but I don't know for sure that we're being followed. And I haven't been told to stay at the house—in fact, quite the contrary, because I asked first."

"Oh, good, because I thought you were saying I'd be wrong to try to dodge them."

"I was teasing. I only want to get a good look at Amanda's stash before I bring the cops in. When I took that stuff to storage, I had no idea she'd turn up dead—let alone in my back yard."

"Well," Mabel said, "my niece Betsy goes to school here, and she works over at The Grind. If I can get hold of her car for a bit, I could maybe sneak around back and pick you up."

"And this is only one of your many lovable qualities. So quick with the brilliant, practical solutions to everyday problems."

Mabel flushed. "Don't be silly."

"Just stating the facts." He grinned as he pulled into the faculty parking lot.

"I texted Betsy. Hopefully, she'll be okay with this. I'll let you know one way or another."

"If you can't get the car, I'll meet you back here in another ten or fifteen," John said.

When they got out of the car, he caught Mabel's hand and pulled her closer. "In case the cops are watching, I think we should let them know you're leaving me here. Lower their suspicions." With that, he gave her a goodbye kiss that rivalled the iconic Times Square V-J Day embrace.

Okay, maybe it wasn't quite the full dip, but still impressive. Mabel wobbled a bit as she headed down the street to The Grind.

Her phone vibrated in her hand. Betsy had replied,

Sure, Aunt Mabel. As long as I have it back by 5. Did you break down?

Since she was nearly to the coffee shop, Mabel didn't bother replying. She pushed open the door and looked around the half-full room at students working on laptops and tablets or talking and laughing over their lattes. Betsy was working behind the counter and caught Mabel's eye over the heads of people waiting for service.

Mabel sighed and got in line, texting John.

Got it.

Five minutes later, she was at the counter. Betsy pulled a monkey key ring from her hip pocket. "Is your car okay, Aunt Mabel?"

"Yeah. I'll explain later. Thanks so much."

"No problem. Hang on a sec." As Mabel turned to leave, Betsy took a foam-topped takeout cup from the barista behind her. "A little gift from me."

"Thank you, baby!" Mabel blew her a kiss. "I'll have your car back by five sharp."

"It's down the block toward the bakery." Betsy pointed.

Mabel spotted the little crayon-blue car immediately. It was a cheap import of unknown but elderly vintage, and its many dents attested to the flimsy material that had gone into its making. "Hi, Rosie." She hoped using Betsy's pet name for the old girl might encourage her to start smoothly.

She climbed in and turned the key. After a heart-stopping moment's hesitation, the ancient engine sputtered to life, despite clearly needing a tune-up. Mabel inched back and pulled out of the spot, glad she was leaving, rather than trying to parallel park.

John already waited in the shadows of the rear entryway when Mabel drove up. He sprinted to the car and slipped inside. "Wow. Will it get us there?"

"Of course." Mabel patted the dashboard. "She's a dependable girl, aren't you, Rosie?"

"How's the gas?"

"Oh, blast. I never thought to look. Of course, it's dead empty. College students."

"Hit the Fill Stop. It's only a couple blocks out of our way."

The gas station took but a moment, as the tank was nearly full. "I can't believe the gas gauge doesn't work. How did this car ever pass state inspection?" Mabel fussed.

"Well, she's full now, so head out Orchard, then left on McKinley. Do you know where it is? Over by the carpet warehouse."

"Vaguely."

Mabel drove with an eye on the rearview mirror but saw no sign of followers. She hoped that meant there weren't any—and, in turn, that John wasn't a serious suspect.

Mabel recognized the storage facility as soon as she saw it. Rows of units stood in ranks atop a hill above the road. At the bottom, a one-room guard shack sat against a high gate in the wire fence surrounding the property.

"It looks like they're guarding the inner sanctum at Roswell. Most of this stuff's probably junk, like musty old furniture and boxes of 1984 bank statements."

John grinned. "Excuse me for preferring the very best for my 1984 bank statements."

The guard opened the window. "Hi," John said. "Unit 7-F."

"Hi, again." The guard, a dreadlocked young guy probably still in his twenties, smiled and nodded as John handed Mabel the card for the gate. She tapped it on the reader and the gate slid open.

"All the way to the top, four rows back on the right, and turn," John instructed.

The little car struggled and gasped its way to the top and shuddered on the turn. Unit 7-F stood on the right, secured with a padlock.

As soon as John got out, Mabel turned around and parked facing out, in case they later needed a jump, or a push in the right direction.

John already had the unit open by the time she got out. There was a lot of unused space, despite numerous boxes and parcels and several pieces of old furniture, including a filigreed walnut pump organ.

He caught Mabel's glance. "My grandmother's. I have no use for it but couldn't bring myself to get rid of it. I still remember her playing old hymns on it and singing."

Mabel ran her hand over the wood. "It's beautiful." She couldn't help thinking it would feel right at home at Grandma's house...if that weren't already full of other long-hoarded keepsakes.

John started pulling parcels toward the door, where the light was better. Mabel, seeing what he was doing, picked up one of the larger paintings and carried it over, as well.

Her phone rang. Lisa's photo appeared.

"Am I interrupting anything?"

"Not really."

"Just confirming our date to look for your maid-of-honor dress."

Mabel grimaced. It would be a small ceremony, and Lisa was having only one attendant. Mabel knew it was her responsibility to step up...no matter how distasteful the prospect of trying on gowns that would at best make her look like a mylar balloon.

"It's on my calendar," Mabel promised. "Hey, Lisa..." She'd been about to tell her about finding Amanda's body but realized Lisa would still be at work. It could wait. "Never mind. Call you later."

John carried the last package to the door as Mabel hung up. "Okay. Let's look through all these and figure out what's here."

"Like hidden messages?" Mabel felt a small rush of excitement.

He laughed. "Right, Ms. Drew."

John opened the first parcel and studied the oil painting of a pastoral scene inside. "I don't see a signature, do you?"

Mabel pointed. "That squiggle by the shepherd's pouch might be something. It's hard to tell."

John squinted and shrugged. As he finished his inspection, he rewrapped the picture with some care. "Can you make an inventory as we go?"

"Oh, sure." Mabel pulled out her phone and as John worked his way through two more packages, she began taking photos, and making notes in the memo app. "What are you thinking?"

"It would take an expert to say for sure, but these look real to me. It doesn't seem likely she owned all this. If she was wealthy enough to own so much original art, why was she living the way she did?"

"According to everybody we talked to, she didn't come from money."

"And she didn't dress like money or—"

"Or pay her private investigator like money," Mabel supplied.

John laughed. "Exactly."

A shadow rolled over the open door.

Mabel looked up to see the young guard, who'd just driven up in a golf cart. "Hi. I'm about to go off duty, and we're not staffed in the evening. Wondered if you need anything before I take off."

John walked over to the cart. "Thanks. No, we're checking through some of this stuff. We'll probably be locking up in half an hour or so."

"Hey." The young man, whose nametag said Jamal, pointed at the packages scattered around Mabel. "Where did you get that?"

"Huh?" She looked around to see what he was indicating.

"That drawing of a man's head."

"This?" Mabel held it up. She floundered and got to her feet. Every joint in her body creaked from sitting on the concrete.

"My client asked me to hang onto a number of things for her," John said, "including that."

Jamal frowned. "I don't know, man. How do I know you're legit?"

John pulled out his driver's license and a folded piece of paper, which he passed over to the security guard. Jamal unfolded the paper and looked it over. "You a PI?"

John, to his credit, shook his head. "Not right now. I was an investigator at the time I worked for her."

Jamal passed the documents back to John, looking troubled.

"You've obviously seen that before?" John asked.

"Yeah. She said it was maybe by Rembrandt when he was young and starting out. Or maybe a student of his."

John and Mabel flashed each other a sharp look. "Who said that?" John asked. "Could you tell me about it?"

Jamal hadn't gotten off the golf cart, and he shifted in his seat. He'd picked up his phone at some point. Mabel wondered if he might be thinking of calling for back-up. It occurred to her the young man was pretty brave to be confronting them alone about what he obviously suspected to be theft, at the very least.

"The woman who was packing up one of these other lockers a while ago. Why would she give you all this stuff?" Jamal said.

"I'm not sure," John said, honestly. "She left it with me and told me to hold onto it till she came back for it. She said if she didn't come back, I was to keep it for my unpaid fee." He gave a quick description. "That her?"

"Think so. Do you have a phone number for her?" Jamal held up his cell phone and waggled it.

John shook his head. "She won't answer. I'm sorry to tell you she's dead."

The shock on Jamal's face couldn't have been more apparent. He clenched and re-clenched his fist convulsively, then rubbed his lower lip with it. "What happened?"

"She was shot. We don't know who did it. She must've either been coming to see me or to pick up her stuff."

Jamal's eyes widened as he seemed to realize where Amanda had ended up.

John nodded. "Mabel and I found her this morning."

The young man dropped his head into his hands. "Oh, man. I saw online they found a body, but there was no name or picture or anything. Didn't know her name, anyways."

John lightly touched his shoulder and the young man startled. "Sorry. Listen, Jamal. I hope you'll trust us, because something bad's going down, and we're trying to figure it out before anybody else gets hurt. The lady's name was Amanda, by the way." He dug the photo out of his wallet and handed it over. "This is who you met, right?"

Jamal nodded. "Yeah," he said softly, running a finger over the photo.

John began talking rapidly, spelling out how Amanda had hired him to surveil her house, Mike had made trouble, she'd disappeared, and all that had happened since—including both murders. "I'm in the middle of all this, and I don't have a clue. But I think it might be right here—in these packages. The thing is I don't have a lot of time to figure it out."

"Okay." Jamal handed back the picture. "I don't know you, but that's a heck of a story to make up on the spot. You want to know about her and that sketch, I'll tell you."

"Mind if we sit?" John asked.

Jamal shook his head.

John dragged out a couple of padded, dining room-type chairs and offered one to Mabel.

Jamal's brow furrowed. "Here's all I know. It isn't much—I don't know where all the rest of that came from." He gestured. "But the drawing—I know that one. And I bet a bunch of the others were what she gave me that day."

"She gave *you?*" Mabel asked. "Seems like she was always giving people artwork."

Jamal quirked an eyebrow at her. "I know, right?"

"What do you mean, she gave it to you?" John asked.

"Kind of like what you say she did with you, I guess. Asked me to hold onto them for her for a couple days."

"Was she a friend of yours?" Mabel felt like Alice, gone through the looking glass. Hadn't he said he didn't even know her name?

"No, no. She…I guess I really ought to go back a couple steps and start over," Jamal said.

"Take your time," John told him. "We appreciate any help you can give us. It may help us figure out who killed her."

Jamal drew a big breath and let it out. "Where to start…?"

He glanced up the hill, out along the double row of storage units, for a moment. "Well, there was this guy who rented a couple units here. He died a few months back, and somebody put in a bid for the contents."

"Do you remember names?" John asked.

"Nah. The guy who died was like Wilson or Williams or something like that—but it would be in the files."

Mabel made a note.

"The man who bid on it—I don't know. The guy who owns this place would. Basically, what happens if someone's behind in their rent so many months, they get a warning to pay up or lose their stuff for the back rent. This renter was behind when he got killed in a car accident. He was living out of state at the time. Nobody came forward to pay the back rent or make a claim on it, when the boss advertised the sale would be coming up.

"When the auction rolled around, all the usual bidders were here. We see the same people all the time. Except this dude nobody seemed to know. He wanted to win bad. Ran the bid way up, and everybody else dropped out pretty quick, so he ended up winning."

"You watched the auction?"

"Yeah. It can be fun."

"Can you describe him? The guy who won?"

He frowned. "Average, white, middle-aged. Medium height, weight. Light hair, but balding a bit."

Mabel shifted in her chair. Jamal's description could easily fit Vin Perdue.

"Anyhow, he won. Wrote a check for the contents. That's Friday. Rules are you have so many days to clear out the unit, you know. So that Saturday, a different dude, younger, arrives with another fella, that girl, and a truck. He's cleared to pick everything up from those units for the new owner."

"All right. Wait a minute." John held up his hand. "Can you describe the guys who showed up with the truck?"

"I didn't really study them, but they were both white. One shorter than me and scrawny, but he sure was strong. He had dirty-colored hair and a couple days' worth of beard the same color."

"Dishwater blond?" Mabel asked.

"Yeah, I guess that's a good way of describing it."

John caught Mabel's eye and shrugged. That description didn't fit anyone she could think of, and it seemed John didn't recognize it, either.

"The main guy was bigger. He had muscles and I dunno…he reminded me kind of like a cartoon superhero. Good looking, or at least *he* seemed to think so. Dark hair and eyes."

Again, John caught Mabel's eye and silently mouthed, "Mike."

"They load up, and the two guys drive out. The girl stays behind because they're coming back for another load."

"I assume this is Amanda?" Mabel asked. She shivered, realizing the temperature was dropping along with the sun, and checked the time. She still had an hour to get the car back to Betsy.

"Yeah. Not too long after, she calls and asks me to come up to the unit they were about to start on and tells me bring the golf cart."

John and Mabel's eyes met briefly. She couldn't believe what they were hearing.

"So, I drive up there, and she motions me inside the unit." He briefly rubbed the top of his head. "I guess I was crazy to listen to her. I mean she might have wanted to kill me or steal my keys or something, but you know…"

John grinned. "I totally get you, man. A beautiful lady can get us to do pretty much anything. Right, Mabel?"

Mabel rolled her eyes but felt the blush creep up her neck.

"Anyway, I step inside, and she drags out maybe a half-dozen or so wrapped-up pictures. Looked like she'd been opening and rewrapping them. She showed me the Rembrandt one."

"What did she say about it?" John asked.

"Just how it could've been painted by him, like I said before. She said all these packages were paintings, and they were too valuable to get stuck in an old truck with a bunch of other stuff and get damaged.

"Then, she asks can I keep them safe in my guard shack till she can come back with a car and take them in a day or two.

"I told her, yeah, I guess. So that's what I did. She told me don't say anything to the men—said she knew about art, and they didn't. Said they wouldn't understand why she needed to protect them. Told me don't tell anyone else—even my boss—because the less people knew, the less people would be talking and maybe the wrong person find out."

"Sooo...did the guys come back? And did they notice some of the paintings were missing?"

"Yeah, they came back, but they didn't say one word about the paintings, at least not around me. I think maybe they didn't know there were pictures in that unit."

"Let's be clear. Neither of these men was the guy who actually bought the contents?" Mabel asked.

"No. They had the right papers—like the bill of sale. I figured they were like paid movers."

"Gotcha," John said. "How long did you end up hanging onto the paintings?"

"Oh, a couple days. Like two nights, and then, she came back with her car, like she said she would. I helped her load them up, and she gave me a big tip."

"If they were so valuable she didn't want anybody to know about them, how come she trusted you?" Mabel asked.

Jamal stiffened. "I'm honest."

"Of course, you are," John agreed. "I believe what Mabel's saying is Amanda didn't know you any better than she knew your boss, but she apparently didn't trust him."

Jamal seemed to think about it. "I don't believe she thought my boss would steal the paintings any more than I would. And we're both bonded, you know. But she trusted me not to tell the two men, and she wasn't sure about my boss. He might've felt like he was responsible to let them know about it. You understand what I'm saying?"

"I do," John said.

"I was crazy to help her." Jamal rubbed his forehead. "I never did anything like that in my life. Did I help her steal this stuff?"

"I don't think so." Mabel looked around at the paper-wrapped packages. "What else did she tell you about the paintings?"

He shrugged. "She knew a lot about art. She said that's what she studied at college. She told me about some of the different styles and stuff. Said it all needed to be stored under the right conditions, and she wasn't going to let those 'bozos' go bang it all up and stick it in a basement or something."

"When the guys came back, nobody seemed to notice anything missing?"

"Nope. Not that I heard of."

"Hey, thanks for trusting us," John said. "You gave us a lot to think about."

"I hope you can figure out who killed her." Jamal nodded toward the pictures. "What you going to do with those?"

John smiled wryly. "Keep them here for now, in that climate-controlled storage Amanda said was so important. But I'll have to tell the police about them, and soon, or I'm going to be even deeper in trouble than I am right now."

"You gonna mention me?"

"Not if I don't have to."

"I don't want to lose my job—but let me know if I can be any help, man. She was just somebody who cared about art, right? Why would anybody want to kill her?"

"I don't know, Jamal. There's got to be something more we don't know yet that can answer that question."

Chapter Twenty-Four

ON THE RETURN TRIP TO BARTLES Grove, John leaned back with his eyes closed, face creased in a frown. After driving in silence for ten minutes, Mabel finally burst out. "What do you think about Jamal's story?"

"My mind's going a hundred miles an hour. We got a ton of new info back there. And that artwork she very casually told me I could have seems to be at the heart of why she ended up dead."

"Which I guess lets all our suspects off the hook—the ones who might have killed Mike out of jealousy over his love affairs...or revenge for that arson."

"Maybe. All we have are theories at this point."

"Well, look at Amanda a minute. You met her. Do you honestly think all this happened simply because she was trying to protect some artwork?"

"Of course not. Naturally, she might be concerned about the safety of the art—she was a fine arts major, so one would think she cared about it. But there's got to be more to it...money, most likely."

"We agree it's hot?"

"Yeah."

"Now what?" Mabel pushed the tired little car to its limit, trying to make it up the last hill into town.

"Two things. Maybe three. One—we find out what we can about the first dead guy—the one who owned the contents of those storage units. Second—we need to know who bought them at the auction."

"Maybe also who the other guy was with Mike the day they loaded all that stuff up and hauled it away," Mabel said.

John gave her a small smile and nodded. "I need you to send me the pictures you took. We should try a reverse image search on those right away. If they're real, they have to be known. I've got a suspicion I'd like to follow up on."

Mabel signaled for the faculty lot.

John climbed out. "Pick you up in front of The Grind."

The angled spots in front of the coffee shop were occupied. Mabel still had fifteen minutes to get the car back to Betsy, so she drove around till she found a spot a block away, where she could pull in without parallel parking maneuvers. She locked the battered little car and gave its hood a loving pat. "Thanks, Rosie."

After returning Betsy's keys with massive thanks, Mabel jogged out to meet John at the curb.

When she finally got home and unlocked the kitchen door, Barnacle dashed outside and nearly flattened her. She never had a chance to clip him to his cable before he was all the way out in the yard, pottying all over the struggling remnants of Grandma Mabel's treasured Van Fleet rose bush, which Acey hadn't already managed to finish off.

Mabel punched in her alarm code and plopped her things onto the kitchen table as Koi wound herself around her ankles and chattered. Mabel suspected Koi was tattling on Barnacle, especially given the overturned trash container, and chewed-up food wrappers strewn across the hall floor.

"Nobody likes a snitch," she told the cat, who slitted her eyes and purred with innocent contentment. "And no one likes overturned garbage, either." She gritted her teeth at the mess.

She stroked Koi's head, then rounded up Barnacle and filled the pet bowls. Both animals dove into their dinner without hesitation, reminding her once again that their love, while sincere, was closely tied to regular feeding.

Next, Mabel turned to her own needs. She hesitated, staring at the contents of her freezer a moment before grabbing a mac-and-cheese and shoving it in the oven. While waiting for that to cook, she worked on cleaning up the vestiges of Barnacle's afternoon snack from the floor.

Once the trash was again secured and toted outside, she flopped down on her couch and turned on the local TV news. Amanda's murder was the lead story, with footage of emergency vehicles and swarming first responders in front of John's bungalow. As the story wrapped up, Mabel let out a breath she hadn't realized she'd been holding. They hadn't identified either Amanda or John. And blessedly Mabel's name hadn't come up, so she wouldn't be getting a call from her mother.

The phone rang. For an instant, Mabel considered the possibility her mother had extrasensory powers beyond those of ordinary mortals.

She let out another pent-up breath when she saw the caller ID. "Lisa—I was going to call you."

"Did I just see your car on the news? That was John's place, wasn't it?"

"Yeah. It's kind of a long story, but everything's okay. I think."

Mabel switched off the TV and gave Lisa the details as best she could, allowing for rapid-fire questions and exclamations. Then, her phone began to vibrate again. "Look, Lisa. I'll call again before bed, but looks like John wants to video chat, so I've got to run right now."

Not to mention she was beginning to smell something scorching in the kitchen. Mabel accepted John's call, while conveniently leaving her own camera off as she ran for the oven.

John popped up on the screen. "Hey, Mabel—turn on your camera."

"In a sec. I'm in the middle of something right now."

"Do you want to hear what I found out?"

Mabel looked up from the stove, where she'd been checking on the casserole, which was still cold in the middle, though the top was already turning brown. "You found something out already?"

He thumped his chest. "Detective."

"Tell me all about it while I tend my dinner."

Mabel turned the stove dial down. This is what came of putting a frozen slab of noodles and cheese into a cold oven and setting the heat at 400 to speed things along. It wasn't simply that she was a less-than-stellar cook. This oven of Grandma's needed to be replaced...though, if she did that, she'd no longer be able to use the oven as an excuse for her cooking disasters. At least, she could keep this particular debacle to herself.

While she contemplated putting foil over the casserole—and concluded she didn't have any—John told her he'd researched the previous owner of the contents of the two storage units. Rather than attempt to start with Jamal's vague "Wilson or Williams," he'd managed to reach the owner of the facility, who identified the man as Addison Winters. Working from there, and some sketchy information, he had located an out-of-state obituary.

"I was lucky his name was a bit unusual. If he'd been a John Wilson, I'd have been searching for months."

"Did the obit give you anything useful?"

"A little. It said he was forty-one. He'd worked as a security guard for a company in New Mexico, where he died, and had previously done security work in Pennsylvania, where he was born."

"How does a security guard afford all those paintings? If Amanda told Jamal the truth, they're originals and valuable, at that."

"Exactly what I asked myself." John grinned. "The obvious way would be working as a security guard for a museum or private collector and stealing the artwork he was supposed to be protecting."

"Of course—but why would he be living and working so far away, if he had all that stolen art sitting back here in his storage units?"

"Maybe he was finding it harder to sell than he'd anticipated. Or he might have been waiting for some time to pass before trying to put them on the black market."

"I'm guessing the obit didn't say who he worked for back here?" Mabel said.

"That would be too easy," John said. "We'll soon figure it out, though. I expect an image search will help."

"This guy steals a bunch of art," Mabel said. "Then, I suppose he stashes it in storage till the heat dies down. And leaves the state?"

"So it would appear."

"Then, he dies. Apparently with back rent due on the storage units." Mabel frowned. "If I'd stashed a bunch of valuable stolen goods in a storage unit, the last thing I'd want is to default on the rent."

"Oh, darn. Hang on." Mabel leapt up, grabbing a silicon mitt, and opened the oven. Her breadcrumb topping wasn't in flames, but it had certainly passed the crunchy stage and moved on to singed. She checked the center. Still only lukewarm.

Deciding to quit before things got worse, she turned off the oven. She could finish her dinner in the microwave, once they were done talking. "Sorry. I'm listening."

John cleared his throat. "Getting back to what you were saying, it's not that he let his rent go into default. From what I can figure, it defaulted because he died, and the storage place didn't know it. They advertised before auctioning off his stuff, but nobody with a legal interest stepped forward to pay the rent and claim the contents."

"Then a stranger showed up the day of the auction and ran the bid up to be sure he won. So he must've known what it was worth. You think he helped Winters steal the artwork to begin with?"

John shrugged. "Here's a puzzle for you. See if you can name the stranger who bought the contents."

From his complacent smile, Mabel guessed he not only knew the purchaser's name, but that it really was deducible. Plus, unlike John, she already knew who Jamal's description fit to a T. "Vin Perdue?"

John nodded. "Brilliant, as always. I cheated. I asked the storage facility owner, and he told me."

"What a dirty trick, making me figure it out for myself." But hey, maybe she *was* brilliant. "Have you had a chance to look into him yet?"

"A bit. I'll catch you up, but turn your camera on first, though. There's no point in video-chatting if I can't see you."

She'd been afraid this would happen. Not only did she hate seeing her face on screen, but what if John saw her guilty expression and wormed out of her what she and Lisa had done?

John smiled. "There you are—that's better. All right. From what I

211

gather, Perdue's generally a shady operator. As we already heard, he's a bit of a slumlord—with rundown rental properties in low-income neighborhoods. He also runs a couple small businesses…a secondhand shop, for one thing, which could account for his buying up storage units. But somehow, he always seems to have more disposable income than you might expect from what he supposedly does for a living."

Mabel concentrated on looking innocent as her mind raced. Perdue had told them Mike drove for that secondhand business. Had he possibly also been Perdue's getaway driver the night of the heist? She cleared her throat. "Yeah, I've been thinking. I'm pretty sure I had some dealings with his rental business when I was a lawyer. Not with him personally, but the company was bad news."

"No kidding? If you were up against the company, you're lucky you never had any direct dealings with Perdue. On the outside, he's your solidly middle-class businessman. But that veneer of respectability is definitely thin. There are a lot of rumors—and even a few charges. Insurance fraud, tax fraud—but the most serious is the arson. Probably also most interesting, for our purposes. That, and dealing in stolen goods out of the back room. You wouldn't want him as an enemy."

"Would somebody like that be the brains behind an art heist?"

"Maybe. More likely, Perdue's working for somebody bigger on up the food chain. Drug and arms trafficking are the two highest-dollar criminal businesses going. Art theft, believe it or not, is third, and it's often used to finance the first two."

Mabel swallowed hard. The clear implications were exploding in her head like firecrackers.

Vin Perdue had somehow been involved in stealing that artwork. Likely with the assistance of that Winters guy. Had Mike been involved? If so, wouldn't he have noticed the paintings were missing?

In any event, Amanda, in turn, had stolen them from the storage units. Then she ran, taking the paintings with her. Vin discovered the paintings missing and came after Mike, who of course, didn't have them at that point. Somehow, he or one of his goons ended up killing Mike, but not having located the artwork, he then came after Amanda, who almost led him to the paintings in John's back yard. Except they were already gone. Now she was dead too.

She focused on John's face, fear making her heart chug erratically. "Vin Perdue is going to come after you next—he or someone worse. He didn't find the paintings in the shed, so he's going to keep looking."

John waved away her fear. "Not necessarily. If he does, I'm not that worried. I won't have the paintings—I hope they'll be safely with the police by that point."

"A—he doesn't know that, and B—I'm not worried about the paintings—I'm worried about you."

"Don't. Mabel, please. I can take care of myself. Vin won't want to kill me, anyway. What he wants are the paintings, and if I'm dead, I can't tell him where to find them, can I?"

Mabel couldn't believe the foolishness coming out of John's mouth. "Excuse me. Two other people are already dead. I don't know whether they're dead because he was mad and frustrated—or it was an accident, or whatever. My point is even if he got the info he wants out of you, why would he leave you alive to tell about it?"

"Now maybe you understand why I told you I'd handle Perdue, and you should stay far away from that part of the investigation. I'm entirely competent to take care of myself, you know?"

Mabel gnawed her lip. It wasn't only John in danger anymore, but she couldn't tell him that. Perdue had seen her—and Lisa. By the end of their ill-advised interview, his suspicions had been obvious. Was there any way he could track them down?

She took a deep breath. The greater risk was to John. And he wasn't sufficiently worried, in her humble opinion. Despite her frustration, Mabel knew when to pivot and take a different tack. "All right, you're a total he-man. Let me ask this. How do you plan to prove Vin Perdue's a double murderer? What's your next step, oh, great one?"

"I'm going to need to get the artwork safely into police custody, as soon as possible," he said. "But let's wait till tomorrow, after we've tried identifying the paintings. I don't have a lot of confidence in the police's desire to focus on Perdue instead of yours truly.

"Between now and my possible incarceration, I'll see if I can pinpoint any of Perdue's movements during the critical time periods. Maybe I'll get lucky and find a clear nexus between him and Mike or Amanda around their times of death."

Mabel wasn't comforted. It all sounded very iffy…except for the part about the police likely continuing to focus on John as their best suspect.

"Mabel, stop looking like that. There's still a lot I can do…as long as I'm not in jail. Besides, the police will do at least the minimum look into Perdue. He has a sordid criminal record, which I do not, after all."

"Not for homicide he doesn't."

He laughed. "Well, I don't, either. And he has a lot of criminal and other associates who might very well know something."

"Please be careful," she begged. "You're the only…*you* I've got."

"And you're the only you I've got too. Don't worry. I have no intention of getting myself thrown in jail—or worse—and miss out on our next fifty years of madcap adventures."

Mabel scowled. "If you do, I'll never forgive you."

It wasn't till she was brushing her teeth later that she remembered this had been the night of the monthly historical society meeting. *Maybe next month. Then again, maybe not.*

Chapter Twenty-Five

MABEL SAT AT HER TABLE EARLY the next morning, laptop open, as she tried to figure out how to do a reverse image search. She'd woken around six-thirty and not been able to go back to sleep. Lisa was supposed to pick her up at ten for her maid-of-honor fitting, but after tossing a while, she figured she might as well get something accomplished before that nightmare began.

She was a bit offended by one of the first articles that came up, which contained the opening line, "Of course, most users know how to do a reverse image search using," blah, blah, blah… Mabel did not believe that for a minute. It sounded to her like techy snootiness.

Finally, she found a video, "Reverse Image Searches for Idiots," which broke the procedure down step by step. Bingo.

Of course, all the images were on her phone, and not on her laptop, which caused more lost time. Finally, her first image loaded, and she clicked to search.

To her amazement, the picture popped up over and over, filling the page with the repeated image of a sturdy girl holding a basket of cheeses, her plain blue dress and yellow apron glowing in a beam of sunlight, white head covering reminiscent of a seventeenth-century Madonna. Mabel was stunned to see the first image caption, *Girl with Cheeses*, Jan Vermeer, Art Museum of the Alleghenies, and quickly clicked on it.

A page within the art museum website came up, boldly headed **Art Theft.** Mabel's heart chugged.

Her eyes raced down the page. A major art theft had occurred at the museum the previous spring, before Mabel moved to Medicine Spring. Nearly a dozen paintings had been stolen, including Vermeer *Girl with Cheeses*. Mabel didn't have to upload any more photos to conclude where at least several of the stolen paintings now resided—in John's storage unit.

A knock sent Barnacle barking and flinging himself at the kitchen door. Startled, Mabel looked up to see Lisa peering through the glass.

She jumped up to let her in.

"Didn't you get my text?" Lisa asked. "I've been sitting out there for over five minutes."

"No, I'm so sorry." Mabel looked at her phone. "I must've left it muted. I'm ready, though. Give me a second to grab my stuff."

Lisa glanced at the computer screen. She raised her eyebrows. "You planning on trying to supplement your income with reward money?"

"There's a reward?" Mabel froze, coat halfway on.

Lisa laughed. "Only a million bucks. Where have you been for the last year?"

"Not here," Mabel said. "I was still at the law firm in Pittsburgh when it happened, working ten hours a day, six days a week, trying to get ahead." *For all the good* that *did me.*

"Come on, let's go." Lisa tugged Mabel's sleeve. "We can talk in the car."

Mabel checked the animals' dishes and grabbed her phone, purse, and travel mug. She set the alarm and jogged to the car. Lisa was already waiting. The moment Mabel closed the passenger door, they started backing down the driveway.

"Okay. The reward," Lisa said. "Mabel. You were right there at the museum with me while Mr. Comstock was talking about it. Remember?"

Mabel frowned. "No." Good grief, was she losing her memory?

"The evening security guards were overpowered by three men who tied them up in the basement. They'd come in earlier, while the museum was still open, and hid till the place cleared out, undoubtedly with some inside assistance."

"I never heard any of that. It must've been while I was out talking to Danny in the lobby."

"Danny—I think he might've been one of the two guards that night," Lisa said.

"How did I never hear anything about this?"

"To be fair, you weren't living here. And you probably could've missed it, if you had a couple busy weeks and weren't paying a lot of attention to the news."

But John would've known. He'd said he had a "suspicion." He must've been thinking about this robbery.

"Comstock said the museum was beginning to lose hope the paintings would be safely returned, because they were too hot to sell, and too dangerous to hang onto. He also said they couldn't survive most ordinary storage, long term."

Mabel's mind raced. At this moment, John was holding onto stolen paintings with a million-dollar reward on them. With a bounty that high, what must they be worth? Two people who'd gotten hold of them before he did were now dead—three, if you counted Addison Winters. John was connected to both Mike and Amanda. Were the paintings safe? Was he safe?

Lisa had already moved on to chatter about her wedding plans. They were coming together rapidly, because, as Lisa said, fifty-year-old brides can't waste time planning extravaganzas two years out.

It was hard for Mabel to concentrate on anything but those paintings. She'd never dreamed they were *that* valuable. And here was John…apparently embroiled in grand theft, plus a double murder.

It now seemed clear the biggest danger to John wasn't being arrested. What if whoever killed Mike and Amanda now realized John had the paintings?

The killer must know, because where had they killed Amanda? Right in John's back yard.

As Lisa pulled into the parking lot in front of Dress to Kill, Mabel texted John.

The paintings stolen from Art Museum of Alleghenies! $1 million reward!!! Where are you?!

Women of all ages and sizes crowded the shop—mothers and daughters, girlfriends, salesclerks. Even crying toddlers and pouting little girls, being fitted for flower girl and first communion dresses. Mabel despised crowds, making this perhaps the worst possible place for her to be right now, as her panic over the paintings was escalating.

Lisa identified herself at the front counter. "Fielding wedding. My dress is on order? I brought my maid of honor for her fitting."

The woman behind the counter smiled and nodded. "Let's bring up your order. It will help the associate in coordinating your theme."

Moments later, a plump middle-aged saleswoman whisked Mabel and Lisa toward the back, while Mabel was checking her phone. John hadn't responded to her text.

"Would you ladies care for some coffee or tea? Or maybe a soft drink or bottle of water?"

Mabel shook her head. She didn't want anything to prolong the agony. Still, she ended up waiting for the clerk to locate a chilled bottle of water for Lisa.

"Would you please relax?" Lisa said. "You're making me nervous."

"I'm sorry. I can't help it," Mabel said.

"I know you don't like to shop, but this is important to me."

"It's not that. I—I'm worried about John."

Lisa laughed and patted her hand. "Don't worry. He'll propose one of these days."

Mabel stared at her. "I'm not worried about his proposing. It's—"

The clerk passed a bottled water to Lisa. "Please have a seat right here. Not you, dear," the woman told Mabel. "You and I are going to go grab a few dresses to model for your friend."

The next few minutes became a blur as the clerk suggested dresses and held them up against Mabel's chest, squinting as if she could already envision the fit. Mabel wasn't sure why, but she'd always found salesclerks—especially the ones selling women's clothing and cosmetics—very intimidating. Her mind immediately shut off, and she had a tendency to buy things she ended up hating the minute she got the bag to her car.

"All right, dear." The sales associate shepherded Mabel into a dressing room. "I'm going to hang these right here, and you can get started. Once you have the first one on, you can come on out and let your friend see how it looks. If it doesn't fit, give me a call, and I'll see if I can find it in another size for you, all right?"

As the door closed, Mabel eyed the collection of dresses with dread. Lisa's chosen colors were peach with mauve and sage accents. Peach was a great color for Lisa. It was less kind to Mabel.

She held up the first dress—a ballerina pouf of below-the-knee chiffon with a fitted strapless bodice. She would die a thousand deaths, walking down the aisle in that.

Maybe she should start with another dress and work her way up to the ghastly, orangey, poufy skirt that would make her hips look like she was being judged in the "biggest pumpkin" contest at the county fair. She checked the one behind it—silky, clingy, and shiny. Mabel could imagine the heads turning, checking to see if that big orange balloon coming at them was tethered to any handlers.

Finally, she took a deep breath and slipped one over her head. Of course, it didn't fit, and she had to call for assistance. And, of course, instead of bringing her the dress in another size, the clerk came running back with a foundation garment that would supposedly totally reshape the body the good Lord and a love of fried food had given Mabel. Even worse, she started trying to shove Mabel into it.

"Thanks, but no, thanks," Mabel said firmly, wriggling away. "If the body I've already got doesn't fit, it's a no go."

From the recesses of her purse, she heard her phone buzz.

"Excuse me a moment."

Mabel dug through her purse and came up with her cell. John had texted.

Yeah. I saw same re: the museum heist. With police. Will call later.

Mabel chewed at her lower lip. Should she ask if he'd been arrested?

"Shall we try this one?" The clerk shook the shiny, slinky dress at Mabel.

This was Lisa's day, Mabel reminded herself. Reluctantly, she put her phone back in her bag. John had said he'd call. She'd just have to wait.

After a horrifying hour, Lisa and the clerk decided on a simple tea-length dress with a fitted bodice, boat neckline, and bell skirt. It was not entirely flattering, given the color still made Mabel's complexion look like mud, but it was the least unflattering of the lot. Mabel tried not to wince as she passed over her credit card for the down payment. Lisa was her best friend, she reminded herself, and this was a once-in-a-lifetime occasion.

"Let's find you some shoes," Lisa said, right as Mabel was anticipating the sweet smell of freedom. If there was anything Mabel hated worse than clothes shopping, it was shoe shopping.

"Don't you make that face," Lisa said. "You don't like shopping. You don't like shoes. Your woman card should be revoked."

"Look, I don't want to be difficult, but I'm no good at choosing clothes or hairstyles. This is your big day. Why don't you pick out some shoes you think would work with the dress, and if they have them in my size, I promise I'm okay with it."

Lisa's face fell. "Well, all right. But that kind of sucks all the fun out of it."

Mabel felt a pang. "I'm sorry. My mind's somewhere else today, and here I am, ruining your wedding plans."

Lisa frowned. "Are you okay? Something's wrong, isn't it?"

Mabel started to say she was fine, but then realized Lisa truly was her closest friend. If anybody could understand, Lisa would.

"John's in a lot of trouble."

"Oh, honey, why didn't you say so? Do you want to talk about it?"

"Yeah, maybe." Mabel checked her phone again, but John hadn't sent any more messages. She forced a smile. "But let's find those shoes first, huh?"

Chapter Twenty-Six

"YOU WANT TO GRAB LUNCH SOMEWHERE?" Lisa shot Mabel a sidelong glance as she prepared to pull out of the parking lot.

"I don't know." Mabel checked her phone again. Still nothing.

"I know it was rough on you in there," Lisa said. "You were a trooper. Thanks."

Mabel forced herself to focus on her best friend. "I guess you're worth it. But this marriage better last because I am *not* doing this again."

Lisa laughed. "Promise." She pulled into the street. "Let me buy you lunch, okay?"

Mabel checked to make sure she had taken her phone off mute.

"Mabel." Lisa's voice drew her back. "Your uncharacteristic lack of interest in lunch has me a bit worried."

Mabel heaved a sigh, but it didn't relieve the hard spot in her chest. "I'm sorry. Lunch would be great."

"How about fish and chips at Old Tom's?"

"Sure."

Old Tom's sat along Cloud Lake, next to a small marina. It wasn't fancy, but it had a reputation for good fish, burgers, and steak. Its second greatest attribute was the outside deck, which afforded a spectacular view of the lake and opposite shoreline in the summer and early fall. By late fall, of course, the deck was long closed, despite the occasional unseasonably warm day.

Still, since the place wasn't as busy this time of year, Mabel and Lisa were able to grab one of the plank tables next to the big windows overlooking the water. With the sun glittering on the ripples, Mabel could almost imagine it was a July day—except for the mostly bare trees along the far shore.

They ordered their drinks and waved away menus, having already settled on fish and chips. A few men sat at the bar across the room, talking and glancing at the big screens mounted along the ceiling, which featured nonstop sports. A few other tables were occupied, but given the sprawling room, it felt as if Mabel and Lisa had private seating.

As she set her purse on the floor, Mabel casually checked her phone again.

"Go ahead and put it on the table," Lisa said. "I can see what you're doing."

Mabel groaned. And put her phone next to her place setting.

The waiter returned with their drinks. Mabel took a deep swallow of Coke.

"Okay, Mabel. Spill."

Mabel squirmed. She wasn't sure how to explain. Or how much she should share. But, after all, Lisa already knew about their finding the bodies. It wasn't that big a distance to the whole story.

Quickly, Mabel sketched out how Amanda had left John with the paintings. And about meeting Jamal at the storage facility. When she got to *Girl with Cheeses*, Lisa's eyes widened.

"Wait." Lisa held up one hand and darted a look around them. She leaned in and dropped her voice. "Are. You. Trying. To. Tell. Me…John has the stolen paintings from the art museum?" she hissed.

"Shh…yeah." Mabel gulped. "I think so."

Lisa sat back as the waitress approached with two sizzling plates of fish and chips. As soon as she'd walked away, Lisa shoved the food aside and inched her chair close to the table. "Mabel." Her voice was serious. "Are you completely sure—completely—that John is uninvolved in all this?"

Mabel's stomach flipped. She had never expected this reaction. "Lisa! Of course, I'm sure. John wouldn't…" Her voice trailed off. Wouldn't what?

"He wouldn't do any of this stuff." She waved an arm to include murders, art heists, and deceiving Mabel.

Lisa didn't say anything, but her face spoke volumes. Mabel read both pity and concern. Suddenly, the plate of fish lost its appeal.

"What would be his motive?" Mabel asked, maybe as much to herself as to Lisa. "He didn't know anything about the paintings. Amanda up and left them with him. We only heard later, from the guard at the storage facility, how she got them."

Lisa sighed. "Hear me out. And I'm only saying this because I care about you. If I've seen one case of a man with a secret life, I must've seen a hundred."

"*True Crime Solved*?"

"*True Crime Solved*…all the shows, really. *What I Didn't Know. Dead at the Altar. Crime Reports.* Several different podcasts. Woman brings home a new boyfriend. She's head over heels. At first, he charms everybody. Then after a while, things start to change."

"Nothing has changed," Mabel said through tight lips.

"Are you sure?" Lisa laid her hand over Mabel's.

Mabel pulled away. "He's exactly the same as always. And he has zero motive to kill anybody."

"Didn't you say that Mike guy cost him his license?"

"Temporarily. And John admits it was mostly his own fault."

"What about…money? How sure are you he didn't know about the paintings? Or the reward? That case got a good bit of publicity."

"Come on, Lisa. I was there when the paintings first showed up in his shed. I was there when he was trying to figure out what they were."

Lisa didn't respond. She picked up a fry and swirled it in the ketchup.

"He didn't know," Mabel said. "Besides which, he is not the type of person to kill anybody for money…or anything else."

"I understand. I like John—but try to remember we still don't know him all that well. Keep your wits about you, okay?" Lisa pushed Mabel's plate back toward her. "Your food's getting cold."

It did smell good. Reluctantly, Mabel picked up her fork. Maybe it would be better to give up and eat for a while, instead of trying to talk to Lisa about this. She didn't know whether to be upset with Lisa—or admit she had a valid point.

Lisa passed the malt vinegar. "Are you mad?"

"No. It's all just super upsetting. To tell the truth, I'm most worried the killer might come after John."

Lisa's eyes widened. "Well, now the police are in the loop, maybe that won't be a problem anymore."

"If the killer realizes that fact. I wonder what's going on. Wouldn't you think the police would remove the paintings from storage and at least hold them as evidence?"

"Oh, right. They're stolen property, but I bet the police won't return them to the museum right away—"

"Because they're evidence in a homicide," Mabel concluded. "Two homicides."

Mabel's phone rang. She jumped. John's ringtone.

She fumbled for it.

"Hey, where are you right now?"

She told him. "Are you okay?"

"I'm fine. I'm over at the storage locker with the police right now, and they're taking the paintings down to the station. Someone from the museum will be coming over to authenticate them and work out proper storage for the time being."

"Are you still a suspect?"

"Of course. But don't worry about it. I think we'll flush out the killer—especially now the police are confiscating the paintings."

"Will that be publicized?"

"I don't know how they'll play it," John said.

Mabel hesitated, then asked the other question gnawing at her mind. "Do you think they'll give you the reward?"

"I'm not even going there right now. The main thing is getting Amanda's murderer behind bars—and I want my license back."

"Right." Still, the thought of a million dollars was awfully hard to push entirely out of her mind.

"Will I see you later?" she asked.

"Maybe. I'm not sure when the police will be done with me, so I can't give you a definite time."

"Come on over when you can then. I can, uh, make dinner."

John laughed. She might have been offended, if she hadn't known she wasn't much of a cook.

"Go ahead and eat when you're ready, if I'm not there, and I'll pick something up on my way."

When she didn't immediately say anything, he cleared his throat. "I've got to go. How about I bring dessert?"

"What kind?"

He laughed again. "Let me surprise you."

When Mabel got home, Barnacle met her at the back door, transported by joy over her return. She supposed he could never be sure whether she was merely going to the mailbox or leaving him forever. Koi sat beside her empty dish, fixed Mabel with a pointed look, and delivered a soft but firm meow.

"Guys—let me get inside." She shoved at Barnacle, who pawed at her and danced on his hind legs. As soon as she'd set her purse down, she clipped him to the run-out cable. Then, she apologized to Koi and grabbed the animals' bowls.

Barnacle wasn't due to be fed till evening, but Koi liked to graze all day. Undoubtedly, Barnacle had cleaned up her breakfast leftovers, so Mabel refilled her bowl and tossed a few kibbles into the dog bowl too. Both animals had a strict sense of fairness, and would never tolerate an empty bowl while the other was being fed.

It grew dark and Mabel switched on the table lamp. Dinner hour passed. She rummaged through the fridge and located her leftover mac-and-cheese. While it reheated, Mabel dug out some printer paper and began creating a bubble diagram. It felt like the only way she could visualize all the suspects and the evidence in a logical way.

After scribbling a while, she sat back and stretched, still horribly confused. There were two murders—Mike and Amanda. An art theft. It seemed highly unlikely that Amanda and Mike both were involved with the paintings without a direct link back to the theft. And both ended up dead.

The art theft came first. Over a year ago. Who could've been involved? It came down to a few likely suspects.

Mike already had a criminal record, and he'd worked at the bar right across from the museum and hung out with the guards.

Amanda, the art major, ultimately ended up with the paintings...at least, till she got herself killed and they landed with John. But if, as Lisa had said, Amanda's old boyfriend Danny was one of the guards who'd gotten tied up by the robbers, he'd surely have recognized Amanda. In the unlikely event she'd been one of them.

Was one of the robbers female? No, Lisa said Phil from the museum had specifically told her there were three men.

Anyway, Danny obviously would have known Mike too. Did that eliminate Mike, as well? Or did it suggest Danny was in on it?

Danny's being tied up didn't necessarily clear him. Lisa said the police suspected someone with inside information or connections had set up the theft. Danny, as well as Addison Winters, could have told the robbers when it was safe to come to the museum, let them inside, and helped them hide when they got there.

He might even have set aside his differences with Mike—or even Amanda—and been working with them. Over a million dollars' worth of art might erase a few hurt feelings. But he loved art...and of course, so had Amanda. Would either have risked damage to something irreplaceable like *Girl with Cheeses*?

Or had one of them coveted the Vermeer—or another of the pictures, like the possible Rembrandt—enough to steal and possess it?

Mabel scribbled some more. Okay. Either Mike or Amanda—or both—could have been involved in the theft without being on the premises. They could've fed inside information, which they'd picked up from Danny or the other guards, to the robbers.

Whether or not Danny took part, common sense said the late security guard, Addison Winters—who ended up dead with the hot paintings in his storage locker—had been involved.

Finally, they had Vin, a notorious criminal and more likely

ringleader than Mike or Winters. And he'd ended up with the stolen art when he outbid all comers for the storage contents. Jamal had told them Vin wasn't one of their regular bidders—but he'd clearly wanted the contents of these units badly. Mabel put checks next to him and Addison Winters. Both were definites, in her opinion—but who else had they been working with?

Vin reputedly never wanted to get his own hands dirty. So, assume he'd planned this thing—probably, as John said, on behalf of someone even higher up—and sent his underlings in. The vibes Perdue gave off when she'd mentioned Mike's name suggested this was another job Mike had somehow been involved in.

She scowled. If Mike had participated in the heist, he darn sure would've noticed Amanda's pilferage from the storage unit.

Who had killed Mike? And why? At this point, it looked like it had more to do with the art theft than his womanizing.

Suppose while working for Vin, Mike had helped himself to a few paintings—or Vin thought he did—and Vin found out? Anybody who'd set up an arson would hardly balk at murder.

But...

Mabel was relieved when John's headlights flashed outside her kitchen windows. She couldn't wait to see him and learn what the police said. Maybe together they could make sense of all these suspects and motives.

He came inside carrying a pecan pie and a half gallon of vanilla ice cream, which she knew was a lot richer than what John normally ate. She wondered whether it was for her—or if spending hours with the police had driven him to a sugar and fat binge. Mabel cleared a spot, and he set it on the kitchen table before giving her a hug. She rested her cheek against his cool jacket shoulder, as he patted her back.

Mabel searched his face. "You okay?"

John nodded but didn't quite meet her eyes. "Tired, that's all. Ready for dessert?"

"Sure." Mabel was always ready for dessert–but not ready to drop the subject.

While she got out plates and forks, John opened the pie and ice cream. She handed him serving utensils.

"Tell me what happened. Did you call the police or…?"

"Did they slap the cuffs on me?" He grinned and passed her a skinny slice of pie topped with a small glob of ice cream.

"Of course not!" Mabel waited, listening all the same.

He took pity. "No, I still walk the earth a free man. I called them right away, once I was pretty sure the paintings were from the AMA heist."

"That should show your innocence."

He shrugged. "They still questioned me for over an hour. I think they suspect I was using the artwork to divert from the murders."

Mabel set her plate down. "Without a lawyer? Why did you let them do that?"

"I want to help—I don't have anything to hide. I want answers too."

Mabel couldn't believe what she was hearing. "That doesn't matter. You know better. Don't you ever do that again."

John put the ice cream in Mabel's freezer. She sadly watched it go. Then he calmly sat himself down with his tiny sliver of pie and dab of ice cream. "Like I said, I want to help solve this thing."

Mabel took a bite of her sample-size dessert and immediately regretted not dishing up her own serving. "They're solving it, all right," she said dryly. "But you may not like their solution."

"That's why we're helping them out."

"How? What more can we do? We can bet Mike—and maybe Amanda—were involved in the heist, one way or another. But they're both dead. So is Addison Winters. Unless somebody else was involved we don't even know about, I think we're down to Vin—and maybe Danny—for their murders."

"You don't think Chad or Buffy could've killed Mike out of jealousy?" A smile twitched at the corner of his mouth.

"Of course. But I don't think it makes sense all these unrelated crimes are going on, and then they end up coming together that way."

"And you don't see any possible connection between Chad and the art theft, I take it?"

Mabel had never considered that. "He's a rich lawyer."

"People aren't always as rich as they appear. For all we know, he could be up to his eyeteeth in debt."

"Of course. But an art heist is complicated to pull off, and the return's iffy. People like him, in my experience, have easier ways of getting money. Like ripping off their clients or committing insurance or tax fraud."

"I bow to your superior knowledge of crooked lawyers."

Mabel threw up her hands. "Hey, I knew some crooks."

John reached for her empty plate. "Can I rinse that for you?"

Involuntarily, Mabel's eyes drifted to the fridge.

John laughed. "You want another smidge?"

Mabel jumped up. "You stay there and relax. I'll get it."

John winked, obviously aware she wanted to control her own portion size. Barnacle crawled out from under the table and looked at her plate with longing.

She placed the knife to carve off another narrow slice, but after a furtive backward glance, moved the knife to make it a smidge larger. Once she'd covered it with ice cream, it wouldn't look so bad. Naturally, sufficient coverage might require a slightly more generous scoop of ice cream.

When she plopped back down at the table, she asked, "What's next?"

He considered. "Well, my instincts tell me Vin's the most likely candidate for multiple murders."

"Except," Mabel said, and licked ice cream off her fork, "he's not really a do-it-yourself kind of guy."

John shook his head. "No, I have to agree. In fact, if Mike were still alive, he'd probably be the most likely candidate for Vin's hired gun."

"Danny struck me as awfully wimpy to have killed two people," Mabel said. "Goodness knows I've been wrong before, but he seems like a typical grad student to me."

John shrugged. "Maybe yes, maybe no."

"Are we boxing ourselves in?" Mabel asked. "I mean we're presuming we've already talked to the murderer, and isn't it possible there's somebody else out there we missed?"

He slowly shook his head. "I did a lot of snooping around and sure, there may very well be another murderer out there, but if so, I think he was most likely working for Vin."

Mabel ate in silence, digesting what he'd said. After scraping the last crumb from the plate, she sighed and laid down her fork. "Back to Perdue, then?"

John nodded. "Everything fits. He's a known criminal, and he worked with Mike—likely even in connection with this art theft. Mike helps himself to some of the stolen artwork—or Vin thinks he has when Amanda absconds. Which is the likelier scenario, given what Jamal told us. If Mike had his hand in there, he'd darn well have known how many pieces of art there were and noticed what was missing. Hence, I'm guessing his involvement was probably grunt level, like transporting the loot without any real clue what he had.

"One of Vin's hired thugs comes after Mike. Maybe Mike is carrying—he has a permit, not that it probably would've mattered to him. Things go bad, and Mike ends up dead."

Mabel chewed her lip. "Don't forget all the other reasons Perdue might've wanted to take Mike out either… like eliminating a witness to his crimes, especially the arson. Or maybe getting rid of a blackmailer. But what was Mike doing up on the mountain? And what about Amanda—why was she killed?"

"I have no idea why he was up there unless he was lured somehow. As for Amanda? Mike probably threw her under the bus, don't you think?"

"Yeah." Mabel heaved a sigh. "He'd been stalking her when you were working for her. You saw that firsthand. Once he caught up to her, looks like she ran—and kept the paintings with her. Do you think she planned to sell them?"

He shrugged. "I'd guess yes, but she was a nut about art, so anything's possible. Maybe she planned to line her walls with it and have a secret private art gallery."

"Would she be willing to die for that?"

"I doubt dying was part of the plan."

"No, I guess not." She placed her chin on her hand and thought for a moment. "If Vin's the most likely suspect, how do we prove it?"

He tweaked her nose. "There's no 'we' here, darlin'."

Mabel considered objecting to preserve her street cred, but she really didn't want to. "Are you going to talk to him?"

He shook his head. "Not before I get a better idea of how likely he was to mastermind an art heist, who all he was involved with, and where he might've been when the murders occurred."

"I thought we agreed he'd likely have paid someone else to bump them off."

John shrugged. "Depends how it went down. Whether or not it was planned."

Mabel yawned. She was feeling a bit dizzy with exhaustion.

John got up. "Hey, you need to get to bed. For that matter, so do I." He gathered plates and forks. "Lock the door after me, and don't forget your alarm. I'll call you tomorrow."

Mabel couldn't help smiling, as Koi jumped to the counter and settled herself to lap ice cream puddles from the top plate as Barnacle sat and whined below. She trailed John to the kitchen door, where he pulled her to him.

"This will soon be over. We're close. I can feel it." He brushed back her hair and kissed her forehead.

She hoped he was right, but she didn't feel much closer to an answer than when they'd started.

231

Chapter Twenty-Seven

MONDAY AFTERNOON, MABEL UNLOCKED JOHN'S BACK door with the key he'd dropped off that morning. It felt weird, entering his house when he wasn't there. She paused at the security keypad to punch in the numbers he'd given her.

Mabel stood a moment in the tidy kitchen. Smells of coffee, toast, and a whiff of lemon lingered.

Apart from the low hum of the fridge and a small creak, probably due to the house's settling, silence filled the air. It had a muffled, almost physically stuffy quality.

She glanced at the clock above the sink. By now, John should be in Wilkie, or somewhere beyond. When he'd called, he told her he had a lead on someone who claimed firsthand knowledge of the arson, and conceivably also the museum heist. He wanted to run the guy down as soon as possible, and she'd been his second call. The first had been to his regular sub at the college, who'd agreed to proctor his scheduled exam.

Mabel set her purse on the table with a wary eye out for Billie Jean. She'd only ever had one marginally positive interaction with the hate-filled cat.

"I hate to ask you this," John had said, "but she needs medication three times a day, and I'm going to miss the afternoon dose. You don't need to handle her."

This had been purely academic information, since Mabel couldn't "handle" Billie Jean in any way, shape, or form, whether she needed it or not.

"All you have to do is mix five units with some tuna and leave the room. She'll eat it. Most likely."

The floor tiles creaked as Mabel checked the fridge, then the lazy

Susan cabinet below the counter, searching for tuna. She found a can—water-packed, of course, which was why John didn't have an ounce of extra fat on his body. The medicine and oral syringe sat on the counter, and Billie Jean's dishes were on a vinyl placemat in the corner.

Mabel mixed the potion, casting an apprehensive look over her shoulder for signs of the cat. Odd she still hadn't appeared, whether to attack Mabel or come investigate the sound and smell of the tuna can being opened.

Mabel looked up, half-expecting to see the cat crouched atop the fridge, poised to launch herself downward in a tempest of teeth and claws. Nothing.

Billie Jean was the Mary Higgins Clark of feline suspense.

Mabel covered the leftover tuna with foil and set it inside a nearly empty fridge, then put the spoon into the dishwasher basket. She hesitated, jingling her keys.

Two thoughts bounced around her brain. One, unworthy though it might be, was that this was a perfect opportunity to snoop a bit. The other salved her conscience quite nicely. What if Billie Jean had been accidentally shut inside a bedroom or closet somewhere? She'd not only be missing her medication, but likely her litter box, as well.

She'd better check, to be sure.

Mabel wandered through the downstairs, casually scanning the reading material next to John's armchair...biographies, socio-political nonfiction, and a couple Carl Hiaasen crime novels. She wondered if he had any hesitation, choosing between Chernobyl, Theodore Roosevelt, or Hiaasen for bedtime reading. She wouldn't.

Was there a book on his nightstand?

"Here, kitty, kitty. Billie Jean?" Mabel tried to make her voice friendly and inviting. She hoped she wouldn't scream if Billie Jean flew out of hiding.

John's vintage oak desk was orderly. The blotter, a relic of fountain pen days, held a pewter mug full of colorful gimme pens emblazoned with names of local banks, car dealers, and other businesses. Papers sat corralled in a wooden inbox. John's holster, she couldn't help noticing, was missing from the back of the desk chair. She knew he kept another, unloaded weapon, a wartime relic of his father's, in that old Cuban cigar box on the bookshelf. No need to snoop there.

She wasn't really snooping, she assured herself. She was looking for the cat. Firmly, Mabel averted her eyes from the file drawers. Obviously, no cat there.

Casting a glance around, as if John might be capturing all her movements on a nanny cam, she jiggled a desk drawer. Locked. She jerked her hand back. Just because she hadn't seen a hidden camera didn't mean there wasn't one. After all, "hidden" implied not readily visible, and John was a pro.

Exaggerating her movements for the benefit of the camera that was possibly there, Mabel peered under the couch, one arm up in a defensive posture in case Billie Jean actually lay in wait there. She shone her cellphone light all around, but the cat was nowhere to be seen.

"Billie Jean?"

There were two doors in the entry. Mabel checked the small closet. A couple of coats and umbrellas, and one pair of winter boots. John's house was remarkable for its sheer quantity of unused space. The other door, which she guessed led to the basement, was locked.

Oh, well. Not much choice but to head upstairs, she told herself.

Trailing one hand over the polished banister, she climbed the creaking stairs. As she climbed, Mabel felt a prickle of apprehension, knowing Billie Jean was undoubtedly lurking somewhere unexpected, ready to attack when Mabel was least prepared.

The bungalow was one-and-a-half stories, with sloping ceilings on the second floor. As she reached the top of the steps, Mabel paused to scan the two small bedrooms on either side. The sparsely furnished room to the left, visible through a partially open door, appeared to be a spare room. The other must be John's bedroom. That door was closed, so possibly Billie Jean had been accidentally trapped inside.

Curious about John's private sanctum—and of course, anxious

too, to liberate the cat—Mabel eased open the door. She could imagine herself living here...if she and John ever did, well, get married. It was such a cute little house, and perfect in every way.

John's bed was a full-size, obviously vintage, in a heavy, dark walnut frame. A red-and-white quilt in double wedding ring pattern was topped by white pillows. Mabel ran her hand over the worn fabric. Had it come down through his family?

Billie Jean was forgotten as Mabel crept over to inspect the nightstand.

Her hand was still extended toward the night table when impulsively, she drew it back, kicked off her moccasins and stretched out, eyes closed, on the bed. John's bed. Where he presumably dreamed of her.

Mid-sigh, she remembered the ever-present threat of Billie Jean, and her eyes flew open.

As they did, a door shut with an audible clack.

Mabel thrashed upright, expecting a whirlwind of fur and claws, which didn't come.

She turned to the bedroom door. Her eyes widened at the sight of a pistol, leveled right at her. Her heart thudded. Buffy Westermann's gun hand was rock steady. Calm and unsmiling, Buffy met Mabel's eyes.

"Paintings?" Buffy asked, in the same flat tone she might have used to inquire as to the whereabouts of the bathroom. She was beautifully dressed for the occasion, in what appeared to be a coral cashmere tee, perfectly fitted jeans and buttery soft-looking leather jacket.

Mabel was nowhere near as calm as Buffy seemed to be, and her brain refused to process information. "How did you get in here?"

Mabel heard a click—was the safety being released, or whatever one did to prepare to shoot? She swallowed hard and coughed on her spit.

"I know your partner has the paintings, so where are they?"

"Partner? You mean John?"

Buffy took a step closer. "That's whose house this is, so yeah. Your detective partner. Where did he put them? I don't have all day."

What little active gray matter Mabel could summon churned uncomfortably. She could identify Buffy. Therefore, Buffy was not going to leave her alive.

"The museum paintings?" Mabel asked, stalling for time because she had no other options.

"Yes," Buffy hissed. "The museum paintings. I need them."

"The police have them."

Something flickered in Buffy's cool eyes. "Nice try, but I doubt that."

Mabel shifted. She was sitting on the bed, and her right leg was cramping, but she was afraid to make any abrupt moves. "It's the truth." She eyed Buffy. "What makes you think John would have them?"

"I know he has them, so let's skip all this. Take me to them, and I can get going."

Buffy had closed the distance to John's bed. "Now." She prodded Mabel's shoulder with the gun barrel. "Move it."

Mabel staggered to her feet. Her right leg was now asleep, pins and needles all but collapsing her. Still barefoot, she hobbled ahead of Buffy's gun, feeling like a lurching ogre next to her sleek captor, who looked remarkably like a sexy Bond villain.

Desperate, Mabel tried to think. She couldn't take Buffy to the paintings because they weren't there. If she could get to John's antique pistol, maybe she could bluff Buffy into dropping hers. If the Shawnee County PD didn't have it too…

The stairs were agony.

"Pick up your feet."

"I can't. My leg fell asleep." Mabel looked back. "Why are you doing this? You don't need money."

Buffy snorted and gave her a shove that nearly sent her tumbling. Mabel caught the railing. "You have no idea what I need."

None of this made any sense. Mabel paused again, gripping the banister. "Are you trying to leave Chad?"

"What are you talking about? Move it."

Mabel stumbled the last couple steps and caught the newel post to steady herself. She hobbled around to face Buffy. "I mean it's obvious Chad's loaded. Unless you're planning to split, why would you need to commit armed robbery for hot artwork?"

Buffy stepped up to Mabel and jammed the gun into her stomach. "You may like playing detective, but this isn't a police interrogation, so shut up." Buffy had appeared cool, but close up, Mabel could see the sweat beaded on her forehead and upper lip.

Mabel's mind raced. Buffy had barely been on her suspect list. What was going on? How had she gotten into the house? Where would she leave Mabel's body? Would John come home and find her?

"This way." Mabel slowly turned. She knew she was postponing the inevitable blast of gunfire and hoped she'd die at once. She endorsed Woody Allen's famous statement that he wasn't afraid to die—he just didn't want to be there at the time.

Mabel's glance flicked over the gun. It was still aimed right at her.

"No sudden moves. My trigger finger's getting tired." Buffy's wrist, Mabel now noticed, had deep-looking scratches. Had she already killed Billie Jean?

Mabel needed that antique gun, to have even the slimmest chance of bluffing her way out of this. How could she do this? Buffy was not going to believe John had hidden several paintings in a cigar box. Considering Buffy was more nervous than she'd first appeared, was she nervous enough to shoot?

"Over here." Mabel gestured. "Th-there's a secret panel behind the bookshelves."

Steady. Even Mabel could tell she didn't sound convincing.

In her agitation, Buffy seemed not to notice. She motioned impatiently with the gun. "No sudden moves. Get that panel open."

Trying to move smoothly, Mabel stepped between John's desk and the bookshelves. Her heartbeat crashed in her ears as she reached toward the cigar box with its bright image of a leaping tiger.

To her despair, Buffy pressed close, still wielding the gun at gut level.

I'm going to die. How could she grab the weapon and turn it on Buffy without making any sudden moves? Buffy believed the paintings were two feet away at this point. She'd no longer feel the need to keep Mabel alive, if Mabel became problematic.

"The switch is hidden in here." Even as she said it, Mabel thought Buffy would have to be pretty dumb to fall for that.

It felt as if her chest would explode. Mabel eased her hand toward the box lid. If only she had self-defense skills, maybe she could spin around and kick that gun right out of Buffy's hand.

But she didn't.

Please come home, John. Please bring him home, she silently prayed, though she knew that was highly unlikely.

As her fingertips touched the smooth, paper cigar-box label, a booming knock shook the front door. Mabel jerked back. She screamed, but it came out in a squeak.

Buffy spun toward the door, and the gun no longer pointed at Mabel's stomach.

The booming continued, and a furious male voice demanded, "Open this door! Buffy! Come out of there!"

An expletive erupted from Buffy's perfect coral lips. Her smooth veneer cracked, and she seemed to lose all interest in Mabel or the paintings.

Seizing her chance, Mabel ducked around the far end of the desk and bolted for the back door. To her shock, Buffy chose the same moment. And the same escape route.

They collided in the kitchen entry in a flailing of arms. Mabel's breath left her body in a whoosh on impact.

Skinny as Buffy was, she was insanely strong. She shoved Mabel backward, still gasping for breath, as they scrambled toward the outside door.

Mabel might've let her go, if she hadn't been as terrified of the man outside, now throwing his full body weight against the front door in an apparent attempt to break it down. Buffy's obvious fear, despite the fact she was armed, fed Mabel's adrenaline. She didn't want to be the closest target in the line of fire if that door gave way.

Mabel clawed at Buffy, trying to reach the freedom of the back yard. Buffy popped through the overcrowded kitchen entry like a liberated champagne cork, stumbled, and crashed to the floor, taking Mabel with her.

With a stream of unladylike profanity, Buffy broke free.

All of a sudden, the front door burst open, as the frame cracked and splintered at the hinges. Chad Westermann burst through with the intensity of an enraged bull.

"Buffy," he snapped, "stop right there or I'll stop you myself."

Buffy hesitated, then turned back, pistol dangling from a limp hand. Her eyes were calculating.

Chad cast a glance at Mabel, still panting for breath on the kitchen floor. "What is this?" he snarled. "A threesome?"

Mabel wanted to say something indignant and scathing, but her mouth opened and closed, and her lungs refused to join the team.

Chad shook his head, still staring at Mabel. "What a dog."

Mabel narrowed her eyes in a glare, but he didn't seem to notice.

He looked back at Buffy. He was breathing hard. "Where is he?"

"Don't be silly." Buffy managed a smile. "It's nothing like that. Let's sit down and I can explain."

Mabel, recovering her wits, scooted backward toward the corner behind the built-in breakfast bar. Her forgotten cellphone fell from a hip pocket and with fumbling fingers, she scooped it up and dialed 911.

Buffy and Chad were too focused on each other to pay her any attention.

"Where's the sleaze ball hiding? Too scared to come to your rescue." He sneered. "Is he in here?"

Chad threw open the pantry door and a furious Billie Jean exploded forth.

Chapter Twenty-Eight

BILLIE JEAN RACED BETWEEN CHAD'S LEGS and crashed headlong into Buffy. The agitated cat yowled and slashed at Buffy's pantlegs.

Buffy yelped and clutched at her left leg. Billie Jean had managed to hook a claw into the denim and was thrashing, trying to pull it out. From Buffy's shrieks, Mabel could only assume Billie Jean had also hooked flesh.

Buffy let her gun drop with a thud and clutched at the captive paw, trying to release it. Then her scream shot up an octave and she frantically shook her left leg and right hand, which was gushing blood.

"She bit right through my hand," Buffy wailed.

Chad ignored his wife's cries and stormed up the staircase, in apparent search of John.

"Are you there?" a female voice came through the phone. "911. What's your emergency?"

Transfixed by the feline-human drama, Mabel had forgotten she'd dialed the phone. In a few words, she reported her location and that she was dealing with an armed intruder. The rest of the story would have to wait.

Cautiously, she crept forward and snatched the gun, then faded back into her corner. Billie Jean had freed herself from Buffy's pantleg and stalked queenlike toward her food, plume of tail blown out to majestic proportions and waving behind her.

For once, the cat showed no interest in attacking Mabel...perhaps since she'd already drawn her quota of blood for the day. She paraded by and sniffed her dish of tuna.

Billie Jean's lip curled in the characteristic feline response to rank smells, and she began scratching the floor as if to cover a litter box deposit. She turned and hissed at Mabel.

"Sorry!" Mabel found herself apologizing to the cat. "It's tuna. You like tuna. And maybe a little bit of medicine. It's good for you."

Buffy bypassed the roll of paper towels by the sink and grabbed John's clean dish towel to wrap her bleeding hand. She paid no attention to Mabel, if she saw her at all, and didn't pause to look for her gun. After a hesitating glance toward the staircase, and the swearing and banging sounds from upstairs, Buffy whirled and slipped out the back door.

Mabel wavered only a moment between following Buffy's lead or confronting Chad. The police were coming, and meanwhile, self-preservation was job one.

The back yard was already empty. Mabel slunk around front to watch for the police. Chad's massive Escalade now blocked her car.

She laid the gun in the grass next to the driveway and dialed her phone. John picked up on the second ring, at the same time Mabel heard the brief blast of a squad car siren. The police must not want to stampede the intruder, she thought, and were only using the siren as needed, to speed through intersections.

"Where are you?" she asked.

"On my way home. Be there in about half an hour. I got some good info on Perdue."

Mabel jumped back as a speeding cruiser squealed up to the curb, blocking the Escalade. "Hey, I've gotta go. Can't talk right now, but we've had an incident at the house. Uh, your house."

Over John's sputtering, she assured him she was fine, the cat was fine, the house was fine. For the most part. She clicked her phone off and stuffed it into her pocket as two male officers poured out of the cruiser, guns drawn, but to her relief, pointed downward.

"You the homeowner?" asked the cop tagged Domingues.

"No, I was cat sitting."

"Did you call 911?"

"Yes."

"Intruder still in there?" The other officer, whose tag read Federovich, nodded toward the house.

"One is." Mabel pointed as Chad's face appeared in the upstairs hall window. Domingues seemed to spot him the same time she did. "Back here and stay down," he told Mabel, pulling her behind the cruiser.

A second police car, and then a third, skidded into position.

Wow. More officers, two in bulky Kevlar and helmets, emerged. The Bartle County Sheriff and Bartles Grove PD had responded along with Medicine Spring.

"The intruder's armed?" Federovich asked.

"I'm not sure." She took a tentative step back toward the yard, to pick up the gun.

"Stop right there," a female voice ordered.

Mabel realized she was a potential suspect herself until she'd been cleared. "I was going to pick up the gun over there. The second intruder dropped it when she ran."

"I'll handle that."

Police were circling the house. Chad's face had disappeared from the window.

The sheriff's deputy, who'd taken custody of Buffy's gun, questioned Mabel, keeping one eye on the house. Mabel gave her the basic information, trying without a lot of success, to condense.

An officer banged on the broken doorframe. "Police. Come out with your hands up."

"I'm coming out, I'm coming out," Chad said, his voice higher than Mabel had ever heard it.

Mabel raised a cautious eye to the cruiser's side window as Chad emerged through John's mangled front doorway, sweating and blustering. Unless Buffy reappeared, waving another firearm, it was probably safe to get up.

"She knows what's going on," Chad growled, pointing a shaking finger at Mabel as she tried to straighten her stiff knees. "Tell them."

"Both hands on the hood of the cruiser," one of the county cops told him, as another deputy moved in to pat Chad down.

"I'm Chad Westermann. Take your hands off me. I need to pull out my ID."

"On the hood, I said. I'll get your wallet."

"I'm Chad Westermann." He repeated his name slowly and loudly, but the officers seemed to pay no attention. "Westermann. Are none of you hearing me? Call the police chief—he'll explain it to you."

A grizzled older officer raised an eyebrow. "Seeing as the chief's nowhere around here, maybe we ought to ask her like you said first." He jerked a thumb toward Mabel.

"Idiot," Chad sputtered. "Chief DeRoy will explain to you who *I* am."

"Doesn't really matter at the moment." The older cop pointed. "Over there, sir."

Mabel and Chad were separated for questioning, while the few neighbors home at midday came out onto their porches to watch and take pictures and video. It wasn't long before a WXAT chopper was hovering over the scene.

Looks like I'm going to be on Country Morning again.

The sheriff's car was first to disperse, and moments later, John pulled into the vacated spot. He burst from his car and looked around rather wild-eyed at police, news copters, neighbors, and his busted door, before his gaze settled on Mabel.

"Homeowner," John said, hands in the air. "What the devil's going on here?"

Chad emitted the sound of an enraged bull and lunged in John's direction.

"That does it, buddy. We'll finish with you at the station." Federovich shoved Chad against the cruiser and cuffed him.

"You're arresting me? On what charges? Do you know who I am?"

"Disorderly for now," Domingues said. "And yeah, we know. You already told us like ten times."

Chad dug in his feet and tossed his head in John's direction. "He's fooling around with my wife. I'm gonna kill you!"

"Resisting," Domingues said. It took both officers to stuff Chad into the back of the squad car.

"What's that lunatic talking about?" John cast a bemused glance at his wide-eyed neighbors. "I don't even know his wife," he assured them.

He gestured at the house. "What happened to my door?"

Mabel shifted her feet. He had trusted her to medicate his cat, and now his house was trashed, his reputation on the block was ruined, and Billie Jean had never even taken her medicine.

"It's kind of a long story."

Chapter Twenty-Nine

BY LATE AFTERNOON, THE POLICE WERE through with Mabel and John, the neighbors had scattered, and John had made a rough job of sealing the hole in his front door. "At least, I know Chad can afford to replace it." He stacked his tools on the porch to be carried back to the shed later.

Mabel sat on the porch swing, one foot tucked up and the other dangling. Restless, she was using it to push herself back and forth. "I'm so sorry," she repeated. "Your poor house. Your flowers…" The police had trampled the once-perky rows of red geraniums lining the front walkway.

John shrugged with apparent nonchalance, but not before she'd seen him grimace. "Not your fault. The frost will soon take them, anyway."

Though the evening was mild for late fall, she knew he was right. It made her feel a little better, but still…

John sat, and the swing creaked and settled a bit lower as he pulled one end of the red-plaid fleece blanket over his lap and put an arm around Mabel's shoulders. "I'm the one who should apologize. I feel like ten times a fool for letting you walk into that situation. I was too quick to write off Buffy. And I put way too much trust in my security system."

"Why would you suspect Buffy of being anything but a rich, bored housewife?"

He glared at the wreckage of his geraniums. "There was a clue somewhere. There always is. I just didn't see it."

"Do you think she killed Mike and Amanda too?"

"I wouldn't be surprised if the ballistics come back to her gun. How did she connect me with those stolen paintings? If we knew that, and why she was so hot to get her hands on them, maybe we'd have a better idea."

"She was planning on leaving Chad, I think."

"There's got to be more to it than that. Even if they had an oppressive prenup, armed robbery is plain nuts."

"You think they'll find her?"

"Sure. They already found her car a couple blocks over. She's going to need money if she goes on the run, so they'll watch her bank accounts—and her phone. But if she's smart, she'll switch to a burner."

Mabel's thoughts drifted back to the day's biggest loss, at least from John's perspective. "I'm sorry about Billie Jean."

He tweaked the end of her nose. "It's the Westermanns' fault for leaving my back door open and busting a hole in the front. She'll be back when she stops being mad."

Mabel remembered following Buffy out the back door. If it had been left open, it was Mabel's fault. She swallowed the words and said a silent prayer for the evil cat's return. "She probably saved my life. If she hadn't attacked when she did, Buffy could still have turned around and shot me. She wasn't going to leave a witness."

"She took better care of you than I did," John said. "You're what matters. Don't worry about her—she'll be back. It's not the first time she's taken off."

Mabel was torn. She didn't want to leave John with his ransacked house and missing cat, but she'd been gone all day. Someone had to feed her animals and give Barnacle his long-overdue constitutional.

"Look, I've got to get home now, but do you want to come over for dinner?"

He kissed her forehead. "I'd love to, but I need to hop online and see what I can find out about Buffy Westermann."

"But you never told me what you found out about Vin Perdue."

"Right now, I feel like Buffy's more important. She connects to both Mike and the stolen paintings, as much as Perdue does. We can talk tomorrow. I'll buy you breakfast at the Coffee Cup if you'd like."

"Okay." Mabel accepted his hug without a lot of enthusiasm. She never turned down breakfast, but she still felt disappointed, and maybe a bit blown off.

Locked in her car, she considered texting Lisa, but it was late enough now that maybe she'd be home. Mabel dialed.

"Hi, what's up?"

"Are you home? Can I come over for a bit? I need to talk."

As she drove away, she felt the neighbors' eyes following her.

That evening, while eating a therapeutic bowl of cherry-vanilla ice cream, she saw herself on WXAT's evening news. The aerial footage from the station chopper showed Mabel as a small, disheveled figure crouched behind a police cruiser. Her phone started ringing during the segment and continued after it had ended.

While she'd turned down Lisa's offer of a place to camp overnight, she was glad she'd taken time to drive over and see her earlier. Mabel ignored the calls from reporters, as she'd waved away the microphones shoved in her face in front of John's house earlier despite knowing interviews would probably be good PR for her book. She sighed at the other caller IDs—her sister Jen, both Nanette and Cora from the historical society, and at last, her mother. She had to pick that one up, or she knew either the police or her longsuffering father would soon be on her doorstep for a wellness check.

"Again?" Mom sputtered the instant Mabel answered. "Are you all right?"

Mom never waited for a reply till she ran out of steam, so Mabel waited, gnawing on her lower lip.

"What on earth do you think you're doing, tangling with armed intruders? Are you *trying* to get yourself killed? Or is this some stunt for that murder book you think you're writing?"

Mabel cleared her throat, but Mom bulldozed right over her. "Your dad will be over there in about an hour. Now, no excuses. That woman's still on the loose. You'll be safe here. Just pack an overnight bag for now, all right? I'm making a pan of sticky buns for breakfast. How does that sound?"

"Mom." Mabel finally broke through her mother's sales pitch. "Look. I can't leave right now. I have my animals here— No, I'm not bringing them over there. I'm in no danger. The woman who broke in isn't after me."

She listened to her mother run on for a moment, then tried again. "No. Dad can't drive in the dark. You know that. Please don't worry."

Mabel was limp by the time she'd managed to convince her mother not to dispatch Dad, who by this time of night was already in his pajamas, watching ancient TV reruns. He could thank her later.

She didn't want to return any more calls tonight. The reporters could go find someone else to harass, and Nanette and Cora would have to wait till tomorrow. Quickly, she tapped out a couple of quick text messages to Jen. Her entire day had been hijacked, and she couldn't begin to think of writing anything tonight.

Barnacle laid a pleading paw on her leg, but Mabel, feeling guilty, shook her head. "I'm sorry, buddy. I'll make it up to you tomorrow, okay?"

All she could think about right now was Buffy Westermann. *Had* she killed Mike? Amanda? Was it all about the paintings? How could anyone be that desperate for money?

Yes, she was probably trapped in her marriage. It was easy to imagine what a boorish husband Chad must be, and knowing what she did of him, their pre-nup was sure to be oppressive. Whether or not Buffy could afford to leave Chad, Mabel suspected the problem ran far deeper than money. With Chad's ugly temper, he'd never take her leaving with grace. Even killing people to get enough money to leave him might not buy her freedom from a man like him.

Mabel cleared space on the kitchen table and opened her laptop. She began searching Buffy's name, looking for clues.

Barnacle heaved a sigh and sank onto her feet. Though illiterate, he could read the clues well enough to know he wasn't getting a walk anytime soon.

The first results were all about today's debacle at John's house and the resultant BOLO—"be on the lookout." Mabel scanned those articles, anyway, in case some ambitious reporter had already dug up something useful.

Not much appeared, beyond references to Buffy as a young society matron—terminology that struck Mabel as old-fashioned in the extreme. That was typical Bartle County. Right now, the drama of the home invasion staged by the two Westermanns was the most compelling news fodder, Mabel guessed, but if Buffy remained on the run, maybe tomorrow would bring more background.

A deeper dive led to older articles about Buffy's activities on various charity boards, and even further back, an unsuccessful run for town council in Medicine Spring eight years ago. That was before Mabel's time, so she made a note to return Nanette's call. Nanette would know.

There was nothing beyond maybe ten years back. Mabel stewed over that a while. She made herself a cup of tea and picked up her phone. Then she put it back down. John was doing his own research. If he turned up something significant, she'd know soon enough.

Unthinking, she took a big sip of tea and gasped. Too hot.

Koi, who'd been off somewhere on cat business, reappeared, leaping onto the table next to the laptop. She sniffed Mabel, then tapped her hand. Eyes still on the screen, Mabel stroked her.

Maybe it was the repetitive petting motion that dislodged the thought, but all at once, the obvious occurred. Of course, Buffy would hardly be Ms. Westermann's given name.

I had a stressful day. No wonder I'm not thinking clearly, she reassured herself.

While even the news media—and Buffy's own political campaign—had been using the probable nickname, Mabel should've known better. Also, Westermann would be her married name, so anything from before her marriage would be under something else altogether.

How could she find out Buffy's original name?

At least, she knew Chad's name, and it wasn't a common one. She couldn't find a newspaper article about the wedding, so maybe it hadn't been local. Their marriage record must exist somewhere though. But where? Mabel recalled John's telling her she could do ancestry research right through the local library website. *Nothing ventured, nothing gained.*

After resurrecting her library card from the cluttered depths of her big, slouchy purse, Mabel logged in. Koi yawned and rolled over next to the laptop, seeming satisfied that Mabel had finally gotten the message.

The genealogy database was easy to navigate, but it still took Mabel a while to narrow her search terms. After that, the marriage license came right up.

Mabel's heart sank. Buffy's maiden name was listed as Serena Marie Adams. The name still told her nothing, and further searches turned up little additional information, apart from odds and ends like local school news, showing Serena Marie—Buffy—had made the honor roll. An hour went by, with Mabel scrolling through pages of unhelpful results, before she turned up something curious.

As often happened to Mabel whenever she tried to do computer research, the search engine deduced she didn't know what she was looking for. Besides the results for Serena Marie Adams, she found herself looking at an entry for another "Serena Marie" altogether. Or was she?

Mabel clicked on the article, which turned out to be little more than a captioned photo, showing the four winners of a middle-school science fair. What were the odds of two Serena Maries, the same approximate age, attending the same school district? The picture was small and pixelated, but Mabel believed she saw a resemblance.

She could've searched "Buffy Westermann" the rest of her time on earth and never unlocked nearly the entire first half of Buffy's life—the years lived as Serena Marie Sedlak.

That name could not be a coincidence. Frank Sedlak, the homeless arson victim, was likely related to Serena Marie, aka Buffy—and given their ages, Mabel would guess he was her dad. Mabel pondered the name change from Sedlak to Adams for a moment. Conceivably, she'd been adopted, especially if her biological father had been living on the streets.

Mabel checked her phone again. *Nothing.* She couldn't wait any longer to talk about what she'd found out.

Her call went to voicemail.

Mabel remembered Buffy's cold eyes, glittering with insane determination. What if even now, she had John cornered? What if he was lying unconscious? Or worse.

Maybe she should take a ride over there and check for herself. After arguing with herself a bit, she concluded she'd get no rest till she was sure John was okay.

Koi glowered, ears flattened.

"What?"

The cat meowed silently. Mabel looked away from Koi's unwavering glare.

She gathered her keys, flashlight, and purse. Barnacle sat, attentive, by the door, having recognized the signs of a car trip.

She rumpled his ears and considered. The presence of a big, loyal dog might be comforting.

No. If Buffy had picked up another gun, she might decide to shoot Barnacle. Mabel would never forgive herself if that happened.

"Stay and guard the castle, buddy. We'll go for a good walk tomorrow." *If I live.*

Dusk had fallen, and the wind had come up. The forecast had said rain later tonight. Mabel buttoned her pea coat and threw the hood over her head. The wind lifted and swirled dry leaves and a stray plastic bag, which glanced off her shoulder as she ran for the car.

John would laugh at her overreaction. Before putting the car in drive, she tried his number once more. Nothing.

Mabel made the short trip in record time. Still, she hesitated as she contemplated approaching the house. What if John was ignoring her calls on purpose? Would he be mad she'd come here instead of waiting for tomorrow, as he'd told her?

And what would she do if Buffy had returned? Mabel couldn't go barging right up to the house. She needed a plan.

The house looked dark. Its windows reflected her headlights as she pulled to the curb half a block away. Mabel turned the engine off and tried John's number again, but he didn't answer. She sat and thought.

John's car was nowhere in sight. Therefore, he was probably elsewhere, safe and sound. She should turn herself around and go on home, where she could be safe and sound too.

Why was she so indecisive? John never seemed to waffle the way she did.

No. As long as she was already here, she could at least take a look around for any signs of a break-in. She could also see if Billie Jean had returned to John's back porch, where he'd earlier left her dishes and bed.

Mabel got out and shut her door as quietly as possible. A single streetlamp along with the neighbors' lights cast enough of a glow to see where she was going, without turning on her flashlight.

A drizzle had started while Mabel sat debating whether to get out of her car. Alas, she hadn't brought an umbrella or raincoat, so she pulled her hood back up. She trotted toward the darkened house with its crude front door patch and slipped around the side, trying to avoid the front security light.

Where was John? Clearly, he'd gone someplace without letting her know. Not that he owed her an account of his every move, but she'd invited him to dinner, and—

The moment Mabel stepped into the yard, everything flooded with light. Instinctively, she threw one arm up over her eyes and stumbled backward into the shadows.

"Freeze."

Mabel let out an involuntary screech and spun around into a blaze of high-intensity LED light.

"I said freeze."

Mabel froze, eyes squeezed shut tight against the flashlight beam.

The fireworks effect imprinted on her retina still dazzled against the inside of her lids. Her heart chugged erratically, and she couldn't seem to get a decent breath.

"You. Good grief."

Mabel raised a cautious eyelid.

Detective Lieutenant Sizemore of the local PD had lowered her flashlight and was holstering her service weapon. She gestured wearily at two uniforms behind her. "May as well pack it in for tonight, thanks to this one."

Even with her vision still spangled with patriotic red, white, and blue splotches, Mabel could read disgust on all three faces. She put an unsteady hand up against a porch post and watched the officers fade into the shadows as they presumably headed for a cruiser somewhere.

As luck would have it, Sizemore didn't fade away.

"What brings you down here this evening, Ms. Browne?"

"I, um, wasn't able to reach Mr. Bigelow and became concerned. I also was wondering if Billie Jean came back."

Sizemore's left eyebrow elevated. "Mrs. Westermann?"

"Oh." Mabel pushed away from the house. "No, sorry. I meant the cat. She got out during all the excitement earlier."

"Well, let me allay your concern about Bigelow. He's vacated for the night so we could surveil the house without civilian interference." It might have been Mabel's imagination, but it seemed as if Sizemore bore down on the phrase "civilian interference."

"I'm sorry," Mabel mumbled, and pushed damp hair behind her ear. A chilly gust of wind rustled the dying leaves that still clung to the neighbor's oak tree. An involuntary shiver passed over her.

"Go home. Stay there."

Sizemore stood aside and Mabel plodded toward the street.

Her phone rang as she reached the pavement. She snatched at it, but not quickly enough to muffle the *Hot-Blooded* ringtone before Sizemore could hear it. She might've imagined the snicker behind her.

"What's up? I saw you were calling."

Should she ask him where he'd been? Why he'd ignored her calls? Should she tell him what had happened, thanks to his failure to keep her in the loop?

"Mabel?"

The events of the last few minutes had taken the luster off her big discovery about Buffy. "I'm, uh, kind of in the middle of something here."

"Sorry I missed your calls. I was busy with the police, then camped out at my office, doing some research online. The police decided to set up a sting to try to catch Buffy if she came back to the house."

"Yeah." Mabel grimaced. "I know."

"Huh?"

She had reached the sidewalk, and the rain had picked up again. Mabel sheltered the phone as best she could with her hood. She snuffled, unsure whether her nose was running or if those were raindrops trickling down her chin.

"Never mind." Mabel used her sleeve to swipe at her face. "Hey, I think I found something out about Buffy."

Sizemore's hand was on her upper arm, and her voice was in Mabel's ear. "Did you now?

"Like what? Who is that?"

Sizemore, now brandishing a sturdy umbrella, gestured at the phone, then pried it from Mabel's hand. As Mabel stood in the rain, Sizemore spoke into the cell. "Bigelow? You can come on home now."

John's answer was inaudible, but Sizemore replied, "Your girlfriend blew our plan. You might as well come home and we can both hear her big discovery, as long as I'm already out here." The sarcasm dripping from "her big discovery" was impossible to miss.

Again, John's answer was unintelligible, though Mabel heard sputtering.

"Oh, you'll hear all about it when you get here. We'll be waiting out front."

After another listening pause, Sizemore said. "Okay. See you soon."

She clicked off and passed the phone back to Mabel. "Your boyfriend says you know where the key is, and we should go on in."

Mabel nodded. The last thing she wanted was a private sit-down with Sizemore while waiting for John. The next-to-last thing she wanted was seeing John's face after this most recent debacle. Twice in one day. Could anyone be a bigger rolling disaster area?

As they stepped inside, she sighed. At least it felt good to be out of the rain. She entered the security code, then peeled off her jacket and hung it carefully on the vintage coat tree by the door, arranging it over the drip mat.

Sizemore parked her umbrella and plopped down on the couch. She'd pulled out her own phone and was scanning it.

"Don't you have a partner somewhere?" Mabel blurted, as the silence lengthened.

"Yep."

"Shouldn't he—er—she—er—come in too?"

"He's home with his family. We're off duty. I live down the street, and when I heard they had somebody, I couldn't resist heading over."

Mabel now realized the detective was wearing a red Cornell sweatshirt and blue jeans. She stared. This was the closest to the human side of Lt. Sizemore she'd ever seen.

Mabel's phone pinged and she glanced at the text—

Make some coffee or tea if you want.

She cleared her throat and Sizemore looked up.

"Would you like a hot drink?"

"If you have tea, sure. I've been fighting a bit of a sore throat."

"Oh, me too," Mabel said. "I think it's post-nasal drip. From my allergies, you know..." She trailed off, realizing she was rambling, and Sizemore was back to looking at her phone.

Well, this was at least a reprieve from sitting there in silence, waiting, for the next half hour. Grateful, Mabel scurried into the kitchen and threw the light switch. To her surprise, the room was already cleaned up, for the most part, and back in order.

She set about boiling a pot of water, then opening cabinet doors in search of tea. Nothing. Where had John gotten the coffee when he'd made that breakfast pot?

Pantry.

Seconds later, as Mabel reached for the door pull, a demonic growl from under the table sent her airborne, and she shrieked. Nerves already frayed, Mabel clutched at her shirt with both hands, scrambling backward.

Sizemore burst into the room, weapon drawn.

The tea kettle shrilled.

"It's okay," Mabel gasped. "It's B-Billie…John's cat."

With shaking hands, she turned off the burner, wanting nothing more than to sink to the floor for a while. Instead, she backed onto one of the bar stools, and took some deep breaths.

Billie Jean, in a graceful display of hydraulic capabilities, vaulted to the top of the refrigerator and began grooming her impeccable fur.

Sizemore holstered her firearm and shook her head. She left the room without a word.

When her breathing had slowed a bit, Mabel got back up. She walked over and eyed the cat. "I'm glad you're back. Thanks for earlier."

The cat continued to groom.

Mabel checked the pantry shelves and found several types of tea. Most were loose-leaf, and she wasn't sure how to brew them. John also had a box of Irish breakfast teabags. She grabbed a couple of those, threw them into mugs and poured the water over them.

She didn't really want to go back into the living room with Sizemore, but it couldn't be avoided. Mabel stuck her head around the door. "What do you take in it?"

"Nothing."

The box said to brew for three to seven minutes. Mabel decided five was a safe compromise and set the timer.

When the buzzer sounded, she startled and half-stumbled off the bar stool. She'd overfilled the mugs and they sloshed as she carried them into the living room, scalding her hands. It struck her that she was going to have to calm down if she continued to serve hot beverages to the lieutenant.

Sizemore lounged in a corner of the sofa, browsing through a book she'd apparently pulled from John's shelves. Mabel plunked the mugs down on a couple of coasters and inspected the red marks on the backs of her hands, then sank into the adjoining armchair.

"Thanks." Sizemore didn't look up. "Bigelow has an interesting library there."

Mabel had never studied John's bookshelves. She looked over at the appealing floor-to-ceiling shelves, surrounding a comfy-looking armchair and Victorian floor lamp in the corner. She'd love to curl up there with a good book...or John.

But right now, she couldn't concentrate on anything but how much trouble she was in. Not only with the police, but maybe John too.

"You familiar with the Thaw case?"

"Huh?" Mabel raised an eyebrow.

"Harry Thaw? Shot Stanford White in 1906 in front of bunches of witnesses but got off on mental issues."

Mabel's hands had stopped hurting, but they were still sweating. She rubbed her palms on her jeans. Was this turning into a book discussion?

"Sounds familiar."

"Vintage crime of the century," Sizemore said. "Like your Sauer ax murders, but a few decades earlier. This one had a celebrity vic— Stanford White, an ultra-famous architect—and sex." She held up the book, *The Girl on the Velvet Swing*.

"Wow. Who's that?"

"Evelyn Nesbit. She was White's lover before marrying Harry Thaw. A fact that didn't sit well with Harry Thaw. He was a Pittsburgher, by the way. Not every day a local boy shoots a celebrity on the roof of Madison Square Garden in front of hundreds of witnesses."

Despite herself, Mabel was intrigued. She made a mental note to borrow that book—if Sizemore didn't do it first.

"I haven't been doing as much reading as I'd like to, lately. First, dealing with my grandma's house, my new career, and of course, the..." She'd almost said "murders."

Sizemore either didn't notice how she'd trailed off, or more likely—though surprisingly—decided to give Mabel a break. "New career?" She laid the book down and picked up her mug.

"Uh, yeah. I was a lawyer for a lot of years, but now I'm writing."

Sizemore arched an eyebrow over the steam rising from her tea. "Oh? What are you writing?"

Mabel started explaining about her volunteer book but got tangled in the details. "Well," she mumbled, "I guess I've been sidetracked lately, because of the Sauer thing, and then, I realized I ought to do a book about that. True crime. Since I sort of had a front seat, you know..."

Sizemore grinned. "Oh, I know."

Mabel cast a longing eye at her tea but was afraid to pick it up. Her hands were still too unsteady.

"That's very interesting, Ms. Browne. I'll be sure to pick it up. But here's a piece of advice."

Mabel looked up.

"Writing about true crime doesn't make you a detective. Being an ex-lawyer doesn't make you a detective. Trying to involve yourself with criminals can make you—not to be crude about it—but it can make you dead."

"I don't 'try to involve myself,'" Mabel sputtered. "Criminals keep involving themselves with me."

"You should never have been here tonight. You not only blew what we had taken care to set up, you're darn lucky you didn't get hurt."

"But—"

The door opened, and John blew in on a gust of wind. Rain had soaked the shoulders of his black Patagonia jacket and spattered his well-fitted jeans.

Mabel froze with her mouth open. She both wanted to run away and into his arms for reassurance. With a quiver of apprehension, she met his eyes.

"Hi, Lieutenant," he said, but his eyes never left Mabel's. "You okay?"

There was no question whom he meant.

"Yeah," Mabel said miserably. "I'm sorry. I hadn't heard from you, and I was worried when you didn't pick up, so—"

He waved it off. "It was my fault. I didn't keep you in the loop."

John peeled off his coat and tossed it onto the coat tree, then settled on the couch next to Mabel. He squeezed her sweaty hand. His were cold and rain spattered.

Sizemore cleared her throat. "Okay. I'm blaming both of you till further notice. I need to get home yet tonight, so could we cut to the chase here?"

"Sure," John said.

"If Westermann was going to return tonight, that's pretty much off the table now. We can try watching the house, but if she did happen to approach tonight and saw what went down, she isn't likely to try again. She'll know we're surveilling. So we go to plan B."

"Do we have a plan B?" John asked.

"First, there is no 'we.' Second, there is no 'we.'"

Mabel shifted in her seat. "What if I can help?" She cringed reflexively.

Sizemore snorted. "We already had this discussion, Ms. Browne, didn't we? And stop ducking like that. I'm not going to hit you."

"Well, here's the thing." Mabel tried to square her shoulders and look confident. She had good information. "Maybe you all know this already, but I discovered something earlier this evening."

She laid out what she'd learned about Buffy's probable origins. "I'm not 100% sure," she said, "but Sedlak isn't the most common name in the phone book."

Sizemore mouthed something, and Mabel cleared her throat. "All right, we don't use phone books anymore, but you know what I mean."

Clearly, Sizemore did know what she meant, given the quick glint of interest—or perhaps mere surprise—Mabel had seen in her eye.

"You can go ahead and make that 100%," John said. "I reached the same conclusion tonight, but I was able to confirm a birth record."

"If you keep an eye on Buffy's father, she may turn up at the hospital," Mabel said.

Lt. Sizemore smirked. "Give us a little credit, okay?"

She got up then and shook John's hand. "I've got to be getting home." She nodded at Mabel.

As she reached the door, Sizemore looked back. "Nice work, Citizen Patrol." Then, she spoiled it by adding, "But don't do it again."

Chapter Thirty

As soon as John had closed the door on Lt. Sizemore, he held out his arms for Mabel. "It's late on an awful day. You poor kid—and all of it for me."

Despite her best efforts, Mabel began to cry, an unattractive snuffling sob. "You've got to be kidding. I screwed everything up."

"No, you didn't." John sat on the arm of her chair, holding her against his heart. "You didn't make Buffy come break in here. You didn't..."

His voice trailed off.

Mabel pulled back to meet his eyes. He handed her a tissue, and she blew her nose. "Yes, I did. If you were about to say I didn't just ruin a good chance to catch Buffy Westermann, then it's not true and we both know it."

"Let's say you didn't know you were interrupting a sting operation. Anyway, that's as much my fault as anybody's. This came up unexpectedly, and it never occurred to me how things might look to you. Don't cry."

The tissue was thoroughly soaked. Mabel pushed away and averted her face before she could saturate John's shoulder. She dabbed at her eyes and blew her nose again. "I never cry."

"I know you don't." He passed her another tissue. "It's only the letdown after all that adrenaline."

Mabel wiped the adrenaline from her eyes and nose. She couldn't look at him. "Do you think the police will put a guard on Sedlak's hospital room?"

"I hope so."

"The police already figured it out, didn't they?"

John hesitated before nodding. "Yeah, I'm sure they did."

Billie Jean flowed into the room and wound her body around Mabel's legs. "Are you kidding me?" Mabel reached down and laid a cautious hand on the cat's silken head. Billie Jean spat and lashed out, then slipped from sight beneath the couch.

"She's moody." John's voice was apologetic.

"Well, so am I." Mabel laid her head back on the cushions and closed her eyes. "Do you think the cops will go visit Sedlak yet tonight?"

John shrugged. "All I know for sure is you and I don't have the manpower to do it ourselves."

Mabel shuddered, imagining Detective Sizemore's catching her at the hospital. "As if."

"It'll be all right. You've been through enough on my behalf. Come here." He reached out his arms and Mabel melted into them. She rested there as he talked into her hair. "From now on, our investigation is done, okay? I'm quite unlikely to get charged at this point, so let's relax and let the police do their jobs. You get back to concentrating on your writing, and I can get back to concentrating on you."

Mabel liked the sound of that. She liked it even better when he lifted her chin and administered a toe-curling kiss.

To her disappointment, he leaned back and tucked her hair behind her ear. "I think it might be a good idea if we called it a night. Maybe we can do a movie or something tomorrow—what do you think?"

"Sure." It appeared he was kicking her out, but she felt his reluctance. Was it because he found her impossible to resist?

John smiled. "You decide what you'd like to see. Or if you want to do something else, you can let me know, deal?"

Mabel nodded. She floated toward the front door, concentrating on regular breathing while walking at the same time—a frequent reaction to one of John's kisses.

He helped her into her coat, then gripping the lapels, pulled her against him. "Sleep well." He kissed her again, this time on her forehead. "I'll call you tomorrow."

Except for the lights over the back door and kitchen window, Mabel's house was dark when she pulled into her driveway. Rain sluiced down her windshield and tiny balls of hail pattered on the roof and danced on the hood. For a few minutes, she sat, wondering if she should wait for the downpour to let up.

Despite her weary body, her mind still churned through the day's events and her own contribution to the debacle at John's. She was probably too agitated to sleep even if she ran inside and went straight to bed. And getting pelted by cold rain wouldn't help.

Still, she felt trapped out here, her breath starting to fog the glass and close her in. Barnacle and Koi would've heard the car and they'd be waiting for her to come inside.

Mabel gathered her things. She wouldn't melt.

As she turned to open the door, Mabel jerked at the sound of a sharp rap on the window. Even through the rain and shadows, she could make out the shape of a pistol aimed against the glass at her. Behind it stood Buffy, dressed in rain-streaked black like a wannabe ninja.

Her face was a stony mask. "Open," she mouthed.

Mabel flung her purse back on the seat and hit the door locks. She fumbled with the key, her only thought to throw the car into reverse and escape. She jammed it into the ignition, but before she'd even had time to turn it on, she heard a loud report.

The left front wheel lurched downward.

Another shot. Mabel's rear window shattered.

Dimly, she heard barking coming from the house, as Barnacle reacted to the commotion outside.

"Open the door," Buffy said.

Mabel hesitated, but what options did she have?

"Hands up."

Mabel raised her right hand as if she were about to testify in court. Would she ever get the opportunity to testify against Buffy? Would she live that long?

With her left hand, she opened the driver's door. Buffy eased back, keeping the gun pointed at Mabel. Her hand shook, which was unnerving.

Mabel sensed it would take very little for Buffy to shoot again. "Okay," Mabel said. "Okay."

Buffy blew raindrops off her lips. She gestured toward the kitchen door with her gun hand. "Let's go."

Mabel had slid her phone into her pocket when she gathered her things. Unfortunately, she doubted she could get her hands—now high in the air in the approved fashion—on it to dial.

"Now, when you step inside, the first thing I want you to do is lock the dog up. Got it? Or I *will* shoot it."

Mabel thought fast. Or, at least, as fast as she was able to, under the circumstances. Buffy had ordered her to lock up Barnacle first. Which meant she probably wasn't thinking about disarming a home security system. This, given the ramshackle appearance of Mabel's house, wasn't surprising.

"You don't need to shoot my dog. He's very gentle."

"I don't care if he's a toothless hamster. Right away. Grab him and lock him in somewhere."

"Okay. Sure." Mabel unbolted the back door. With one hand, she flung it wide, to hide the blinking red light of the security panel. With the other, she grabbed Barnacle's collar as he squirmed with delight. Already, his barks and growls had diminished to happy whining.

Buffy seemed afraid of dogs, because she drew back as Barnacle made a friendly lunge at her. Mabel heard a click from her pistol hand.

"Take it easy," Mabel said, in what she hoped was a soothing tone. "I'm going to stick him in the basement."

With Barnacle fighting her every step of the way, Mabel dragged him toward the cellar door. Fleetingly, she thought of darting down there herself, but knew that old door wouldn't hold.

As she shoved the struggling dog through the door and slammed it shut, the alarm began shrieking. Buffy did the same.

"Turn it off!" She waved her gun hand at Mabel. A blood-stained gauze wrap marked the spot Billie Jean had sunk her teeth into. Mabel raised her hands and sidled past Buffy, who was showing the whites of her eyes like a skittish horse. She closed the back door and considered the panel, then jabbed in the wrong code.

This time, Buffy rammed the gun into Mabel's ribs. "Off."

Mabel fumbled as she reentered the code. "Sorry. You're making me nervous."

"I'm considering making you dead."

With Buffy watching, Mabel punched in the correct code. If she lived through this, she was going to have to change it.

The alarm stopped shrieking. Almost at once, the phone rang.

Mabel moved toward it, but Buffy gestured for her to stop.

"Look," Mabel said. "That'll be my security company. If I don't answer, the cops are going to arrive in the next five minutes."

"I don't have time for this." Sweat had beaded on Buffy's forehead, and her glare threatened to break through the Botox. "Answer that thing."

As Mabel picked up, Buffy hissed at her. "No funny business."

Mabel had never heard anyone say that in real life.

"Hello? Yeah, hi."

Mabel kept a wary eye on Buffy. "Everything's fine. I, uh, came in and was soaking wet and juggling things."

Buffy jiggled the gun at her.

"No, no. I'm fine. Thank you. Good night."

As Mabel hung up, Buffy motioned her toward the kitchen table. "Sit."

Barnacle whined and scratched at the basement door.

"Settle down," Mabel called. "It's okay."

She sat. How long would it take for police to arrive? As soon as Mabel had failed to say her safe word, they should have been summoned.

Buffy cast a disgusted look around the worn furnishings and deposits of clutter.

"This was my grandmother's house. I haven't had a chance to get it in shape yet." Mabel clamped her lips shut. Why was she apologizing to a homicidal maniac?

"Now," Buffy said. "We have unfinished business. I need that artwork. And you know where it is."

Mabel worked on a flat expression.

"Hel-LO!" Buffy waved a hand in front of Mabel's face. "Are you having some sort of seizure?"

Mabel shook her head.

"You know where it is. So, this is what we're going to do. You are going to help me get what I need. Either you tell me how that's going to work, or we'll have to take another route."

"I...can't."

Buffy seemed to be working on a scowl, but the Botox reduced it to a squint. "Okay. Surprised you'd choose a hostage situation, but it's a way to go."

"Hey, wait a minute. I never—"

Barnacle's barking rose to a frenzy, and the scrabbling and banging at the basement door along with it.

Buffy shot a look in that direction. Mabel's heart chugged in her throat. She hadn't noticed anything, but she suspected by now, Barnacle was announcing the arrival of the police.

Mabel gave an awkward little laugh. "He doesn't like being down there."

Buffy's head swung the other direction, as if she might have heard something else.

Mabel strained her ears, but all she heard was Barnacle. She'd felt insulted when her fiftieth birthday had arrived to a flurry of mailings from AARP and hearing aid companies, but now she wondered. Maybe her hearing really was starting to go.

Mabel jumped in her seat at a burst of loud pounding at the front door. She'd heard that, all right.

"Police. Open up."

Buffy's eyes were calculating.

Mabel felt weak with relief. Ignoring the door wasn't an option.

"Tell them you're okay—it was a false alarm."

"I can't do that. I mean I can do that, but they won't buy it. As soon as I didn't give my safe word, they knew I wasn't alone in here."

Sweat gleamed on Buffy's upper lip. "Try it, anyway."

Mabel slowly got to her feet as Buffy gestured toward the door. Barnacle must've heard them walking because the barking escalated.

"Crack the door and tell them you were getting ready for bed and you're not decent."

Mabel swallowed. She got up, feeling as if her body were detached from her brain, and floated toward the door.

Buffy followed. Mabel felt the heat of her and the brush of the gun barrel.

More banging at the door. "Police. Welfare check."

"Don't try anything. I'll kill us both. I've got nothing to lose."

Mabel put her hand on the doorknob and cleared her throat. "I'm okay," she called. "False alarm."

"Please open up, ma'am."

She cracked the door and caught a glimpse of the young male officer—Jerry?—who sometimes accompanied Lieutenant Sizemore. "Sorry. I was getting ready for bed. I'm not, uh, decent."

There was movement on the porch and Sizemore stepped in front of the male officer. Mabel caught the gleam of her drawn service pistol.

Mabel drew a quick breath. Sizemore was off duty, still in her civilian jeans. And she was a detective. She would not be answering calls for a welfare check.

"Let me in, Ms. Browne. We're both of the female persuasion, so no need for false modesty."

Mabel mouthed, "No." She didn't want to get shot. She didn't want to get Sizemore shot, either. "I can't."

"All right, Ms. Browne. If you're sure. Sorry to disturb you."

She knows, Mabel thought. But what could she do?

"Thanks for coming," Mabel said. "Sorry to drag you out here."

She closed the door with a last desperate look at Sizemore, who either failed to notice, or had an admirable ability to maintain a flat stare.

"All right, Browne. Let's chat." Buffy motioned Mabel back toward the kitchen with her gun hand.

As she sank into her chair, Mabel's mind raced. Apparently, Buffy was so stressed and hyper-focused on forcing the location of the artwork out of Mabel that she wasn't thinking clearly.

It was dark outside. The kitchen light was on, and Mabel had thrown on the hall light as she and Buffy headed to the front door. Anyone outside and paying attention had to have a clear view of what was going on in Mabel's house.

She strained for sounds of police movement, but all she heard was Barnacle, whining, barking, scratching at the basement door. "Quiet," she yelled, then immediately regretted it. It didn't matter whether she could hear the police or not—but it was definitely better that Buffy didn't. The noisier Barnacle was, the less likely Buffy would hear anything but him.

To her good fortune, Barnacle was disobedient, as usual.

"So spit it," Buffy said. "Where are my paintings?"

Mabel raised her eyebrows. *My paintings?*

"I don't know what to tell you." Mabel dropped her forehead into her hands and massaged her now-aching head. "I told you the police have them all."

"I know what you told me, but I don't believe you," Buffy spat, right before cracking Mabel's head with the gun barrel.

Mabel saw stars.

"Nobody finds multi-million-dollar artwork and turns it right over to the cops. Even you and your dumb boyfriend aren't that stupid."

Mabel touched her temple and winced. Her headache had turned to a massive explosion of thudding pain. "Did it ever occur to you that some people are honest?"

Buffy's laugh was raucous. "No."

"Besides, turning the paintings in to the police doesn't mean we won't get the reward."

"But it does mean you wouldn't be able to ransom or sell them for ten times that."

She grabbed Mabel's collar and forced her to meet her eyes. "We're going to wait half an hour. That should be long enough to be sure the cops are nice and far away. If you tell me where the paintings are before then, all good. If not, I'm going to start shooting. Maybe your toes. Maybe an arm."

"My neighbors will hear."

"Your neighbors are a block away and shut in their houses on a rainy night."

Would the police make their move before Mabel lost her toes?

A faint sound made Mabel hold her breath.

Barnacle whined and scratched at the basement door. Mabel looked up and saw Koi streak from the front hall and dart underneath Grandma's Hoosier cabinet. Probably, she'd been curled up in a box on a high shelf in the junk room. It was one of the cat's favorite new hideaways, since Lisa had started reorganizing.

Could you bleed to death from having your toes shot off? Mabel swallowed hard and tried to think of a story that would delay Buffy's itchy trigger finger.

"You know," Mabel said, "it's true the police do have those paintings, but—"

Buffy swung at Mabel's head again, but this time Mabel ducked.

"Ow!" The sudden movement hurt, anyway. "I *said* 'but,'" Mabel snapped. She was getting sick and tired of Buffy's attitude. "You know you catch more flies with honey than…"

She trailed off and held up her hands to ward off another blow. "Okay. *But*," she repeated, "there may still be a couple at the storage unit up on Route 50. The ones John squirreled away for himself." *Forgive me, John, for slandering you.*

Mabel watched Buffy think. Skepticism flickered across her face, chased by greedy flashes of hope.

"Can you get in?"

"No, John is the only—I mean, well...I'd need to lift a key. I'm pretty sure the day guard would remember me."

"I am NOT waiting till tomorrow." Buffy screamed.

"I think..." Mabel's mind, in fact, was a blank. "I..."

A sudden crash from the hallway saved her from having to complete the thought.

Buffy whirled and fired.

The shot shattered the glass on the picture hanging next to the hall entry—an autumn scene of a covered bridge Grandma had cut from an old calendar and framed. The victim, a hole through its midsection, crashed to the floor.

"Lower your weapon. Drop it or I'll shoot."

Mabel, feeling unheroic, dove underneath the table.

A beat later, to her relief, Buffy set her gun on the floor next to Mabel's foot. Mabel let out her breath. Subconsciously, she'd been waiting for a shoot-out.

"Keep your hands up where I can see them. Get on the ground."

Sizemore jerked her head toward the floor. "Now—I said down. I *will* tase you."

Buffy muttered under her breath, but Mabel couldn't make out anything but a few swear words. All the same, Buffy eased onto the floor and sat next to Mabel.

"On your stomach."

"This floor is disgusting," Buffy said. "I don't even like sitting on it."

"Tough," Sizemore said. "On your belly. Next time you do a home invasion, pick a cleaner house."

"It's not that bad," Mabel said from under the table.

"It's covered in animal hair," Buffy muttered. "I'm getting it in my mouth."

Barnacle howled from the top of the basement steps, putting in his two cents.

"Maybe if you hadn't broken into my house, I'd have had time to sweep," Mabel said.

Sizemore gave a piercing whistle. "Ladies—take it up with Martha Stewart. Come on out, Ms. Browne. The coast is clear."

Mabel tried to straighten her legs, but her body screamed with pain. "Wait a sec."

At last, she managed to sidle, crablike, from beneath the table, then eased to her feet, clinging to the back of a chair. She hoped she'd been subtle enough that no one had noticed her graceless exit.

"Can I get up now?" Buffy called from the floor.

"Soon enough," Sizemore told her. "Hands behind your back."

"Come on," Buffy snapped. "You're treating me like a common criminal. Do you know who I am?"

"Yes, I'm afraid we do. When you behave like a common criminal, it doesn't matter where you live or what kind of car you drive. You're in a lot of trouble, Ms. Westermann."

As Buffy began erupting again, Sizemore made a quieting noise. "Your husband's a lawyer. I'm sure he'd remind you—you have a right to remain silent." As she continued the Miranda warning, another officer helped Buffy to her feet and cuffed her.

Mabel felt tension ooze out of her body, only to be replaced by an all-over tremble she couldn't contain. Koi emerged from under the Hoosier cupboard and rubbed herself against Mabel's ankle, oblivious to everything else going on in the kitchen. Mabel picked up her purring cat and buried her face in the soft fur.

Barnacle barked and whined, obviously wanting to join the party, but Mabel knew better than to let him out before everyone had left. Above all the commotion, including Buffy's complaints the cuffs were too tight, Mabel's phone began playing *Hot-Blooded*.

She silenced the ringer, but not before Sizemore smirked and winked.

"May I…?" Mabel gestured toward the front of the house.

"Go ahead," Sizemore said. "We'll get your statement later."

As she reached the living room, Mabel answered the call.

"Are you watching TV?" John asked.

"No. Is there something going on?"

"No—but it sounds kind of noisy. Do you have visitors?"

"You have no idea."

Chapter Thirty-One

THE WAITRESS, WEARING JEANS AND A white T-shirt topped with a brown Coffee Cup Diner bib apron, slid a short stack of pancakes and side of turkey sausage links in front of Mabel a couple of days later. Mabel reached for the pitcher of warm maple syrup. She wondered if John had noticed she was ordering healthier portions these days.

Alas, probably not. Across the booth from her, he peppered his Popeye special, a poached egg on a bed of steamed spinach and sprouted-grain toast.

Mabel sighed and took a luxurious stretch before tucking into her late breakfast. "I slept like a baby last night. Like the weight of the world's been lifted."

John grinned. "For me, it has." He reached across to squeeze Mabel's hand. "Have I told you how amazing you are? I'm grateful Buffy didn't hurt you."

"A few times. It wasn't like I did that much. I just always seem to end up in the path of felons, and they and the police do the rest."

"You're always doing that," John said. "You put yourself down, and you shouldn't. It was your idea there might be a crazed family member working on their own, right? And even Lt. Sizemore complimented the way you handled Buffy. She said you deserve a lot of credit for that capture."

Mabel hunched a shoulder, feeling embarrassed, and went back to her pancakes. "Have you heard anything about the reward money?"

John rolled his eyes. "Apparently, the committee in charge of it is debating whether I qualify, since the stuff was dumped on me."

"Oh, come on. That's ridiculous," Mabel sputtered. "It was missing, and you found and turned it in."

He shrugged, seeming unconcerned. "I suspect the real problem might be someone who pledged the money and now can't come up with it. At least, I'm no worse off than I was before I found it."

With effort, Mabel turned her thoughts away from the fading vision of riches. She wanted to enjoy her breakfast without indigestion. "How about your license? Any news there?"

He shook his head. "I don't see any other obstacles, though. My suspension will be over the end of January, and then the board will review my record. Which," he added, "is clean, except for the original offense."

"That's great," Mabel said. "You think you'll quit teaching?"

He shook his head. "I like it, and I expect business will be slow for a while. How about you? What's next?"

Mabel sighed. "Writing, I guess." She hadn't meant to sound glum, but even she could hear it. "I won't be doing any more dog training, that's for sure. I'm not cut out for crouching in the woods. I'm going to need a new place to volunteer. And I have to keep working on the true crime book—not to mention the house. The health department really will show up one of these days, if Linnea has any say."

When they'd finished eating, John signaled for more coffee. "The breakfast crowd's died down. You want to debrief right here?"

Mabel looked around. Their booth was in a quiet corner by the coffee station, anyway. "Sure. I basically know what happened, but did you find out any more about how the murders went down?"

One huge advantage John had as a longtime PI was his contacts within the area police departments. They hadn't helped him much in the case of Mike's murder, which had occurred out of county. But Amanda had been found in his own back yard, and Buffy's recent shenanigans had all happened right here too.

"Yeah. Buffy's lawyer made a proffer of evidence to the DA in exchange for a plea deal. Hopefully, it'll go a long way toward nailing Vin Perdue for both the heist and the arson."

"All right," Mabel said. "Here's what I know so far—you can catch me up from there, okay? Buffy was Frank Sedlak's daughter. Her mother died early on, and she grew up in homeless shelters and foster homes. In time, he lost his parental rights. She got adopted in high school."

"Yup. Despite her unconventional childhood, she was smart, and her good grades got her into college. For a while, she worked on distancing herself as far as she could from her past, worked in IT for a bit, and—"

Mabel looked up. "IT?"

John grimaced. "I talked to my guy. He thinks she bypassed my security system by hacking in and silencing the alarm. If you do it right, it's like nothing ever happened."

"Looks like we underestimated her there too." Mabel promised herself not to make that mistake again. "Sorry. Go on."

"Anyway, she ended up marrying Chad. As the years went by, she began thinking of her father. She could understand his situation better— that a lot was due to some underlying mental problems, along with PTSD from his military service. Because Chad was so status-driven, Buffy never confided in him, but she started trying to reconnect with her dad and help him out as she could. When she saw how he'd been hurt in that fire, she blamed herself for freezing him out so long he was reduced to sleeping in deserted buildings."

Mabel scowled. "I still don't get the armed robbery...not to mention the murders. We both saw that house. Even with a lousy pre-nup, didn't she have enough money to provide whatever he needed?"

"*She*, as I understand it, didn't have much at all in her own name. Chad controlled her with money, and all she had was a monthly allowance."

"Is that why she went to work at the Timbers?"

John shrugged. "Maybe in part. Not to mention she was probably bored out of her skull and needed something to do. Of course, she met Mike there and got involved with him. The police think she figured out his connection with the fire at some point after that—maybe she heard the gossip. Or he told her something, never realizing her father had been the burn victim."

"So she wanted revenge."

"Crazed with it." He shook his head. "As I'm sure you noticed, she's not the most stable person out there. A lot of people have mental illness, and very few of them are criminals. Buffy Westermann is different. She behaves more like a sociopath—I'll be interested to see if she gets evaluated and what that turns up."

John ran a fingertip along the rim of his empty coffee mug. "She didn't admit it, but I wouldn't be surprised if she hatched a plot to kill Mike, the moment she found out he'd torched that house. When he started bragging about the museum heist she decided to work him for a chunk of the proceeds."

"Like how? Blackmail?"

"I don't know that she's admitted to that. But there's no question she thought he owed her and her father. Vin Perdue signed Mike's death warrant when he came after Mike."

Mabel tried to fit Perdue into the picture but failed. "I don't get what you mean."

"Mike was still alive at that point because Buffy wanted to get her hands on either the paintings or a lot of money, and she needed him alive for that. Except as soon as Perdue discovered the paintings had vanished, he sent his goons after Mike. According to Buffy, Mike dissolved into a sniveling mess, and she knew right away he had no idea where those paintings were. He'd never so much as touched them. Called him a big, dumb blowhard.

"She said she could see the light go off in his 'numb skull' at that point. He babbled to Vin's guys that he was only the driver, and he had no clue what was in those lockers. He threw Amanda under the bus on the spot. One of the goons laughed and said bringing his girlfriend along on a job was his 'first fatal mistake.' Said Vin wasn't stupid, and that's why he didn't trust Mike to be in on the heist in the first place. He told Mike he better come up with the paintings and fast, or he'd wind up dead."

Mabel lifted her coffee cup but realized it was already empty.

"Hang on." John snagged a couple of refills.

"Okay, so Mike was after Amanda." Mabel warmed her hands around her mug. "Vin and his guys were after Mike—and probably Amanda too, before long. If you're right that the heist was above Perdue's pay grade, he probably had somebody more powerful after him now too. It's a miracle either Perdue or Mr. Big didn't get to Amanda first." She gulped. "Or you."

"Right." John smiled. "But they didn't. Professional criminals tend to be a bit more cautious than loose cannons like Buffy."

"If I follow the action, based on what Jamal told us, Mike and that other guy had taken away the first load, and Amanda stayed 'to keep an eye on things.' Right?" Mabel raised a questioning eyebrow. "Either the guys had opened the second locker already, or maybe they gave her the key and she was supposed to move stuff toward the door for them to pick up when they returned. I'm sure she recognized right away that the brown paper packages were paintings, and—being she knew the art world—probably also made an immediate connection to the museum theft. By the time the two bozos got back, the paintings were gone, but they never missed them."

"Yup."

Mabel frowned. "What I still don't get is how on earth Mike and Buffy ended up at the overlook. That's not an easy hike, and neither of them strikes me as the outdoor type."

"She lured him there. At that point, Mike and Buffy were both desperate to get their hands on the pictures, but naturally, she convinced him they were working together, and she only wanted to help him. She told him she could force the paintings' location out of Amanda, and she'd show him the 'perfect spot' to do it—easy disposal, remote, and no interference."

John rolled his eyes. "Of course, she says now she never intended to kill anyone. Just give Mike the big scare he deserved."

"I almost feel sorry for the stupid guy." Mabel sipped her coffee. "But not quite."

"I know, right? She said they'd march Amanda up there at gunpoint, make her tell, and then eliminate her on the spot."

"I know Mike was weak and mean, but was he really okay with killing Amanda?"

"All we've got is Buffy's version of the story. I sense he wasn't the killer she is. But she did say he believed Amanda wouldn't hesitate to turn them all in if they managed to get the paintings from her. So maybe self-preservation kicked in, especially if he didn't have to pull the trigger himself."

"So, Buffy got him up there and just shot him?"

John nodded. "She claims it was an accident—tripped or a struggle over the gun or something—and it discharged."

Mabel rolled her eyes. "She hated him, and she didn't need him anymore. In fact, he was likely to spill his guts on her if things went bad, which also made him a liability." She shuddered. "How can a human being be so cold?"

"One of the cops said he heard her mutter, 'He should've been skeletal remains by the time he turned up—if he ever did.' But she was capable of love, I guess."

That was true, Mabel thought, improbable as it seemed. "For her dad."

He nodded.

"Now what about Amanda?"

"Buffy trailed her to my place, and there was another struggle and another 'accidental' shooting. Amanda wouldn't give up the location of the paintings. I guess they were always her first loyalty."

"It reminds me of that famous line from the *Fargo* movie. When Marge says, 'All those people dead and for what? A little bit of money.'"

"You could've been one of them." John picked up her hand again. "I'd never have forgiven myself."

"Well, I wasn't," Mabel told him. "She didn't even shoot off my toes."

"Before we go, I've got something to show you." John reached inside his jacket, which lay next to him on the seat. He pulled out a fat envelope. "Funny you mentioned *Fargo*. This somehow got misrouted. Arrived in yesterday's mail, via Minot, North Dakota."

He passed the envelope to Mabel, then waved a small key. "This was in it."

Mabel looked back and forth between the envelope and key. "This is from Amanda."

"She still didn't pay me. But she knew she was in mortal danger, so before anything could happen to her, she mailed me that. It was probably the last thing she did. Go ahead and read."

Wide-eyed, Mabel read.

I'm sorry to tell you this, but those packages I left with you aren't mine. If anything happens to me, they need to be returned to the Art Museum of the Alleghenies. I wish I could pay you. If I live long enough, I will, but it'll take a while.

In the letter, Amanda explained her side of the story, calling Mike "a big mistake." She went on to implicate him in both the arson and at least to a degree, in the heist, along with Vin Perdue and several others.

When I saw those paintings, I just couldn't let anything happen to them. I know I should have turned them right back in, but I guess I went a little bit crazy. I'd never have done anything to harm them, but you can't understand the feeling it gave me, holding onto them for just a little while as if they were mine. I kept thinking I'd turn them in, but they'd been missing so long already, and I couldn't figure out how to do it without the risk of getting caught and either killed or arrested for stealing them.

Mabel looked up at John. "The key is for a locker at the bus station?"

"Hopefully, the evidence she squirreled away, along with Buffy's testimony, will go a long way toward making sure Perdue pays for both the art theft and the arson. It's probably a long shot, but I'd love to be able to nail somebody higher up along with him."

Mabel opened her mouth to say, "Poor Edith," but stopped herself in time. John still didn't know about her and Lisa's escapade. It was probably better that way. Besides, nobody was hurting Edith but Vinnie himself, with his own poor life choices. "Maybe Charlie Maier can finally go home," she said instead.

John grinned and nodded. "It's hard to get a conviction overturned, but now he has a chance. I've been thinking about talking to the museum people. If they can scrounge up any of the reward money, even if it isn't the full amount, wouldn't it be great to see Frank Sedlak gets it? I'll rest easier if we can ensure he'll be taken care of."

Mabel envisioned a sky full of bills with wings, flying away. She squeezed John's hand. "I think that's a wonderful idea."

"Want to come see what's in that locker?"

Mabel grinned. "Let's go."

Chapter Thirty-Two

JOHN PULLED TO THE CURB IN front of the Wilkie bus station. Rain clattered on the hood of his car and bounced up from the pavement. "Hop out here, and I'll park."

With a leery eye on the downpour, Mabel pulled up her hood. "Meet you by the lockers."

She'd assumed Amanda would have stashed her parcel of evidence at the big bus station in Pittsburgh. That Wilkie still boasted a bus station of its own had been a surprise.

Once through the main door, she could see everything the facility had to offer. *Guess I don't have to ask my way to the lockers.*

The station was a single, low-ceilinged room with three rows of polished wooden benches at the center. A group of men and women in Amish garb with stacks of luggage occupied the front row. Behind them sat a young mother, rocking an infant carrier with her foot, and a probable college student playing on his phone. Metal lockers lined the back wall, along with two vending machines.

John came through the door, shaking water off his sleeves.

"We were lucky." Mabel pointed. "According to the sign out there, the station's only open twice a day, when there's a bus due."

John grinned. "Luck didn't enter into it. I checked before we left. Shall we?"

Mabel rubbed her hands together, tingling with nerves and excitement. "Maybe it's more stolen goods."

"Could be. But whatever it is, Amanda said it was evidence."

They scanned the lockers until they spotted the correct one. It sat at about chest level. John turned the key and reached inside. From where Mabel stood, it appeared empty. She stuck her head around to peer over his shoulder.

John laughed. "Hold your horses, Miss Nosy." He pulled out a fat manila envelope and tucked it under his arm. "I think we'd better take this out to the car before we open it, don't you?"

Nobody seemed to be paying them any attention, but she supposed he was right. "Where are you parked?"

"Just a block up. Do you have room for this in that satchel of yours? I don't want to get it wet."

Mabel opened her overstuffed slouchy purse, eyed the envelope, and frowned. "Um…"

John rolled his eyes and shook his head. "Never mind." He unzipped his jacket then tucked the packet inside. "Let's go."

The run to the car felt longer than a block, with wind tossing the rain sideways. Mabel felt her feet squish inside her shoes as she stepped in and slammed the door.

"Whew! That rain is cold. Bet it turns to snow later." John gasped and wiped droplets from his face with one hand. "Let me get the heater going."

The windows were already beginning to steam up as he opened the envelope flap, screening the car's interior from passersby. "Ready?"

"Good grief. Just take it out." Mabel tried to snatch the package from him, but John was too quick.

"Foiled again." He grinned, peeking inside. "What have we here?"

As Mabel fidgeted, John relented and handed her a white, unaddressed business envelope. "Should I open it?"

"Hang on." He pulled a plastic zip bag full of paper, a photocopied news clipping, and a lonely flash drive out of the manila envelope, then felt around the interior and shook it out. "Guess that's it. Go ahead— there may be more of an explanation in there."

With shaking hands, Mabel tore open the letter. "It's from Amanda. Looks like she might have written this sometime before the one she sent you, but it covers some of the same territory."

John shrugged. "She might not have been sure who'd be reading it."

Mabel began reading aloud as Amanda told how she'd been attracted to Mike, a handsome, fun older guy. He wasn't constantly broke like Danny the grad student, and bragged about the "easy money" he made doing odd jobs on the side. But things had changed, several months into their relationship, when she'd moved in with him late that spring.

Amanda was smart enough to realize Mike was being overpaid for his so-called odd jobs and began putting two and two together. She became uneasy, especially after overhearing a few phone calls from Vin Perdue or one of his henchmen.

I got into his email one day and started nosing around. He'd received several from an anonymous account that seemed to track with some of the suspicious phone conversations. I saved those to a flash drive, which you'll find with this letter. I suspect the account could be traced to Perdue—if so, I think you've got him. They'll tie both him and Mike to receipt of stolen goods, among other criminal activity. You'll see what all they were involved in, as you read through them.

Some of the papers in the plastic bag came from Mike's trash. One of them—the one on top—he kept squirreled away. I think he was holding onto it in case he got arrested for the arson in the enclosed clipping. He probably figured he could use it to implicate Perdue in exchange for a plea deal. That's the one that scared me to death. It's why I decided to dig out all the other notes and bundle this stuff up. I want it to be shared with the police if I don't live long enough to figure my own way out of the mess.

"What's the paper on top?" Mabel grabbed at the plastic bag, but John held it away.

"Prints."

"I wasn't going to open the bag. Can you read it through the plastic?"

John squinted. "Not really. Can you?"

Mabel looked, and her heart began to chug. All the papers in the bag looked like they'd come from a notepad. What she could see on top was scrawled in blue Sharpie. She remembered Vin Perdue's desk...covered in notes this size, scribbled in bold blue ink. She opened her mouth to tell John but thought better of it.

Mabel cleared her throat and returned to reading Amanda's letter.

The handwriting on the notes looks distinctive enough for a handwriting expert to give an opinion as to who wrote them. The note on top, as far as I can make out, is a checklist for the arson. It has an oily thumbprint on it—probably Mike's—and still kind of smells like maybe oil or kerosene.

"She talks about the artwork here. More or less what she had in the other letter you got." Mabel skimmed that section, then continued.

I was all set to bail on Mike, and then I found the paintings, which complicated things. I doubt Mike had much to do with those, but Vin sure did, because he came after Mike when they disappeared. I feel bad about that, because Mike's dead now, and maybe that was my fault.

If you got this far, I'm likely dead too. But hopefully there's something in here that can be used to make Perdue pay for his sins. I'd love to see him sent up for that arson. For the art theft too, but I'm guessing he was never the mastermind there. Maybe he'll flip on whoever that was to save his hide.

"Aw, she died thinking she caused Mike's death."

John's mouth was tight, but as he took the letter back from Mabel, he managed a smile. "Mike certainly contributed to his own fate. But whatever mistakes Amanda made, at least she made a big step toward setting things right at the end."

He returned everything to the packet and put it on the back seat. "We'll drop this off at the PD in Bartles Grove on our way home."

Mabel rubbed a spot clear on the passenger window. "Hey, look. The sun's back out."

"Good sign. Let's do something fun tonight. What do you say?"

On the ride home, they debated how to spend the evening. Mabel was in favor of pizza and a movie. John pointed out that the torrential rains in Wilkie didn't seem to have hit Bartles Grove. "It's probably nice in Medicine Spring. It'll be dark, but we could grab Barnacle and take a walk through town where we have the street lights."

"I'm kind of tired. Let's save the walk for when we have a lot of daylight."

John grinned. "Promise you'll go? Maybe we can take him up to Clear Creek Park next weekend."

Return to the scene of her disastrous outing as a canine search and rescue volunteer? "Maybe."

"It'll be fun. You can show me your family's cabin, okay?"

"Sure." Perhaps by next weekend, her frayed nerves would have recovered from everything she'd been through in the past few days.

Mabel's phone rang, and she had to dig through her bag to retrieve it. "Oh, no. It's Acey." She could almost hear the ping as the last of her strained nerves began to snap.

John flinched. "You sure you want to answer that?"

Mabel's hand hovered over the "off" button, but she had to know. "Hello…?"

"Hi, there, little lady. Hey, you didn't set much store by that row of bushes back of your yard, didja?"

His use of the past tense didn't go unnoticed. Mabel's jaw tightened. "Yes. I do. Those are Concord grapes my grandfather planted. They're at least fifty years old."

She heard him spit tobacco. "Past their prime, then, were they?"

After Mabel finally convinced Acey he'd done enough for one day and to please go home, she collapsed against the seat back and closed her eyes. She considered looking up pruning recommendations for Concord grapes but feared what she'd find out. Besides, Acey hadn't expressly told her he'd cut the vines down. For all she knew, he'd set fire to the grape arbor. Or replaced the whole thing with an ornamental stand of invasive kudzu.

"Are you okay?"

"Of course. Everything's just dandy." Her giggle ended on a snort.

"So…no pressure, but what do you think about taking Barnacle up to Clear Creek next weekend?"

Mabel thought about her poor grapevines and about all the work waiting for her at the house—not to mention her faltering writing career. The likelihood of her frayed nerves healing by next weekend was slim indeed, especially with Acey "helping."

"Come on, Mabel. The fresh air and exercise will be good for us." John gave her an irresistible sidelong grin. "Do it for Barnacle."

Hopefully, she wouldn't break a leg or get eaten by bears. In any event, resistance was clearly futile. When your life's already gone to the dogs, she reasoned, you might as well go with the flow.

"Oh, all right." Mabel smiled back. "For Barnacle."

AUTHOR NOTE

Thank you for reading *Mabel Goes to the Dogs*—I hope you enjoyed it! I've had so much fun with Mabel's adventures in volunteering, which always keep me learning right along with her. This book took me into two very different worlds—art theft, and canine search and rescue.

I love dogs, and they've always been part of my life. My own volunteering has included Australian cattle dog rescue (dog evaluation, home evaluations, fostering, medical fostering, and transport), as well as dog-walking and both medical and hospice fostering for our local humane society. When I was planning this novel, I thought about using my previous experiences. But then, I decided to explore canine search and rescue. While most of my research occurred online, I was very fortunate to get a timely call to go out—much like Mabel—and hide in the woods for a dog-training day.

I'd offered my services probably a year previously, simply out of curiosity and a desire to help, but never heard back. At that point, I had no idea of writing a book involving search dogs. But when the call to come out for a day with the dogs finally arrived, the timing was perfect. I couldn't have been more impressed with the three dogs who found me—from the gray-muzzled elder to the eager puppy. Their abilities are simply remarkable, as was their enthusiasm for what they do. It was truly an honor to watch them work.

I became interested in the realm of art theft after listening to the *Empty Frames* podcast, about the stunning 1990 heist at the Isabella Stewart Gardner Museum in Boston. The robbery is to date the largest property theft in the world (pegged by the FBI at an astounding $500,000,000). The $10,000,000 reward remains unclaimed, though new clues occasionally emerge. For more about this fascinating case, you may visit the museum website, www.gardnermuseum.org. The theft was also featured in a Netflix documentary, *This Is a Robbery*.

I also greatly enjoyed *The Rescue Artist*, which won the Edgar Award for nonfiction from Mystery Writers of America. It is a rich source of information about stolen-art trafficking, as well as an entertaining read. The book details the bold 1994 theft of Edvard Munch's *The Scream*, from the National Gallery in Oslo, as an international audience was focused on the opening of the Winter Olympics at Lillehammer.

As an additional aside, I might also mention that Mabel's efforts to control her anxiety with "ANT therapy" is based on the research of psychiatrist and neuroscientist Dr. Daniel Amen. The essential concept is that our anxious thoughts are both damaging and, more often than not, untrue. Centuries before Dr. Amen was born, St. Paul also counseled us in our troubles to turn our thoughts to positive things, the first of which is "whatever is true." (Philippians 4:8) That remains good advice today!

If you enjoyed *Mabel Goes to the Dogs*, I hope you'll come back for Book Three, *Mabel & the Little Green Men*. We've included a sneak preview following this note. (And if this series is new to you, you may wish to go back and check out Book One: *Mabel Gets the Ax,* as well as the prequel novella, *Mabel & the Cat's Meow*.)

As always, if you liked this book, I would greatly appreciate your leaving a review, however brief, at Amazon.com, Goodreads, Christianbook.com, or other sites for book lovers. Reviews are so important to readers looking for their next literary adventure! I hope you'll also come see me at one of the following sites. (Check out the link on my website to sign up for my newsletter, which will give you insider stories and chances for giveaways.) Hope to see you there!

susankimmelwright.com
facebook.com/susankimmelwrightwriter
instagram.com/susankimmelwrights
twitter.com/SKimmelWright

DISCUSSION QUESTIONS

1. Have you ever volunteered? Did you have any memorable experiences (good or bad)? Did your volunteer experience turn out to be a significant event—or even a long-term commitment—in your life? Why or why not?

2. Mabel isn't perfect. Do you like main characters with flaws, or do you prefer to escape from real life with characters who have it all together? What is it about flawed characters that you feel increases the value of a book?

3. Mabel and Lisa have been best friends since kindergarten. Do you have a best friend—and how long have you been friends? Are you still in touch with your childhood best friend? If not, did anything happen to separate you, and is there a way you might be able to reconnect?

4. Was any scene in this book especially memorable to you? Which one, and why?

5. Did the ending surprise you? If you guessed who the murderer was, what was the point where you figured it out?

Now, a Sneak Peek at Book Three
in the *Mysteries of Medicine Spring* Series

Chapter One

A GUST OF WIND ROCKED MABEL'S car as she rounded the bend, skirting an old stone arch bridge, now no longer in service but preserved for its historic value. It stood spectral against the dark hemlocks and bare-trunked oaks and maples. To her left stretched fields of corn stubble and hay bales. She glanced at the dash clock and sighed. Already after eleven pm, and she still had another twenty miles to the outskirts of Medicine Spring, and another two from there to home.

The tri-county tourism meeting had run late, due to a long and bitter argument about paying for TV ads. That, and a chairman who didn't—in Mabel's opinion—use the gavel enough.

The historical society members were supposed to take turns attending the monthly tourism meetings, but Mabel suspected she'd be getting the assignment nearly every month. Some of the other members claimed conflicts, and the rest pled cataracts and poor night vision. Mabel, at fifty, was their token young member.

She had only joined the society initially to get experience for the book she was writing—trying to write—for seniors on the joys and satisfactions of volunteering. In less than three months, she'd lost her long-time job as a low-level attorney, launched a new writing career funded by an inheritance from her late Grandma Mabel and a fat settlement from the law firm for age discrimination. And she had gotten herself involved in two murders…or was it six? She wasn't sure how to count them.

It was November now, and only a few leaves still clung to trees, whipping up and down like hands waving. The wind was wild. It was so dark out here in the countryside, away from the light pollution of the towns. A clear, star-pierced sky showed a near-full moon to good advantage—what Native Americans had called the beaver moon, in honor of the active critters who were getting ready for the coming winter.

Driving along the lonely stretch of road, lit only by the moonlight and Mabel's headlights, she realized she was getting sleepy. She rolled her window down.

As she climbed the next hill, she gradually became aware of a humming sound. Was it her engine? Mabel's heart sank. The last thing she needed right now—with Grandma's rundown house to fix up, and no job—was car trouble. Let alone, way out here by herself.

At the top of the hill, she reluctantly pulled over. The tires lurched over the grassy verge and when she jerked to a stop, the car tilted to the right. At least, she hadn't slid into a ditch. The fields fell away to either side now, a ghostly landscape of rolled hay bales wrapped in white plastic that gleamed in the moonlight. Dark stands of trees encircled the distance.

Please don't let this be car trouble. She turned off her engine, praying it would start again.

Still, the humming continued. Mabel patted her phone. It wasn't that either, but the bad news was she also had no signal up here if she needed help.

Mabel stuck her head out the window, looking for power lines. There were wires above her, but they were quiet. Her brain fixated on something else.

Up there in the clear indigo sky, an array of lights sat in a curved formation like a boomerang. What was that constellation? Mabel never seemed able to find anything but the Big and Little Dippers. Even Orion, which her sister Jen told her was also easy to find, always eluded her.

Or was it a plane? Might that explain the humming?

As she stared in fascination, she realized the lights seemed to have moved closer—much too close for a constellation. Maybe about the altitude of a private plane, with a pilot scanning for a safe landing place like those fields.

The lights flashed red, white, and amber in a sort of rhythm. *Okay.* Stars definitely did not do that. In fact, she'd never seen a plane do that, either.

As she watched, one of the amber lights broke away and descended in an eye blink, to settle several yards above her car. The humming intensified and seemed to vibrate the car, and Mabel as well.

She jerked her head back inside. The hairs on her arms stood up.

The light bathed the car in a warm glow. *It's a drone,* she told herself. *It's a drone. It's just a drone. Probably delivering somebody's order of foot powder. Or mapping the roads.*

Mabel fumbled to start her car, but nothing happened. Not so much as a click. It was completely dead. Even the dashboard icons didn't flash on.

Surely, her battery wasn't dead. It couldn't be. She'd had to replace it the week before her scheduled state inspection, which was only two months ago.

The humming continued. Mabel felt as if the sound and vibration were inside her body, and her brain felt more and more detached from reality.

Dreaming. She must be dreaming. She was not out here in the middle of a cheap sci-fi B movie.

Was the car in park? Once she'd accidentally left the car in gear, and then freaked out when it wouldn't start. It had to be something simple.

Again and again, she tried the starter. *Nothing.*

Mabel stomped the brake, wiggled the steering wheel, and turned the key. And, just like that, the car started. As if not a thing was wrong with it.

Mabel threw her car into gear and hit the gas. The tires spun and squealed in the tall weeds and grass, and the car leapt forward, lurching over the bumps and back onto the pavement again.

As Mabel tore down the road, the amber glow, which still hung over her, suddenly sharpened, and the car flooded with intense white light. Was she being abducted by aliens?

She was so isolated up here. It was chasing her—whatever this hovering thing might be. And she knew she couldn't outrun it in a high-mileage hatchback.

Mabel clenched her slippery hands on the steering wheel and stood on the accelerator. She tried to take calming breaths, but her chest was so tight, all she could manage were shallow gasps.

This wasn't something that typically happened to normal people. People who encountered strange lights in the sky like this had a tendency to wind up on early morning talk shows, telling about being beamed onto flying saucers and probed by little green men with bottomless black eyes

The car skidded as Mabel took the next curve too fast. Heart pounding, she fought to bring it back under control. But just as suddenly, the light shot away—straight up into the sky.

The last time she'd looked, she had left the other lights behind her, still hanging in their precise array in the sky. Now, she wasn't going to take time to look back and see if they'd sped away, too. All she cared about was getting down from the lonely hills and back into town, where the lights were the warm and friendly ones of lamps left on for latecomers, or TVs flickering in darkened family rooms.

Mabel pushed her car for the next ten miles, bucketing over potholes and abandoned railroad tracks, till she reached the commercial stretch outside Marklinton. The strip malls were still lit up, even though everything was closed at this hour, except for a combo gas station and convenience store.

Suddenly, she wanted desperately to stop. To go inside and use the restroom. To talk to another human being.

Mabel turned off and pulled as close to the building as she could. She wasn't going to get out and pump gas, even though her tank was down to only a quarter. Somehow, she didn't want to stand out there, alone and exposed, just in case…

Just in case…what? In case a spaceship came down from the sky and tried to abduct her? How silly.

Never mind. She had enough in her tank to get home, it was late, and she was overtired and imagining things. She simply didn't want to waste time pumping gas. With her luck, it would be one of those slow pumps that took forever to produce one gallon, two gallons, three gallons, while her hand ached from holding down the trigger on the handle.

When she got out of the car, she realized she was wobbly. Mabel put a steadying hand on her car before hustling inside the station.

The garish lights smacked her in the eye, but they were good lights.

Mabel smiled at the young clerk, who seemed absorbed with his phone screen. He hadn't bothered to look up after the first glance, which she presumed had been merely to make sure he wasn't about to be robbed.

Mabel checked her phone. She'd charged it on the way to the meeting earlier, but now it was stone dead.

After a quick trip to the restroom, where the mirror showed a pasty-faced stranger with wild eyes, Mabel returned to the store. She took her time browsing through the snack aisles, which ordinarily was one of her favorite road trip activities.

Tonight, her heart wasn't in it, though she finally selected a package of crème-filled snack cakes, a bag of red-hot potato fries, and a Coke for the caffeine jolt. When she brought them up to the register, the clerk took a moment to finish whatever he'd been reading on the screen. He set the phone down with an audible sigh.

"Good evening." Mabel smiled.

The young man—Tyler, according to his badge—grunted and picked up the snack cakes to scan.

"Must get boring here by yourself at night, huh?"

He shrugged one shoulder. Maybe he was mute. Poor fellow.

"Hey." Mabel chuckled a bit from embarrassment. "Did you ever notice anything in the sky around here at night… like something weird?

I was just up there." She gave a vague wave behind her. "And the strangest thing happened."

"Seven-fifty-six," he said, having recovered the power of speech.

"I'm sorry." Mabel dug out the money. "I, well..." Her voice trailed off as she realized he was looking at his phone again.

"Have a good night." She rolled her eyes and headed back out into the night.

CPSIA information can be obtained
at www.ICGtesting.com
Printed in the USA
BVHW091126120522
636877BV00011B/460